TOUCH OF INNOCENCE

COVENTRY SAGA BOOK 5

ROBIN PATCHEN

JDO PUBLISHING

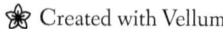

For Savannah Patchen
Welcome to the family.

CHAPTER ONE

THIS WAS SUPPOSED to be her solitary space.

Grace Mullen didn't mind, though. Ever since she'd met eight-year-old Lily during a walk in the woods a few weeks earlier, the girl had been Grace's shadow, showing up at her secluded cottage every afternoon when she finished her schooling. Grace had taken to hurrying through her work in the mornings so they'd have time to visit. Not that Lily ever had much to say. She was a quiet child.

Some might say too quiet.

Troubled, even.

There'd been a time when Grace would have used her curse to see what Lily was hiding. Just a touch of Lily's hand could evoke a vision of what had put the pensive look on her beautiful little face. But that time was long past. Grace had vowed never to suffer that anguish again.

She wouldn't complain about her new friend, though she wasn't accustomed to having a friend a third her age. She didn't even mind Lily's support dog, a Cavalier King Charles spaniel named Regis, though the animal left his hair all over her hardwood floors. He was a charming little thing with his bright royal blue collar and matching oversize tag emblazoned with one of those circle peace symbols.

No, Grace didn't mind Lily or the dog. It was just that, ever since Lily had started coming around, things had gone missing.

Okay, not missing exactly. Grace had found her slippers the night before, but not in her closet where she kept them. They'd been under the bed.

Strange.

Now, after she set the kettle on the stove to boil, she searched for her favorite mug. It wasn't in the cabinet where she kept it or anywhere else in the small kitchen of the cozy home she'd rented a year before.

A glance into the breakfast room revealed no mug. Beyond the windows, clouds were gathering. One learned to enjoy the sun when it shined on the western slope of the Cascades. As spring turned to summer, the sun would peek out more and more. It had been a dreary winter, but Lily's presence the last few weeks had brightened Grace's world.

On the back deck, the girl was coloring in one of the books Grace had bought her, little legs swinging beneath the café table. She was a gorgeous child with thick brown hair and the biggest, greenest eyes Grace had ever seen, so unlike Grace's blond hair and bland gray eyes.

Lily had to know what was keeping Grace so long. Why hide her mug?

Why hide her slippers?

She searched the small living area and the guest room. No mug.

When she stepped into her bedroom, Oliver, her pale gray cat, blinked his blue eyes at her from his spot on her bed. He stood, adjusted his position, and settled himself again. After scratching him, she got down on her knees and checked under the bed.

No mug.

Her house wasn't that big, and she'd hardly brought anything to fill it. Where could the child...?

She checked in the closet. There on the floor, beside her slippers, sat her favorite mug. Emblazoned with the words *Freedom*

Home for Girls and Women, it was the only souvenir she'd kept from her time there.

Grace snatched it and headed back to the kitchen. She hadn't talked to Lily about moving her things before, but it was time to mention it. She didn't like the idea of Lily poking around in the bedroom when Grace wasn't present.

By the time she returned to the kitchen, her kettle was whistling. She poured hot water over a tea bag, then added honey and milk. The perfect afternoon treat. With a glass of lemonade for Lily, she returned to the back deck.

The little girl looked up, her emerald eyes bright. She tapped the princess drawing in her coloring book.

"Look at that," Grace said. "I love the colors you chose."

The girl beamed, taking the offered glass.

"Sweetie, would you do me a favor?"

Lily nodded, her jaw open as if she were afraid of what Lily might ask.

Grace squashed her curiosity and concern. She was just a neighbor. Not a counselor. Not a mentor. Just a neighbor.

"Would you please not move my things without asking me?"

Lily blinked a couple of times, then nodded.

"Thank you."

Lily returned to her coloring as Grace settled beside her.

"How was your schoolwork today?"

She shrugged.

The day they'd first met, it had taken Grace a solid ten minutes to get a word out of her.

"What was the most interesting thing you learned?"

Lily set down her crayon and looked up. "Did you know flowers have boy parts and girl parts, just like people?"

"Is that right? What are they called?"

She tilted her head to the side. "The boy part is the stamen, and the girl part is the pistil. They're not like people parts, though, because every flower has both, and people only have one or the other."

3

"What a good memory you have." She was trying to think of a follow-up question, but Lily wasn't finished.

"They don't look the same as boy and girl parts, either. And they don't work the same way."

Before Grace could fully internalize what the child had said, her stomach filled with acid. Did most eight-year-olds know that much about the human reproductive system?

Maybe.

Grace's worry was probably unfounded. Lily was home-schooled and clearly intelligent. Perhaps she was more advanced than normal eight-year-olds. And anyway, what did Grace know about normal eight-year-olds? She'd never been one herself. A *normal* one, that was.

Lily's gaze stayed on Grace's face, and the light in her eyes dimmed as if she could read Grace's thoughts. She returned her focus to her coloring book.

"That's so interesting," Grace said. "What else did you learn?"

Lily shrugged, but eventually she shared other things she'd studied that day while Grace nodded and smiled and tried to ignore the worry whooshing through her insides like a river over-flowing its banks.

It probably made perfect sense that Lily understood human anatomy. That was not a red flag. Grace had a bad habit of assuming trouble where none existed. She'd spent so much time among broken and damaged girls that she could hardly differentiate between those and the healthy ones. Another reason her decision to leave Seattle had been wise.

Whatever was going on, Lily was not Grace's responsibility.

Her cell phone rang, and she snatched it up, eager to think about something else. But a glance at the screen had her groaning. She wanted to think about something else, but not that.

She rejected the call, but it rang again seconds later. When she rejected the second call, it rang a third time.

Lily giggled. "I don't think they're gonna stop."

"Unfortunately, you're not wrong. I'll be right back."

Grace swiped to connect and stepped back into the house. "Mama Lucy."

"Thank God you answered." The older woman sounded genuinely distressed. "Allison was in a car accident. She's in the hospital."

Grace barely knew the woman the girls home had hired to replace her. "Is she going to be okay?"

"Yes, but she broke a number of bones. It's going to be months before she can come back to work. I was hoping—"

"I'm sorry, but no."

Mama Lucy sighed, and Grace could imagine the disappointed look on the face of the white-haired woman who'd loved her so well. "Sweet daughter."

Grace's heart warmed at the words. Mama Lucy had called her that from the first day they'd met. It didn't matter that she called all the girls in her care the same. To be called daughter...It had meant something. It still did.

"You are needed here," she said. "You have a home here. You are loved here."

"I can't do it anymore. I'm sorry."

"These girls...Nobody connects with them like you do."

Grace didn't doubt that was true. Hers was a unique ability, no question. But to connect and to heal—those were different gifts. She'd only been given the first. And without the second...

"I can't help them." Grace leaned against the counter, settling in for the coming debate. "You know it and I know it."

"You *can* help them," Mama Lucy said. "You've helped many of them. Your insights are invaluable."

"My insights are useless. I've proved that."

"What happened with Celia—"

"No." She couldn't go there. Couldn't stand to hear the girl's name. "I can't talk about her. I won't."

"It wasn't your fault." Mama Lucy's words, delivered so many times before, held only compassion. "You can't save everyone."

"I can't save *anyone*. I'm sorry. I can't. You'll have to find somebody else."

Before her old friend and mentor could respond, Grace hung up, hating herself for her rudeness but knowing she had no other choice. Mama Lucy wouldn't stop trying to change her mind, but Grace wouldn't be convinced. What happened with Celia...

She couldn't survive that again.

It took so long for Grace to compose herself after the call that she half expected to find Lily gone when she stepped back outside. But the girl was still there, crayon dragging against the cheap paper. When the screen door slammed, Lily flipped the page quickly.

Was she hiding something?

Grace was being ridiculous. She sat beside Lily again. "Sorry about that. Old friend from the city."

Lily considered the crayons in the box Grace had bought—a sixty-four pack with as many colors as a girl could want. Lily chose a bright orange and started filling in flowers on an untouched page.

"Tell me about your friends," Grace said.

The girl said nothing.

"What's your best friend's name?"

Lily glanced her way, a slight smile on her lips. "Grace."

"Aw, what a sweet thing to say. You're my best friend too." It was true. At the moment, Lily was Grace's only friend. "Do you have any friends at church?"

"We don't go anymore."

Grace didn't either. She hadn't found a church since she moved here. She should. She knew that. Knew it wasn't healthy to avoid all human interaction. But all the stuff she'd learned in her counseling classes seemed theoretical and somehow irrelevant to her actual life. She didn't need community, no matter what the books said. She needed to be left alone.

Though she enjoyed Lily's company.

A low *meow* had them both turning toward the black-and-white cat that had taken to visiting in the afternoons. Grace had set out some food and water earlier, and Sylvester—Lily's choice for a name—helped himself.

Regis stood and padded across the deck to greet him. It had taken a few days, but the animals had gotten used to each other.

Lily waited until the cat finished its meal before sitting cross-legged beside him to pet him. The cat purred in response.

Probably jealous, Regis crawled into Lily's lap, and she alternated between petting the animals.

While Lily was occupied, Grace flipped the pages of the coloring book, curious about what the girl had hidden earlier. She found an image on the inside back cover and studied it to be sure she was seeing it right.

It was crudely drawn but clear enough. A bed. A girl on the bed who had one elbow propping up her head, one little stick-figure knee stuck in the air, the other flat against the mattress.

There was nothing wrong with the picture. And yet, there was.

It was not a normal way for anybody to recline on a bed. It was posed.

It was...provocative.

Nausea churned, and she slammed the book shut and closed her eyes.

No.

She couldn't do it again. She wouldn't.

Lord, please don't ask it of me.

When she opened her eyes, Lily was standing beside her, eyes round as marbles.

Grace pressed on a smile, wishing she could pretend she hadn't seen what she'd seen.

But couldn't.

"I saw your picture."

Lily tugged the book out from under Grace's hand, opened it, and colored again.

"Was that you?"

She shrugged.

"Were you going to sleep?"

A shake of her head.

"Were you playing a game?"

"Daddy's a photographer. He puts pictures of me on his website."

Grace forced a normal tone. "Do you know his website's name? I'd like to see them."

She didn't say anything, just kept coloring.

Grace asked, "What's your daddy's name?"

"Myron Bowman."

Grace went inside for her laptop and returned to the deck. "I'm going to see if I can find them."

When Lily looked up, Grace smiled at her. "Go ahead and keep coloring. I'll let you know if I see your pictures." She opened her browser and searched.

Sure enough, there it was. Myron Bowman Photography. She clicked the link, stomach churning with worry, but what she saw surprised her.

Sweet, innocent photographs. Not just of Lily, though there were plenty of the beautiful girl, but other children, families, weddings, special events. The man was an artist.

Grace's fears were unfounded.

"Your daddy's good," she said.

"I know."

Ah, the confidence of children.

A low knock sounded on the wood behind her, and she swiveled in that direction, snapping the laptop closed as if she'd been caught.

Standing on the ground beside the deck, a man smiled up at her, but the smile seemed forced. He looked to be in his midforties, if not older, tall and slender with short-cropped blond hair and blue eyes. He was attractive in an unassuming sort of way. He focused on Lily. "So this is where you've been running off to every afternoon."

Lily jumped to her feet, eyes wide. "I'm sorry, Daddy. I'm sorry."

"We have to hurry, sweetheart. You have a dentist appointment." He rounded the deck railing and took the three steps up to join them on the platform. "Pick up after yourself."

The girl was already shoving crayons back in the box as fast as her little fingers could manage it.

Grace stood. "I didn't realize you didn't know where she was."

Hands behind him propped on the railing, he crossed one ankle over the other. The pose said he was relaxed, but the expression on his face—tight smile, squinting eyes—said he was anything but. He was trying to convince Grace—and maybe Lily—that he wasn't angry. "She told me she was exploring. I didn't know she'd made a friend." Considering his daughter had been lying to him, he had a right to be angry.

Grace was about to introduce herself when Lily threw her arms around Grace's waist. "I love you, Miss Grace."

She *loved* her? They barely knew each other, but her innocence and honesty had Grace's eyes filling.

Grace patted her little back. "Come back and see me, but you have to ask your daddy first."

Normally, at that point, Lily would run into the woods back to her own cabin, which was just a few hundred yards down their country road. But today, before Grace could stop her, the child grabbed her hand.

She said something, but Grace didn't hear the words.

The images and impressions that flashed in her mind were louder than anything going on in the real world.

A bed.

A camera.

A man's hands adjusting her. Moving her this way and that.

Lily in front of a mirror wearing a bright red silky teddy, crossing her arms over her flat chest.

A stuffed animal held over a camera, bright lights. *Smile at the lion, sweetheart. Blow him a kiss...*

Fear. Shame.

Lily took her hand away, and the images dissipated.

Grace blinked to clear her mind, to bring herself back to the present.

Lily's father was focused on Grace, lips pressed closed.

She couldn't think of a thing to say.

He stepped forward, hand outstretched. "I should have introduced myself. Myron Bowman."

She didn't want to touch him. She could make up a story, tell him she was afraid of germs, even pretend she didn't see it. She'd been rude to Mama Lucy. She'd have no trouble being rude to him.

But she had to know.

As much as she told herself it wasn't her problem, the instant Lily's images had invaded her mind, it had become her problem.

She steeled herself, forced a friendly smile. "Grace Mullen." She slid her hand into his.

The images came too fast. Boys and girls and beds and flashes and...

Myron ended the handshake, and mercifully, her vision cleared.

"Thanks for letting her hang out." His words were kind, but his eyes were squinted, his lips tight in the fake smile.

"I love having her." Grace's voice sounded perfectly normal. "She's welcome anytime."

"Bye, Grace." Lily hurried away, Regis on her heels.

Myron followed his daughter, shooting Grace one final look before he disappeared into the woods.

When they were gone, she collapsed in the chair and dropped her head into her hands. *I can't do this again. I can't.*

But after what she'd seen, as much as she hated to face it, she had to do it again. Lily was worth Grace's pain.

CHAPTER TWO

"Hold please."

Grace paced across her small kitchen, fear keeping her moving. When she was finished, she'd collapse.

She was usually so careful about protecting herself, about not letting anybody hold her hand. With most people, she could shake hands without getting much more than general impressions, but every once in a while, she'd see visions that revealed trauma or abuse, whether on the part of the victim or the perpetrator.

They left traces on Grace's psyche. And they made her care far, far too much.

She'd let her guard down, but she wouldn't be sorry, not if the authorities could protect Lily.

A detective came on the line and introduced herself as Detective Eckmann. "How can I help you?"

"I have reason to believe my neighbor, Myron Bowman, is taking inappropriate photographs of his daughter." And a lot of other children, but she didn't say that.

Considering how little Grace knew, the conversation took much longer than she'd anticipated. After explaining the picture Lily had drawn, she tried to tell the woman about the impressions she'd gotten without telling her how she'd gotten them. She tried to make it sound as if she'd gotten the notion from what Lily had said —without actually lying, which was both wrong and probably, when reporting a crime, illegal.

Most people, when told about Grace's visions, decided *she* was the one who needed help, not the victims she was trying to protect. Not that Grace could blame them. She'd always been an insightful child, but after she'd given her heart to Jesus when she was a teen, she'd started seeing things. She'd thought she was going crazy until she'd prayed about the images and realized they were her spiritual gift. When she'd plucked up the nerve to tell Mama Lucy, her mentor had agreed. Discernment, prophesy, some combination of the two. Grace had quit trying to define it and quit trying to explain it.

After a few years, she'd quit using it and quit calling it a gift.

The detective sounded skeptical. "So the girl told you he was taking lewd photos of her?"

"Not in so many words," Grace said. "I'm a child counselor, so I know what I'm talking about. Lily drew a picture and told me about it, and based on that, I believe that her father is taking pornographic photos of her. And maybe worse."

"Okay. Please hold."

Grace had no evidence that the girl was being physically or sexually abused, but it was entirely possible. The images she'd gotten from Myron, all those children...

In Grace's visions, she could only see through the other person's eyes, and most of what she'd seen through Myron's came from what he saw through a camera lens. She didn't know exactly how her visions worked, but she'd employed them enough to know that, when she held on longer, the visions went deeper, revealed more.

She was glad she hadn't held on longer to Myron Bowman's hand. Because another aspect to her so-called gift was that she felt what the other person felt.

From Lily, she'd felt fear and shame.

From Myron, she'd gotten arrogance and triumph.

The detective came back on the line. "There've been no other complaints against Mr. Bowman."

"I'm curious, detective. How many people does Lily need to trust enough to tell what's going on before you take it seriously?"

"I take every complaint seriously, ma'am." The woman's words were delivered with authority and just a hint of impatience. "I just wanted to tell you what we know. I've already called the county. They're better equipped to investigate. Do you think Mr. Bowman has any idea what his daughter has told you?"

Grace remembered the suspicion in the man's eyes. "It's possible."

"Okay, I'll pass that along. Somebody from the county will contact you."

"Today, or—?"

"I don't know when exactly. They'll need to get a warrant to search his place. Hopefully, they'll find evidence, and the child will be removed."

Removed. Sent to foster care unless there was a family member who'd take her. Lily'd never talked about grandparents or cousins or even her mother. Who made up this child's safety net?

Did she have one, or would she be relegated to whatever home was willing to take her? Would that be better for her, or worse?

Whatever happened, Grace had done her duty. She'd done as much as anybody would ask of her.

Anybody on the planet, that was.

She tilted her head back and focused above. *Can I be done now? Please?*

THE FOLLOWING AFTERNOON, Grace was returning home from her twice-monthly trip to town, the cargo area of her Land Rover filled with supplies. She purchased much of her produce from the local farmers market, which she visited on Saturdays, but she forced herself to go to the grocery store every couple of weeks.

She'd considered having all her groceries delivered. Then she'd never have to leave her home.

Which would be a mistake. She knew that.

She needed to heal, not make her problems worse. Adding agoraphobia to the list of her issues...Bad idea.

So, twice a month, she traded her yoga pants for jeans, slipped into a blouse, chose cute shoes, and even dabbed on a little makeup. She pushed her cart through the superstore, smiling at strangers and acting the part of a typical member of society.

She yawned as she made the last turn-off toward her house. Pretending to be normal was exhausting.

There were only a few houses this direction, hers being the last before the pavement ended at the base of a mountain. Lush forest gave way every half mile or so to narrow driveways leading to small cottages. These were mostly summer homes for people who yearned to escape the craziness of Seattle just an hour or so west. Few people stayed year-round. The Bowmans were year-rounders.

Grace was glad she'd met Lily and discovered the girl's terrible secret. When the authorities found evidence of Myron's illicit activities, the child would be removed to a safe place, and Grace's part in the drama would be over.

She slowed as she reached the Bowmans' driveway. Two police cars were parked on the side of the narrow road, an unmarked sedan in the driveway.

Grace's stomach pinched. She'd done that. She'd brought all those people down on Myron. *Let them find the evidence, Lord. Protect Lily.*

She was almost past the second cruiser when she saw Myron standing beside a uniformed police officer, Regis sitting obediently at his feet.

Why wasn't Regis with Lily? He never left her side.

The officer was saying something while Myron met Grace's eyes through her windshield and glared.

She averted her gaze.

He knew. He knew she was the one who'd called them.

Of course he'd guessed it. Who else would Lily have told?

Grace's hands trembled. Her whole body trembled, but she wouldn't regret what she'd done. No man should exploit his child the way he had. Reduce her to no more than an image for men to ogle over. Reduce her to a profit-making machine.

Not just Lily, but other children as well.

Myron Bowman should be incarcerated for the rest of his earthly days.

She didn't regret it, but fear pulsed with every beat of her heart. What if she'd only made things worse?

CHAPTER THREE

GRACE HAD FORCED herself to finish her transcription assignments that afternoon, but the droning voices and medical terminology hadn't had the numbing effect they usually did. Her thoughts never strayed far from Lily and Myron Bowman.

Had Lily been taken away?

Had Myron been arrested?

Why hadn't the county investigator called?

When she finished her work, she warmed a bowl of tomato soup and sat at the small kitchen table to eat. Lily hadn't come by, of course. She probably never would again.

It was funny how quickly Grace had grown accustomed to the little girl's presence. The hours between dinner and bedtime now felt interminable. Maybe it was time to step out of the cocoon she'd created for herself, find a church, meet some people.

Maybe it was time to rejoin the human race.

She tried to imagine attending a local congregation. Walking in the door, greeting people.

Shaking hands.

She shuddered, all the images she'd seen the day before coming back.

She'd have to keep her hands in her pockets, tell people she feared germs. Maybe wear thin gloves. People would think she was weird. Well, she *was* weird.

But she could go to church. She'd done it before, back in Seattle. She'd had friends, had community, had a church family. Maybe Sunday she'd find a place to worship.

Even as she had the thought, she doubted she'd do it. Someday, she'd step out of her cocoon, but not yet. She wasn't ready.

She flipped on the TV and forced herself to focus on two episodes of the show she was binge-watching, though her thoughts never strayed far from Lily and what had surely unfolded down the road.

She was headed toward her bedroom to change into her pajamas when a knock sounded on her back door.

What in the world...?

The only people she knew in this town were Lily and Myron. If it was the second, she'd call the police. But if it was the first...

Heart pounding, she reached the window that overlooked the back deck and flipped on the outside light.

Lily glanced at the bulb, then to the woods. She looked terrified.

Grace unlocked the door and pulled her inside, the spaniel right on her heels. "What are you doing here?"

"He's gonna take me away. I don't wanna go, Miss Grace." She wrapped her arms around Grace's waist and held on tight. "Please, can I stay with you? Daddy's gonna take me away again."

Grace extricated herself from the child's thin arms and crouched down to meet her eyes, holding Lily at arms' length. "What do you mean? What's happening?"

"The police came. Daddy sent me straight to bed after they left. He thinks I told someone, but I didn't tell anybody anything. I wouldn't, not ever."

"Did he hurt you?"

She shook her head. She'd come in nothing but a thin nightgown and slippers, and her skin was cold to the touch and prickly with goose bumps. Grace quickly surveyed the child's arms and legs but saw no signs of injury. She draped a throw blanket from the sofa over her.

"What do you mean, he's taking you away? Is your father planning to move, or—?"

"He got a...a thing to put stuff in. I peeked out the window and saw it. One of those orange box things attached to the back of his pickup. It's in the driveway."

"A trailer?"

"He's putting in his cameras and computers. He's gonna take me away again." Her big green eyes filled with tears. "I don't wanna go. I don't wanna go again."

"Did you tell the police the truth?"

She shook her head. "He said he'd kill Regis. If I ever tell anybody, he'll kill Regis." She scooped up the dog, tears sliding down her cheeks.

"I'm going to call the police. You need to tell them everything."

"I can't. You don't know...He did it before. I said something to my teacher once. Back when I went to school. I didn't mean to, but she got nosy and I told her something I wasn't supposed to, and she talked to Daddy, and..." Lily sniffed, dropped her head, and sobbed. "He killed my dog. My first dog. Please don't make me go back."

Grace pulled her close, but the child's spine was stiff with terror.

What kind of man would use a dog's life to control his child?

Fear had Grace's heart pounding.

"You have to hide me, or I have to go," Lily said, "before he realizes I'm gone."

"No." Grace pulled her closer. "You're not going back there."

Voice muffled against Grace's sweater, Lily said, "You promise?"

How could she make that promise?

How could she not?

"Yes, I promise."

Lily collapsed against her, and Grace scooped her up, blanket and all, and held her close.

Now what?

She had to get Lily to tell the authorities the truth. But until then, she had to take her to a safe place. Maybe, if she called the authorities and told them what was going on, they'd return to Myron's house. They'd search the trailer—surely there'd be some evidence. They'd realize Lily was being exploited.

One step at a time.

She settled Lily on the couch. "I need to gather a few things. Stay here." She ran into her bedroom, grabbed a duffel bag from her closet, and tossed in some clothes, enough to last a couple of days. She added her toiletry bag. Back in the kitchen, she shoved some snacks into her purse, grabbed her laptop and charger, and took everything out to the garage, calling over her shoulder. "Come on, Lily."

Grace tossed her things into the SUV's cargo area.

Dragging the blanket behind her, Lily stepped into the garage, Regis on her heels. Grace helped them both into the backseat and put the child's seatbelt on her.

She returned to the house to find Oliver at the door, looking at her with those big, blue eyes. She scooped him up, grabbed his bag of food, and threw them both onto the passenger seat.

She met Lily's eyes in the rearview mirror. "You ready?"

Lily nodded, poor Regis crushed against her chest.

What am I doing?

This was insane. This was...

This was *kidnapping.*

No. She'd call the authorities and tell them everything as soon as she and Lily were safe.

She hit the garage door opener, and the door slowly lifted.

A truck blocked her driveway, a trailer attached at the back.

Myron.

He was walking down the driveway to her garage, something long and dark and menacing in his hand.

Rifle? Shotgun? She didn't know the difference. She did know, based on the murderous look in his eyes, he wasn't afraid to use it.

Thank God she'd backed in to more easily unload her groceries. "Hang on." She shifted into drive and mashed the gas.

Her Land Rover lurched out of the garage.

Myron planted himself in the middle of her driveway and lifted his weapon. She aimed right at him. At the last second, he jumped out of the way, firing a second too late. The gunshot reverberated in the quiet night.

She was almost sorry she hadn't hit him.

She could ram his truck, but she didn't want to damage their only means of escape, so she jerked the wheel, and the car lurched onto the grass and up the small hill toward the road.

In the rearview, she saw Myron standing. Aiming.

"Get down, Lily." Grace's voice sounded weirdly calm.

She angled around a tree.

A gunshot rang out. She didn't think he had hit her vehicle, but she couldn't be sure.

Her SUV bounced up between the trees, down the drainage ditch and up the other side. When she'd bought this vehicle, she'd figured she might need the off-roading abilities to navigate the country roads during bad weather. She'd never imagined this.

But the Land Rover handled the bumps and dips, and she reached the road and floored it.

In her rearview mirror, she saw Myron limping toward his truck.

She drove as fast as she dared along the narrow road, thankful Myron's truck had been pointed the other direction. With the trailer on the back, it would take him several minutes to turn it around.

She angled onto the highway that led to town, checking her rearview every few seconds.

No headlights back there.

She'd lost him. They were safe.

CHAPTER FOUR

Myron limped to the road and watched until long after the tail-lights had disappeared around the corner. Perhaps he should have fired again at the SUV. He'd been willing to take out the woman when they were headed uphill, toward him. Her lifeless foot would have slipped off the gas. The truck would have slowed to a stop. He'd have retrieved Lily and run. They'd have been long gone before the authorities found the body.

But she'd been smart. If he hadn't jumped out of the way, would she have braked?

He'd been afraid to fire at the back of the truck and possibly cause an accident that might injure his Lily. A broken limb would have been rough. A cut across the perfect little face, tragic.

He should have been better prepared. He should have realized, now that Lily had someplace to go, that she would run to the woman when she discovered they were moving. He should have understood the connection between the woman and the girl.

He'd underestimated Lily's desire to stay in their cabin in Washington.

He'd underestimated Grace Mullen in every way.

A woman hiding out in the woods, avoiding contact with all

mankind? It had never occurred to him that she'd risk so much for the sake of a stranger.

He'd been studying her, watching her, for weeks, ever since Lily had met Grace in the woods that day. He'd thought he understood her. Tonight, she'd surprised him.

Frankly, he was impressed.

He realized as he hobbled to his truck where he'd made his mistake. With no family nearby, no friends, no neighbors checking on her, Grace Mullen had nothing tying her to the community. In that respect, they were alike, he and Grace.

In other respects as well.

Like Myron, Grace Mullen was capable of living a solitary lifestyle.

Like Myron, Grace Mullen was perfectly at home in her own skin.

And like Myron, Grace Mullen was willing to go to whatever lengths necessary to gain her desire, even when those lengths required great dedication and courage.

Yes, he'd underestimated Grace Mullen.

Fortunately, she'd underestimated him as well.

CHAPTER FIVE

FIVE MONTHS LATER.

Andrew Middleton wasn't sure why his father had summoned him to his office in Nashua, New Hampshire, that late August morning, but he figured something serious had come up. Why else would Dad call on him? Their relationship had been contentious for years, and no matter what Andrew did, he couldn't seem to heal the wounds.

Despite Dad's shortcomings—and they were myriad—Andrew wanted nothing more than to repair the rift. After all, he wasn't perfect, either, and the first Andrew Middleton—Drew to those who knew him well—was the only dad Andrew had.

The eight-story brick-and-glass building rose above the surrounding establishments, the name *Middleton Enterprises* emblazoned on the side. Many folks had never heard of their company, though they'd probably gotten bills from one of their many subsidiaries. Dad had started the medical billing company back in the nineties, and it had quickly become the most successful of its kind. Since then, Dad had expanded to other services for medical practices and hospitals. His company had become one of the largest medical support businesses in the nation. Though there were branches from New Hampshire to Los Angeles and everywhere in between, Dad had kept the corporate office right there in Nashua, where it had begun.

Andrew flipped on the blinker and turned into the parking lot, catching sight of a police cruiser behind him, its spinning red and blue light bright in the morning sunshine.

He figured the officer would scoot on by, but the cruiser stayed on his tail.

No. No, no, no.

This couldn't be happening.

Andrew pulled into the first parking spot available, only to realize that he was right in front of the glass-fronted lobby.

No doubt the people inside were watching the scene unfold. The receptionist, who'd worked there since Andrew was in little league, would certainly recognize him and was probably spreading the news already.

He pulled his driver's license from his wallet and then located his registration and his proof of insurance and set them on the dashboard. Weren't those what police officers asked for when they pulled people over on TV shows? He'd never been pulled over himself. But he'd had enough experience with cops and armed guards that his heart was trying to pound out of his chest.

The cop had parked right behind Andrew's BMW. When he stepped out of the cruiser and started toward Andrew's car, Andrew lowered the window, letting in a whoosh of warm air. He left the documentation on the dash and settled both hands, fingers splayed, on the steering wheel.

The man bent at the window and looked inside. "Good morning."

Andrew offered a smile that he hoped looked authentic. "Officer." At least his voice didn't give away his fear. He'd had a lot of practice sounding confident when he felt anything but.

The man nodded to Andrew's hands. "You have no idea how many people are digging through their stuff when I approach their window."

Andrew had learned the hard way to show himself as

nonthreatening. He moved slowly as he retrieved his documentation and handed the cop the items.

He studied the license. "Any idea why I pulled you over, Mr. Middleton?" At the name, his glance slid to the name on the building, then back.

"I don't think I was speeding." He *knew* he hadn't been speeding. He was meticulous about obeying every law.

"You got a brake light out."

Andrew almost laughed, but there was nothing funny about the adrenaline pulsing through his veins. Would he ever get past the fear?

"Did you know?" the cop asked.

"Not a clue. I'll take it right in and get it fixed."

"I'll be right back." He walked to his cruiser and slipped inside, where he'd no doubt call in the information on Andrew's driver's license. What would he learn? That Andrew was an upstanding citizen who'd never so much as gotten a speeding ticket?

Or that he'd spent six long, torturous months behind bars?

His record was supposed to have been expunged. He'd been cleared of all the charges, and his lawyer had assured him that the felony conviction wouldn't follow him. But what if the judge's ruling hadn't been obeyed? Or red tape had held up the change in status? What if the cop thought Andrew was a felon? Or worse, thought he was supposed to still be in jail. Sure, Andrew would be able to prove he'd been released, eventually.

But not until after he'd been yanked from his car, cuffed, and arrested. Right there, in front of his family business. All the employees.

His father.

Andrew wasn't sure which he dreaded more—the wrath of the armed police officer, who wasn't a prison guard but looked enough like one to get his hands trembling—or his father's disappointment.

He did know he hated himself for his weakness. It was no wonder Dad wanted nothing to do with him.

Finally, the cop approached.

Again, Andrew placed his hands on the steering wheel. *No threat here, Officer. No reason to use force.*

The cop leaned down and handed Andrew's documents through the window. "You're all set. Get that brake light fixed."

"Will do. Thanks."

After the cop had driven away, Andrew breathed deeply.

It was nothing. A busted brake light. He'd have it fixed by the end of the day. He was talking himself down when the building's glass entry doors opened.

Dad stepped onto the sidewalk. As usual, he wore a suit and tie, his wingtips shiny as they clipped across the pavement. His gray hair was thinning on the top, trimmed on the sides. He'd gained some weight in the previous few years, and his oversize belly stuck out between the sides of his suit coat.

A look of disgust marred his face.

Excellent. So much for repairing their rift. If anything, that scene had only driven another wedge between them.

Andrew climbed from the car. "No big deal," he said when Dad was just a few feet away. "Broken brake light."

Dad froze on the sidewalk, setting his feet as if preparing for a fight. "You'd think, after what happened, you'd be more careful."

Andrew tamped down the surge of irritation, thanking God, not for the first time, that he'd gotten his height from his mother. He had a good six inches on his father's five-eight, though Dad had always seemed larger than life. "You check your car's brake lights daily, do you?"

"If I'd spent six months in prison—"

"For a crime I didn't commit."

"A crime you didn't *knowingly* commit, which isn't exactly the same thing."

"Thanks for that, Dad. If I ever start to feel too good about myself, I'll know exactly where to go."

Dad pressed his lips closed.

The door behind him opened, and Chet stepped outside. Charles Middleton, Dad's second son, the one born to his second wife, the woman Dad had chosen over Mom despite the marriage vows.

Chet...The name sounded like it should be branded on the outside of a box of crackers. *Cheddar Chets.*

Chet smiled at Andrew, his eyes dancing with glee. "Didn't take you long to get in trouble with the law again."

Andrew ignored him and focused on his father. "What do you need?"

Their father shifted to face his other—preferred—son. "This doesn't concern you."

"I don't know why you called him," Chet said. "I've got it under control."

Dad's smile was tight. "Son, take care of that stuff we talked about."

Son. When was the last time Dad had called Andrew *son*?

Dad turned back to him. "Come on inside."

When Dad's back was to him, Chet glared. Andrew waited for him to stick out his tongue to complete the childish moment. He ignored his idiot half brother and followed Dad into the building.

Silently, they walked through the lobby, took the elevator to the top floor, and pushed through the glass doors that separated the corporate offices from the rest of the company. Andrew smiled at familiar faces along the way, trying not to look guilty, despite the scene he'd just been a part of.

Looking confident when he felt anything but—that was Andrew's special skill, and he'd employed it often in this building.

Harrison Ackerman, Middleton's CFO for as long as Andrew could remember—and Dad's oldest friend—stepped out of the office beside Dad's. Andrew hadn't seen him in years and surprised that the once brown hair had grayed. He smiled and held out his hand. "Haven't seen you in a long time."

"Uncle Harrison." Andrew shook his hand, thankful for the friendly reception when everybody else had acted as though they didn't remember him. As if he hadn't been in this building a million times during his growing-up years. As if they didn't all know the most shameful thing about him.

"What brings you here today?" Harrison asked.

Andrew shifted his gaze to Dad, who said, "Got some catching up to do." He clasped his friend on the upper arm, then preceded Andrew further down the hall.

Finally, they reached Dad's opulent corner office with its view of the city, the river, and the forest in the distance. It was beautiful, so contrary to the frustration churning in Andrew's gut.

Dad sat heavily in his leather chair, and Andrew settled in one of the two chairs opposite the carved, ornate desk. If they were a real family, they might relax in the sitting area to the side, maybe share a drink and a laugh. But he and Dad hadn't been family in a long time.

"How's your little company doing?" Dad asked.

"My *little*"—he stopped short of adding *wildly successful* —"company is doing quite well, actually." Andrew loved his job at BNB in Coventry. He loved his role there, which combined his business acumen with his medical experience. Though he'd once thought he wanted to be a physician, he realized the job he was doing was exactly the role he was created for, whether Dad respected it or not. "Right now, we're developing a product that could revolutionize treatment for diabetes."

"Good, good." Dad leaned forward, propping his elbows on his desk. He tented his fingers. "You're right. What you said outside. When I got the call that the police were out front, it brought back what happened before. I was worried."

Worried that Andrew would get arrested again, thrown in jail again, convicted again? Did Dad think it would be another miscarriage of justice? Or did Dad worry Andrew had broken the law?

But another truth nudged its way in. Dad had gotten the news, hurried along the hallways, taken the elevator, and burst outside. He could have just waited in his office, away from prying eyes.

He could have kept his distance. He hadn't.

Maybe that meant something. Maybe there was hope.

Andrew asked, "Who called you?"

"Bernice called Harrison, who told me."

The busybody receptionist just couldn't wait to share the news. Andrew was surprised she'd call the CFO, though. What was their connection? Or did Bernice simply know Harrison would want to know?

Who else had she called? Would the woman be as conscientious to share that the cop had left without incident?

Doubtful.

Why did Andrew care what any of them thought? The only person in this building whose opinion of him mattered was sitting right across the desk.

"If I want you to move on from all that mess," Dad continued, "then I ought to do the same."

Dad hadn't always been so quick to judge, so quick to bring up the past. Their relationship hadn't always been so strained.

"I never meant to hurt you."

Dad's expression softened. An instant later, he shifted, and the hard-nosed businessman was back. "I want you to do something for me."

Andrew sat forward, hating his own eagerness. "Okay."

"Since you got that MBA, maybe you can make sense of this." He bent toward the floor beside him and lifted a box. He dropped it on his desk. "For some reason, Middleton Billing is bleeding money, but I can't figure out where."

Middleton Billing Company, MBC, was the corporation's bread and butter, the enterprise Dad had started first. After Chet graduated from college, Dad put him in charge, and Andrew had wondered if he'd done so because the business had been practically running itself and turning a profit for thirty years. Even Cheddar Chet couldn't screw it up.

Apparently, he could.

Andrew stood and peered into the box. It was about half full of accounting notebooks, manila folders, and random paperwork. He riffled through it a minute, then lifted his gaze to Dad's.

"Please tell me this is the paperwork to back up your electronic files."

Dad sat back in his chair. "We got all the other subsidiaries working in the new accounting program, but Chet's been struggling to get his feet under him. You know he's never been great with numbers. Harrison's been working with Chet since he took over, trying to teach him the ropes. Chet's got his talents, but book-keeping isn't one of them. Harrison figured Chet would do better to work with paper files until he really understood what all the numbers meant."

"You're saying"—Andrew gestured to the box—"this is it, all the records?"

"For the last several years. Before that, the company was making a tidy profit."

Andrew set the box on the floor beside him and sat again. "Before Chet took over."

Dad's expression darkened. "He's doing a decent job. He's just missing something."

"If MBC is losing money, then he's not doing a decent job. He's doing a lousy job."

Dad straightened in his chair. "He doesn't have your quick mind, that's true. He's not as naturally talented as you are. That's why I wanted..." The words faded. Dad tapped some papers on his desk against the wood before setting them to the side.

"I know I disappointed you."

"If you'd finished medical school..."

Hot shame rolled down Andrew's back. He'd screwed every-thing up. He knew that. He certainly didn't need Dad to remind him at every opportunity.

Dad waved his own words away. "I never wanted that for you. I wanted you here." He knocked on his desk. "Here, in this business, stepping into the legacy I built for you. When you wanted to go to medical school, I realized business wasn't your dream. But now..."

"I need to forge my own way. Surely you can understand that. That's what you did. You didn't follow Pop's footsteps."

"Your grandfather was a *plumber*." He said the word with scorn. "I own a multimillion-dollar corporation. It's not exactly the same thing."

"Grandpa might not have built what you have, but he was a good man."

"I know that. I'm not saying..." Dad sat back and shook his head.

Why did they always do this? Why did every discussion have to end in discord?

Because neither approved of the other's decisions. Which was one of the reasons Andrew hadn't wanted to work for his father, to have this kind of conversation every single day.

Dad glanced at his watch and stood. "I'm hoping you can get back to me by the end of the week."

"Why not have Harrison do it? Or one of his underlings. Surely there's somebody more in tune with the business than I am."

Dad's gaze flicked to the side, to the ceiling, before meeting his again. "I want fresh eyes on it." That wasn't all, but Andrew had no idea what Dad wasn't telling him.

He grabbed the box and followed Dad to the door. "Shouldn't be a problem. Should I call you or Chet with questions?"

"Call me. I know how you boys like to fight." Dad delivered the words with the slightest hint of a smile. Andrew had never gotten along with his half brother, and now that he would be double-checking the man's work, he wondered if he ever would.

"Okay, then. Assuming this is pretty well organized, I should have some information for you by Friday."

He'd figure out what Chet had done to screw up MBC. He'd finally been given a way to make his father proud, and he wasn't going to blow it.

By the time Andrew had his brake light repaired and reached the condominium development where he lived in Coventry, the sun was inching below the tall pines. Children played in the playground. A couple of older kids skateboarded along the sidewalks. Neighbors walked dogs. The clubhouse parking lot was half-full, probably for some community event the complex had planned. Even though he was one of the few single people there, he joined the fun whenever he could. He needed people, needed friends. But it had been a long day already, and he hoped to start digging into MBC's books before bed.

He parked outside his place, one of four he owned in this area —the others were rental properties—and climbed from his BMW. After unlocking his front door, he returned to the sedan for the box, only then noticing a black SUV in the spot across the way.

A brunette stepped out the condo's front door. Cassidy. She saw him and lifted a hand in a wave before turning to speak to someone inside. A moment later, she jogged his way. "I'm glad you're here. I want to introduce you to your new tenant."

Andrew wanted to dive right into Dad's paperwork, but meeting this woman was necessary. After all, she would be living in one of his properties, even if Cassidy and her husband, James, had signed the lease and paid the rent.

He lifted the box a bit. "Just let me set this down, and I'll be right over."

When Cassidy turned, he caught sight of her baby bump. She was five months along with her first child and glowing. James had all but popped a button when he'd shared at their game night that she was expecting. They were one of those couples that almost made Andrew believe happy marriages existed.

He dropped the box in his living room and jogged across the street. He knocked on the open door. A "come in" rang from inside, and he stepped into the condo, which had been empty when he'd handed over the keys to Cassidy a few days before. Now, it was filled with furniture. Not the renter's furniture, though. Cassidy and James had collected pieces from friends and family and garage sales.

Cassidy had known the renter back in Seattle. How she'd ended up on the East Coast, he had no idea. Not that it mattered to him, as long as she took care of his property and didn't cause any trouble.

There were no boxes, no crates, no plastic containers. There'd been no moving truck outside. Either the woman had already unpacked everything—and stowed all evidence of having just moved in—or she owned next to nothing.

Cassidy stepped into the living room from the kitchen, wiping her hands on a towel. "Glad you made it before I left. She's upstairs getting changed. It's been a long day."

"Moving's never easy." He glanced around at the too-tidy space. "Though they seem pretty settled."

Cassidy shrugged and walked past him to the bottom of the stairs. "Grace, your landlord's here."

Before she'd finished, a little girl hurried in through the back door. She had brown hair in braids and great big green eyes the color of springtime. She rushed across the space, then froze a few feet from him and looked up. The smile she'd worn faded.

A little dog stopped at her feet, sat, and glared up at him as if he were an enemy.

"Hi there," he said. "I'm Andrew."

The child looked from him to Cassidy, saying nothing.

Footsteps on the stairs had him glancing that direction. Then taking a longer look.

Whoa. Cassidy had described her old friend as if she were one step away from homelessness. He'd expected a bedraggled woman, wan and drawn, with limp hair and dull eyes.

The woman descending the staircase had only gender in common with the image in his head. Long wavy blond hair, eyes the blueish-gray of a morning sky. Milky skin free of unnecessary makeup. Far from haggard, she looked healthy and strong. Beautiful.

He hoped he'd schooled his expression by the time she reached the landing. He held out his hand. "Andrew Middleton."

She glanced at it, then at Cassidy, who dipped her head as if giving permission. Or encouragement.

The woman slid her slender fingers against his palm. "Grace."

He'd barely gotten a grip before she yanked her hand back. But her face registered...relief?

Okay, that was weird. Was she afraid of him?

The little girl bumped against Grace's legs, and the woman lowered her gaze to her. "Did you introduce yourself?"

The girl looked up at him and swallowed. "I'm Lily."

"Nice to meet you, Lily. That's a pretty name. And who's this?" He crouched down and held out his hand to the dog, some kind of little spaniel, he thought.

"That's Regis."

The dog sniffed Andrew's hands, then nuzzled. He rewarded the animal with a scratch behind the ears. "Nice to meet you, Regis."

The child scooted closer to Grace and stepped slightly behind her.

He wasn't sure what their story was, but he didn't need to read the whole book to know they were both wary. He stood and stepped slightly away, trying to appear as nonthreatening as possible. "I hope you have everything you need."

"We do," Grace said. "Cassidy's been very generous."

"She's like that." Andrew glanced at his friend, who waved off the words. To Grace, he said, "If you need anything, I'm right across the way." He pointed to his condo. "Number thirty-three."

"We'll be fine." The words were curt, and the quick "thank you," she added didn't sound particularly thankful.

"Okay, then. I'll leave you to it." He swiveled and stepped through the door and across the parking area, eager to eat dinner and dive into that box.

The sound of footsteps following him didn't bode well.

Cassidy called, "Can I talk to you for a sec?"

He stopped on his front stoop. "Friendly folks."

She ignored that, leaning on the railing across from him. "Keep an eye on her for me, would you?"

"I don't think she'd appreciate that."

Cassidy's gaze flicked to the new tenant's condo. She lowered her voice, not that there was anybody close enough to overhear. "I'm worried about them. I haven't gotten to the bottom of what's going on, but..." She bit her bottom lip and shook her head. "Anyway, just let me know if you see anything weird."

He had better things to do than babysit. But Cassidy was a friend, and how hard could it be? "Sure thing."

Cassidy gripped his elbow. "Thank you. For that, for renting to a stranger, for allowing the pets."

Against his policy, but for friends, he'd allowed it. He'd moved to Coventry without a single acquaintance. The people at his new church had pulled him right into their group. James and Cassidy were only two of the crowd that had made Andrew feel at home in this town. What were a few stains on the carpet compared to friends?

"I'm happy to do it," Andrew said, meaning it. "And I'll keep my eye on them." He glanced around at his condo community and chuckled. "Honestly, the whole world's watching around here. If anything *weird* happens, I won't be the only person to witness it."

Cassidy didn't laugh with him, though. She seemed uncharacteristically serious when she nodded. "Just keep an eye out."

The way she said it, the tone, had his amusement fading. "I don't need any trouble."

"Don't worry. She won't be any trouble."

CHAPTER SIX

After Cassidy left, Grace passed the used furniture Cassidy had been so gracious to provide and peeked out the window.

Across the parking lot, Andrew was leaning against the door-jamb, staring at her door.

The man had taken her by surprise. She'd known Cassidy was friends with Grace's landlord, but still, she'd expected someone older, someone thicker around the middle. With his brown hair and those dark, brooding eyes, Andrew was not only younger than she'd expected but much more handsome.

But handsome men weren't necessarily good. Some people would call Lily's father handsome, and he was a monster.

And the way Andrew was staring at her place?

Despite the flash of insight she'd had when they shook hands—she'd not seen any pictures, but she'd felt only bright and good emotions—he seemed far from safe.

She closed the blinds, then double-checked the front door. It was locked and dead-bolted. They were hidden here. Myron wouldn't find them. And Cassidy wouldn't have introduced her to a man who wasn't trustworthy.

It would be fine.

Lord, please. Please let us stay here.

After Lily bathed and read for the night, Grace led her to her bedroom and got her settled. She looked tiny in the twin bed. It had been a long day, and the girl was half awake, her dog nestled against her side, her thumb in her mouth. If Grace didn't know her age, she'd guess that Lily was five, not eight-going-on-nine, as the girl had told her when they'd first met. She'd taken to sucking her thumb after their terrifying escape from her father that first night. Grace had decided not to encourage her to quit just yet. When the child felt safe, she'd lose the habit.

Assuming she ever felt safe again. But they'd been running for so long.

Grace had called the police not long after she'd escaped Myron that night, telling Detective Eckmann that he'd shot at her, but somehow, the authorities had never located the man and his trailer.

Grace hadn't admitted that she'd kidnapped Lily. When Grace called back to get status reports—even months later, nobody'd seen the man—she hadn't mentioned that Lily was with her. The detective had never asked about the child.

Grace spoke a prayer over Lily and said, "I'll be right across the hall if you need me."

For five months, they'd shared hotel rooms, often sleeping in the same bed, always trying to stay one step ahead of Myron. That first night after they'd escaped, they'd made it all the way to Idaho before finding a place to sleep. She'd been sure they'd be safe there.

But then Myron had shown up. If the dog hadn't alerted her—Regis had proved to have super-canine skills—he might have caught up to them.

How had he found her, though? For the life of her, she couldn't figure it out.

She'd sold her Land Rover and purchased a RAV-4 with cash. She'd ditched her old phone and replaced it. She'd purchased false papers for herself and Lily. And now, they'd moved all the way across the country.

Maybe they'd be safe.

Maybe they had been since that first night in Idaho. Maybe it hadn't been Myron who'd broken the window on her old Land Rover in Little Rock. Maybe Grace had just imagined him in that hardware store in Kansas City.

Maybe she was crazy. But over and over, she'd felt the compulsion to run.

"I like this place," Lily said, drawing her back to the moment.

She kissed the child's forehead. "Me too."

"Can we stay here?"

If only Grace had a good answer for that. As far as she could tell, Myron had never reported Lily missing. Grace didn't believe she was a fugitive, but she'd been careful to keep her head down whenever she saw a police officer, just in case. If she was caught, would they throw Grace in jail? Return Lily to her father?

She had no idea.

When she first took Lily, she'd had every intention of going straight to the authorities with her and encouraging her to tell them the truth about her father. But Lily wouldn't even open up to Grace. How could she expect the child to open up to strangers?

Please, let us be safe here, Lord. Because they couldn't keep running. Lily would never flourish if she couldn't put down roots and let them grow deep.

The trust in the child's eyes made her heart ache. "You think Daddy is okay?"

The question didn't surprise Grace. Myron was Lily's father, her family. Of course she missed him. That didn't mean she was safe with him.

"I'm sure he's fine." And then she added the question she'd asked whenever Lily brought up her father. "Do you want me to take you to him?"

Lily's little eyes rounded, and she shook her head. "I wanna stay with you."

Grace brushed Lily's hair back on her forehead. "That's what I want too." Whatever happened, Grace wouldn't let Myron get his daughter back, but the child needed to process her feelings. Lily deserved to know the truth about herself, that she was precious and loved, not an object to be used and threatened and hurt. She deserved to grow up in a safe home around people who loved her. Grace couldn't be that person. She just couldn't figure out how to get Lily to a family who would love her without getting herself thrown in jail and Lily returned to the father who'd exploited her.

"Get some rest and wake me if you need me."

Lily sat up and opened her arms, and Grace pulled her into a hug. She comforted the child, but she was always careful not to get too close. Not to hold her hand. She was loosening her grip when Lily said, "I love you, Miss Grace."

She leaned away and forced a smile. She didn't know what she felt for Lily, but she knew it couldn't be love. Not the real kind, the kind that made a difference in the world. Grace's love had never been enough for anybody. She didn't understand what was wrong with her, why she was defective. But she always had been. Always would be. And her heart couldn't stand another loss when one more person deemed her *not enough.* "You are loved, sweet girl."

Lily curled around her dog and closed her eyes. Within seconds, her breathing had evened out.

The innocence and trust of children. Good thing Lily had no idea how inept her chosen savior was.

Grace was exhausted too. They'd driven two hundred miles that day, much of it in traffic, and then spent the afternoon and evening getting settled. After a cup of chamomile tea—her nightly ritual—she climbed the stairs to ready herself for bed. In the shower, she lifted her heart in thanksgiving, knowing that if she didn't focus on the good, she'd get swallowed up in the bad.

Thank You for bringing us here. Thank You for Cassidy, for this home. For our health. For the money You've provided. She would never attribute the money in her bank account to the family that had given it to her. God was her provider, not that man. *Thank You for the new car, for keeping us safe all these months from Myron.*

Was he still on her tail, or had she finally shaken him off?

Please, God, keep protecting us. And protect my heart. Help me not to get attached to Lily.

God knew what Grace needed. He knew what she could handle, and she could definitely *not* handle getting emotionally involved with another at-risk girl.

Help us to fit in here, to make a home here.

Andrew's image floated in the hazy bathroom air. She didn't know what to think about the landlord across the parking lot. For five months...Actually, since long before Lily'd come into her life, Grace had managed to avoid people. Now, she had Cassidy and her husband, James, and Cassidy had alluded to other friends she thought Grace should meet. Could she avoid them, or would that seem rude and ungrateful?

And then there was Andrew watching from across the street. She didn't know what his story was, but despite the peace she'd felt in their brief touch, she didn't trust him.

Protect us, Lord. Hide us.

CHAPTER SEVEN

MYRON'S PLAN had been perfect. The more settled Grace and Lily got at that crappy by-the-week hotel in Kansas City, the more his plan took shape. He'd had no doubt that Grace would eventually rent one of the apartments she'd toured, probably the one closest to the most highly rated schools in the area. She cared about things like that, and she seemed to believe Lily needed to be around people. The more Myron watched Grace Mullen, the more he was coming to understand her.

Grace and Lily would move in. Lily would start school in the fall. They'd grow complacent just in time for all the pieces of his plan to fall into place.

He'd been in town, purchasing new deadbolts for the basement rooms and chatting with the kid behind the counter. He'd learned long before that the way to divert suspicion was to chat and charm. Smile and schmooze. Act like he belonged. Not arrogant or haughty but humble and generous, the kind of guy people wanted to like and hated to think ill of. That was Myron. Even his name—carefully chosen for its meekness—invited people to trust him.

"Keeping out the boogie man?" the clerk asked, ringing up the best lock the Kansas City hardware store sold.

Myron chose his most ingratiating smile. "That's what I'll tell my daughter. She's coming to stay with me. I'm trying to get the place ready."

"That's awesome, dude," the kid said.

An older lady behind Myron had laid a hand on his arm. "What a good father you must be."

He'd dipped his chin. "I sure hope so. She's been with her mother for so long, I'm afraid she'll hate being with me."

"You just love your little girl, and she'll come around." The woman spoke the words with authority, squeezing his forearm as she did.

"Oh, I intend to, ma'am." He did love Lily. Loved her like he'd never loved another of his muses. She'd put new spark in what had become his humdrum life, taking boring photographs of mediocre faces for magazine spreads, shooting portraits that hung in ritzy homes from coast to coast. On the side, capturing lewd photos of children for the real income.

But Lily had given him something to live for. With Lily as his subject, his work, which had always been excellent, had become stellar. Groundbreaking. He wasn't taking photographs. He was capturing beauty.

Sadly, the only people who got to experience his artistic genius were men who weren't buying because they appreciated his brilliance. At least they paid well.

Yes, it had all been coming together.

And then, in the worst kind of coincidence, he'd stepped out of the hardware store and almost run smack dab into Grace.

He'd averted his gaze, pulling his baseball cap down over his eyes. But he'd seen a spark of recognition in her eyes.

Grace and Lily had escaped that night. He'd seen the tears running down her cheeks as she'd loaded the sleepy child into the car.

All the work he'd put into his plan, and he'd have to start all over. He'd be more careful next time. Neither Grace nor Lily would see him until he was ready to reveal himself.

Patience. He just needed patience.

CHAPTER EIGHT

ANDREW PUSHED BACK from the desk in his home office and slammed his laptop closed.

He'd been working on entering years of numbers into accounting software and trying to analyze what he found, but the more he entered, the less clarity he had.

Children's laughter floated in through the open window. It was unseasonably warm for late September, nearly seventy degrees and, from the sound of it, the rest of the people in the complex were enjoying the sunshine and the changing leaves. A walk would do him good, clear his mind.

He shoved his feet into sneakers and stepped outside, closing his storm door but leaving the other door wide open. Studying and working in Boston had taught him to be cautious. Six months in prison had taught him to be paranoid. But slowly, living in this small town, in this close-knit community, he was learning to trust again.

And anyway, he'd only be gone a few minutes.

As he'd guessed, the playground equipment in the park in the center of the complex was crawling with children. A group of guys played basketball on the half court. Two older couples were enjoying a game of doubles tennis. Surrounding it all, adults watched, standing in clusters or sitting at picnic tables. One woman had brought snacks, and kids clustered around her, little hands reaching for brightly colored packages.

As Andrew passed, the woman, Becky, who lived on the next street over, smiled at him. "Goldfish?"

He patted his belly. "Trying to quit."

"But it's fish. Brain food!" She laughed and returned her attention to the brown-haired girl waiting patiently beside her.

Oh. It was Lily. She looked so different, so much more relaxed than when he'd first met her. He wouldn't have recognized the child if not for the dog at her feet. Andrew's promise to keep an eye on his new tenants hadn't taken much of a toll. He'd barely gotten a glance of them in the month since they'd moved in, just waving a couple of times when they'd left at the same time in the morning, him for work, them to get Lily to school.

When Lily got her crackers, she thanked the woman and jogged away, the little dog at her side.

The table she approached was the farthest from the playground, the only one not surrounded by people. Grace sat alone, her focus on a laptop. She looked up when Lily stopped at her side and opened the crackers. After she handed the bag back to Lily, the girl bolted toward the playground, shoving food in her mouth as she went.

Another girl called her name, and Lily joined her. They climbed one of the ladders and disappeared among the children.

It seemed Lily fit right in.

Grace, not so much. Did she want to stay separate from everyone, or was she simply too shy to join?

Andrew chatted with some neighbors, shook a couple of hands, greeted a few of the kids, and then headed for the lone woman.

She must have heard him coming because she looked up, wariness in her expression that didn't fade when she saw who it was. In case she'd forgotten, he said, "Hi, Grace. Andrew."

"I remember." She'd pulled her long hair into a ponytail and wore no makeup. She was fresh-faced and beautiful, despite the unfriendly expression.

"Mind if I...?" He nodded to the bench across from her.

She shrugged. "Help yourself."

He settled in and gazed at the kids on the playground. "Lily seems to be having fun."

But Grace had returned her attention to her laptop. "Yeah. She's made a lot of friends." Her expression softened when she lifted her head to watch the kids. "It's a relief."

"This place is pretty special."

Her only response was a shrug.

"What are you working on?"

"Just..." She pressed a couple of buttons and closed the laptop. "Sorry."

"What do you do?"

"Medical transcription."

One of his father's subsidiaries was a medical transcription service. He could ask who she worked for, maybe find a connection, but he didn't like people to realize his relationship to Middleton Enterprises until they knew him better. He wanted to be known not for who his father was or how much money he had but for who he was and what he could contribute. "You like the work?"

"It keeps me busy."

"And pays the bills," he guessed.

She nodded.

"How about you?" he asked. "Made some friends on the playground?"

Her lip quirked at the corner, the only indication she found his comment even slightly amusing. "I'm content."

As in, *I have plenty of friends*? Or as in, *I don't need friends*?

He didn't ask those questions, though. "Do you go to church?"

She shook her head. "Tomorrow, if Cassidy has anything to say about it."

"That's where I go. I hope you make it."

Her gaze flicked back to her laptop. Obviously, she hadn't chosen a table away from the crowds because she was shy. She simply didn't want to get to know her neighbors.

Fine by him. He slid off the bench. "Well. Good to see you."

She offered a closed-lipped smile that said she felt just the opposite, and he left her there, walking toward the basketball court. Maybe he could join the game, clear his mind of the unfriendly woman and the work he'd left at his condo.

Difficult problems never got solved by being stared at. Andrew'd discovered that he usually needed to walk away, to let the facts bubble in the cauldron, so to speak, until the solutions rose to the top. He'd told his father he'd have an understanding of MBC's numbers within a couple of days. It'd been weeks, but he didn't have everything he needed, and Chet had been dragging his feet about forwarding the accounting books that somehow hadn't made it into the box. Without them, Andrew was having a very hard time getting a clear picture of what was going on.

He shot baskets with Thomas and Garrett, two of his friends from church who also lived in the complex, along with a bunch of teens who thought their slurs of *old man* were hilarious, as if late twenties were akin to late seventies. The kids were winning, but Andrew's team was catching up when he heard a scream from the playground.

A dog barked furiously.

Andrew turned, ball in hand.

Lily was lying on the ground beneath the monkey bars.

At her table to the side of the playground, Grace didn't even look up from her laptop. Granted, she was as far from Lily as she could be and still technically be at the park. But shouldn't she have one ear tuned in to the child in her care?

Andrew bounced the ball to Thomas and maneuvered through the crowd of children surrounding Lily. She'd pushed herself to a sitting position and was supporting one arm with her other hand.

Her dog was at her side, whining now.

Andrew crouched beside her. "Hi, Lily. Remember me? I'm Andrew. We met your first day here."

She looked at him, tears dripping from her wide green eyes. "I fell."

He wasn't about to examine the arm, but by the way it was already swelling and how she was supporting it, he guessed it was broken. "Come on. Let's go find your..." Not mother. Foster mother, if he remembered right. The child needed a real mother, because the woman who was supposed to be caring for her obviously didn't.

Lily seemed paralyzed by pain or fear, so he scooped her up and carried her to where the woman still worked. Maybe she was doing medical transcription, and had earphones in. But he saw nothing in her ears that would explain her not having heard the scream.

He called, "Grace!" as he approached.

She lifted her gaze, then slammed the laptop closed and stood. "What happened?"

"She fell. She was screaming."

But Grace didn't respond or defend herself as she hurried to meet them, holding out her arms as if she would take the girl. Andrew wasn't relinquishing Lily that easily, not until he knew Grace would take care of her. "I think her arm's broken. She needs to go to the hospital."

The little color in Grace's face drained. "Oh. I...Let's just have a look. Maybe it's not—"

"I'll drive."

"What? No, no. I can take her."

But Andrew wasn't listening. He marched toward his condo, the child whimpering in his arms, the so-called mother on his heels almost as close as the ever-present dog.

"I've got it." Grace caught up with him, her laptop tucked beneath one arm. "I can handle it."

"Yeah. That's really obvious, based on the way you didn't even know she was hurt."

Grace's eyes widened. She blinked several times.

Great. Just what he needed, another weepy female.

"I'm happy to do it." He tempered his voice, tried to sound kind. "If I drive, then you can be with Lily." They reached his condo. He needed to dig his car keys out of his pocket, but how, with the child in his arms?

He was afraid that if he put her down, Grace would snatch her and take off. Would she get Lily the care she needed? So far, she hadn't proved to be all that great a parent.

Foster parent, he reminded himself. Maybe she wasn't that great at parenting, but she was trying. More than most folks without kids of their own. More than he was. He needed to adjust his attitude.

"Okay. If it's no trouble..." Grace set her laptop on top of his car and held out her arms. "Come here, sweetheart."

He shifted the child to Grace. Lily whimpered but didn't cry out again. After yanking his keys from his pocket, he clicked to unlock his car and opened a back door. Grace placed Lily inside and put on her seatbelt. The dog hopped in before he could stop it.

"Give me your keys," he said, "and I'll put the dog in your condo."

"No!" Lily looked stricken at the suggestion.

"Regis stays with Lily," Grace said. "She needs him."

"They won't allow him in the hospital." Andrew worked hard to keep his tone level. "It would be cruel to leave him in the car for as long as it'll take."

"Of course." Grace dug her keys from her pocket and handed them over.

Andrew managed to wrangle the wiggly dog out of the car, grabbed Grace's laptop, and hurried to her place, where he deposited both. He locked his front door, and two minutes later, they were on the road.

"Closest ER is in Plymouth, about twenty minutes from here." He glanced in the rearview to Grace in the back seat. "We could try an urgent care closer, but I don't know which ones have X-rays. Do you have a preference?"

"I don't have my purse or my wallet." She looked stricken at the thought. "I should have had you grab them."

"Don't worry about it." He'd pay cash for the visit if he had to, as long as Lily got the care she needed. But foster kids probably had medical care provided by the state. He didn't know how that worked.

He expected Grace to argue, but she didn't. Not that there was a choice. He wasn't going to put off getting Lily help so they could return for the woman's purse.

The child whimpered, and Grace spoke gentle words over her. He could barely make out what she was saying, but it sounded like...Was she praying?

He strained to listen and picked up words that confirmed his guess.

So maybe Grace wasn't the world's greatest mother, but it seemed she was a believer, and she truly cared about Lily. Those two things would smooth over a lot of jagged edges.

"Ma'am, I need to see some form of ID." The woman behind the desk where Grace sat seemed utterly unsympathetic.

Seated nearby in the waiting room, Andrew patted Lily's good hand. "I'll be right back, okay?"

She nodded, still holding that arm protectively, and he approached the desk. He sat in the chair beside Grace and smiled at the stern-faced woman on the far side of the plexiglass partition. "Ms. Barker," he said, reading her name tag, "we took off in a hurry to get the child here. Can I give you my information? I'll be happy to act as the responsible party."

The woman glared at him. "We need the child's insurance information. I can look it up. I just need the name of the insurer."

As if she hadn't spoken, Andrew slid his driver's license through the small opening. The woman snatched it up, lips pinched. Then, her expression shifted so fast, Andrew had to grit his teeth.

"Oh, Mr. Middleton. I didn't recognize you."

As if they'd met before.

"Yes, this will do." She went from lemons to sugar in a matter of seconds. "Sorry for the misunderstanding." She took down his information and passed some paperwork across the desk. "If you'll just—"

"Wait." Grace was looking from the woman to him and back, curiosity in her eyes. Or was that suspicion? "I can handle it. I'll just need to bring back—"

"That's fine, ma'am," the woman said. "Just whenever it's convenient for you."

Andrew glanced up from the paperwork he'd already started filling out. "What's her last name?"

Grace blinked a couple of times. Swallowed. "Smith. Lillian Smith."

He wrote the name down. "Why don't you go sit with her?"

Grace still seemed suspicious, but she nodded and returned to where Lily sat in the busy waiting room. There had to be twenty-five, maybe thirty people. They'd be lucky if they were out of there by morning.

But ten minutes after Andrew handed over the paperwork, a nurse called Grace and Lily back. As they stood, Grace sent Andrew another one of those curious glances.

Nearby, others' looks weren't so friendly.

Andrew ignored all that. "I'll just wait here."

"You gotta come." Lily grabbed his hand and held on. "Please, you saved me."

Saved her? Far from it, but he didn't hate being seen as a hero in the eyes of a child. He glanced at Grace for permission. Her lips were pressed so tightly, they'd turned white. How was it this woman could still be so attractive, even when she was practically shooting fire out of her eyes?

"It's fine," she finally said.

Way to make a guy feel welcome.

But he joined them anyway, feeling protective of the little girl he'd *saved*. And maybe the child's foster mother. If they'd been pushed to the head of the line because of his last name, he didn't complain. He couldn't blame the staff for that, considering his last name was plastered across the entrance to the heart center on a higher floor. His father's generosity—and ego—knew few bounds.

Grace lifted Lily onto the bed in the exam room and stood by her side. The room itself was barely larger than a walk-in closet and filled with equipment. A curtain had been pulled closed between them and the hallway outside. There were no exterior windows.

A nurse did an initial examination. "Did you get hurt fighting a big lion?" she asked.

Lily giggled. "I fell off the monkey bars."

"Those monkeys." She tsked. "They're such a nuisance. I'll send someone in to get some pictures."

Before the X-ray tech came, though, a different woman entered. She gave Andrew an apologetic smile then focused on Grace. "Sorry. We just have a few more questions. When a child gets hurt...You know how it is."

Grace's smile was tight at the corners. "Okay."

The woman turned her attention to Lily. "Can you tell me what happened?"

Her gaze flicked to Grace as if seeking permission. "I fell."

The woman asked a few more questions, and Lily answered them honestly. Abruptly, the woman asked, "What's your name?"

"Lily Bow—"

"Smith." Grace laughed, but the sound was forced. "Lillian Bonnie Smith."

Lily shoved a thumb in her mouth and nodded.

The woman squinted at Grace, who seemed to be trying to look natural, but the fear radiating off her was so palpable that Andrew could almost taste it.

"I was there when it happened." He stood from his seat in the corner. "Andrew Middleton."

The woman didn't respond. Apparently, she'd already known who he was, and she wasn't impressed. It made him like her a little more. Though she hadn't said so, he guessed she was a social worker, someone sent to make sure Lily hadn't been abused. At some point between when they'd walked in and when they'd been ushered back to the exam room, something they'd done had set off alarm bells.

Probably Grace's lack of identification.

And her obvious fear.

"Grace and Lily are my new neighbors," Andrew said. "Like Lily said, she fell off the monkey bars. The accident took place at the community park. There were a lot of witnesses. I'll be happy to give you their names, if you'd like to follow up." He rattled off Thomas and Garrett's names, then added some of his neighbors and the kids he'd been shooting baskets with. "I don't have all their numbers"—he pulled his phone from his pocket—"but I have a few." He scrolled through his contact list and read phone numbers.

The social worker made notes on her clipboard. When she looked up again, she smiled. "Thanks. That should do it."

Finally, she stepped out, her suspicion satisfied.

Andrew's was anything but.

A man who had probably been waiting just outside the door pushed a mobile X-ray machine in and smiled at Lily. "We need to take a few pictures of that arm, okay?"

Lily yanked her thumb out of her mouth. "Will it hurt?"

"I'll do my best to make sure it doesn't." He pulled open the curtain to reveal the window between the room and the hallway. "You two'll need to step out. You can watch from there."

Grace kissed Lily on the forehead and left. Andrew followed

and stood beside her, watching through the glass as the man, joined by two other techs, got the X-rays they needed.

"You want to tell me what that was about?" Andrew kept his voice low, not even glancing Grace's way when he asked the question.

"What do you mean?"

"Don't do that."

She said nothing.

He forced a deep breath for patience. "We both know Lily wasn't about to give her middle name. You jumped in to keep her from revealing the truth. I'm sure you have a lot of skills, but lying isn't one of them."

Again, Grace said nothing.

"I covered for you in there."

"You told the truth." Her words were whispered but vehement. "You know I didn't hurt her."

"And *you* know that, if I hadn't intervened, that social worker would have latched onto Lily's slip-up. The child's about as skilled at deception as you are."

Grace crossed her arms tightly over her stomach. "You need to let it go."

"No, I don't." Andrew wasn't about to look the other way when a child's safety was involved. "You need to tell me the truth, or I'll call that social worker and tell her my suspicions."

"Which are what? What do you suspect?"

Fair question. He wasn't sure exactly, but something was going on.

Finally, Grace turned his way. Her eyes were wide and red-rimmed. "Please, don't."

But he wasn't compromising on this. He wasn't going to be an accomplice to another crime because he refused to ask the glaring questions. He'd compromised in the past, and that decision had landed him in prison. He didn't care that Grace was a friend of Cassidy's. He didn't care how attractive she was, how adorable the little girl. If Grace was breaking the law, he'd report her. End of story.

She must've seen the determination in his face. Her shoulders sagged, and she turned back to watch Lily through the window. "Not here. And not in front of Lily."

"Fair enough." He'd wait for the answers. Until they got back to their condos, and not a minute longer.

CHAPTER NINE

It was well past dinnertime by the time they left the hospital, Lily sporting a purple cast and chattering about everything from her dog to her latest school project.

Though it wasn't easy after all that had happened, Grace engaged in the conversation, asking questions and responding with appropriate remarks.

Without her permission, Andrew found a drive-through. "What'll it be, Lily?"

Grace said, "I have food at home. We don't need to stop."

Andrew sent her a tight smile. "This'll be easier."

She started to remind him that she'd left her wallet at home, but she doubted he'd forgotten. And based on the way the hospital staff had practically fallen over their own feet trying to please him, she guessed he wouldn't worry about being reimbursed.

Despite the fact that he lived in a condo, it was obvious he came from money. Not that she cared. The fact that he was wealthy only made her trust him less. Money didn't make a person good or righteous. Often, it only provided a means for people to feed their ugly desires.

After Lily told him what she wanted, he turned to Grace. "For you?"

"It's not exactly health food."

"One burger and fries never hurt anybody." He glanced at the rearview mirror and winked. "And our girl deserves a reward for being so brave, don't you think?"

Our girl.

Lily wasn't even Grace's girl, much less Andrew's.

But Lily pleaded. "Please, Miss Grace?"

She heaved a sigh. "Fine. A chicken sandwich—grilled. No fries."

Andrew ordered the meals, adding fries to all their orders. When she protested, he said, "If you don't want them, I'll take them." And then, maybe just to irritate her, he added an order of chocolate chip cookies.

Lily shouted, "Yay! My favorite!"

Anything with sugar was Lily's favorite. Didn't mean it was good for her, especially so late in the evening.

Grace wasn't happy, but she was self-aware enough to know that her irritation stemmed more from guilt and fear than from anything Andrew had done. Guilt because Lily had gotten hurt on her watch. Because she hadn't even known the child was injured, being so intent on finding some clue about what Myron Bowman was up to. Not that she had the slightest idea how to cyber-snoop, but she had to try.

Fear...Her fear stemmed from Andrew's questions. He knew she was lying, and he wasn't going to let it go.

Should she trust him? Or should she and Lily run. Again.

For the first time since they'd escaped Lily's monster of a father, Lily seemed happy. Content. At peace. She fit in at school. She had friends. How could Grace take her away from all of that?

But if Andrew started asking questions...Worse, if he started digging into who they really were...

How could Grace *not* run?

The scent of food had her empty stomach churning. All she wanted was to be alone, to think, and to figure out what to do.

But after Andrew parked outside his condo, he grabbed the

fast-food bags and carried them to Grace's door.

"Why don't I just take our dinners," she said, "and you can head home? I'm sure you have better things to do than hang around with us."

"That's okay." He stopped on her stoop and faced her. His easy smile seemed genuine enough, but she doubted it anyway. "I'd love to chat."

"Let's do that tomorrow."

"Tonight works." He winked at Lily, who stood one step down, wide-eyed gaze looking up and flicking between them, practically bouncing with excitement. "Besides, I promised to sign that cast. Do you have a Sharpie?"

"I have magic markers! Hurry up. I'm starving."

Grace was obviously not winning this argument.

She unlocked the door, and Lily squirted between them and bounded through, crouching down right inside to show her cast to Regis. It had been hard for Lily to be away from her dog the first few days of school, but since then, she'd grown accustomed to leaving him at home. Grace had worried that the trauma of the emergency room would frighten the child, but she'd handled it well.

Though Grace hated to admit it, Andrew's presence had helped to calm Lily's anxiety.

It had only raised Grace's.

From his perch on the back of the sofa, Oliver issued a loud meow. He got one look at Andrew and bolted up the stairs.

"Fraidy cat," she murmured. She wished she could hide right along with him. She tapped Lily's bottom with the toe of her shoe. "Scoot in, sweetheart. Let us by."

Lily pulled Regis into her arms, unfazed by the cast that covered her forearm, and led the way to the kitchen.

Grace followed, and Andrew pulled the door closed behind them. "I forgot you had a cat."

"He's not a huge fan of strangers."

"I'm guessing that runs in the family."

She turned and glared, but Andrew paid her no mind.

They sat at the small, well-worn kitchen table, Lily carrying the conversation. Despite Grace's insistence that she didn't need fries, she managed to eat most of hers, along with all of the chicken sandwich. She was nervous and worried, but also hungry. The food settled her a little.

By the time they finished, Lily's eyes were drooping. "Can I have a cookie?"

"We'll save them for tomorrow. It's a little late for sugar." She shot a look at Andrew, who had the grace to look chastised.

"Good idea," Andrew said. "A treat for after church. Do you want to go to church with me?"

Lily nodded, then looked to Grace for permission with wide, pleading eyes.

She managed to stifle a frustrated growl. "Let's see how we sleep tonight. It's been a pretty eventful day. For now, why don't you go put on your pajamas and brush your teeth."

"But I don't wanna go to bed."

It took thirty minutes to get the child read to, prayed for, and tucked in. The whole time, Grace thought about the man in her living room. He'd flipped on the TV, and the sounds of highlights from some football game carried up the stairs.

She took her time, lingering until Lily's eyes closed.

By the time she returned down the stairs, Andrew had made himself at home on her couch.

Oliver, the traitor, was curled on his lap.

Andrew turned as she reached the bottom. "He warmed up to me."

"Never trust a cat's intuition."

He chuckled and ran his hand along the soft fur. "Oh, I don't know. This one seems to have good instincts." He lifted the animal and set him on the couch before standing. "Kitchen?"

It'd been hours since he'd insisted she tell him the truth about herself and Lily. In all that time, she still hadn't come up with a good story.

She couldn't tell him the truth.

But he wasn't wrong when he'd called her a terrible liar. She'd had a lot of practice in the previous few months, though. She was getting better.

Not that it was a skill she'd ever planned to master.

"I'll leave the TV on." He lowered his voice. "So she doesn't hear us."

Grace sighed and led the way to the kitchen table on the far side of the open-concept room. She sat where she'd be able to see the staircase.

Andrew sat catty-corner to her.

All the amusement and kindness faded from his expression. "Explain."

She would stay as close to the truth as she could. "I have custody." Not *legal* custody, but he didn't need to know that.

"Then why are you lying about her name?" When she gave no answer, he continued. "Cassidy gave me the impression that you're in trouble. She didn't tell me why or what kind, and I didn't think it was my business. But now..." He leaned forward and rested his forearms on the table. "Look, I trust Cassidy, but I need to know what's going on."

"You could just mind your own business."

"You're living on my property. I've provided you an address. Because of that, you were able to enroll Lily in school. And earlier today, I vouched for you. I've provided you *legitimacy*." His exhale was long and frustrated. "This is my business."

She disagreed, but he wasn't exactly giving her a choice. "Lily's father is a pornographer."

Andrew's eyebrows lifted, and the scowl melted off his face. He sat back, blinked. "Oh, man." He swallowed, swallowed again. "Did he...?" His eyes lifted as if he could see the innocent child upstairs. "Poor girl."

"Problem is, I can't prove it."

"How do you know?"

"She told me." Sort of. Grace couldn't explain how she'd

learned the information. Andrew wouldn't believe her anyway. "Her father wants her back, and he's not worried about the legality of it." She thought about the gunshots that had rung out as they'd escaped. She thought about that moment when he'd caught up with them at the hotel in Coeur d'Alene, banging on her car window as she backed out of the parking spot. His face, contorted in rage...He hadn't carried his gun at that moment. If he'd had it, she had no doubt he'd have used it.

"So you're trying to keep him from finding you," Andrew guessed.

"I'm trying to protect Lily. I've given up everything—my home, my life"—her security, her sanity, or so it felt sometimes—"to protect that child."

"Okay." His gaze flicked up to the ceiling. "Okay."

Had she convinced him? Would he let it go?

But Andrew shook his head. "Do you plan to hide forever? Or is there some endgame here?"

She propped her elbows on the table and dropped her head into her hands. That was the question that had dogged her every single moment since she'd snatched Lily.

Truth was, she didn't have an endgame. She'd been looking over her shoulder for so long that she hadn't had time to look forward.

They'd been in New Hampshire for a month. She felt safe. Lily was thriving. But how long could it last? How long before Myron found them?

Was it wise to stay, or should she leave before he caught up with them?

She didn't know.

"You've told the authorities?" Andrew asked.

She looked up. "Yes, of course. But he threatened to kill Regis if Lily told them anything."

Andrew's jaw dropped, and he shook his head as if that was the tidbit that threw him over the edge. He muttered something under his breath, and she caught just enough to know she wouldn't ask him to repeat it. "But if the authorities don't believe he's doing anything wrong, how did he lose custody?"

She dropped her head into her hands again, hoping he'd blame the movement on fatigue and frustration and not on a desire to hide. She searched for an answer that would satisfy his curiosity. "I'm not sure about all the particulars."

"But they don't believe he's been taking pictures of her."

She shook her head. "I passed along the information, and they searched his property but found no evidence."

"He's smart."

She sat back. "Too smart. Somehow, he always finds us. I think."

"You *think*? What does that mean?"

Was she just being paranoid?

"A couple of times, I've seen him lurking. Or thought I did. Once, our hotel was broken into when we were out. Once, my car window was shattered."

"If he found you, why not take Lily back? Why would he lurk, let himself be seen? Why break into your hotel when you weren't there?"

"I don't know."

Andrew's lips pressed together. He watched her for a moment, then shook his head. "I don't understand."

"Maybe I was just being paranoid." Had she really needed to run so many times? Could they have settled before this? "It doesn't matter. I got us both false papers—not exactly something I knew how to do. That took some time. I bought a new car, a no-contract phone. He shouldn't find us again."

Unless Lily had been contacting him. But Grace had started keeping her phone in her pocket at all times. The child wasn't allowed to touch it.

They should be safe.

And Lily wanted to stay in New Hampshire. She'd asked more than once if this could be their new home. When they were moving from dingy hotel to dingy hotel, no friends, no fun, it was no wonder she'd considered returning to her father. But now, why would she alert her father as to her whereabouts if she was happy?

Grace dug her fingers into her hair and squeezed her fists. She didn't know what she was doing. She hated this, hated her insecurity, her inability to be certain Lily was safe.

Maybe she should just leave the child on Cassidy's doorstep and run. Cassidy would get Lily into the system. The state would find her a good foster home.

Maybe.

Or maybe she'd end up in a worse situation than the one Grace had rescued her from.

"Hey." The gentle word came an instant before Andrew slid his fingers around Grace's wrist and tugged. "Pulling your hair out won't help."

She opened her hand, only then realizing she'd been yanking. The pain in her scalp lessened. She shook her fingers free of the strands—and of Andrew's fingers near her palm. The last thing she needed tonight was visions of somebody else's life. She could barely tolerate her own.

Andrew brushed her hair away from her face, his touch tender. "It's okay."

Grace met his gaze, saw nothing but understanding and kindness there. They held like that for a long moment before she forced herself to look away.

He pulled his hands back and clasped them together on the table.

A beat of quiet seemed to stretch, the only sounds coming from the TV playing quietly in the living area.

"I'm sorry," he said. "I shouldn't have..." But he didn't say what he shouldn't have done, and she couldn't think of a thing he needed to apologize for.

She pushed her shoulders back. "I'm the one who should apologize. You've been nothing but kind today. I'm thankful you were there when I wasn't paying attention. I'll be more careful next time."

"It wasn't your fault she fell. And trying to make a living, under the circumstances, is admirable."

She didn't correct his assumption that she'd been working, nor that she needed the money. She continued with the medical transcription because, when dull medical reports played in her ears, she was able to escape the thoughts and memories and regrets that plagued her.

She felt more at peace typing up other people's medical conditions than she ever did thinking about the condition of her own life.

"Speaking of," she said, "I'll get back to the hospital and pay the bill. But if they should happen to send you something, just bring it over."

He opened his mouth as if to argue, then nodded. "You never asked."

"About who you are? Now that you know all my secrets..."

"My father owns Middleton Enterprises."

"Never heard of it."

"Yeah. In most of the country, few have outside the industry. It's a pretty big company, though, and Dad does a lot of philanthropic work in this state, specifically with hospitals. He and I share a name, so..."

She studied the look on his face. Not pride. Not amusement. "You hate that."

"Only with every fiber of my being."

She let her raised eyebrows ask the question, but he just pushed back from the table. "A story for another day."

He'd heard enough of her secrets, it only seemed fair he share some of his. On the other hand, she had enough to deal with. His story didn't matter to her. No matter the kindness in his mesmerizing eyes.

She forced her gaze away.

Andrew stood. "Thanks for trusting me with the story."

Not that she had, not completely. Not that she could ever trust anybody with the whole truth.

After all, kidnapping was a federal offense.

CHAPTER TEN

GRACE WAS GOING to pay for that.

Myron had followed the neighbor's car all the way to Plymouth. He'd watched as the man and Grace had ushered Lily into the building.

Fuming, he'd waited hours and hours until they emerged, his girl sporting a bright purple cast on her arm.

Had her body been scraped up as well? Would there be scars?

For every mark he found on Lily's body, Grace would receive tenfold. Letting the child play on the monkey bars—didn't Grace know how dangerous that was?

Didn't she understand Lily's worth?

The child had been perfect. Absolutely perfect. He'd made sure of it. He'd lectured her countless times on making sure she didn't harm herself. Didn't get scrapes or bruises or cuts. Didn't scratch at rashes or pick at scabs. He'd done everything in his power not to let anything mar Lily's beauty. Grace had had the child for a few months, and Lily already wore a cast.

Would the skin turn pale and sallow underneath? Would it itch? Would Grace allow her to scratch it? Did the woman not understand Lily's perfection?

No, how could she? She wasn't an artist. She was a drone, typing words onto a screen. Utterly artless.

Myron would have to make sure Grace understood how to protect his property, not let Lily climb all over dangerous playground equipment. Grace would be schooled in the art of protecting beauty.

The more he watched Grace, the more he was certain he'd made the right choice back in the spring when he'd decided not to kill her. He'd had her in his sights. Missing her had been instinct, nothing else. Even then, he'd understood that there was something unique and special about Grace Mullen.

How had she gotten his Lily to open up about Myron's art? That alone required investigation. Grace and Lily had a special connection. With Grace around, Lily might expand her emotional range. Rather than just looking frightened or solemn, he'd be able to capture joy, happiness, desire, expressions he'd seen on his muse's face that very afternoon before her fall.

He could imagine the beauty he'd create.

Grace was a mother to Lily, drawing out emotions Myron had never been able to elicit, emotions he hadn't seen since Annabeth had been with them.

Like Annabeth had, Grace would have other uses.

As much as Myron loved his art, he wasn't one to see children for anything but their artistic value. Yes, he understood that the men who bought his photographs weren't parting with their money because of his genius. But Myron wasn't like them. Those people disgusted him. He'd never touched Lily inappropriately, and he'd kill the man who tried it. She was fragile, like a delicate flower that would wilt unless handled with care.

In protecting Lily, in focusing all his energy on feeding his muse, Myron had neglected the baser part of himself, the part that roared to life more and more as he watched Grace. He had to admit, he was rather excited about the prospect of having someone who could take care of the day-to-day tasks that a child required.

And having a fresh subject to photograph when he needed new ideas—the thought intrigued him.

Grace wouldn't be easy to break. She was so certain of her course that she'd abandoned her entire life to keep Lily safe. What else would she sacrifice to protect the child?

Myron liked the idea of finding out. He liked the idea of having someone in his life who wouldn't cower in fear. He liked the idea of having a woman who wouldn't be controlled the way a child would.

He'd punish Grace for Lily's broken arm. He'd train her in the care and feeding of his muse. He'd enjoy her body for more than just its artistic value.

He liked the idea of a woman who would fight back.

CHAPTER ELEVEN

GRACE HAD LOOKED over her shoulder for more than a week.

Ever since she'd told Andrew the almost-truth about herself and Lily, she'd worried. She was using a false name, just like Lily was, but Andrew knew about her connection to Cassidy, which could lead him to Washington and her past. He was smart. He had resources.

He could find out the truth about them if he wanted to.

Or, he could simply call the police and let them handle it.

Why would he believe anything Grace said?

But Lily was thriving, and Grace felt settled for the first time in a long time. She told herself she was safe there and, most of the time, she even believed it.

It was Tuesday night, and Lily was coloring a map of the US. She'd just filled in the state of Texas—baby blue, her favorite color —when she said, "I used to live in Texas."

Grace dried her hands of dishwater and joined her at the kitchen table. "You did? When?"

She shrugged. "I was a baby."

Lily hadn't talked much about her life before Washington. "What do you remember about it?"

Setting down the crayon, Lily looked up, her little face

scrunched as she searched her memories. "I remember Nana. She was all soft and squishy and had white hair and smelled like fried chicken and peaches."

"I bet she was a good cook."

Lily nodded and picked up her crayon again. But Grace wanted to know more. Maybe there was family out there who could take care of Lily, who could fight for her in court. Maybe Grace could give Lily to them. Not that she wanted to get rid of her. In fact, the longer she kept Lily, the more attached she became. Which wasn't good. Lily wasn't hers, could never truly be hers. The more time she spent with her, the more heart-wrenching it would be when she had to give her up.

"Do you remember where in Texas?"

Lily shook her head. "It was hot, and there were cows and horses we used to drive by. I liked it there, but Mama hated it."

Lily'd never mentioned her mother. In all the time Grace had spent with her, even when Grace had asked, the child had been close-lipped about the woman who'd birthed her.

Gently, Grace asked, "Where is your mother?"

She lifted her tiny shoulders and let them drop. "Daddy said she didn't want me anymore. I was too much trouble."

Grace settled her hand over the child's wrist, careful not to touch her palm, and waited until Lily looked up. "I don't know what happened with your mom, but I can promise you that, if she left you, it wasn't because of anything you did. You are a sweet, kind, and amazing child, and wherever your mother is, she loves you very much. And if she doesn't, then there's something wrong with her, not you. Because you, beautiful girl, are incredibly lovable."

Lily blinked a couple of times, then returned to her coloring.

Grace prayed the words would take root and grow in that tender heart. What kind of father would tell a precious child such a thing?

A beast.

After Grace got Lily tucked into bed, she returned to her

laptop, trying fruitlessly to figure out what Myron Bowman was up to. She'd searched for his name a thousand times since she'd left Washington but never found anything except links to his photography website and glowing reviews about his work. Those hadn't been updated, though. Except on his own website, there were no new photos. No new reviews since before Lily was born.

Grace had figured how to do an image search and loaded a photograph of Lily, but she'd found no photos of the girl except the ones she'd seen when she found Myron's website.

If Myron had taken illicit photos of Lily, he hadn't posted them, at least not anywhere Grace could find.

There was only one photo of Myron, taken when he was a younger man. According to the information in the who's-who article, Myron had been a well-respected children's photographer whose pictures had appeared in magazines all over the world. He'd taken photos of the children of famous people—politicians and tech moguls and movie stars. He'd been sought after.

But that article had been written nine years before. There was no new information about him at all.

If he was so good at what he did, if he was so well known, what had he been doing holed up in a tiny cabin in the middle of nowhere?

She knew the answer to that. Apparently, being famous hadn't been his goal. He was working on getting filthy rich. Emphasis on *filthy*. Or maybe his motivations were even darker. Maybe he hadn't gotten into the pornography game because he wanted to make money. Maybe he'd done it to feed his evil desires.

She shuddered and slammed her laptop closed. If she were smart, she'd confine these searches to the hours when Lily was at school and focus on transcribing doctors' notes before bed, something to calm her nerves rather than set them on edge.

It was pouring outside, and she sat back and listened, allowing the familiar sound to calm her. She never thought she'd miss the rainy weather of western Washington, but there was something soothing about being cocooned in a dry house while the weather raged outside.

She breathed slowly in and out. She was safe. They were safe.

Pulling back the curtain that covered the rear doors—they looked like French doors, but only one of them swung open—she peeked outside.

Lightning flashed in the distance, allowing her to see the expanse that separated her building from the one behind. The trees dotting the space bent in the wind. A few lights remained on at that late hour, but it seemed most folks had gone to bed.

She needed to do the same.

She dropped the curtain, shut off the lights, and made her way upstairs. She'd just brushed her teeth when a loud crash split the quiet.

Then, the unmistakable sound of breaking glass.

The lights went out.

Her stomach dropped to the floor.

Myron. It had to be Myron, using the storm as cover. He'd cut her lights. He'd broken her window.

He was here.

Panic crawled up her throat, tried to escape on a scream. She slapped her hand over her mouth. *Think.*

She stood frozen in the upstairs hallway.

She had to fight.

If Myron was there, she had no other choice.

She dashed into the bedroom and yanked her handgun from the hidden pocket in her purse and checked the chamber.

She'd kill Myron before she let him take Lily back.

If that meant prison, so be it.

She slipped into the hallway, gun lifted and ready. Listening. But the rain and wind and rumbling thunder were too loud. Myron could be walking up the stairs and she wouldn't hear him.

She aimed toward the staircase and inched that direction. She would kill him if she had to, but she'd rather simply grab Lily and escape.

Was it too late for that? Was he inside? Why else break the window? Of course he was.

She fought a wave of hysteria and inched down the stairs, pausing at the landing to peer around the corner. It was so dark, so dark, as she looked for moving shadows in the pale light coming through the blinds.

The staircase was empty.

Where was he?

Everything inside her trembled, but she slowly took a step down.

Cold air and the scent of rain swirled around her. The steady sound of the downpour accompanied the whistling wind and the rustling of branches.

A window *had* been broken. No doubt about it.

He was in her house.

Jesus, please. Please protect Lily.

And me.

She took another step down.

The sound of banging froze her in place.

Banging...on the door?

"Grace! Grace! Are you okay? Open up."

Andrew?

What in the...?

"I'm coming in." The words were shouted a moment before the door opened.

Andrew stepped inside, his keys swinging from the lock, and moved a flashlight around the space.

He must've caught sight of her because he lifted his hands, the beam of his light bouncing off the ceiling. "It's just me. Just Andrew."

She couldn't lower the gun, though. Myron was there. Andrew was going to get hurt. Killed.

"Be careful!" Her voice was high. "He's here. He's going to—"

"It was a tree," Andrew said. "A tree fell. Didn't you hear it?"

Had she?

She'd heard a crash.

She'd heard a *crack*. Then a crash.

"He's not here, Grace." Andrew's voice was low and soothing, so different from her own. "Please, lower the gun."

His words penetrated.

A tree had fallen. A tree had broken the glass.

Not Myron.

She was safe.

"Please?" Andrew said again.

She did as he asked, then sagged against the railing.

She managed to sit before she fell. With trembling fingers, she engaged the handgun's safety. Before she could set it down, Andrew was beside her.

"Here, let me."

She handed it to him, and he walked away, flashlight glowing on the hardwood. He returned a moment later. "I put the gun in the cabinet where you keep your plates. You'll want to stow it before Lily sees it." At her nod, he continued. "It's the kitchen window. Come on." He held out his hand to help her up.

The last thing, the very last thing, she needed at that moment was to touch his hand.

She took hold of the railing and pulled herself to her feet, not even glancing to see his reaction. "Sorry. It's just..." Not that she could explain. "I'm feeling a little off."

"It's okay." She heard no censure in his tone. He wrapped his arm around her waist, then asked, "Is it all right if I—?"

"Yeah. Thank you." She wished she didn't need the support, but she wasn't sure she'd stay standing without it.

She made it down the stairs and into a chair.

Her stomach was roiling.

"Just lay your head down and breathe."

Good advice. She dropped her forehead onto her arms on the table and inhaled and exhaled and told herself she was safe. They were safe.

"Where's Lily? Surely she's not still sleeping."

"It's her superpower," Grace said. "She can sleep through anything."

"Lucky girl." Andrew was moving around. She heard crunching, sweeping. The opening of the drapes. Then a cabinet and another.

"Where's your trash?" he asked.

"In the pantry."

The door opened, followed by the sound of glass clattering into the empty can.

"I'm going to get a tarp. Yours wasn't the only place hit. Thank God the tree landed on the ground and not on somebody's roof."

Grace looked up to see Andrew in the dim light coming through the back window. There were people out there. She could hear voices, see the bouncing of lanterns or flashlight beams.

Andrew was watching her from the kitchen. "Are you okay?"

"I think so."

"Thanks for not shooting me."

"Thanks for not being *him*."

"I do my best."

She added, "And for being here. And for..." She waved past him at the mess in her kitchen. The window over the sink had shattered, and a leaf-covered limb fluttered in the opening.

"Sorry I came in like I did," Andrew said. "I couldn't see from outside if your upstairs window had been hit. I was afraid you were hurt."

Some kind of motor started up outside.

"Hear that?" he asked. "It's a four-wheeler. Probably one of the maintenance guys, already working on getting this cleaned up. I ought to go help."

"Okay." She pushed herself to standing. "Let me just grab—"

"You stay. There are plenty of people around who aren't looking after a child. Men from the community, and maybe even some of the teenage boys, will get it taken care of. We'll just chop off that limb and get the window covered. Hopefully, the lights will come back on soon. Meanwhile, you should be warm enough upstairs."

"You don't have to..." But what was she going to do? She didn't know how to use a chainsaw. She didn't have a tarp. She didn't even own a ladder.

Andrew's smile was gentle. "We've got it, Grace. It's okay to let people help sometimes." He started for the back door, then turned and held out his flashlight. "You need this?"

"I have a couple, if anybody else needs one."

"Good to know." Andrew slipped out the back door.

CHAPTER TWELVE

It took a couple of hours of hard, wet labor, but finally Andrew and other men had the tree cut and dragged away from the condos, the broken windows and damaged siding covered with plastic sheeting.

The power company had been doing its part, and after the electricity came back on, Grace had opened her rear door and offered cups of coffee and snacks to anybody who wanted them. Thank heavens the storm had tapered to a light drizzle. By the time he was done, Andrew wanted nothing more than to crawl between his sheets and sleep.

Instead, he climbed to Grace's patio and knocked on her glass door. "It's just me," he called. "We're all finished."

She opened it and ushered him in, mug steaming in her hand. "So nobody needs this, I guess."

"They're all headed home."

She set the coffee on the peninsula between the kitchen and dining area. "Pretty impressive how everybody came together to help."

"That's what people do in a community. Surely you've experienced that before."

She shrugged. "Not with strangers."

They weren't *strangers*. They were neighbors.

Grace added, "I appreciate you and everybody who helped."

"They appreciated the coffee." He was dripping on the hardwood floor but didn't leave. "Look, uh...Are you planning to stay?"

"No place else to go, and Lily slept through it all. I don't want to wake her."

"But what about...I know you were nervous about her father."

Grace's expression slid into what seemed an embarrassed smile. "Yeah. Sorry about that. I panicked."

"I don't think so. I think you reacted very rationally." In that moment when he'd seen her handgun, and then the fear in her eyes, he'd thought he was a goner. But as terrified as she'd been, she hadn't pulled the trigger. She'd been thinking, responding, fully aware of her surroundings. "I was especially impressed when you didn't shoot me."

"Thank God I didn't. Who'd have covered my window?"

He chuckled, the sound out of place in the quiet. "I'll get the glass replaced tomorrow, but in the meantime, do you really feel safe here?"

Her lips pressed together, and her gaze flicked to the plastic between her and the outside. "We'll be fine."

"I have two options if you don't want to go to a hotel. One, you two can come stay at my place. I have an extra bedroom with a queen-sized bed, which you'd have to share."

She was already shaking her head.

"Okay, then. Option two. I sleep on your sofa."

Still, the head shaking. "It's fine. We'll be fine."

"Considering the way you greeted me a little while ago, I know you don't believe that."

She lowered her voice. "He isn't here."

"You want to believe that, but you don't *really* believe it. If you did—"

"Like I said, I panicked."

"I want you to be safe." For someone who'd practically

collapsed in a puddle of relief earlier, she was being awfully stubborn.

"I think we are."

Ignoring that, he said, "Also, I want you to *feel* safe. But you won't. You'll lie awake all night worrying about that open window. Right?"

Her shrug was slight. "It wouldn't be the first night's sleep I've lost."

Andrew was too tired to have this argument. "Look, Grace. You don't want to stay at my place. I get it. That'd be weird, and you'd have to wake Lily. So either I sleep right there"—he pointed to her sofa, which didn't look nearly as comfortable as his own bed —"or I camp out on your patio in the rain. You decide."

"No, that's not—"

"I'm tired. Decide."

"You don't have any right—"

"Fine. Go to a hotel."

Her shoulders sagged. "I don't want to wake her."

Which left one choice. "I'm going to run home and change into dry clothes. Mind if I walk through?"

She didn't answer. Seemed to be trying to catch up with him.

He tracked water across the floor, figuring if she didn't clean it while he was gone, he'd do it when he returned. He stepped out her door and started to close it. Before he could, he glanced back to find she'd followed and was standing just a few feet away, looking terrified.

He closed his eyes. Shot up a quick prayer. "I just thought of a third option. I'll call Cassidy."

"No. No. She's pregnant. She needs her rest."

Fine. Not Cassidy.

He didn't exactly want to wake his boss at that hour, though Jacqui would certainly do it. "I have another friend—"

"No." Grace shook her head slowly. "You're very stubborn, you know that?"

"So I've been told."

"Don't call anybody. If you insist, you can stay. I don't have any extra blankets, so—"

"On it. Be right back." He dashed across the parking lot before she could change her mind.

GRACE'S SOFA had been more comfortable than he'd anticipated.

But he'd had nightmares about that gun aimed his way, which brought back way too many memories.

Prison and prisoners and orange jumpsuits, living and working and sleeping with one eye open, never sure where the next attack would come from.

Prayer and scripture had helped him dispense with those old fears.

Which had opened his mind to other dreams, those about the pajama-clad woman who'd stood on the stairs looking terrified and helpless.

When Grace came down early the next morning, tiptoeing past him, he'd peeked. Shouldn't have, he knew that. But he wasn't perfect. And she was an enigma, a mystery he wanted to solve. Confident and frightened. Strong and vulnerable.

She was still in her pajamas, her blond hair mussed from sleep. In the low light of dawn, he'd watched her fill the carafe, start the coffee brewing, then pull two mugs from the dishwasher.

Two. One for each of them.

He'd mashed his eyes closed and told himself to get out of there. Which he'd done the instant she'd gone back upstairs.

Though they'd since talked a couple of times and exchanged texts about getting the window repaired, he hadn't been back to her place.

Except in his memories. And his dreams. And sometimes, in new nightmares with faceless men crawling through broken windows.

He needed to stop thinking about Grace.

Something hit him in the head, and he shook himself from the thoughts and turned to Braden, who'd apparently smacked him. He was standing behind him, giving him a curious look. "Where'd you go there?"

"Just thinking."

"Yeah. I saw the steam coming out your ears." Braden nudged him out of the way and reached into his refrigerator to pull out a couple of sodas. "Did you need something?"

Andrew lifted the Coke he'd grabbed before he'd gotten side-tracked by his thoughts. He'd been going to Braden's house to watch sports every Monday night since he'd moved to Coventry.

"Worried about the open house?" Braden asked. The company they both worked for was putting together an event for prospective employees in two weeks.

"Nope." Andrew popped open the can and headed back to the living room, where sounds of the football game and their friends' conversation carried. "It's coming together. We've got thirty great prospects. The event planner's taking care of the details."

"Good, good. Let me know if there's anything I can do to help." Braden settled in the upholstered chair.

Thomas and Garrett sat on opposite ends of the sofa. Reid, Jacqui's husband, reclined on the love seat, stretching his long legs out as if he owned the place.

Andrew grabbed a couple of slices of bruschetta from the plate on the coffee table and settled behind the sofa on the kitchen chair he'd dragged in. Braden's wife, Carly, had classed-up the weekly guys nights. Used to be, they'd have store-bought chips and dip, maybe a platter of cold cuts from James's restaurant. Tonight, Carly'd served bruschetta with whipped feta on toast points along with some kind of warm pizza dip.

Monday night had become his favorite of the week.

The living room was too small for the crowd, but nobody complained. Andrew would offer to have the weekly event at his place, but his living room was even smaller. And he didn't live with a gourmet cook.

James, Dylan, and Fitz sat in chairs like Andrew's. Fitz was the newest member of the group, and the oldest. Apparently, a couple of years past, he'd married Dylan's wife's best friend, Tabby. They'd been living in Rhode Island until Fitz's little sister graduated from high school. That summer, they'd moved to Coventry, where Tabby'd grown up.

Andrew was still trying to figure out everybody's stories and how they were all connected.

"Desi is perfect, of course," Braden was saying about his newborn.

"She could have an ear in the middle of her forehead," Reid said, "and you'd think she was perfect. Now Ella, on the other hand, is amazing." Reid bragged about his daughter for a few minutes. Andrew couldn't remember how old she was. Six, maybe? Seven? A little younger than Lily.

He'd seen the two girls playing together at church the day before. Despite his invitation, Grace hadn't wanted to attend after their trip to the ER, but apparently Cassidy had strong-armed her, as he'd seen Grace sitting beside his friends. If he'd had a hard time concentrating on the sermon that day, he didn't think too hard about the reason.

The football game was a blowout, and nobody was paying it much attention.

Thomas turned to Andrew. "Have you solved the mystery of your father's company yet?"

He polished off the bruschetta, sipped his soda, and settled it on his knee. "I'm missing a few months of data. When I get that—"

"Your dad didn't give you everything?" Reid swung his legs to the floor. "Why not?"

"Not sure he knew. He gave me what Chet gave him." Andrew had already filled them in on what he was doing for his father, something he'd never have done with other friends. But he trusted these guys. They all went to the same church. They'd shared their difficulties and struggles, which had given him the courage to do the same.

"What do you think about that?" James asked.

"I can't decide if Chet's hiding something or if he's just an imbecile."

"From what you've told us," Dylan said, "I'd guess the second."

"It's possible he's not as dumb as I've made him out to be," Andrew admitted. "I don't exactly admire the guy, but that doesn't make him stupid."

Fitz was nodding slowly. He looked a little too much like a Hollywood leading man, a little too pretty. Though Andrew figured that, when he donned his sidearm and his badge, he had no trouble being taken seriously. Andrew was glad he'd gotten to know Fitz before he'd discovered he was in law enforcement, or else he might be nervous around him. "If he's been skimming," Fitz said, "maybe he's too stupid to figure out how to hide it."

Skimming. Andrew hadn't let himself go that far with his theories.

James leaned forward and faced Andrew. "That would be awkward, having to tell your father that your half brother's stealing from him."

"Much as I dislike the guy, I don't want that to be the case. I'm trying to repair my relationship with Dad, not drive another wedge in it."

"But if you discover the truth," Thomas asked, "won't that help your relationship?"

Before Andrew could say anything, Reid said, "Then his dad would have to admit he's been wrong about Cheddar Chet."

Andrew smiled at the nickname the guys had all started using.

"Being proved wrong?" Reid shook his head. "That can be the death knell to any relationship."

"Especially one as tenuous as theirs," Braden added.

"Wow, you guys are a ray of sunshine tonight." Andrew infused the words with amusement, though he feared Reid and Braden were right.

"We'll be praying," Dylan said. "Let me know if you need any help with anything. I'll be happy to lend a hand."

"Appreciate that." Though he hoped he wouldn't need Dylan's skills as a former detective.

"Tell us about the blonde." Garrett turned to face Andrew, eyebrows waggling.

"What are you talking about?"

"Oh, come on, man." Garrett's gaze traveled the room. "You guys saw it, right?"

"The drool?" James asked. "I'm pretty sure the pastor saw it from the pulpit."

The guys laughed, and Andrew joined in, though he wasn't amused. "Grace is attractive, sure. I noticed."

Reid shrugged. "She's okay, if you like blondes. I'm partial to redheads."

Dylan rubbed a hand over his carrot-colored hair. "Thanks, man. I never knew."

Reid shot him a look. "Not that. The pretty kind."

"Aw, you say the nicest things." Dylan's remark earned a laugh from the guys.

"I want to hear more about this blonde," Braden said. "We haven't been at church since Desi was born. What did we miss?"

"She's a friend of Cassidy's," James said. "From Seattle."

Originally, though she had to have been living in New Hampshire for a while. Andrew wondered what'd brought her there. He considered asking James about that, but the last thing he needed was to encourage this conversation. "A neighbor. That's all."

"Sure, sure," Garrett said. "That's all it seemed like when you spent hours repairing her window."

"She's a tenant. That was my condo getting rained into."

"Uh-huh." Garrett's words were filled with skepticism. "That doesn't explain you returning to her place with blankets and pillows."

"Whoa." James peered past Fitz, looking not at all amused. "What's that? We put her up there so you could keep an eye out, not take advantage of her."

Irritation and frustration crawled up Andrew's throat even as heat filled his neck. "I'd like to think you know me better than that by now."

"I'd like to think so too," James said.

Between them, Fitz backed his chair away. "I'm just gonna get out of the line of fire here."

Andrew ignored him. He had no idea what James and Cassidy knew about Grace's situation, and he certainly didn't feel comfortable discussing it.

Maybe James knew more than Andrew did. Maybe less. Either way, he knew enough to want Andrew to keep an eye on her. "She was nervous about intruders." *Andrew'd* been nervous about intruders. "Her window was broken. I stayed on the couch."

James studied him another moment, then nodded. "Yeah. Okay."

The *sorry for accusing you* was apparently supposed to be implied.

Garrett cleared his throat. "I figured it was something like that, what with the blankets and all. I mean, why would you bring your own blankets if you were planning to share her bed?"

The guy was about as subtle as a sledgehammer. "And you," Andrew said. "Do you have nothing better to do than spy on me?"

"You're not that interesting, man." Garrett smirked. "I saw you when I came back from returning the chainsaw to the maintenance shed."

"Anyway," Reid said into the awkwardness, "you like this woman?"

"She's a neighbor."

"Whom you find attractive," Braden added. "Considering that the single women at work haven't caught your eye, I'm eager to meet her."

How did this conversation become about Andrew and his love life? *Lack* of love life? "What are you talking about?"

"You can't have not noticed. Saralyn and Allison? The way they giggle when you walk by?"

"Allison's way too old for me."

"She's thirty-two. And Saralyn's in her twenties and not exactly a strain on the eyes. And single. And definitely interested."

Andrew hadn't noticed. Both women had been friendly, sure, but was there more to it than that?

Allison wasn't his type at all. Saralyn was pretty and smart, but he felt no attraction to her.

Unlike his new neighbor.

"Here's the deal." James's voice was dead serious. "You have a thing for Grace, that's fine, but you treat her with kid gloves. That woman's had a world of hurt in her life. I don't know the ins and outs of it, but I know enough about her to know she doesn't need her heart broken."

"Who's breaking anybody's heart?" How had the conversation gone so far afield? "She's my tenant, nothing more." But even as Andrew said the words, he knew he was lying, both to his friends and to himself. Because he hadn't gone a waking hour without thinking about Grace since their trip to the ER, worrying about Lily's father showing up. Wondering if Grace was thinking about running again. Hoping she wouldn't.

"Mmm-hmm." James regarded him through squinted eyes as if he could read his thoughts. "Just remember what I said."

Andrew wasn't concerned about James's unspoken threat. He wouldn't do anything to hurt Grace.

But maybe, rather than sitting around obsessing about her, he could do something about the danger she was in. Maybe, he could help her prove what she believed about Lily's father. Then if the man showed up, they could get him put behind bars.

Grace and Lily wouldn't have to spend their lives in fear.

Grace could start looking forward. And maybe, if she did that, she'd see Andrew. Really see him.

He was surprised to find he wanted that.

CHAPTER THIRTEEN

IT HAD BEEN a week since the storm. In that week, Grace had relaxed, allowing herself to hope, once again, that they were safe.

But the more she thought about what had happened the night before, the more convinced she was that she and Lily had to run. Maybe the intruder on her back patio hadn't been Myron Bowman. But there'd definitely been *somebody* there. If not for Regis's barking, would he have broken in?

Would Lily already have been taken?

As little as Grace wanted to, she had to assume Myron had found them again.

She spent the bulk of Tuesday morning obsessing over the problem, praying for guidance.

Maybe the Lord was leading her one way or another. She had no idea. Fear had taken hold, and she couldn't keep it at bay.

She considered relocating to another state, but Myron had found them everywhere they'd gone. It was time to leave the country. Maybe, if they were in Canada or Mexico or…France.

Yes, France. She'd studied French in high school and college and spoke it passably. They'd find a place in the country, and she'd enroll Lily in the local school. The child was young. She'd pick up the language quickly.

They could blend in.

Maybe if they were in Europe, Myron would give up and leave them be.

She didn't want to yank Lily away from her new friends and the home they'd built. She didn't want to leave the sanctuary they'd found in Coventry. But if Myron had found them, it was no longer a sanctuary.

What choice did she have?

Lily climbed into the SUV after school that afternoon, chattering at top speed. "It's Jilly's birthday party, and she invited the whole class!" Lily waved the invitation. "It's on Friday night, and there's gonna be a magician! Can I go, Miss Grace? Please?"

Grace fought the tears that prickled her eyes. "Sounds like fun."

"We gotta get her a present. I've never been to a birthday party in my whole life! Can I have a birthday party too? With a magician?"

"We'll see." Not that they could celebrate her actual birthday, which Lily had told her was in January. They'd have to celebrate the one on her fake birth certificate, which was in March. Maybe, by March, they'd be settled, and Lily would have a whole class full of friends she could invite to a party.

Except they'd need to get new papers. If Myron had found them, then he could easily have discovered their new identities.

Would the falsified passports she'd paid six months' salary for get them out of the country and into France? She prayed they were as good as the forger claimed.

Grace managed to act normally throughout the afternoon. She gave Lily a snack and helped her with her homework. When Lily cried because Grace wouldn't let her go to the park to play with her friends, Grace allowed her to watch TV, something she rarely did.

She was just starting dinner when a knock sounded on the front door.

Grace's stomach lurched.

Lily called, "I'll get it!"

"No!"

The harsh tone had Lily stopping, wide-eyed.

"You know you're not allowed to answer the door without permission. We've discussed that."

"Yes, ma'am." Lily fell back onto the sofa with a pout, and Grace peeked through the front window.

Andrew stood on her stoop. When she pulled open the door, he said, "Sorry to stop by unannounced."

Maybe company would make the hours go faster. Not that she was in a hurry to leave, but just to be done with it. To put to rest this town and all the hope she'd made the mistake of feeling. "It's fine. I haven't had the chance to thank you in person for getting that window repaired so quickly."

"My pleasure."

Lily bounded off the couch and hugged his waist, then backed up and held out her cast. "Look at all the people who signed it."

"Wow." He crouched down and looked for a long time. "You've got a lot of friends."

"I know. And I'm going to a birthday party Friday night." She practically bounced with excitement.

"That's super cool. You're going to have a blast."

Lily returned to the couch and the TV show, and Grace said, "Come on in. I was just fixing dinner."

"I don't mean to intrude, but I wanted to talk to you about something."

He settled at one of the barstools, and she pulled a package of macaroni out of the pantry and started a pot of water to boil. She'd already browned the rest of the hamburger meat from her freezer and added it to the spaghetti sauce. "No intrusion. You're welcome to stay."

"I don't want to eat your food."

"It's not a problem. The least I can do after you rescued us." And it wasn't as if she could take it with her.

"That's what I wanted to talk to you about." He'd lowered his voice. "Well, not that exactly, but what you told me about..." He tipped his head toward Lily in the other room.

"What about it?"

"I think your best defense is a good offense."

"Meaning?"

"I reached out to an old friend from school who works for a software developer. They've developed this advanced facial recognition software. I told him what we were looking for, and he said he could run the software on the dark web, see if her image popped up."

Grace wasn't sure if she should be grateful or irritated that Andrew had asked without consulting her.

He must've seen something in her expression because he said, "It's not like I gave him your name. And he lives in Boston. It's not somebody you've met."

"It's nice of you to try to help us, but even if we found her picture, what would be the point? As far as I can tell, Myron's living outside the law."

"You could prove what he's doing, get him arrested and thrown in jail. Exploiting minors is serious business."

"They'd have to find him first."

"Nobody can stay hidden forever, Grace."

Didn't she know it?

It was a good idea. If only they didn't have to run again. Maybe, if Andrew found the proof, and if he could get word to Grace, she and Lily could return to the States. Maybe even to this little corner of the world where Lily had found such acceptance.

Grace had too. The neighbors who'd helped with her window, then all the kind folks she'd met at church...She'd forgotten how much she liked—and needed—to be in a community.

The water started to boil, and she dumped in the macaroni and stirred.

"I just need to get a good photograph of Lily," Andrew said.

She set the wooden spoon on a plate and leaned against the counter. "We can't stay here."

His eyebrows hiked. "What are you talking about? What happened?"

"Last night, we had an intruder on the back patio. If not for the dog barking...I don't know that it was him, but who else would have been snooping around our place? I just...I can't take the chance."

Andrew's chuckle had her blood pressure rising.

"It's not funny."

"Sorry. I know. It's just..." He pulled his phone from his pocket and tapped the screen. Then, he handed it to her. "It's that neighborhood app. I get the alerts."

She read the headline. *Bring in your pumpkins at night!* The story talked about two teenage boys who'd been caught on multiple doorbell cameras in the past. They'd been caught on back-door cameras the night before, apparently thinking they could wreak havoc without being caught if they stuck to the back patios instead of the front.

"If you scroll down, you'll see the parents admitting their kids snuck out last night. They're both grounded."

She read the whole post and all the comments. Sure enough, the kids had been out at the time when Regis had been barking.

She closed her eyes and breathed a prayer of relief. They didn't have to leave. They were safe in Coventry.

She'd almost blown up their entire lives because of a couple of mischievous teenagers.

How many times had she run based on a feeling, a bizarre experience, or the thought that she might have seen Myron in a crowd? How many times had she run based on *nothing*?

When she opened her eyes again, Andrew was watching her. His expression was no longer amused. He held out his hand, and she gave him back his phone.

"If I hadn't stopped by, would you have told me?"

"Huh?" Grace turned to stir the macaroni and the sauce. Truth was, she hadn't planned to tell anybody she was leaving.

"Cassidy, though, right?" Andrew asked. "You wouldn't leave without letting her know where you were going."

With no other excuse to keep her back to him, she turned and leaned against the counter. "It's been a while since I've had anybody..." She shook her head, started over. "We've been on the run so long, just Lily and me, that, honestly, it didn't even occur to me."

His lips pressed together. A moment passed before he spoke. "Can you imagine how that would have been for Cassidy and James? For me? To suddenly discover you gone? I don't know what they know, but I'd always wonder"—he lowered his voice—"if her father had found you. We wouldn't know if you were dead or—"

"I'm sorry. You're right, of course." About Cassidy, anyway. It wouldn't have occurred to her that Andrew cared.

He studied her another long moment, then shook his head slowly. After blowing out a deep breath, he smiled, though it seemed forced. "What do you think about my idea? If we can prove what we believe, we can take the information to law enforcement, and they can keep their eyes out for...What's his name?"

"Myron Bowman." If she could prove Myron was a child pornographer, then if the police caught up with Grace, she'd have the ammunition to take him down. Probably wouldn't save her from paying the penalty for her crime, but Lily would be safe.

"I'll agree to it," she said, "if you promise not to do anything more without my permission. We need to handle this with care."

"Sure. Of course. Whatever you think is best."

He said that now. Would he be willing to hold off on what they learned, assuming they learned anything?

Was it worth the risk?

To get information that would keep Myron from ever regaining custody of his daughter? Yes, that was definitely worth the risk.

GRACE SENT Andrew a photograph of Lily from her phone and called her in for dinner.

"Are you gonna stay?" Lily asked Andrew.

His phone made a swishing sound that indicated a sent message, and his gaze flicked to Grace's. "If it's really okay."

"Sure." Not that it was anything fancy. She hadn't even set the table. While Andrew and Lily filled their plates, she set forks and napkins out, then added the loaf of bread and a stick of soft butter. Not exactly gourmet cooking, but then she hadn't planned on company.

Not that she could have done much better if she had.

Lily kept up a steady stream of conversation, talking about everything from what she'd learned at school that day to how much fun she'd had at Sunday school to what she wanted to get her friend for her birthday. The party that, thanks to Andrew, she'd be able to attend.

Thank God he'd come by. The man had rescued her from a life-altering decision.

Amazing how much Lily had come out of her shell since they'd left Washington. This child who used to be so quiet talked incessantly. Smiled constantly. Giggled frequently and, unlike the first few weeks after leaving her father, slept soundly.

Whenever Grace wondered if she'd done the right thing that terrifying spring night, she thought about the changes in Lily and knew she had. Myron's exploitation had harmed his daughter in countless ways, ways Grace was only beginning to uncover, but praise God for the resiliency of children.

"What do you think, Miss Grace?"

She blinked, scrambling to figure out what Lily was talking about.

Across the table, Andrew said, "I think something craft-related sounds like a great idea."

"Yes." Grace shot him a grateful look. "When I was your age, I used to love friendship bracelets. Do you think she'd like a kit to make those?"

"What's a friendship bracelet?"

Grace explained the brightly colored woven bracelets she and her friends used to trade and wear with pride, remembering those easy days of childhood. She and her mother hadn't had much money, but they'd been happy. Her mom's second marriage had solved the money problem and destroyed everything else.

"Yes!" Lily bounced in her seat. "Can I be excused? Can I get on your computer and see if I can find one? I bet they have them online. Do we have time to order one? Should we go shopping? I love toy shopping!"

Andrew chuckled, shaking his head.

Satisfied that Lily'd eaten all she was going to, Grace said, "Bring me the laptop, please."

Lily did, and Grace opened a browser for her, making sure to close all the tabs related to French cottages and overseas flights. She always used a private window to search for Myron, and that was closed, the history not saved. Lily should be safe to browse. "Don't open any more windows, and don't—"

"Answer any messages," Lily finished. "I *know*."

Lily took the laptop and sat on the couch, where she scrolled through the products Grace had pulled up on the shopping site.

Andrew was still smiling. "She uses more words in an hour than I use all day."

"She's thriving here."

"It's a good place," Andrew said. "When I first moved here, I was a little like Lily. I hid it better, but I was nervous at my new job. After living in the city, and...other places that weren't exactly friendly, I worried about how I'd fit in." His shy smile was even more attractive than the confident one he usually wore. Which was saying something.

"That surprises me," Grace said. "You seem so self-assured."

"I am. Totally self-assured." He winked. "Or at least, I pretend to be, which is practically the same thing."

"Practically."

"Speaking of returning favors..."

"Were we?" she asked, hearing the amusement in her own tone.

"My father's birthday party is this weekend at his place in Hollis."

She'd never heard of Hollis, but she couldn't say so. Andrew'd never asked about where she'd moved from, but considering he thought she was a foster parent, he had to assume it was another town in this state. "About how far is that from here?"

"It's an hour and a half or so, near Nashua. I know it's a long way to go for a party when you won't know a soul there, but..." Again, the shy smile was back. "I could sure use some moral support."

"You don't get along with your father?"

"We've had issues. I'm working on it, which is why I'm going to this thing. Normally, I wouldn't bother, but if I really want to repair our relationship..."

Of course Andrew should go, but did Grace want to? Church was one thing, but to meet a bunch of strangers, to make small talk, to shake hands?

"Before you say no," he said, "you should know Lily would love it. They're going to have a bounce house. I have nephews who are about her age, who never miss an opportunity—"

"A bounce house?" Lily popped up on the sofa. "Can we go, Miss Grace? Can we? Please?"

Andrew said, "Oops."

She laughed. "Sure. You didn't do that on purpose at all."

He just shrugged.

Brat.

Lily's expression was filled with hope.

How could she say no to that?

Andrew's next words were spoken quietly. "I wasn't kidding about the other, though. I could use a friend."

It wasn't as if she had plans. "Oh, all right."

"Yippee! Two parties in one weekend!" Lily returned her attention to the laptop.

Andrew stood and grabbed his plate. "Sorry...not sorry."

"Yeah. Forgiven, not forgiven."

He chuckled. "You done?"

She scooted back from the table. "I got it. You're the guest."

"You cooked." He took the plate from her hand and went into the kitchen, where he dumped the remains in the trash and started filling the dishwasher.

"Seriously, I can do it."

"I know you can." But he kept at it, so she mixed the leftover macaroni and sauce and put it in a plastic container.

"To be honest," she said, "I'm looking forward to meeting your parents. Do you and your mom have a good relationship?"

"Yeah, excellent." He filled the sauce pot with water and added some soap. "But Dad's not married to Mom, not since I was a kid. He traded her in for a younger model."

"Oh. Sorry."

"To his credit," Andrew added, "he's stayed married to Christine for over twenty years. They have three kids."

"Do you have any full siblings?"

He shook his head. "Do you? Full or half or step?"

"No, none. My mom had a miscarriage after I was born. I think she'd have tried again. But my father was killed in Afghanistan in 2002."

"Oh." Andrew looked over his shoulder at her. "That's awful."

She shrugged. "I remember him. Not well, but I remember how I felt when I was with him. He loved me. He was a good father, a good man."

"It must've been hard growing up without him. Did your mom remarry?"

"When I was about Lily's age. They didn't have any kids. Not sure if he didn't want them or she couldn't get pregnant again or what."

Oliver jumped onto the counter and approached the butter dish like a tiger stalking its prey.

"Don't even think about it." She shooed the cat away and covered the dish. "You're a nuisance, you know that?"

"I'm just trying to help," Andrew said.

"Not you, goober."

He continued working on the dishes. "Been called worse."

She shook her head. "Lily, time to take Regis out."

The child hurried in, the dog at her feet. "You coming?"

"We'll stay inside. Stay in the fenced-in area."

Lily's sigh communicated her displeasure, but Grace couldn't let her wander off alone.

Andrew shut the water off. "These are done, if you want to go out with her."

Did Andrew want to join them, or was he telling her he was ready to head home? She was surprised to find she hoped the first, not the second.

Being in New Hampshire had been healthy not only Lily. It seemed Grace had done a little bit of healing too. Craving adult human interaction? It'd been a long time since she'd done that.

"Okay, then," she said. "Grab a coat and a plastic bag, sweetie."

Andrew stood beside her. "I didn't wear one."

She laughed.

"Silly!" Lily said. "She's talking to me!" The child was still shoving her arms into the light jacket when she bounded outside, Regis on her heels.

Grace followed. Behind her, Andrew said, "Can Oliver come?"

"I tried to make him an indoor cat, but he communicated his displeasure with that very soon after I got him."

Andrew held the door open, and Oliver dashed outside and took off.

The temperature was in the fifties but would probably fall quickly now that it was dusk. The community's old-fashioned streetlights lit up as they walked. Lily led the way on their familiar route toward the park, Regis bolting this way and that, then returning to bark at her heels. As soon as the playground equipment was in sight, both child and dog took off to play.

"You're doing a really good job with her," Andrew said. "How did you come to be her foster parent?"

"That's kind of a long story. Suffice it to say, she and I have a connection."

"You do. That day after she fell..." Andrew turned to her, his face barely discernible in the dim light. "I wasn't very kind to you. I'm sorry about that."

"I should have been paying better attention. I was trying to find information about Myron."

"Any luck?"

She shook her head. "I just wish I knew where he was. If he was on our tail or...I always feel like, if I turn around really fast, he's going to be right there."

"Must be scary, living like that."

"I'd like to say I'm getting used to it."

"I hope you don't." His words were serious when he added, "I hope the man's caught long before being afraid becomes second nature."

They watched Lily and Regis play for a few minutes before Grace called the child back. "Bath time and bedtime." Before Lily could argue, she added, "You have not one but *two* birthday parties this weekend. I think you're one blessed kid. So let's not complain, all right?" Grace started back toward their condo, and Lily followed without a word.

Andrew brushed his fingers against Grace's wrist, her only warning that he was about to hold her hand.

She snatched it back and crossed her arms.

He turned her direction, hurt and embarrassment clear in the light from the nearby street lamp.

"Sorry." She was trying to come up with some words to excuse her poor behavior when Lily piped in.

"Miss Grace doesn't like to hold hands." The child said the words as if it were the most obvious thing in the world. "It makes her feel funny." She looked up at Grace. "Right?"

Now, Grace was the one feeling embarrassed. "You're very insightful, sweetheart. It does make me feel funny."

"How come?" Lily asked.

"It's sort of hard to explain."

"Okay." Seemingly satisfied, Lily chased Regis, who'd caught sight of Oliver and had rushed ahead to investigate.

"Would it be hard to explain to me?" Andrew's voice was low and deep, the question almost tentative.

"Yes. But maybe I will someday."

They walked a few feet in silence, and then his hand touched the small of her back. "That okay?"

The gentle pressure felt warm through her sweatshirt, comforting. Oddly intimate.

Maybe she should tell him no. Maybe she should step away, stop this friendship from deepening into something more. But she didn't want to.

Grace was twenty-five years old, and she'd never been in love. She'd never had a boyfriend. She'd never even dated. It wasn't that she was against the idea. It wasn't that men hadn't been interested in her. But she'd never been the slightest bit attracted to anyone. In fact, more than once she'd wondered if there were something wrong with her.

"You're perfectly normal," Mama Lucy had told her. *"It'll happen when it happens."*

Was it happening now? With Andrew? Or was Grace just grateful for the man's kindness?

She'd felt grateful before. She'd never felt *this*.

The hand dropped from her back. "I didn't mean to—"

"It's fine. I mean, it was fine. The hand. On my back."

She sounded like an idiot.

Andrew returned his hand, then slid it around to rest on her side, just above her hip. "How about that? Is that okay?"

She nodded, enjoying the feeling.

He sidled closer until she was tucked against his side. "How about that?"

"How far are you going to go with this?"

"Hmm...Almost sounds like a challenge. And I love a good challenge."

She laughed. "Let's stop here for now."

"Okay. For now. Maybe we'll practice some hand-holding on our date this weekend."

She froze, but he nudged her along. "Don't get cold feet on me now. You already said yes."

CHAPTER FOURTEEN

Myron growled beneath his binoculars as the neighbor wrapped his arm around Grace.

That man had no business touching her.

He had no business being anywhere near Lily.

There was still much work to be done. In the meantime, Grace had better not let the neighbor get too close or too familiar.

Myron would have to step up his timetable, complete the space he was designing especially for his girls. Then, he'd reclaim them both.

And if the neighbor came anywhere near, he wouldn't know what hit him.

CHAPTER FIFTEEN

Saturday morning dragged. Andrew blamed the slow clock on the fact that he spent most of the time after breakfast focused on numbers on his computer screen. Chet had sent—via snail mail, no less—another accounting notebook, and Andrew had spent the morning adding the contents to his software program, only to discover that, once again, Chet hadn't given him everything Andrew had asked for.

Even Cheddar Chet wasn't *that* stupid.

Which meant he was hiding something. His own incompetence, or was there more to it?

Without all the information, Andrew couldn't be sure. He planned to confront, or at least encourage, his half brother at the party that afternoon. If he had anything to say about it, he'd bring the remaining books home with him.

Dressed in a pair of jeans and a sweater Mom had once told him made him look dashing, he was just about to cross the street when his phone dinged.

Praying it wasn't Grace canceling, he glanced at the screen. His friend had gotten a hit on the image of Lily. He clicked the message, and the screen filled with a black-and-white photograph showing a woman holding a toddler's hand.

David's message read, *My software thinks this is your girl.* How sure? Where'd it come from?

David said, *Software's really good, but it's no guarantee. Still getting the details. Get back to you soon.*

Andrew enlarged the photo and gazed at the little girl's face. She looked to be two, maybe three, but even still, he could see Lily in those big eyes.

And the woman holding her hand had to be related, her mother, or possibly her sister, since she looked so young.

It wasn't the kind of image he was looking for, but maybe it was a link to the child's past, a link to her mother, or at least her family.

He grabbed his things and jogged across the parking lot.

If his heart was racing a little more than normal, he'd blame the short run and the photograph, not the eagerness to see his neighbor again.

He rang the new video doorbell. He'd installed it and the one at the back door the day before so that, the next time Grace thought she had an intruder, she could simply check the app.

It was Lily who answered, her eyes teary. "Mr. Middleton, can I bring my dog, please? I forgot to ask, but I don't wanna leave him home alone all day long. Miss Grace said no, but I said you would let me 'cause you're nice."

"Lily." Grace's voice held more than a hint of rebuke as she approached from the kitchen. "That is impolite." She stood beside the child and addressed Andrew. "She'll survive without Regis for the afternoon." To Lily she said, "And we know Mr. Middleton is nice already, even if you can't take your dog. Right?"

The child nodded, big green eyes filling with tears. "Sorry. I didn't mean to be mean."

Oh, man. He'd walked in on something. "It's okay, sweetie. Can I talk to Miss Grace for a second?"

Grace said, "Go to the bathroom so we won't have to stop on the way. And get your shoes on." After Lily ran upstairs, Grace stepped back. "We're almost ready. Sorry about that. I don't think she meant it the way it sounded."

"As if you didn't think I was nice?" Andrew smiled to show he was kidding. "Or she didn't think *you* were."

"Either. Both. I don't know."

He joined her inside, and as his eyes adjusted to the dimmer light after the sunshine outside, he took in her appearance. She wore dress slacks and a pale blue off-the-shoulder top that brightened her gray-blue eyes. She'd curled her hair and even put on makeup. He'd already thought her attractive, but wow.

Wow.

He cleared his throat. "You look beautiful."

"Oh." Her cheeks pinked just a touch. "You said it was a date, so..." She lifted her shoulders, dropped them. "Too much?"

"You look perfect." He lowered his voice. "I was planning on taking Regis, but if you said no, and you want to stick with that answer—"

"You don't have to."

"I don't mind. I know the dog's important, and the party will be mostly outdoors."

Regis, seated at their feet, looked between them as if he understood every word.

"He makes her feel safe. Though..." She chewed her lip, glancing up the stairs. "Lately she hasn't relied on him as much."

"I think *you* make her feel safe, and she feels at home here. That's a good sign. But today, she'll be in a new situation. New people, new experiences. I don't mind. Really."

"I can drive, if you're worried about your car."

"Leather seats are easy to clean. Will Oliver get his feelings hurt?"

That earned a laugh, which had been Andrew's goal. "He'll enjoy having the house to himself." Grace stepped toward the stairs. "Let me just—"

"Hold on. I want to show you something." He opened the photograph on his phone and showed her. "David thinks this is her."

Grace took the phone and studied the image. "Oh, my gosh. I think so." She looked up. "What do you think?"

"Definitely possible."

Grace returned her focus to the image. "It's some sort of fair or festival."

He'd mostly noticed the people, but now he saw what she meant. Booths were lined up on one side of the photograph. A Ferris wheel rose in the background. "The landscape looks flat and tree-less. Doesn't look like Washington. I wonder...Could it be Texas?"

He stepped close and looked, trying to think about the image and not about the floral scent that told him Grace had even put on perfume. "Could be. Why would you—?"

"I'm ready!" Lily hurried down the stairs.

Grace handed him back the phone. "Mr. Middleton said you can take Regis."

The child's eyes lit up, and Andrew felt about ten feet tall. Would that all females were so easy to please.

Andrew followed as his stepmom gave Grace the grand tour of the house. Not that Andrew knew Grace that well, but he guessed she wasn't terribly impressed even as she oohed and aahed and praised Christine's decorating skills and taste.

She might not've been bowled over by the house, but Andrew was bowled over by her. When they'd arrived, she'd conversed comfortably with people she'd never met—shaking hands through a pair of camel-colored leather gloves—while gently handling Lily's incessant *Can I go play now? Please, Miss Grace?* Grace had handled their first hour at Dad's party with...well, grace.

She was well named.

Lily had made fast friends with Andrew's nephews and was outside bouncing in the big blow-up contraption. Before she'd walked away, Grace had instructed her repeatedly to be careful of her broken arm, not only for her sake but that of others. "You don't want to hurt anyone. And you need to stay close. Don't run off into the woods, and stay away from that pool."

Grace seemed reluctant to leave Lily until Christine pointed out the teenagers she'd hired to babysit for the afternoon.

Andrew had introduced Grace to both of his half sisters and his brother-in-law, and of course the nephews. He and Grace had greeted old family friends Andrew had known as long as he could remember. He'd been looking for his father among the hundred or so guests when Christine had cornered them and offered to take Grace on the tour. Because of course, in her mind, everybody would want to see her house.

To be fair, it was rather impressive.

Six bedrooms and seven baths, not including those in the guest house. The place stood alone on five acres, tucked into gorgeous New Hampshire woods, which had exploded in color that week as if even nature bent to Dad's will.

The grounds were perfectly manicured. Bright yellow mums lined the beds and surrounded the ridiculous spitting-cherub fountain in the middle of a perfectly trimmed circle of hedges.

Ostentatious much?

But Christine loved it. And she wasn't stingy with her home, opening it not only for business associates and friends but sometimes for people who found themselves without housing. Students needing a place to stay had lived in the guest room in the south wing.

Yes, his father's house had *wings*.

A missionary family had stayed in the pool house for a year while they regrouped after being booted from some third-world country.

His father and stepmom were good people. They hadn't started out that way, but they'd grown and changed in the years since Dad left Mom. Andrew should be less judgmental.

But the fact that Grace wasn't dazzled by the wealth made him like her a little bit more.

Finally finished with the tour, they'd just stepped onto the back porch when his father's booming voice reached them. "Been wondering when you'd get here."

"Been here for an hour, Dad." Andrew paired the words with a smile as he approached his father and shook his hand.

Dad introduced him to the men orbiting around him like moons. Andrew greeted each, then backed up and urged Grace forward with a tap to the small of her back. "This is Grace Miller. Grace, my father, Drew Middleton."

At some point, she'd put on her gloves and reached out to shake his hand.

"Pleasure to meet you," she said. "Your wife just gave me a tour. What a lovely home."

"Thank you, thank you."

Andrew shifted to the man beside his father. "Grace, this is Harrison Ackerman, CFO of Middleton Enterprises."

"And surrogate uncle," Harrison added as he reached to shake Grace's hand. Harrison clasped Andrew on the shoulder. "Known this fellow since he was in those footed pajamas. Too big for those now, I guess."

"I'm sure he was adorable." Grace's eyes twinkled as she regarded Andrew.

"I'm too old for those now too," Andrew said. "Haven't worn them in months."

Harrison threw his head back and laughed. It wasn't *that* funny.

"And how do you two know each other?" Dad addressed Grace, but Andrew answered.

"Grace is a neighbor. She just moved to Coventry."

"What made you move all the way up there? Too cold for my taste, and so far from the action." Around him, the other men nodded and muttered their agreement.

"I love it," she said. "It's the perfect location. And Andrew's been so friendly both to me and Lily."

His eyebrows lifted. "Lily is...?"

"My foster daughter." Grace pointed across the yard. "She's chasing one of your grandsons."

Dad gave her a cursory glance. "Cute, cute." He focused on Andrew. "Don't leave before we get a chance to talk, eh?"

"Of course." Andrew tapped Grace's back. "Let's go check on her."

After *see you later* murmurs, Andrew urged Grace toward the yard where the kids played. "Nothing like being put on the spot in front of an audience, huh?"

"He seems nice enough, your dad."

They were nearing the screaming children when Andrew leaned in close. "You're wearing gloves."

"It's kind of chilly."

It was in the sixties. Not that chilly. He gave her a look, and she shrugged. "It's the hand thing."

"Germaphobic?" She'd implied her issue with hand-holding was something that needed to be explained, and fear of germs wasn't exactly complex.

"That's not it."

"Since you're wearing the gloves, do you mind?" He held out his hand, palm up, and she slid hers into his. He'd prefer skin-to-skin, but skin-to-soft leather would do. For now.

They reached the yard and greeted his sister and other adults standing nearby, chatting and watching the children. He nodded to one of the many café tables placed all over the backyard for the occasion. "Want to sit?"

She did, and he took the chair across from her. Regis, who'd been standing guard at the edge of the grass, came and sat by their feet.

Andrew patted its head. "This is the most well-behaved dog I've ever met."

"I know, right? And completely devoted to Lily. The first few days she went to school, he sat at the door all day long. His whining made me crazy." She smiled at the little animal. "I've never been much of a dog person, but Regis is winning me over."

"How does a person not like dogs?"

"I like them, just never had one. They always seemed like a lot of work. They *are* a lot of work."

"This from a woman who takes in foster children." He leaned forward, keeping his voice low. "Can I ask you a question?"

"Sure."

"You don't seem particularly impressed by all of this."

She gazed around at the yard, the pool, the crowd, skimming over the three-story house they'd just toured. "That wasn't a question."

He held her eye contact and waited.

"My stepfather was wealthy. Maybe not this wealthy, but he had money."

"You aren't a fan of your stepfather."

With her lips pressed closed, she shook her head.

"I assume there's a story there."

A moment passed, and he feared she wouldn't say anything else.

Finally, facing the yard, she spoke. "My mother fell in love with his money. Maybe him too. I don't know. But definitely his money. I knew...It's hard to explain because I was just a child, but I *knew* he wasn't a good guy. I told Mom, but she thought I was scared or jealous or..." Grace shook her head. "She married him anyway."

"And were you right? Was he not a good guy?"

"He was not."

"In what way?"

She turned to meet Andrew's eyes. "Mom fell in love with his money. He fell in...not love but something much darker...with me."

"Oh. *Oh*." He sat back, tried to process that. Tried to figure out how to phrase his next question. But Grace continued without his having to ask.

"I could feel it, his interest. For years, I could feel his eyes on me. He never said or did anything inappropriate. But... It's hard to explain."

"Okay." He leaned toward her, wanting to know the rest but not daring to ask.

All around them, the sounds of the party continued. Children laughing. People chatting. Music playing. But all he cared about in that moment was the woman who trusted him enough to share this dark memory.

"He was always kind to me," Grace said. "He bought me things. He took me places. He let me have sleepovers with my girlfriends. By all accounts, he was a good father. But I never trusted him."

Andrew wanted to ask how she knew. There must have been hints, looks, something in his behavior. If she picked up on it as a child, how did her mother miss it?

"They'd been married four years when I turned thirteen," Grace said. "It was not long after that birthday that he tried to touch me the first time. He came into my room at night. I pretended I didn't know what he was doing and managed to slip by him, going to my mom. I didn't tell her right away because he was there. I just asked if I could sleep on her floor, told her I'd had a bad dream." Grace's shoulders lifted and fell. "I was afraid. But the next day, when he was at work, I told her exactly what happened."

"Good for you."

Grace's closed-lipped smile was far from amused. "She called me a liar."

"Seriously?" He tried to imagine that. What kind of mother wouldn't at least investigate? At least consider that she might be wrong? Her own daughter was at risk, and the woman...what? Didn't care? "Did he have some power over her? Was he abusive or—?"

"It was nothing like that. He just held the purse strings. Mom had signed a prenup, so if she left him, she'd have nothing, and I don't think she could face that again. Even though I asked her not to, Mom told my stepdad what I'd said. The next time, he was bolder. He said my mother would never believe me, so why not give in to it? 'You might even enjoy it,' he said."

"What a pig."

Grace nodded slightly. "I screamed. Mom came running. He explained away his presence in my room by saying he'd heard me cry out. Suggested I needed counseling and even offered to pay for it."

Grace delivered the words almost mechanically. She'd shared this story before. Still, that she would share it with him meant something.

"He thought I was trapped," Grace said. "But I was smart. Mom went out for a girl's night. He wasn't supposed to be home, but I had a feeling he'd come home early. I found our old video camera. When he came into my room that night, I caught the whole thing on film."

"Good thinking. But..." He dared not ask the question.

"I also had a knife," she said. "And I wasn't afraid to use it. With the camera, I knew that if I defended myself, the whole thing would be on video. I waited just long enough so that there would be no doubt about what he was trying to do, and then I pulled it out and threatened him. He laughed, but he backed off, told me it was just a matter of time."

Andrew tried to imagine thirteen-year-old Grace wielding a knife against a grown man. The image made his stomach drop. He could have really hurt her. Andrew didn't want to think about what that man could have done to her.

"So you proved to your mom you were telling the truth. I'm sure that was tough on your relationship, but..." His words trailed when Grace shook her head.

"She accused me of trying to destroy her marriage and sent me away."

"At thirteen? Are you serious?"

"I went to live at the girls home, which is where I met Cassidy. My stepdad was furious," Grace said. "With Mom, with me. He wanted me in his house. When I was packing, I heard them arguing. He threatened to leave her if she sent me away. But the prenup only protected him if she left, not if he did the leaving. And, deep down, Mom knew the truth. She knew, but she was weak. So she found a safe space for me and left me there."

"I'm sorry." Andrew wished he knew better words, healing words. He wished he could go back in time and fix it for her. "I'm so sorry you had to deal with that. I'm sorry your mother didn't understand your value, how all the gold in the world pales in comparison."

Grace's lips stretched into an almost-smile. "You're a sweet talker, Andrew Middleton."

He shook his head, not allowing even a hint of amusement to grace his face. "Not pretty words, true words. Of you, of Lily... We're all worth so much more than any bank account."

Her gaze bored into him. After a minute, she dipped her head, seemingly satisfied with what she'd seen. "Money doesn't mean to me what it means to most. My stepfather died a couple of years ago, and I inherited half of his fortune. I don't know why he left it to me. Guilt, maybe." She shrugged. "So, to answer the question you didn't ask earlier, no, I'm not impressed with wealth. To be honest, wealth makes me nervous. Men with money to burn often do so in unsavory ways."

"True of women, too, I think."

"My mother's an example of that. The things people do for— and with—money...I want no part of it." Then, she gazed around again. "I don't mean to imply anything about your father. I'm sure he's a good man. I know money doesn't make people evil. You have it, I have it. Some people use it for good. Wealth just makes me wary."

"I understand that." He wanted to take her hand, but she'd slipped off the gloves. Instead, he rested his palm against her forearm lying on the table between them. They watched the kids for a little while, Andrew's mind swirling with what Grace had told him. Because Grace had every reason in the world not to trust men, and yet, for some reason, she'd trusted him.

He didn't know why she'd deemed him worthy, but he vowed he'd never do anything to break that trust.

CHAPTER SIXTEEN

Seated on the back patio near one of the many oversize propane heaters, Grace, Andrew, and Lily were finishing up their dinners. Lily'd eaten an entire hot dog, a handful of potato chips, and enough carrot and celery sticks to make Grace feel like a halfway decent parental figure.

"Is there gonna be cake? I love cake."

Before Grace could answer, Andrew said, "If I know my father, there will be a giant cake, probably chocolate."

"Yay!" Her voice was too loud, and Grace shushed her. In a slightly lower tone, she added, "Chocolate is my favorite."

Andrew, unfazed by the child's volume, asked, "What kind of cake did your friend have last night?"

The question had Lily talking about the birthday party, the cake, the magician, and all the presents. Andrew, kind and gentle soul that he was, kept his attention riveted to Lily as if she were the most interesting guest in attendance. Pretty impressive, considering the crowd of adults all around them. That day, Grace had met doctors, hospital department heads, business owners, bankers, and real estate moguls, not to mention a congressman and the governor.

Apparently, Drew Middleton's birthday celebration was a very big deal.

Yet there was Andrew, conversing with an eight-year-old girl and seeming to enjoy every second of it.

Grace hadn't planned to tell him about her stepfather. But at the time, confiding in him had seemed like the most natural thing in the world. She wasn't one to trust easily, especially men. Living at, and then working in, the girls home, she'd heard many stories—and seen many images—of evil men, and to be fair, some evil women as well. The old adage that broken people break people had proved true over and over. For years, Grace had dedicated her life to healing the broken.

She'd thought she was done with that forever. But here she was, risking everything for a child, again. If anything happened to Lily, she wouldn't be the only broken one. Grace wouldn't be able to put her pieces back together again.

She mentally shook herself. It wasn't her job to put herself or anybody else back together. God was the creator and *re*-creator, not Grace.

A man approached the table. Andrew looked up, and the expression that crossed his features was nowhere near the easy smile he'd worn most of the day. He stood. "Chet."

"Wondered where you were."

"Been here all day. Haven't seen you though."

"Been inside watching the Boston College-Wake Forest game."

"BC win?" Andrew voiced the question, though it sounded more *forced polite* than *interested*.

Chet just shrugged. "Wasn't their best game." He held out his hand to Grace, and dread filled her stomach. Why hadn't she kept the gloves on?

Andrew leaned in and whispered, "You don't have to."

But she could do this. For years, she'd shaken hands. At one point, she'd learned to use the impressions she got to her advantage. She'd learned to keep them from affecting her too deeply. When she'd holed herself up in that cottage, she'd lost those skills. If she wanted to rejoin society, she'd need to relearn them. "Grace Miller." She slipped her palm against Chet's.

No pictures, just strong, dark feelings of loathing and fear.

She snatched her hand back and made her lips slip into a smile.

"This is my brother," Andrew said. "Chet Middleton."

Chet appraised her head to toe. "Where'd he find you? The classifieds?" The man added a laugh.

Andrew's low tone held an unspoken threat. "Watch yourself, cheese nip."

Chet glared at him, then bent at the waist in an almost-bow toward Grace. "Forgive me." He exhaled the stench of beer. "It's just so rare to find Andrew with a woman. I meant no offense."

He'd meant plenty of offense. She didn't bother to respond.

The silence, surrounded by partygoers, felt oppressive.

Andrew broke it with, "Did you bring the information?"

Chet stepped back. "It's a party."

"Just tell me where it is, and I'll grab it."

"I'm having a hard time getting my hands on it."

Andrew stepped closer to his brother. "Are you telling me you can't *find* it?"

"It'll turn up."

"There's this thing we learned in business school," Andrew said. "I understand you didn't get your MBA, but I'm sure they at least touched on it where you went. Where was that again?"

Chet leaned back as if Andrew had landed a blow, and Andrew smiled.

At that moment, she wasn't impressed with either man.

"Anyway," Andrew said. "It's a pretty simple concept. It's called *filing*. It's especially helpful to people who can't be bothered to enter their records into software. I mean, if the only accounting records you have are in seventies-era notebooks, the least you can do is keep up with said notebooks."

"I don't need you to lecture me."

Andrew continued as if he hadn't spoken. "The way it works is, you put the notebooks in files in a big box thing we call a filing cabinet. And you use a certain order. Sometimes, you might file things alphabetically. That means by your ABC's."

Dark red crept up Chet's neck. His eyes narrowed, and fury wafted off of him stronger than the scent of alcohol.

"In the case of accounting notebooks," Andrew continued, "you'd file them chronologically. That means by date. You know, January, February—"

"I know these!" Lily popped up from her seat at the table and recited the rest of the months.

Andrew seemed genuinely surprised to see the child there. He smiled, waiting patiently for her to finish. When she did, he turned back to Chet. "Maybe you should be taking notes."

Chet stepped closer to Andrew, getting in his face. "Maybe you should shut up." His voice was too loud, and people turned their direction. "Maybe you should shove those notebooks right—"

"Watch it," Andrew said. "There are children present."

Chet glared. "That's it. Hide behind a six-year-old."

Lily said, "I'm eight."

Grace took the girl's wrist and shifted to stand between the men and the child.

The murmurs of the crowd died down as people watched to see what would happen next.

Grace slid her other hand into the crook of Andrew's elbow and squeezed. "That's enough, Andrew. This is a party."

He glanced her way, then shook his head and took a step back.

Andrew's dad made his way through the crowd and approached. "You two okay?" His voice held amusement, but she guessed it was forced. "These two and their rivalry." He laughed as one hand came down hard on Andrew's shoulder. He addressed the crowd. "The desserts are ready. You won't want to miss the apple pie."

Slowly, people resumed their conversations, turning away and giving the Middleton men some space.

Grace wanted nothing more than to walk away, but the tense muscles below her fingers told her Andrew hadn't relaxed one bit.

She bent and spoke to Lily. "Why don't you go see what they have for dessert? You can choose one thing. I'll get it for you when I'm done here."

The child's eyes were wide, flicking between the two men.

"It's okay," Grace said. "We'll be right there."

Lily skipped away.

When she was gone, Drew addressed his sons. "What's going on?"

"He's being his normal arrogant know-it-all self," Chet said.

Andrew turned away from his brother and addressed his dad. "I need to get the rest of the information to do the work you asked me to do. Apparently, he's misplaced some accounting notebooks."

"I haven't misplaced them," Chet murmured.

Barely taking his attention from them, Drew called, "Alice?"

The sixty-something woman must have been hovering just beyond Grace's field of vision. When she stepped to Drew's side, he said, "Have somebody run to the office to get the MBC books for"—he focused on Andrew—"when exactly?"

"Third quarter last year through first quarter this year."

She nodded and walked away.

"There." Drew eyed both of his sons. "You two happy now?"

Andrew dipped his head toward his father. "Yeah. Sorry. I didn't mean to..."

Chet swiveled and marched away.

Drew watched him go, shaking his head. "I wish you'd make a little more of an effort."

Andrew's lips twitched, and she could almost hear the unspoken, *he started it*. But he managed to keep the words in his head. "You're right. I'll try."

His father stepped away and got pulled into a conversation.

Andrew met Grace's eyes. "Sorry." He looked embarrassed as he nodded at the chair. "Should we—?"

"Let's not." She wanted out of the crowd. "Let's check on Lily."

After they finished their desserts, Andrew led the way to the edge of the grassy area, where the kids were twirling sparklers in the gathering darkness. Lily seemed to be having a blast.

"I take it there's a story there," Grace prompted.

"Dad asked me to look at the books for the division Chet manages, but Chet has refused to turn them all over. His excuses have shifted every time I've called him on it. First, he said he'd forgotten to include a couple. Then it was his assistant's fault for not getting everything together. Now, apparently, he can't *find* them. Even Chet's not stupid enough to misplace the books."

She waited, but he adding nothing else.

"I think the story goes back further than that," she said.

Andrew watched the children. "Picked up on that, did you?" When she said nothing, he blew out a long breath. "I don't think I've ever forgiven him for being born."

She shifted, but with their backs to the light, she couldn't make out the expression on his face.

"Which is stupid. It's not his fault." A long pause was followed by his low voice. "He was born six months after my parents separated. Their divorce wasn't even final yet."

"Oh. That's rough."

He shrugged. "Dad probably would have left Mom for Christine anyway, eventually. I guess they'd been together awhile. But Chet was the tipping point."

"You're right. That is stupid."

His eyebrows rose. "Wow. Thanks for your support." When she said nothing, he looked back at the kids. "In my defense, I have *tried* to not hate him. But he's eminently hate-able."

Recalling the words Chet had spoken to her, and the feelings she'd had when he'd touched her hand, she understood what Andrew meant. "Not really an excuse, though. He can be a jerk all he wants. *You* don't have to be one."

"I'm usually more self-controlled around him." He reached for Grace's hand but didn't make contact before he let his arm drop again. "When he looked at you like he did, and then said that to you, I actually felt pretty proud of myself for not punching him."

She managed a little laugh. "I think maybe you need to raise the bar on your own behavioral standards."

"Only with Cheddar Chet."

She let her expression ask the question, and he laughed. "Immature, I know. But *Chet.* Doesn't it sound like something you'd store in your pantry?"

That explained the *cheese nip* comment.

Andrew slipped his hand around her waist. "You're right about all of it. I'm glad you were there. I hate to think what words would have slipped out if you and Lily hadn't been listening. You make me want to raise my standards."

She leaned against his side, enjoying the warmth and the connection. Maybe Andrew wasn't perfect, but he was a good man, a kind man. A man she could let herself fall for.

No, she needed to keep Lily's situation—*her* needs and *her* protection—at the forefront. Grace couldn't let Andrew become a distraction.

They'd been casually chatting when Andrew grabbed his cell and glanced at the screen. "It's David. The picture guy." After swiping to connect, he said, "What'd you learn?"

While he listened to his friend, Grace's nerves ratcheted up. If Lily had family out there, Grace wanted to know. She did.

Even if the thought of giving Lily up cut fissures in her heart.

And that was exactly why she had to. She'd already allowed herself to become too attached. The last thing she wanted was to fall in love with another girl.

Maybe she should have just left Lily on Cassidy's doorstep and run.

She'd considered the option many times in the months since they'd escaped from Myron. Each time, Grace had talked herself out of it, certain that, because of what she knew, she would be better able to protect her.

And sweet Lily needed somebody to fight for her, even if Grace, damaged and incapable as she was, happened to be the only option.

Beside her, Andrew said, "Text that to me, would you?" When he hung up, he opened the photo she'd seen earlier again. He tapped the child's image. "Photo was published in a newspaper in a small town in Texas. It went with an article about a county fair and rodeo. The woman is Annabeth Springer. According to the newspaper article, she's Lilianne's mother."

Lilianne. Grace took a closer look. The woman looked young, late teens or early twenties. Thin and beautiful with light hair and a big smile.

A text lit up on the screen, and she handed the phone back to Andrew, who clicked it, then handed the phone back. "The article."

Grace perused it. Written seven years prior, it talked about the fair, which had games and rides and food trucks galore. The author seemed proud that his little town had attracted a crowd of thousands. She enlarged the photo and read out loud the caption beneath. "*Annabeth Springer with daughter, Lilianne, enjoying the festivities.*" She handed the phone back to Andrew. "Annabeth didn't like Texas."

His eyebrows lifted. "Let me guess. One of your weird but accurate *feelings?*"

"Not this time. Lily told me she liked Texas, but her mother hated it."

"That explains why you mentioned Texas earlier. I was beginning to think you were psychic."

She'd been called exactly that more times than she cared to admit. Mama Lucy had always corrected the girls, saying Grace was *gifted*.

She'd amended the statement in the years since Celia died.
Cursed.

"Lily told me about her grandmother, who apparently smells like fried chicken and peaches."

"Delicious memory."

Grace wished she knew more. She needed to pass Lily off to somebody who could love her properly. Somebody who could hold her hand without losing her mind. It wasn't fear of Myron that kept her from wanting to keep Lily.

Well, it wasn't *only* fear of Myron, though she wasn't a fool. The man was obviously dangerous.

No. Her fears went much deeper than that. Back to Celia, tears streaming down her cheeks, despondent look in her eyes. *It ain't your fault,* she'd said. *Ain't nobody was ever gonna help me.*

Andrew gripped her shoulders, and she blinked away the memory.

"You okay?"

"Yeah. Yeah. I'm fine."

As Andrew studied her, she was thankful to be standing in his shadow, knowing he wouldn't be able to see the expression on her face. Because she didn't have the energy to hide it. She needed a moment to regroup.

He watched her another few seconds, then faced the kids again. The sparklers were dying, one by one, but the kids didn't seem to care. They'd started a game of tag. Lily was *it*, chasing down a taller girl Grace hadn't met. She caught up to her, tagged her, and then bolted away, giggling all the while.

Andrew's hand slid around Grace's back again. "David got an address for a family named Springer in Freedom Hills, Texas. It's about an hour outside of Austin."

"Your facial recognition guy is also a detective?"

"He did a little digging. He's a good guy."

"How much are you paying him?"

Andrew shrugged, gaze flicking to hers. "I wasn't going to tell you because I figured you couldn't afford to hire him."

"I'll pay you back. Can we trust him?"

"What do you have to hide? You're not the one breaking the law. You're just trying to keep Lily safe."

"We're using false documents."

"You can trust him. You can trust *me*."

She hoped that was true. Prayed it was true.

"Since money is apparently no object," Andrew said, "how about we fly out tomorrow, learn what we can?"

She stepped away, missing the warmth of Andrew's arm on her back but needing to think. "We can't do that. Those papers, remember? I don't know that they'll get us on a plane."

"But you could use your real IDs, right? Surely her father doesn't have access to flight records. I don't know how that works, but—"

"I don't either." She latched onto his words. She thought the false papers she'd bought would hold up, but she wasn't willing to risk it. If they didn't, then those IDs would no longer be good. Assuming she wasn't taken into custody, she'd still need to buy new ones, which would mean relocating. It was one thing to risk it to leave the country, but when the plan was to return to the home she was building...

"I think we need to do it," Andrew said. "I've got a work thing next weekend, and I'd hate to wait two weeks. But if we left tomorrow, got back Monday, we'd only miss one day of work and school. I have the time off, and how much could Lily miss in one day?"

Before Grace could respond, a booming voice came from behind her.

"Where you going?"

She turned to see Andrew's father approaching, holding something under his arm. "Sorry. Didn't mean to startle you." He held the something out—a notebook. "This just got here. Should be everything. If it's not, call me, not your brother."

Andrew took it. "Thanks. Hopefully, once I get these numbers input, I'll get a sense of the big picture."

"The sooner the better. Ridiculous how long this has taken." He turned to Grace. "Taking a trip together?"

"Nothing like that." Andrew answered before she could, and though his words were spoken kindly enough, she heard the hint of impatience in them. "Grace is trying to locate Lily's extended family."

Grace winced, fearing the questions Andrew's words would

garner, but Drew asked none of them. "If you're only going to be gone until Monday, you can take the jet."

Andrew's face registered surprise. "Actually, Dad, that would be great." He turned to her. "I mean, if it's okay with you. It does solve some problems."

A private jet? Her stepfather'd been wealthy, but not private-jet wealthy.

Drew chuckled, apparently reading her expression. "We have offices all over the country. When you figure in the amount of time we don't waste going through security and dealing with layovers and canceled flights, it's actually pretty cost-effective."

"I don't want to be any trouble," Grace said.

"No trouble at all. I'm glad to be able to help." He turned to Andrew. "Get Alice the details, and she'll contact the crew."

"Okay, I'll do that. Thanks, Dad. It means a lot."

Drew cleared his throat. "Happy to. Least I can do."

When he wandered away, Grace leaned close to Andrew. "He's a very nice man, isn't he?"

"Sometimes that gets lost in all the family drama. But yeah, he can be."

She followed the older Middleton's trek across the grass. Andrew looked nothing like his father, who was shorter and rounder and had a lot less hair. There was tension between them, but even still, she saw the resemblance, not in their looks but in their kindness.

She looked up to the man at her side. "All you're doing for Lily and me...I don't know how to thank you."

"I'd sure like to hold your hand one of these days."

The thought didn't bring the tension she might've expected. The one time she'd touched Andrew's hand, she'd only felt comfortable. But she didn't want to pry into his past without his permission.

And to get that, she'd have to tell him the truth.

CHAPTER SEVENTEEN

MYRON STARED through the binoculars from his spot in the woods surrounding the condominium complex, his blood pressure rising by the moment.

What was Grace doing up so early on a Sunday morning?

She couldn't have discovered him. He'd kept himself carefully hidden. But if on the off chance she had...

Was Grace about to run again?

The notion brought a flash of anger. Everything he'd done to prepare this place for her, and she was about to throw it all away.

He'd thought for sure she was settling in to stay this time. The rented condo instead of the cheap hotel. The way she'd gotten to know the neighbors.

Myron had no idea where she'd gone with the man, Andrew Middleton, the day before. When they'd started spending time together, Myron had learned his name. It had been late the night before by the time Middleton's BMW had parked in front of the condo across the lot from Grace's. While Grace unlocked the front door, he took the sleeping child in his arms and carried her inside, closing the door behind him.

His Lily, so comfortable in the arms of another man.

Grace would pay for that.

She was getting far too close to Andrew Middleton.

Meanwhile, everything was taking longer than Myron had hoped, and the more he delayed, the more difficult it would be to take Lily and Grace and disappear unnoticed. Even if nobody else did, Middleton was sure to miss them. And he'd raise the alarm, which would set law enforcement looking for them.

Which was the last thing Myron needed.

Why had Grace chosen this town? Of all the possibilities, why Coventry, New Hampshire? There had to be a reason. He just hadn't figured it out yet.

He would, though. It was only a matter of time. He needed all the information he could get if he wanted to whisk the girls away without being caught.

The house he'd procured needed more structural work than he'd thought it would, and contractors were hard to come by up here in the middle of nowhere. Myron would do the work himself, but hiring people, getting to know them—while keeping them at a safe distance—was a great way to prove he belonged in the community. By the time he brought his girls home, he would be well known and well respected. Nobody would suspect him of a thing.

But considering that Grace was readying to leave so early on a Sunday morning, something was definitely wrong. Rather than work on building out the basement rooms and installing the cameras, it looked like Myron would have to figure out what Grace was up to.

It would put off the work for one day, but even with that, the place should be ready soon.

And then, their lives would start over. With Lily and Grace where they belonged, Myron would capture beauty like he never had before.

CHAPTER EIGHTEEN

It was after three the following afternoon by the time they exited the six-lane highway onto a two-lane country road about an hour outside of Austin, Texas. Grace had been shocked when they'd first stepped off the private jet onto the tarmac. It was October, but the temperature hovered in the mideighties, the air heavy with humidity. Was this a normal autumn day in Texas?

Despite the short night of sleep, Lily had been her usual chatterbox on the flight and when they'd driven through the city. Now, she was quiet. Grace turned to watch her reaction in the backseat while Andrew followed the directions on his phone.

The child's eyes were wide as she gazed out the window at the passing landscape. The world was flatter here than in New Hampshire, but not as flat as Grace had expected.

When they crested a hill and got a miles-long view, Andrew quipped, "There's a reason they don't call it 'mountain country.'"

He wasn't wrong. The landscape was dotted with short, scrubby trees that covered low, rounded hills. This so-called hill country was nothing like what she'd grown up with in Washington and paled in comparison to New Hampshire's White Mountains. Though it wasn't very green, there was a rugged beauty that brought to mind the pioneers, farmers, and ranchers who'd battled the heat and tamed the land.

Grace kept her voice low, hoping not to pull Lily too much from the view outside. "Does anything look familiar?"

Her narrow shoulders lifted and fell.

Poor child was exhausted. She'd fallen asleep on the ride back to Coventry the night before but had woken up when they got to the condo. It'd taken Grace a half hour to get her back to sleep.

And then she'd had to wake her at seven for the flight. Though Grace was rarely impressed by wealth, flying in a private jet was nothing like flying commercial. The plane was tiny but well equipped with extra-wide seats and plenty of leg room. She and Lily had sat across from Andrew, a table between them. Lily colored and Andrew transferred numbers from the notebook he'd been given the night before into accounting software on his laptop. Grace had read her Bible and then prayed for the day, that the Lord would lead and direct them. The galley in the back had been stocked with breakfast pastries and boxed lunches, sodas, bottles of water, and a carafe of hot coffee, so that when they arrived in Austin, they didn't have to waste time getting lunch.

Andrew navigated through the small downtown area with its charming storefronts pressed together like boxes in a pantry and looking like a scene out of an old western movie. One corner held a mechanic's shop, where classic cars in various stages of repair were lined up in the lot.

He made a few turns. They passed what looked like a new neighborhood, two-story brick houses side-by-side with matching garages and driveways. But when he clicked on his blinker, he turned not into a neighborhood but onto a narrow drive that led to a small house built of gray rocks.

In the backseat, Lily gasped.

"Have you been here before?" Grace asked.

The child nodded.

Andrew parked. Before he turned the car off, Lily climbed out and walked toward the front door slowly.

Grace caught up with her there, studying the child while she gazed at the little rock house.

It looked abandoned. No cars in the drive. Overgrown landscaping. The grass had been mowed, but not recently. The windows were cloudy.

She didn't think Lily was seeing any of the disrepair. "What do you remember?" Grace asked.

Rather than answering, Lily walked up the front steps and tried to turn the knob.

"Sweetie, I don't think anyone's home. Even if they are, you have to knock."

Lily looked up at Grace as if she'd forgotten she was there. "This is Nana's house."

Grace wasn't sure if the knot in her stomach was a result of hope or dread.

If Myron had reported Lily missing, then would the authorities have found Lily's extended family? Would Nana call the police the instant she saw Lily on her doorstep?

Was Grace about to be hauled off to jail?

Was Andrew? She should have thought this through. All of it. Yet...she had prayed about it, and this had felt like the best next move. If she could return the child to family, even if it meant the loss of her freedom, it would be worth it.

And Andrew wouldn't be in trouble. He didn't know the truth about Grace and Lily.

It would be all right. She had to trust that, whatever happened next, it would be all right.

Andrew approached and stood at the bottom of the three steps leading to the stoop.

After a deep breath for courage, Grace pointed to the doorbell. "You want to ring it?"

Lily pushed the button, and the ding carried through the door.

Nobody answered. No sounds from within to indicate anybody was home.

Lily rang the bell again.

Grace stood beside her, not wanting to rush the child.

Andrew approached one of the windows, stood on tiptoe, and peered inside. He looked over his shoulder at Grace and shook his head.

The place must be empty.

"What was it like the last time you were here?" Grace hoped the open-ended question would stir Lily's memories.

She finally pulled her focus from the door that hadn't opened and stepped back to the grass. Slowly, she walked toward the side of the house. "There's a peach tree in the backyard."

"Will you show me?"

Lily led the way.

A chain-link fence surrounded the backyard. Andrew opened the gate, and they walked through. Sure enough, a short tree's overgrown limbs practically touched the ground.

Stopping in the middle of the area that was more dirt than grass, Lily spun slowly, then pointed to the opposite corner. "There was a swing set there. Mama used to push me on the swing. And we had one of those horsey things you could get on with another person."

"Did you ever ride it with anyone?"

She shrugged. "I think. A girl, maybe."

"Friend? A cousin?"

Without answering, Lily walked toward where she'd played as a little girl. Or maybe she'd been a toddler. Most of the shrubs in the back were dead, but the fence was lined with some sort of green plant that seemed to be thriving.

Andrew stepped to Grace's side and watched the child wander around the space. When she returned, tears streamed down her face. "I wish Nana was here."

Grace crouched down and opened her arms. "Oh, baby, I do too."

"Where is she?"

"I don't know." Grace swallowed a lump, praying the woman

was still alive. Praying they'd be able to locate her. "We'll try to find her, I promise."

Lily held onto Grace's neck as if she feared somebody was about to rip her away. What had happened to separate Lily from the family who'd lived here? Why weren't the Springers in the child's life? Were they looking for her? Did they care?

When it seemed clear that Lily wasn't going to let go, Grace lifted her and settled her on her hip. She was a little big to be held that way, but Grace wouldn't complain. She loved the feel of Lily in her arms.

Beside her, Andrew was scrolling on his phone.

How could he do that in such a moment? What could possibly pull his attention away from this heartbroken child?

Then, he looked up and settled his hand on Lily's back. "Can I show you something?"

Grace felt the nod against her neck.

Andrew pointed to the plants at the fence line. "Those are flowers. They aren't in bloom right now, but when they are, they're beautiful."

Lily lifted her head from Grace's shoulder and peered at the plants.

Andrew lifted his phone. "Here's what they look like when they're blooming."

Grace and Lily both gazed at his screen to see an explosion of bright orange flowers.

"Pretty," Lily said.

"You know what's so cool about those flowers? Even when nobody takes care of them, even when nobody prunes them or waters them or does anything for them, they grow. Look around." He lifted his arm to indicate the rest of the rundown yard. "Everything else is dead or dying. But not those. They're thriving."

Grace's eyes filled with tears. She knew where he was going with this, and she loved him for it.

"You know what kinds of flowers those are?"

"Huh-uh. What kind?"

"They're lilies."

Her eyes widened. "Like me?"

"Just like you, Lily," Andrew said. "No matter how hard life is, lilies grow strong and beautiful."

Lily squirmed, and Grace set her on her feet.

She ran to the plants to investigate while Grace swiped the tears from her eyes. "You're a pretty amazing man, Andrew Middleton."

"That was one hundred percent God," he said. "I don't know a daylily from a dandelion, but the word popped into my head."

He could brush it off all he wanted, but she was impressed. Even if God had given him the information, Andrew had run with it. He'd used it to plant another seed of truth in Lily's heart. After this latest disappointment, Grace prayed it would take root.

THEY WERE JUST CLIMBING into their rental car when an SUV pulled into the driveway and parked behind them. A woman climbed out. "Hey there," she called.

Grace stepped away from the sedan. "Hi."

"I live next door." The woman pointed toward a copse of oaks and a house beyond it. "What're y'all doing here?"

Before she could answer, Lily said, "I used to live here with my nana. Do you know where she is?"

The woman smiled at Lily but shook her head. "I'm sorry, I don't. We moved here about a year ago, and this house has been empty the whole time."

"Real estate records say the Springers still own the house." Andrew stepped forward. "You ever heard of that family?"

"I wish I could help you. You ought to go see Ruby Lind. She lives on the other side of me. She's been here since statehood, I think." The woman smiled with the words. "Just go on past the brick ranch—that's my house. Ruby lives in the white house on the same side. She knows everything about everybody."

"We'll do that," Grace said. "Thanks."

The woman climbed back into her oversize car and pulled away. When she was gone, Andrew said, "Guess we're going to see Ruby Lind."

Two minutes later, they parked in front of a white house that looked even older than the stone one they'd just left. A wide front porch wrapped around it in both directions. This house's landscaping was well-tended, the house freshly painted. The lack of cars in the driveway—there was no garage—didn't bode well. "Sit tight," he said. "I'll go knock."

When nobody opened at Andrew's knock, Grace pulled a piece of paper from her purse and penned a note, asking Ms. Lind to please call her as soon as possible. She turned to Lily, who was staring back in the direction of the rock house, though it was out of sight from where they sat. "Stay here. I'll be right back."

Worry niggled at Grace as she exited the car. Had it been a mistake to bring Lily on this trip? She could have left her with Cassidy, but with the threat of Myron, she'd been nervous for both Lily's sake and Cassidy's. But had bringing Lily raised hopes in the child, hopes that would be in vain?

Grace prayed not.

Andrew turned as Grace climbed to the porch. "Nobody's home."

"Figures." She held out the note. "Maybe we can stick it in the door?"

He took it and left it wedged between the screen door and the jamb. "Assuming they use this entrance, they shouldn't miss it." He turned and reached for her hand, then pulled his back and shoved it in his pocket like that'd been his plan all along.

She wished she could hold hands like a normal person.

"The library?"

"Here's hoping we'll learn something."

The library was housed in a one-story gray-brick building with a porch that ran the length of the front. A giant brass star surrounded by a circle adorned the entry, the same star she'd seen fifty times already since they'd left the airport. Seemed Texans were pretty proud of that star.

The outside of the library looked old and dingy, but inside it was new and modern. Lily, who'd never met a library she didn't like, picked out two books to read while Andrew talked to the librarian about what they were looking for. When he gestured to Grace from the circulation desk, she ushered Lily toward him. "Come on, sweetie. You can read while Mr. Middleton and I try to get some information on your grandmother."

The child settled into a cushy chair nearby while the librarian, a tall slender woman with gray hair, pulled up old newspaper articles and showed them how to search. When they were set, the woman said, "I'll go find those yearbooks while you look."

After she walked away, Grace said, "Yearbooks?"

"Thought it wouldn't hurt to see if we could find a better photo of Lily's mother. And maybe see if Myron is in any of them."

"I'd guess that he's significantly older than Annabeth."

Andrew shrugged. "They have yearbooks going back a long time. If he's in them, we should find him."

They searched the newspaper archives for the name *Springer* and found very few references. There was the article about the fair with the photograph they'd already seen and Annabeth's birth notice. She'd been born to Buck and Darla Springer. Grace did the math, figuring out how old Annabeth would be now. Sure enough, Lily's mother had only been nineteen when Lily was born.

There were no engagement or wedding announcements for Annabeth, but considering that she'd still had her parents' last name when Lily was a toddler, Grace wasn't surprised by that.

They found Buck Springer's obituary. He'd died not long after Lily's birth. They didn't find an obituary for Lily's grandmother or Annabeth.

After the article picturing Annabeth and Lily at the fair, the Springers were never mentioned again.

"Not a lot there," Andrew said.

The librarian left a pile of yearbooks on the table, and Grace found the one from the year before Lily was born. They were thin, indicating the size of the small high school. She skimmed past the younger grades and then slowly flipped through the color photographs of the seniors.

"There she is," Andrew said.

Grace's gaze landed on the teenage Annabeth Springer. Grace could see Lily in the shape of the girl's nose and mouth, in the high cheekbones. Her skin was milky and clear, her eyes pale blue.

She glanced at Lily, who was flipping through a picture book. Did the child get anything else from this woman? Her intelligence? Her kindness?

Where was Annabeth now? How could she have left her daughter and never looked back?

Or was there something else going on? Maybe she'd become addicted. Maybe she'd been mentally ill. Maybe...maybe she just didn't care.

Andrew tugged the book closer and leaned over it, then glanced at Lily and back. "Wait..."

She tore her gaze away from the image to focus on Andrew, whose lips were pinched closed as he looked from the child to the photo.

"What?" she said.

He kept his voice low, practically whispering when he said, "You have that picture of Myron?"

She opened her phone and found it. She'd taken a screenshot of his portrait from his website. In the picture, Myron was younger by a decade than the man she'd met. Midthirties, blond hair, blue eyes. Handsome.

Andrew studied the photo, then studied the picture of Annabeth.

"What?" Grace couldn't figure out what he was seeing that she was missing.

Still with his voice low, he said, "Lily has brown hair and green eyes."

"Yeah. And...?" But she saw what he'd noticed.

Both Myron and Annabeth were blond-haired and blue-eyed.

"The chances of that are astronomically low," Andrew said. "The hair color, maybe. But two blue-eyed parents having a green-eyed kid?" He shook his head. "And when you figure in both of those—the hair and the eyes?" Again, he studied the two photographs and the little girl sitting not five feet away, "It's a statistical impossibility."

"You're saying it's *impossible* that they're her parents? Because she looks like her mother. Didn't you notice—?"

"I'm saying it's impossible that they're *both* her parents," he said. "I agree she favors her mother."

"Which means..."

"Myron Bowman is not her biological father."

Could it be true?

Had Lily been kidnapped? If so, why hadn't the image search turned up her picture in more places? Surely, if she'd been kidnapped, photographs of her would have been distributed to law enforcement. Amber alerts would have gone out. A photo of a missing child would be on the internet, somewhere, wouldn't it?

But no such photo existed.

Andrew said, "Maybe he's her stepfather."

"And then Annabeth just...just left her with him? A little girl with a man?"

Andrew swiveled to face her. "Maybe she didn't know what kind of a person Myron was. She trusted him to take care of her."

How could she? How could any woman leave any daughter with any man?

The question must've shown on her face because Andrew, in that low gentle voice she was coming to love, said, "Some of us can be trusted, you know."

He was right, of course. Between her own history, her work in the girls home, and her so-called gift, she'd had too much experience with evil men. It was easy to forget they weren't all that way. Andrew wasn't. She slid her fingers over his wrist on the armrest. "I know. You're right. But to take the risk, however low it might have been…What kind of mother would do that?"

"Maybe she had no choice."

Lily was still engrossed in her book, but Grace lowered her voice anyway. "She said Myron told her that Annabeth left because Lily was too much trouble."

Andrew's jaw dropped a moment before his lips pressed together. It wasn't that he had nothing to say. She could see the effort he expended to not voice what he was thinking.

She flipped through the yearbook, searching for other photos of Annabeth. Skimming the names beneath the group photos, she found no mention of Lily's mother. The teenager hadn't been involved in band, any of the clubs, or any of the sports teams. She didn't participate in the school plays or sing in the choir. She wasn't pictured in the homecoming dance or the prom spreads.

In a careful study of snapshots, she found one other photo of Annabeth. In the foreground, two cheerleaders in uniform had their cheeks pressed together, giant grins on their faces. In the background, Annabeth was sitting alone, hunched over a book, long, lanky legs bent and crossed at the ankles. She'd glanced toward the camera but wasn't smiling.

She was gorgeous. Perhaps she'd been shy. Or perhaps that photograph didn't accurately depict the teenage Annabeth. Maybe she'd had lots of friends but somehow never got caught in photos.

After searching for Myron Bowman—no mention of anybody with his last name—she set the book aside.

While Andrew returned his attention to the library computer, Grace flipped through the previous yearbooks. She located Annabeth's image among the students' portraits in each of her grades but found no other images of her. It seemed that she'd managed to attend four years of high school without ever joining anything. Without making any mark whatsoever.

Considering her graduating class had fewer than a hundred people, that was almost impressive.

She glanced at yearbooks going back to a decade before Annabeth started high school but found no mention of Myron or any other Bowmans.

Beside her, Andrew pushed back his chair and shook his head. "There's no record of a Bowman family owning property in Freedom Hills, no mention of him in the newspaper."

"I didn't find him in the yearbooks either."

"So he wasn't from here. How in the world did he meet Annabeth?"

"No idea. This tiny town, an hour from Austin..." She opened Annabeth's senior yearbook and found her image again. She really was beautiful. Shockingly beautiful. "Myron's a photographer. I wonder if he ever took her picture. Maybe..."

"Maybe she wanted to be a model," he said.

Grace found the photo where Annabeth was caught in the background.

He looked at the image. "She was tall and slim."

"A model's body," Grace said.

They said nothing, just gazed at the girl in the photo, who looked so much like the one seated just a few feet away. Aside from the hair and eye color, Lily was a younger version of her mother.

Would she grow up with that same willowy body? With those same drop-dead good looks?

A target for evil men?

Not Lily. Grace would die before she let the girl be exploited again.

Misunderstanding her shudder, Andrew slipped his arm around her back and rubbed her shoulder. "I swear, indoors in the South is colder than winter in New Hampshire."

Grace's chill had nothing to do with the air conditioner.

CHAPTER NINETEEN

ANDREW WATCHED Grace and Lily on the far side of the low table. Lily'd fallen asleep moments after the jet reached cruising altitude, her head in Grace's lap, her thumb in her mouth.

They'd originally planned to stay the night in Austin. Andrew had been looking forward to taking the girls to dinner and spending the evening with them, but Grace had suggested they see if they could return to New Hampshire immediately so Lily wouldn't miss school and he wouldn't miss work. Little though he'd wanted to, he'd called the flight crew, who'd had the jet ready by the time they returned to the airport.

Grace gazed down at the child, brushing tendrils of brown hair away from her cherubic face, expression filled with love.

He'd always been good at reading people, but his first impression of Grace had been so far from accurate it was laughable.

It was obvious that, despite how hard she seemed to try to keep it from happening, she'd fallen completely in love with Lily.

Maybe that wasn't such a bad thing. If they could prove Myron wasn't Lily's father, then maybe Grace could try to get custody. But it all felt so convoluted. If Lily wasn't Myron's daughter, then whose was she? Where were her real parents? Were they looking for her? Praying for her safe return? Were they praying at that very moment, begging God to take care of their child?

At least God had gotten Lily out of Myron Bowman's grasp and into Grace's protection.

He hadn't broached the subject with her yet, but obviously Grace would need to call the social worker and tell her what they'd learned. The state would take it from there, wouldn't they? A simple paternity test could put the matter to rest. Assuming Myron ever turned up. But maybe he was long gone. Maybe he'd given up on Lily. If he wasn't actually the child's father, then would he dare come around again?

Was he a kidnapper as well as a pornographer? Either way, he needed to be punished for his crimes.

Too bad hanging wasn't still a thing.

Though Andrew could think of even more appropriate punishments, which involved the removal of toenails without the benefit of painkillers.

That would be a start. Still not as bad as someone like Myron Bowman—

"What are you thinking about?" On the far side of the table, Grace studied him with narrowed eyes.

"Nothing." He didn't figure explaining the torture he'd subject Myron to would be appropriate conversation even if Lily was sound asleep. And it wasn't exactly romantic. Not that he should be thinking about romance.

Truth be told, when he wasn't contemplating hurting the man who'd hurt that child, he *was* thinking about romance. And why not? Grace was single. He was single. They got along well, had the same values.

He'd first been attracted to her because she was beautiful. Now, he knew that beauty went much deeper than skin-level. He was attracted to her looks, no doubt. But he was falling for the woman behind the face.

Falling for her like he'd never fallen for another woman.

Lily shifted, and Grace took the opportunity to slip out from beneath her head. She stood and watched until Lily settled back into a deep sleep.

"She's a sound sleeper." Grace tipped her head toward the seats across the aisle. "I'm going to—"

"I'll join you." He grabbed two bottles of water from the fridge in the back and took the chair beside Grace's, handing her one. The seats swiveled, and he angled to face her.

"Thanks." She palmed it open and sipped. "I know you weren't thrilled to be headed back tonight."

He thought he'd hidden that well, but Grace was astute. "Just enjoying your company."

Her smile was shy. "Feeling's mutual."

No idea what to say to that, he just held her eye contact, trying to read her thoughts. She didn't seem immune to him. Did she feel half of what he felt?

Did she feel the attraction that pulsed between them?

"I appreciate all you did today," she said. "All you've done for us. Without your help, I could never have figured out half of what we learned."

Though he cared about Lily, they'd talked enough about the girl. "It was my pleasure."

Grace gazed out the window and said nothing else.

Her hand was lying casually on her armrest. More than anything, he wanted to slip their palms together. He'd never in his life, not even as a middle school boy with his first crush, wanted to hold someone's hand like he wanted to hold hers.

He trailed his fingers over her forearm.

Slowly, Grace turned to him. But she didn't pull away.

He reached the back of her hand and traced the tiny veins, then made little circles on her skin, feeling a zing of satisfaction when he saw goose bumps rise at his touch.

Into the silence, while his fingers trailed along her skin, he asked the question that had been hovering in the back of his mind for days. "Will you explain to me why I can't hold your hand?"

Though she didn't move, the muscles of her arm tensed, and he knew he had only seconds before she extricated herself from his touch.

Very lightly, he wrapped his thumb and forefinger around her wrist, keeping it on the armrest between them. "It's okay. You don't have to."

She didn't pull away. After a moment, he let go, and his fingertips resumed their exploration.

That she didn't move—it was something. It wasn't what he wanted. To be honest, holding her hand wasn't *all* he wanted, either. But he felt like he'd never get to the kisses, the embraces he craved, if he didn't understand her fear of touch.

And that was what it had to be. A fear.

Maybe he could make her feel comfortable with him. Maybe he could prove to her that he wasn't a monster. That he'd never hurt her. That he'd never do anything to make her fear him.

For now, if that meant that he confined himself to touching the back of her hand, he'd do it. He'd do whatever it took.

That was who he was, after all.

When his father had cut Andrew off because he refused to promise to work for the family business when he graduated from college, Andrew had gotten a job to pay his own way.

When he'd been convicted of a crime he didn't commit, he'd worked in the infirmary, proving his skills until he was trusted with as much responsibility as was given to any inmate.

When he was released but had lost his place in the premed program, he'd redirected his goals, double-majoring in biochemistry and business and earning a scholarship to pursue his MBA.

At work, Andrew was tireless in his pursuit of BNB's goals, and the company's increased profits reflected his efforts.

Soon enough, he'd know why the family business was losing money. He'd get to the bottom of that mystery and prove his worth to his father.

When Andrew decided to do something, he did it. In that moment, he decided he wanted Grace. And Lily, if the girl was part of the package. God had brought these two into his life, and he wasn't going to let them go.

If that meant starting with tracing tiny circles on the back of Grace's hand, then so be it. He could be patient. The best dreams were worth waiting for.

Fighting for.

And Grace...? Andrew had a lot of dreams for his life, but she was definitely the best of them.

He didn't know how much time had passed before Grace pulled her arm out from beneath his touch and swiveled to face him. "I'll tell you if you promise to keep an open mind."

His heartbeat raced. She'd trusted him with the story of her stepfather. Now, she was willing to trust him with this. "Of course." Though why she thought he'd need to be open-minded to hear about her fear of touch, he didn't know.

"Remember I told you about how I knew my stepfather was a bad man?"

He dipped his head. "You're very intuitive."

"Not...exactly."

What did that mean?

"It's that I get...When I hold people's hands, I get these..."

"What?" He leaned toward her. "It's okay. You can tell me."

"Visions."

He sat back. *Visions?*

Her eyebrows hiked. "You promised to keep an open mind."

"It's open, but...."

"I see things, feel things. Not every time, and the visions aren't always intense. When I was young, it was just feelings. The feeling I had when I first met my stepfather? It was lust, though I don't think I had a name for it back then. But I knew it was a dark feeling. Like..." She rubbed her lips together. "I don't know how to explain it. I sort of feel what other people feel, and sometimes I see what they saw, like their memories. When Lily grabbed my hand, I saw her looking in a mirror, hair and makeup done up like one of those kids who do fashion shows. But she was wearing this little—"

"Don't tell me." He hated to be rude. "I don't want that image in my head."

Her cheeks turned red, and she angled away.

"I'm sorry," he said. "I don't mean...She's so innocent. I don't want to see her like that. I try to guard against that kind of thing."

She nodded slowly, turning back. Her gaze was intense when it met his. "As do I."

By her tone, he knew her words held deeper meaning, but he wasn't grasping it. He wanted to, though. Because what she was describing was impossible.

Impossible, but Grace wasn't a liar, and she wasn't crazy. Which left only one option. She was telling the truth.

"You saw Lily..." he prompted, hoping she'd be vague.

"In the mirror, and then on a bed, looking at a camera. And just by the way it felt, I knew. And then Myron came over and introduced himself, and I shook his hand, just to be sure. And it was like...like a Rolodex of photos that flipped. Children, always children. Beds and lights and cameras and..." Her voice trailed, and she added, "Sorry. Too much information."

"No, it's..." He tried to come up with an end to that sentence.

"It's not usually pictures. That's really rare, and weirdly, always related to some sort of abuse or trauma. Usually, all I feel is strong emotion. Mama Lucy—she's the house mother where I used to live—she and I did a lot of thinking and praying about it. She thinks it's the person's strongest emotion or most frequently felt emotion. If I hold on a long time to somebody, I can sort of clue into everything they're feeling. But in quick handshakes, quick touches, I don't think I feel what they're feeling in that second. I feel what they *often* feel, if that makes sense."

He considered that, then remembered the night before. She'd worn gloves when she'd shaken everybody's hands. Except one. "When you touched Chet's palm...?"

She licked her lips, looked away. "I don't share what I learn. It's not exactly fair, is it? To use it against people?"

He didn't push the issue. "Is that why you wear gloves? To protect people's privacy?"

"It's more like what you said earlier. It's to protect myself. My heart. It's been a part of me as long as I can remember, so I never thought about it as invading people's privacy. When I was little, it was just impressions. It's gotten stronger over the years. Especially since I became a Christian."

He was almost afraid to ask his next question. Her slight smile gave him the courage. "When you shook my hand? Could you tell me that?"

"No pictures. Just an impression."

"Which was?"

"Ambition, but it was a...a glowing emotion." She looked down like she was embarrassed about what she'd said.

As if that was any weirder than the rest of it.

"Meaning?"

"Emotions are rarely neutral. Usually, they're either dark or light. Some are so dark, they feel like pits. When I touch somebody whose emotions are that dark, it feels heavy, like I'm being pulled down. And then others' emotions are so bright that they glow."

"Is it the intensity of the emotion?" he asked. "Am I freakishly ambitious? Dangerously, like Hitler or something?"

Her laugh loosened some of the knots in his stomach. "Not at all like that," she said. "More like...like with Barney. My stepfather. I've gotten the impression of lust plenty in my life. But with Barney, it was that bottom-of-a-pit feeling I get. It was evil."

"I see. So glowing is...good?"

"Yes." She nodded to emphasize the point. "Yes, glowing means it's good. Because emotions are morally neutral, right? It's not the emotion that's good or bad, it's where it comes from and what you do with it. Ambition is a great example. Hitler was ambitious and deep-pit evil. Einstein was ambitious in his own way, I think. But his, I assume, was glowing. Not that those would be their defining emotions. I'm just trying to give an example." She shook her head.

"Anyway, with you I felt glowing ambition, but I also felt kindness. Generosity. Everything about you was good. I felt no dark-pit emotions. Not that you're perfect, but there was nothing about you that worried me or scared me. I knew you were safe."

"You still feel that way?"

She nodded. "The more I get to know you, the more I believe my initial impression was correct."

She'd rested her arms on the armrests again. He settled his hand on her forearm. "If shaking my hand wasn't bad, would holding my hand be?"

Her gaze flicked to his fingers, resting lightly against her skin. "I just never know when I'm going to get a vision or...Once I get to know a person, it feels sort of intrusive."

"But now I know." He inched his hand closer to hers. "I don't mind if you intrude." Though a tiny part of him worried about what she'd perceive in him. He cataloged his feelings. She'd probably pick up on his desire, but he was pretty sure it was...bright, not dark. To use her terms.

All he felt for her was good. All he wanted for her was good. Would she know that?

Would she trust him more?

She swallowed, then flipped her hand over.

He slid his palm against hers, reveling in her smooth skin, in the warmth that traveled up his arm, straight to his heart.

Only a second passed before she said, "My initial impression was correct." She smiled and leaned toward him. "You are a good, good man."

He couldn't think of a thing to say. She was so close that he caught a light scent of mint on her breath. What did she feel coming from him?

Did she know the depth of his feelings for her?

If she did, the fact that she hadn't pulled away meant something.

Maybe she felt something for him as well.

He stared into her eyes, thankful to be holding her hand but unwilling to settle for that.

Ambitious. Her assessment was correct. The instant he got what he wanted, he created a new goal. And the new goal now...

His gaze flicked to her lips. They looked so soft. He longed to feel them against his own. Her mouth spread into a slight smile, and he looked back into her eyes. "Is it...? May I?"

She nodded, and he closed the distance between them.

When they connected, he had to fight the urge to pull his hand away. Because all the feelings shooting through him...

Let them be bright, Lord. Let them be good.

Desire, overwhelming desire. Protectiveness. Need.

With everything in him, he wanted more of this, more of her.

Afraid he would scare her away with the intensity of his feelings, he knew he needed to pull his hand from hers. But before he could, she tightened her grip.

Fine, then. She would know it all. One way or another, there was no hiding from Grace.

His other hand found its way into her hair, the silky strands brushing against his rough skin. He deepened the kiss, leaning closer to her, only then realizing he was kneeling on the floor in front of her. When had that happened?

He didn't know. He didn't care.

He needed to get himself under control.

He managed to pull his lips from hers, but only to trail kisses along her cheeks, toward her ear.

She tilted her head to the side, giving him more access.

He groaned.

He had to stop.

With all his self-control, he managed to sit back on his heels. Had he frightened her with the intensity of his desire? He'd frightened himself. He'd never felt this for another woman. Never even come close.

He was afraid to meet her eyes. But her hand still held his.

Slowly, he lifted his gaze to hers. She was watching him, her expression beautiful and filled with...was that wonder?

Maybe. Maybe that was what she felt. He wanted to know. He'd never in his life wanted so much to know what was going on in another person's mind.

He leaned forward and rested his forehead against hers. Trying to catch his breath. Trying to understand what he'd just experienced.

Knowing that after this, he would never be the same.

CHAPTER TWENTY

GRACE WAS FALLING.

Falling, though she hadn't left her seat.

Andrew's forehead pressed against hers, his hand still holding hers.

She'd never experienced anything like that. The kiss...the kiss alone had been utterly...

Mind-blowing.

Life-altering.

It was ridiculous. It was only a kiss.

Only it wasn't, because as his lips had moved against hers, she'd felt what he was feeling. Those emotions had all gotten mixed up and jumbled and...

"Grace." His voice was low and rough, and she felt another wave of desire, not knowing if it was from him or from her or some combination of both.

She slid her fingers through the hair at the back of his neck, and he groaned.

Everything in her wanted to kiss him again. Kiss him for the rest of her life.

He shifted, nuzzled his head against her neck. "I need to know..." His words trailed, but she felt his fear.

"Yes," she said. "Yes to all of it."

His fear was replaced with elation, and she almost giggled.

She had to stop.

She pulled their joined hands away from her body and let go. In the last second before his palm separated from hers, she felt his disappointment. He lifted his head and leaned back, meeting her eyes. She saw apology there.

She slid her hand around the back of his neck. "I want to know how *I* feel," she said. "It's all mixed up. I need to know—"

His lips cut off her words.

And she felt awash in feelings again. All bright and beautiful.

Not nearly enough time had passed before he pulled away. Breathless. He leaned back to see her face, eyes wide and expectant.

A blush heated her cheeks, and she started to look down.

"Uh-uh. No fair."

She had no reason to fear. She knew that. She knew *him.*

"Desire," she said. "More than anything, like I've never felt before."

A grin spread across his face.

"Safe. Protected. Cherished. I felt...joy. Just pure joy."

He pressed his hands to the sides of her face. "I've never felt so *known.*"

"I've never felt so..."

Despite everything, she was afraid to name the emotion, afraid it was revealing so much.

But he wasn't afraid. Unlike her, he was brave.

"Loved," he said. "I hope that's how you felt. As crazy as it seems—"

"I don't understand, but I feel it too. How did this happen?"

"I don't know. I'm just glad it did."

Yes. And yet...

Lily.

She glanced across the aisle at the sleeping little girl.

"Don't do that," Andrew said.

"Now who's reading minds?"

"I see it in your eyes. You're pulling away from me. You're putting her between us."

"She *is* between us, Andrew. I have to keep her there until she's safe."

He gazed at Grace a long moment before he sat in his seat again and leaned his head against the headrest.

"You understand, don't you?" she asked.

"We're going to find her family." He turned and held his hand out, palm up.

She took it, felt conviction, confidence.

"We're going to prove Myron isn't her father," Andrew said. "We're going to make sure she's safe. I promise. But we're going to do it together. You and me. Don't put up a wall between us, Grace. It's too late for that."

He was right. She felt it. She *knew* it.

Because at some point at thirty thousand feet, in the sky somewhere between Texas and New Hampshire, she'd fallen in love.

But until Lily was safe, she couldn't let herself be ruled by that. She couldn't let that matter. Lily was the priority, and if Grace had to run again, then she'd run.

Even if it meant leaving her heart with this man. Even if it meant never seeing him again.

"You DON'T LOVE ME!" Lily's shrill scream sent Grace's pulse racing.

"Keep your voice down," she said. "And don't talk to me in that manner. It is unaccept—"

"What're you gonna do, get rid of me? That's what you're trying to do anyway. I hate you. I *hate* you." The child swiveled and pounded up the stairs, hair half brushed in preparation for school that day. The sound of a slamming door reverberated through the small condo.

Grace collapsed on the couch and dropped her head into her hands. She hadn't meant to hurt her feelings. She'd only asked what else she remembered about her nana and other family members at the old rock house. Apparently, the questions had clued Lily in to Grace's real motives.

What do I do, Lord?

Grace *was* trying to get rid of her. She had to find somebody to take her. The little fantasy she'd been entertaining—the one where she and Lily lived happily ever after—had shifted during the flight the previous day, after the kiss she refused to think about.

Kisses.

Mind-blowing kisses and all the overwhelming emotions that went with them.

Ever since then, her fantasy family of two had morphed into a family of three. Andrew, Grace, and Lily, making a forever home together, complete with a little house surrounded by snow-covered New Hampshire mountains, cozy winter nights with a flickering fire in the hearth, a child curled up on a fluffy white rug, arms wrapped around Regis, Oliver lounging nearby. Grace had fallen asleep with the scent of wood smoke hovering in her imagination.

But the nightmares had been worse than ever.

Celia gripping Grace's hand, all the girl's thoughts and feelings on display for Grace to experience. She'd done everything in her power to protect her, to love her.

It wasn't enough. It would never be enough.

She hadn't been able to save Celia. And she couldn't save Lily.

The child needed somebody who could. Which was why Grace had gone to Texas that weekend—to find the girl's family, somebody who could take her. Even if it broke Grace's heart to think of giving her up, Lily would be better off with somebody else.

And, truth be told, so would Andrew.

That...that thing that people had, the thing that connected them with others, that enabled them to love? Grace didn't have it. Never had.

She'd never felt connected to her mother. She'd loathed her

stepfather. She'd had no siblings to love. All those years in the girls home, whenever she'd started to feel connected to somebody, they'd been taken away from her.

Grace was mature enough now to admit the truth. Those who hadn't left, Grace had walked away from. Because connection invited deep feelings, and deep feelings were dangerous.

They weren't worth the cost.

One time, only one time, she'd allowed herself to truly love another person. She'd poured her heart and her soul into saving Celia.

And look where that had led.

Which was why Grace had holed herself up in that cottage back in Washington. She should never have left.

She'd been a fool to think she could save Lily. She needed to pass the child off and get away. Fast.

She lifted her head, realizing that Lily was no longer screaming.

Grace pushed herself off the couch. Upstairs, she knocked on Lily's closed door. "Sweetheart, are you all right?"

When Lily didn't answer, Grace opened the door and peeked inside to find Lily curled around Regis on her bed, her back to Grace. She was sniffing quietly.

"I'm not trying to get rid of you." Grace sat on the mattress beside her, rubbing her back. "I'm trying to find your family. Your nana. Don't you want to find her?"

A few beats passed before Lily's little shoulder lifted and dropped in a halfhearted shrug.

"I'm sure she wants to find you," Grace said, hoping and praying that it was true. That the woman was alive and well and wondering about her granddaughter. Maybe even searching for her.

Lily pushed herself up and turned to face Grace, her gorgeous green eyes rimmed in red. "My own mama doesn't even want me. Maybe Nana doesn't either."

Grace opened her arms, and Lily nestled against her. "Sweet

child, you are amazing and priceless, worth more than all the gold and silver in all the world. I bet your grandmother is out there right now wondering where you are." *Please, let it be true, Lord.* "Shouldn't we do everything we can to find her?"

"I guess." Lily leaned back and gazed at Grace. "But I wanna stay with you. I love you."

"Oh..." Grace pulled her into a hug again. It wouldn't hurt to say the words. They were only words, after all. They didn't mean anything. But she couldn't make herself do it.

Despite what she'd almost let herself believe the night before, Grace wasn't capable of real love. Real love didn't just understand others. Real love was powerful. Real love *saved*. She didn't possess that kind of love. She never would.

"You are so loved," Grace finally said. "And so incredibly lovable." She patted the child's back and then extricated herself and stood. "But if you don't hurry up and get ready, you're going to be late to school."

Lily sighed. "I don't wanna go today."

"Sometimes, we have to do things we don't want to do. Growing up is about learning to do the hard things. Maturing is about learning to do the hard things with a good attitude. And you, young lady"—she tapped Lily's little nose—"are growing up and maturing right before my eyes."

With a giant sigh, the child lumbered toward her closet.

"I'm making pancakes."

Even the promise of her favorite breakfast didn't lighten Lily's spirits.

An hour later, after Grace dropped Lily at the school, she dialed Cassidy's number.

Cassidy answered with, "So...Texas? With Andrew?"

"How in the world—?"

"Reid and Jacqui kept your dog. Reid stopped by The Patriot for breakfast and talked to James, who'd heard from Reid, so—"

"Telephone, telegraph, tell—"

"Pretty much anybody in Coventry. We're a pretty tight-knit crew. So, you and Andrew?"

"It's not like that." At least it shouldn't be. "We're trying to find Lily's family."

"Uh-huh. And Andrew went because—?"

"He's a really nice guy. And his father's company owns a private jet."

"Oh." That stunned her into silence, if only for a moment.

"So we were able to get there and back in one day," Grace added.

"Any luck?"

"Maybe. I'm hoping to get a call from somebody with information about her grandmother. If that doesn't pan out, then I'll have to expand the search." It was too early to get to the real reason for reaching out, so she shifted gears. "I wondered if today might be a good day for me to come by and check out the youth center." Cassidy had asked her more than once to stop by for a tour. Grace hadn't done it because she knew that Cassidy would start with a tour but would quickly move on to telling her all the reasons she should go to work there, or at least volunteer. She'd hinted that the local youths could use Grace's gifts.

Grace wouldn't be sucked in, but maybe she could talk Cassidy into helping her find a temporary home for Lily.

"I'll be there by nine o'clock," Cassidy said. "Stop by anytime after that."

Rather than drive back to the condo in the meantime, Grace found a little coffee shop a couple of blocks off the main drag. Cuppa Josie's was located in an old Victorian house. When Grace stepped inside, the scents of coffee and baked goods wrapped around her like a soft scarf. A line snaked from the door to the glass-fronted counter at the far end of the largest space. Behind it, Grace glimpsed the kitchen, the only modern area in view. The furniture was old and used. Not antiques, not valuable. Just comfortable and worn. Scratched and faded tables, arm chairs, side chairs. The hardwood floor was scuffed.

It felt as if she'd just walked into somebody's granny's house.

Behind the counter, the twentysomething woman who seemed to be running the show didn't fit the bill.

Grace ordered tea and a lemon scone, then snagged a padded chair in front of the bay window overlooking the street.

The sweet pastry was the perfect accompaniment to the bitter tea, and she was glad she hadn't had time to eat her from-a-box pancakes that morning.

She watched the world spin around her. A group of gray-haired men got coffee, and one of them took out a deck of cards as if it made perfect sense to play gin rummy over breakfast.

Two women, one bouncing a toddler on her hip, chose an old burgundy sofa against the far wall. They bent their heads together in serious conversation while the child ate a chocolate-covered éclair, getting as much on his cheeks as in his mouth.

One man came in wearing a scowl. So many people greeted him, teased him, and squeezed his shoulder in morale-boosting grips that, by the time he left, he walked with a bounce in his steps and a smile on his face.

People came and went, greeting each other by name. The owner guessed many orders before the customers had a chance to speak them. They joked and laughed, and some, as they left, hollered *Thanks, Josie* over their shoulders.

This was what community looked like.

And as usual, Grace was on the outside looking in. Never quite belonging. Because she wasn't normal. She wasn't like the rest of these people, for whom friendship came so easily, people capable of true love.

She wanted to be part of them, always had. But she'd never been able to make it work. The one time she'd tried had ended with abysmal failure.

At a quarter after ten, she entered the brick building that housed the youth center, struck by the gleaming floors and modern equipment.

Cassidy approached from an office behind a long counter, arms held wide. "How are you, my friend? I'd hoped I'd see more of you, but life has been so busy."

Grace gave her a quick hug, careful of the baby bump that was bigger than the last time she'd seen her. "How are you feeling?"

"Excellent. I was so tired the first trimester, but I almost feel like my old self again now." She rubbed a hand over her growing belly. "Except for this little guy doing karate kicks in there." She hooked her arm with Grace's. "Come on. I'll show you around."

Grace had expected the place to be empty, but there were three teenagers in one of the rooms, heads bent over schoolwork. An older woman raised her hand in a wave as they walked by.

"They were *invited* to leave school," Cassidy explained when they were out of earshot of the teens, "and their parents can't afford private schooling, so we opened a little classroom. Marjorie tutors them."

"Suspended?"

"Expelled. And well deserved. But they're figuring it out."

"All three of them?"

"Partners in crime. They're lucky they're not in juvenile detention. They obeyed and did the work at first because that's their next stop if they don't. They do the work now because Marjorie loves them, and they want to please her."

"Amazing how well that works, huh? We learned that from the best."

"Mama Lucy." Cassidy's voice held wonder as she said the words. "My goal is to love as well as she did."

Grace wished she could say the same. Her goal was to not let herself love. But then, Mama Lucy's love worked.

The youth center was amazing, as Grace had known it would be. Cassidy had been a wonder when she'd run the girls home in Seattle alongside Mama Lucy. No matter how hard Grace had tried, she'd never been able to fill Cassidy's shoes.

When they finished the tour, Cassidy led her into the office and indicated a comfortable chair across from her desk. "You need some coffee?"

"I had tea before I came by." She looked around at the well-appointed space. "You either have a really generous town or a really generous group of benefactors."

"Yes to both." Cassidy leaned back in her chair and rubbed her baby belly. "HCI—Hamilton Clothiers—donates most of what we need to stay afloat."

"Oh, that's right. They have an office here or something?"

"Their corporate offices and their factory. All their clothes are made right up the street. The owner, Chelsea, is a dear friend. I think you met her, the one with the—"

"English accent." Now that Cassidy had mentioned her, Grace remembered meeting the pretty blonde at church. "She owns HCI?"

Cassidy nodded. "Her parents started it, and she inherited."

"She's young to have lost both her parents."

"There's a story there," Cassidy said. "Not mine to tell. Anyway, the town is generous too. They contribute, volunteer...I'm very fortunate."

"The kids are very fortunate."

"True. So it practically runs itself. But I'm about to go on maternity leave." She gave Grace a knowing look. "I need somebody—"

"It can't be me, Cassidy."

"It could be, if you wanted it to. You have a gift."

"It's not a gift. It's a curse, and I'm doing my best not to let it destroy me."

She studied Grace through squinted eyes. "What happened to you?"

Not a story Grace planned to tell Cassidy—or anybody. "I was hoping you could do me a favor. I need to find a place for Lily while I search for her family. We didn't learn much this weekend, but Andrew is convinced that the man who claimed to be her father can't be related to her."

Cassidy leaned forward. "What? Why does he think that?"

"Both he and her mother have blue eyes, and Lily has green.

Apparently it's nearly impossible. Not completely, but..." She shrugged. "He didn't explain all the genetic stuff, but he seems to know what he's talking about."

"What are you hoping for?"

"She has a grandmother out there somewhere. I need to find her. Maybe I can reunite them."

"Why can't you keep Lily with you?"

"It's just..." She swallowed hard. "This weekend was rough on her, going back and finding nothing but an empty house. I think she'd be better off with a more stable family than running all over the country with me."

"This search can't be done from here?"

"I don't know what it'll take. I don't want to hurt her."

"So you're looking for a family to take her for a couple of days? Or longer, or—"

"Permanently. I mean, not permanently, but until I find relatives."

Cassidy sat back and studied her closely.

Grace forced herself to hold her old friend's gaze.

Finally, Cassidy said, "You don't think it'll hurt her if you dump her—"

"I'm not trying to dump her. I'm trying to make sure she's taken care of."

Cassidy leaned forward, as if to impress her with her words. "You do that by taking care of her. Yourself."

"I'm not...I can't." A sob crawled up Grace's throat, but she swallowed it back. "She deserves somebody who can." Grace's voice cracked as the words came out.

A long moment passed before Cassidy shook her head. "What happened to you?"

"Can you help me? Do you know anybody—?"

"I don't know anybody who'd be willing to do that. How did you get custody, anyway?"

Grace hadn't told her friend the story. She hadn't wanted to put Cassidy in the position of having to choose between doing what was legal and doing what was right. Now, she pushed back in her chair and stood. "It's a long story."

"I'd like to hear it." Cassidy stood as well. "I have all day."

"I'll figure something out." She stepped toward the door.

"Grace?"

She turned. "I appreciate all you've done for me. For us. I shouldn't have come to you."

Shouldn't have come to Coventry at all. What was she doing there? All those people who knew everything about everything? It was just a matter of time before somebody figured out the truth.

Cassidy said, "Don't leave."

"I've taken up too much of—"

"I mean, don't leave Coventry. Or at least, don't leave without telling me. Please. I'll do whatever I can to help you and Lily. You have people here who care about you. James, me. Andrew."

The mention of his name set butterflies in flight. But the weight of anxiety pushed them back down.

"Just promise you won't leave without saying good-bye."

Grace nodded and hurried out the door. She was the one who was supposed to be intuitive, but Cassidy had seen right through her.

Her fight-or-flight instinct had kicked in, and everything in her whispered *flight*.

CHAPTER TWENTY-ONE

MYRON FINALLY UNDERSTOOD THE CONNECTION.

Grace had come to Coventry because of Cassidy Sullivan. According to her bio on the youth center's website, Cassidy Sullivan had worked at a home for troubled girls in Seattle.

The same place where Grace used to work.

Though solving that mystery brought a level of satisfaction, it was nothing to the satisfaction he'd felt after learning where Middleton had taken Grace and Lily the day before. He'd followed at a safe distance, not in his Missouri van but in his black sedan, the kind nobody looked twice at, until the BMW had turned into a parking lot near the airport in Manchester.

A bribe slipped to the right person, and Myron learned the private jet he'd seen through his binoculars beyond the unassuming building had been bound for Austin.

There was only one reason for Grace to go to Austin. They must've found out about Lily's grandmother.

Myron should have taken care of the woman years before.

He'd never wanted to harm the lady. He took no pleasure in causing pain. But Grace had left him no choice. Darla Springer would pay for Grace's poor choices.

CHAPTER TWENTY-TWO

ANDREW LEFT the office late Monday afternoon. It'd been a long, busy day. Andrew, Jacqui, and Braden had studied the résumés and educational backgrounds of the prospective employees coming to tour the lab the following weekend. Though all of them would be considered for positions at BNB, there were a few whose résumés had risen to the top, and Andrew was eager to meet them, to try to get them to at least consider a move north.

The young people—all in their final months of earning either bachelor's or master's degrees—would arrive in Manchester on Friday afternoon. They'd be treated to meals and cocktails and tours of the area, including emphasis on the good schools and affordable real estate. Though Jacqui and Braden would be there, Andrew and the event planner were in charge. Andrew would have to stay in Plymouth Friday through Sunday.

Which meant, as much as he wanted to take Grace on a real date, that would have to wait.

Unless...If he could find a babysitter for Lily, Grace could be his date for the dinner Saturday night. Reid and Carly would be there—Jacqui's husband and Braden's wife. So why not?

He sent a text to the event planner, telling her about his plus-one, and when she responded with a thumbs-up, his spirits lightened. On his way home to Coventry, he dialed Grace's number.

Her quick *hello* sounded rushed and frustrated. Definitely not the reception he'd hoped for.

"Everything all right?"

She blew out a breath. "Yeah, fine."

"What's wrong?"

Grace lowered her voice. "It was such a busy weekend. I'm sure Lily will be better tomorrow. She's just tired and cranky."

"Tired, I can understand. But I feel anything but cranky."

"Yeah." Grace's single word held no amusement.

"I could pick up dinner, and—"

"Don't you have your game night?"

They were expecting him, and it promised to be a good game, but still...."I could skip this one."

"No. Don't."

"Wow." He tried to sound lighthearted when he added, "You really know how to make a guy feel wanted."

"We're eating dinner now. Then, it'll be bath time and an early bedtime."

In the background, Lily whined, "I'm not tired. I don't wanna go to bed."

Grace sighed.

"You sure I can't help?" he asked.

"I wish you could."

"I could come over after you put her to bed." He felt a little pathetic, but his desire to see Grace overcame any embarrassment. And anyway, she already knew how he felt.

He was still coming to grips with that. The thing she'd told him was weird, and he wasn't sure what to do with it. He couldn't figure out if she'd been given an incredible gift or if she just had a really wild imagination. She was obviously intuitive, but...

But nothing. He trusted her. She believed she had a gift. Who was he to tell her she was wrong?

"I would love to see you," she said, sounding almost like she meant it, "but Lily had a rough night last night, and tonight's shaping up to be about the same. I think I'd better get some sleep. This is one of those days I just want to be over."

"Okay, then." Andrew kept his voice chipper, hiding his disappointment. "I'll call you tomorrow." He'd wait to ask her to join him for the company dinner when she was in a more agreeable state of mind.

Though he was sorry he wouldn't get to see her, he figured he could use the time between when he got home and when he had to leave for Braden's house to look at MBC's financial records.

Two hours later, he parked on the street in front of Braden and Carly's house, mind spinning with all he'd learned.

The news was not good. Not good at all.

Reid answered Braden's door with, "Howdy, pardner."

Jacqui and Reid had kept Regis while they'd been gone. Dad was generous, but not generous enough to allow a dog on his private jet. They'd picked Regis up on their way home from the airport the night before, but Andrew hadn't seen Reid. Apparently, the man had been saving up his teasing for tonight.

"Having just been there," Andrew said, "I can confirm that that is the worst Texas accent I've ever heard."

Before Reid could come up with a witty response, Garrett said, "Texas?"

And then Braden, from his chair, said, "He flew with his new girlfriend to Texas for the weekend."

Andrew hadn't made it off the front step yet. "With all the gossip, I feel like I just stepped into the high school girls' locker room."

Reid stepped back to let Andrew enter. "Spend a lot of time there, did you? Fixing your pantyhose and whatnot?"

Andrew couldn't help the chuckle. "Idiot."

"Moron."

James added, "Putz."

Carly came down the stairs, little Desi in her arms. "You guys watch your potty mouths." She stopped on the landing and squeezed Andrew's hand. "Pay no attention to them. They're living vicariously through you."

He peeked at the perfect little baby. She looked so much like her mother it was eerie. "My life's not that exciting, little one. Pay no attention to these people."

When he focused on Carly, her eyes sparkled, and a grin stretched across her lips. "So, how was Texas?"

He blew out a long breath and reached for the door handle beside him. "Maybe I'll just see you guys next week."

That brought laughs and insincere apologies, but he allowed himself to be pulled in, though he didn't respond to their ribbing or the questions about Grace. He wasn't ready to put a name to what they had. He certainly wasn't ready for the teasing that would surely come if he did.

The conversation moved past Grace and on to sports, politics, and the economy. It was halftime before Reid asked, "Any update on your father's company?"

Andrew couldn't stop the groan that escaped at the thought of what he'd discovered. He nodded toward Fitz, who'd snagged a spot on the couch. "You were right. He's skimming and too stupid to cover it up."

"Remind me...This is your brother?" Fitz asked.

"Half brother."

"How'd your dad receive the news?" Reid asked.

"I just figured it out. I haven't yet calculated how much has been taken, but there's no doubt. The numbers just don't add up. They did the first few years Chet was in charge, but the last eighteen months or so—"

"You have a guess?" James asked.

"Raw estimate—seventy-five to a hundred grand."

From his chair beside Andrew's, Thomas whistled.

Shaking his head, James said, "I had a server working for me last year who used to pocket cash every so often. The numbers were a little off whenever she worked, and I couldn't figure out why. I thought she was incompetent or something. When I finally realized what was going on...It was just a couple hundred bucks, but I was furious. I can't imagine if my own kid did something like that."

"It's such a betrayal," Reid added. "To have someone you work with, someone you trust..."

"Yeah," Andrew said. "I don't want to be the one to tell Dad."

"You're sure it was him?" Braden leaned forward and propped his knees on his elbows. "No chance anybody else could have done it? A manager? Someone in accounting who figures he's an easy mark?"

Andrew shrugged. "All I know is what I'm seeing in the books. I don't know who has access to the accounts. I guess my dad'll have to figure all that out."

"He had to know something like that was going on," Fitz said. "Maybe he wanted you to confirm what he already suspected."

Andrew considered the idea, then discarded it. "Dad hates that Chet and I don't get along. I can't imagine that he'd have asked me to do this if he thought there was any chance—"

"Why ask you, then?" Fitz shifted to face him better. "Think about it. Your dad wants his two sons to get along but then asks one to investigate the other's work. Why?"

Andrew had asked himself that question more than once. "Maybe he figured nobody at Middleton would tell him the truth."

"And he knew you'd be honest," Reid said. "You wouldn't sugarcoat it. You wouldn't worry about your father's reaction."

Andrew couldn't help the bark of unamused laughter. "He'd be wrong about that."

Snagging a slice of cheese off the tray on the coffee table, James said, "It's not your fault your brother's a thief."

"Still sucks you have to be the one to break the news to your dad, though," Reid added.

But Andrew did have to, sooner rather than later. Once he finished cataloging what he'd learned and adding up the discrepancies, he'd set up a time for the two of them to get together. This didn't feel like news he should deliver over the phone.

~

ANDREW KNOCKED on Grace's door at five thirty the next afternoon, the heavy wind whipping through his light jacket. He'd left work early in hopes of catching Grace and Lily before dinner. He shifted the steaming hot pizza box into his other hand, telling himself to be patient and calling himself all kinds of idiot for not having tried calling again.

But he'd dialed her a couple of times that day, and Grace had rejected his calls.

He couldn't read her feelings, not the way she could read his, but when he'd kissed her on Sunday, he'd never felt so connected to another person in his life. On the jet, she'd claimed to feel the same.

But by the time they'd landed, he'd felt her pulling away. Putting up walls. Putting distance between them.

After two days, that distance felt as wide as the Atlantic.

If she planned to end what they had before it'd even had a chance to begin, Andrew wasn't going to make it easy on her. If she didn't want him, then she was going to have to spell it out. Until she did, he would pursue her.

Finally, the door swung open, and Lily stood in the entry, tear streaks on her cheeks. Before he could say a word, she turned and yelled, "I told you. It's Mr. Middleton."

"And I told you you're not allowed to answer the door without permission." Grace approached from behind, a frown marring her pretty face. "It's not safe."

"I looked through the window!"

"You didn't ask—"

"I hate you!" The girl swiveled and bounded up the stairs, leaving Andrew on the stoop holding a pizza and feeling like an intruder.

Grace took the child's place at the door. "Sorry about that. We're having a hard day."

Maybe he should have taken the hint when she'd rejected his

calls. He held out the pizza like a peace offering, not that he'd done anything wrong. Not as far as he knew, though the way Grace was peering at him made him happy the would-be dinner separated them.

"It's not a good night for company."

"It's the perfect night for company. You both need a buffer." He lifted his free hand to his chest and offered a smile. "I volunteer."

She almost smiled at that.

"Please?" He lowered his voice. "I miss you."

Her gaze flicked to the staircase. He couldn't see what she was looking at but guessed Lily was there when Grace said, "Can you be polite?"

The child must've answered properly because Grace stepped back. "If you dare."

Figuring that was the best invitation he was going to get, he stepped inside. "Half cheese, half pepperoni. I didn't know what you ladies would like."

"She's pepperoni all the way, but I prefer cheese. Or pineapple."

"That's not a pizza topping." He walked past her to the kitchen. "It's a garnish for piña coladas."

No response from Grace. Not even a chuckle.

Lily and Grace were quiet as they ate, leaving him to make conversation. But what did he have to say that an eight-year-old girl wouldn't find boring? He did his best, and Grace at least rewarded him with an occasional smile.

No matter how many questions he asked, he couldn't get either one of them talking.

Finally, Grace shooed Lily away for a bath. "Wash your hair and your body, and use soap."

The child rolled her eyes and then disappeared up the stairs.

When she was gone, Grace collapsed in her chair and ran her fingers through her hair. It seemed as if she'd expended all the energy she had for the day.

Unfortunately, it wasn't even six thirty.

He stacked their plates on the far side of the table. "What's going on?"

"She does this...this thing. She'd been doing it since I first met her. She finds items that are important to me, and she hides them. She doesn't steal them. She just moves them to weird places."

"What do you mean? Like what?"

She shrugged. "A mug. My slippers." She touched her earlobe. "My favorite earrings. I've always been able to find them before. I've asked her and asked her to stop, and she finally did. She hadn't done it since she took my keys the first week we lived here."

"I take it that's changed."

"She hid my laptop. I can't find it anywhere. And she absolutely refuses to tell me where it is or even admit she did it. Not that she's ever done that."

"So she's never actually confessed to taking your things? Maybe she didn't."

Grace sat up. The spark in her eyes could've lit a blaze. "Who else could it be?"

He refused to rise to her level of anger. He didn't know if Lily had done anything wrong. He *knew* he hadn't. "I'm only saying, maybe she doesn't realize she's doing it. Maybe it's...subconscious or something."

"You know I have a degree in child psychology."

"I didn't know that. You don't talk much about your past."

"Oh." She sat back. "Well, I do. And it's not subconscious. I don't know why she does it, but she does. She's never even argued with me about it before. She's never told me where anything was, but she never denied having done it. No, this is just stubbornness. She's mad at me, and she's found a way to get back at me."

"For what?"

Grace stood and snatched her purse from where she kept it hanging from the pantry door. "Honestly, I don't have the energy for this tonight. Let me pay you back for the pizza."

"What? It was—"

"If I pay you, then I won't feel as guilty about asking you to leave."

He stood as well, stepping around the table to get nearer to her. "What's gotten into you? Lily's eight. Her behavior matches her age. Yours, on the other hand—"

"Don't scold me like a child."

"Don't act like one."

She yanked a twenty from her wallet and held it toward him. "Take it."

He squelched the words that came to his mind and forced himself to breathe. Slowly, he approached and wrapped his hands around her fists, careful not to touch her palm-to-palm. The last thing she needed was to add his feelings of frustration and hurt to whatever she was feeling in that moment. "Just take a breath."

She held her glare, the fury in it hot enough to leave a mark. A moment passed until, finally, she deflated.

He pulled her close and wrapped her in his arms. "It's okay." Though he wasn't sure exactly what *it* was, and he had no idea whether it was okay or not.

"I'm sorry." Her words were muffled against his button-down.

"I didn't mean to question you. You're doing your best. You're doing a great job with her. And you obviously know Lily a lot better than I do. I was only trying to help."

When she backed up, he wiped a tear trickling down her cheek. "Hey, now. What can I do?"

"Nothing. Just...the pizza was good. I'm sorry we're both so out of sorts."

He urged Grace back into her chair and took his own, pulling it closer to her so he could keep his voice low. "Did the trip to Texas bring this on?"

"She thinks I'm trying to get rid of her."

"Well, that's ridiculous. You're a foster parent. She understands what that means, right?"

Grace's gaze slid toward the stairs. "It's complicated for a little kid. She's grown attached to me."

"Like you have her, of course. How could you not fall in love with her? Knowing you could lose custody of her any day has to be tearing you up. What you're doing is so noble."

Grace flinched as if he'd wounded her.

"It is," he pressed. "What you're doing with her is amazing." He slid the tip of his finger from her temple to her jaw. "You're amazing."

She seemed to lean into his touch.

And then, suddenly, she backed away. Stood. Shook her head.

Before she could speak, he stood as well. "It doesn't hurt to have a friend. Someone you can lean on and confide in. I want to be that someone for you."

He expected her to argue or order him out of her house.

But she didn't, and he wasn't going to leave unless she forced him to. Instead, he slid his hand around her upper arm. She seemed almost weak as he led her to the living room and settled her on the sofa. He sat beside her and pulled her against his side. "See, it's not so bad."

She cuddled there but didn't say anything.

Grace just needed to rest for a few minutes, not think about all the worries pressing in on her. Rather than question her further, he snatched the remote and found the Food Network. A few minutes passed while they watched a chef make the perfect fried chicken.

Beside him, Grace said, "I need to find my laptop."

"You want help looking for it?"

Her head shook against his chest. "I'll figure it out. Or I'll get her to find it for me."

"Let me know if you change your mind." When she didn't respond, he asked a question that'd been dogging him since Monday morning. Keeping his voice low, he said, "What did her social worker say?"

"Oh. Uh...I haven't called her."

He shifted to look at her. "Why not?"

"And tell her what?"

"That you think Myron isn't her real father."

"We have no proof, just your suspicion. We need more information."

"Right. But don't you think...?" He was confused. "What would it hurt to tell her?"

"It's complicated. These things are complicated."

That was the second time she'd brushed off his questions with that response. He was a pretty smart guy, though. He was pretty sure he could keep up.

And it didn't seem that complicated to him. But Grace wasn't in the state of mind to listen. Rather than argue, he said, "You know what you're doing."

She left his side and settled against the arm of the couch a good foot away. "If that neighbor, Ruby, doesn't call me back soon, I'm going to hire somebody to track down Darla Springer."

"Maybe you should call the Freedom Hill Police Department. Maybe they know something."

She blinked a couple of times. "Why would they?"

"If the girl was kidnapped—"

"Then we'd have found information about that online, don't you think?"

"But if Myron isn't—"

"We don't know he isn't her father. All we have is your suspicion."

His suspicion was based on pretty solid facts, but saying so wouldn't help.

"How about the county clerk's office? They'd have birth records. Maybe they could tell us her birth parents."

"I tried that." The words were sharp, irritated. "Called them yesterday. It's private information. They won't release the records to me."

"Okay." He tried to keep his voice calm and kind. "I have a friend whose specialty is finding lost people. You probably met him at church. The redheaded guy married to the woman with the English accent."

"Chelsea. Who owns HCI. Husband is..."

"Dylan."

She nodded, and some of her ire seemed to drain away. "Cassidy was talking about them today."

"Dylan could find the grandmother. Probably in a matter of minutes. Maybe even Lily's mother." At the flicker of hope brightening her expression, he added, "He used to be a detective, and a darn good one. I know he'd be willing to help."

Grace swallowed, and the hope he'd seen in her eyes dulled. "I'll keep it in mind."

"I could call—"

"That's okay. I can get his number." She stood. "I'm sorry. I just can't do this tonight. I need to get Lily in bed, and I need to find my laptop."

He stood as well, feeling off-balance and confused. This night hadn't gone the way he'd hoped. No matter how hard he'd tried, everything he'd said was wrong. He wanted to help, but Grace obviously didn't want that.

The chasm between them only seemed to be growing.

"I'm sorry if I...I shouldn't have shown up uninvited."

She walked to the door and opened it. "The pizza was delicious. Thank you."

On his way over that evening, he'd hoped they might share another kiss. The hope of that had blown away almost immediately. The hope that he could leave with him and Grace still on friendly terms—even that felt chilled in the cold wind seeping in beneath the storm door.

He considered grabbing the pizza box to toss it out so she wouldn't have to make a trip to the dumpster, but the way she was looking at him—like a nasty rash she'd do anything to be rid of—had him striding toward the door. He paused in front of her. Wanting more than anything to take her in his arms, he settled for leaning down and kissing her temple. "I'm sorry you're having a hard day. Call me if you need anything."

She nodded but didn't force words past her lips, which were pressed so tightly together that they'd turned almost white.

He had no idea what was going on behind those guarded eyes. No idea how he could bridge the gap she seemed intent on keeping between them.

"Good night." When he reached the bottom of the stoop, he turned to wave but found the door already closing between them.

THIS WAS PROBABLY A TERRIBLE IDEA.

Andrew parked outside the old house on the edge of the lake and knocked on the door. So unlike the condo community where he lived, this place was not in a neighborhood at all. In fact, if not for the campground a couple of hundred yards up the road, James and Cassidy's home would be completely secluded.

James answered the door and held it open. Andrew'd called on his way, and Cassidy'd told him to stop by, so he was taken aback by James's glower.

"Did she not tell you I was coming?"

He shook the expression off his face. "She's had a long day, and with the baby coming, she needs to rest."

"I promise to keep it brief."

"See that you—" He cut off his own words and plastered on a smile as Cassidy stepped into the entry from the living area. "I'll be in here." James stepped into the living room, and a moment later, the TV came on.

"Don't mind him." Cassidy glanced through the door at her husband, speaking low. She rubbed her growing middle. "The bigger I get, the more protective he gets."

"Can't blame him for that," Andrew said. "I just had a couple of questions."

She led him through the dining room and into the sizable eat-in kitchen. She perched on the edge of a chair. "Obviously, I won't divulge any confidences."

"I know." He sat and angled to face her. "I just hoped you could give me some background."

Cassidy studied him with those striking blue eyes, her gaze penetrating enough that he fought not to squirm. "You've got it bad, huh?"

He tried to shrug off the question, but she seemed as insightful as Grace. "I'm not gonna lie. And I'm not gonna tell you anything I haven't told her yet. Suffice it to say, I'm moving toward Grace, not backing away. She, however..." He wasn't sure how to say what he was trying to say. He settled for, "I don't think it's because she doesn't have feelings for me."

Cassidy dipped her head, acknowledging that.

"We shared a pretty...intimate moment."

At that, her eyebrows rose.

"Not *that* intimate. A kiss. Or a few. I thought..." He felt like an idiot, talking about this with a woman he barely knew. That he was there was a testimony to how desperate he was. "Is there some reason why she wouldn't want to get involved with me? Or maybe it's just me. Maybe she's just not that into me."

"She had some issues in her past. I thought she'd worked through them, and I obviously can't tell you—"

"She told me about her stepfather," Andrew said. "And how she ended up in the girls home."

Cassidy's eyes widened with surprise. "That was a lot, Andrew. She obviously trusts you. She must care for you, or she wouldn't have shared that. It's a pretty personal story."

His heart raced like a schoolboy's hearing his first crush liked him back. With every tick of the wall clock, he felt more like an idiot for being there. But something was keeping Grace from diving in with him, and seeing as how he was already drowning in his feelings, he'd really like her to do more than dip her toes in the water.

Cassidy's tone was careful when she said, "Grace is...special. She's incredibly insightful, almost to the degree that it's hard to comprehend."

"She told me that too. About the..." Then *he* felt the need to tread carefully. Maybe Cassidy didn't know. He held his hand palm up, and she sat back.

"She told you that? About her gift?"

"Sunday. She sort of demonstrated." He swallowed the rest of his words, remembering the moment when they'd kissed, when he'd felt all the feelings, knowing she was feeling them too. It had been more intimate than anything he'd ever experienced. Considering they'd stopped at a kiss, that was saying something.

"Huh." Cassidy looked beyond him, head shaking. "Did she tell you about Celia?"

"Who?"

"Ah. After I left Seattle, she took over my position at the girls home. She was so good with the girls, better than I could ever hope to be, because she understood them in a way nobody else could. But there was this one girl. Celia. She'd run away from home after suffering repeated abuse at the hands of her father and her older brother. She was only thirteen, and she'd already attempted suicide multiple times before she came to us." She blinked a couple of times, then said, "This isn't personal about Grace, so..." After a long pause, she continued. "It's okay if I tell you. I hope, anyway."

"You can trust me."

"And Grace can trust me. I'm trying to be sensitive to what she'd want. I don't think she'd mind your knowing, especially considering everything else she's told you. I suspect her having kept quiet about it is more because she doesn't like to talk about it. Or think about it.

"Anyway, Grace did everything in her power to reach Celia. She poured herself into that child. The thing is, some people are so broken that they're crushed. Celia was crushed. She'd given her life to Christ, she knew where she was going, and she was ready to get there."

"Oh, no."

"She was still alive when Grace found her, but she'd lost a lot of blood." Cassidy rubbed a vertical line across the inside of her wrist, and a sick feeling settled in Andrew's gut. "Grace called 911 and went with her to the hospital. She held her hand the whole time, weeping and praying and begging Celia to fight."

His mind picked up on one part of that, shining a spotlight on it. "Holding her hand."

Cassidy nodded. "Experiencing it all."

"And being able to do nothing about it."

"Grace quit the next day. She moved out of Seattle and never looked back."

No wonder she seemed so broken. No wonder she was trying to keep her distance.

What must she have felt in her body, in her heart, as Celia's life had slipped away?

How could Andrew—how could anybody—help to guard Grace's heart?

He didn't know, but he was willing to try. He was willing to dedicate his life to protecting her, to keeping her from getting that invested in another person even while encouraging her to use her gift. How, he had no idea, but with God's help, he'd figure it out.

Had she picked up on some brokenness in him, something that reminded her of Celia? He didn't think so. Maybe she feared connection to anybody.

He thought back on all the interactions he'd noticed between Grace and Lily. Grace cared for the child, but she kept her distance too. He'd never heard Grace say that she loved Lily—not to Lily's face or speaking about her. She held her, but never for very long. She managed all the girl's physical needs but seemed to distance herself from the emotional ones.

He'd chalked it up to the desire to not get too attached, knowing Lily would eventually go to someone else. But maybe there was more to it than that. Maybe she was afraid to connect with her.

He remembered Lily's innocent comment the previous week. *"Miss Grace doesn't like to hold hands. It makes her feel funny."*

Grace never held Lily's hand.

"That does shed some light," Andrew said. "But I'm confused.

When did she move to New Hampshire? And, if she was so intent on keeping her distance...She must have healed to some degree to become a foster parent."

Cassidy leaned back. Confusion flickered in her eyes, but she masked it quickly. "I don't have all the details, only what Mama Lucy told me. And Mama Lucy knew nothing about that. I have no idea how she got custody of Lily."

At least some of his questions had been answered, but he felt like more had presented themselves. Why would a woman intent on protecting herself take custody of a little girl, even if she understood Lily's background? It was one thing to turn Myron in for what she suspected, but then to take responsibility for Lily?

She must adore the child.

And yet she kept her emotional distance.

He didn't understand.

But he would. He'd do everything in his power to get to know Grace, to figure out what made her tick.

Strange as her gift was, rocky as her history, he was falling for her more and more every day. If she tried to put up walls between them, he'd work just as hard to tear them down.

CHAPTER TWENTY-THREE

THE NEXT MORNING, Grace stared at the laptop sitting innocently on the kitchen counter as if it'd been there all along.

It hadn't been there when she'd gone to bed. Which meant Lily had gotten up at some point in the middle of the night and returned it.

After she'd shooed Andrew away the night before, she'd spent hours looking for that laptop. All the internet searches she'd done in hopes of figuring out what Myron was up to...Did Lily know how to access the browser history? Had she seen everything Grace had found on her father?

Her maybe father.

Her *probably not* father.

Grace had obsessed for half the night over all the stuff Lily might've seen. Because trying to find a child pornographer could often lead to iffy images at best, images Grace clicked away from the instant they loaded. She'd always been so careful to erase her history before she let Lily on the computer. But had she done so after her last attempt to locate Myron?

It'd been days. She had no idea.

She scanned the browser history now, and it was empty. Had she done that, or had Lily?

Did Lily even know how?

No games were open. No toy store sites. Maybe Lily hadn't opened the laptop at all. Maybe she'd just taken it and hidden it. It was password protected, but Grace hadn't always been careful to guard that password. If Lily'd wanted to see it, she'd only have had to watch Grace's hands as she'd typed it.

Was she that clever? Was she that determined to use the computer?

Grace didn't think so.

What if she'd decided to contact Myron? Grace had continued to be very careful about not giving Lily access to her cell phone, just in case that was how Myron had found them before.

As the weeks had passed, Grace had wondered more and more if she'd only ever imagined Myron breathing down their necks. Maybe, after that first night in Coeur d'Alene, they'd lost him, and he'd never caught up with them again.

But she'd been so sure. At the time. Why doubt now what she'd believed then?

Grace clicked into her email and read the sent messages. Nothing she hadn't sent herself. Then, to be safe, she went to the trash and looked to see if anything had been deleted since she'd last been on the computer. Nope.

So either Lily was more deceitful than Grace had ever imagined, or she'd done nothing with the computer at all.

Which tracked with the other things Lily had taken. It wasn't as if she'd used Grace's favorite mug or worn her favorite earrings. She'd just hidden them.

Grace closed the laptop, then her eyes. *Lord, I need You. I need wisdom. I need direction. I'm so confused.*

She didn't know what she was doing. The world kept shifting, and just when she got her feet under her, it tilted again.

The laptop was back. If Lily had seen something she shouldn't have...

Then she had. It was over, and there was nothing Grace could do about it.

But she didn't feel at peace. She didn't feel relaxed. She just felt more off-balance than ever.

Lily lumbered down the stairs and plopped into her chair at the kitchen table, eyes half open. Grace had learned the hard way to brush the child's hair before she woke up completely. When Lily was fully alert, she'd squirm and complain that Grace was hurting her. But half-asleep, she sat compliantly.

Grace grabbed the hairbrush from the downstairs half-bath and started pulling it through Lily's long, dark locks. On Monday, she'd made the mistake of asking about her grandmother during this time, which had set off a firestorm. She never had gotten Lily's hair brushed properly.

Today, she kept her mouth shut.

When she finished, Lily's hair was in pigtails that fell past her collarbones. The child perked up. "You found your laptop."

Grace settled in the seat catty-corner to her. "Thank you for bringing it back."

She shook her head vehemently "I didn't take it, Miss Grace. And I didn't put it there." She seemed not defensive but genuinely perplexed.

Grace had pooh-poohed Andrew's suggestion that Lily was taking and moving things without being aware of it, but maybe he was onto something.

But if that were the case, then that meant Lily was suffering from some sort of dissociative disorder. Grace had seen no signs of that in the child.

Much as she'd thrown her degree in Andrew's face the night before, her bachelor's in child psychology didn't qualify her to diagnose such a unique and complex issue, much less treat it.

Did Lily need psychiatric care?

"Where did you find it?" Lily asked.

Grace jutted her chin. "There. On the counter."

Lily stared at the space, the color draining from her face. "What is it?"

"I didn't take it."

"Okay." Grace kept her voice light even as worry clawed at her insides. Dissociative disorders were thought to be caused by extreme trauma. She hadn't let herself dwell too much on what Myron had required of the child so he could get his photographs and videos. She didn't want to think about it now. But if Andrew's theory was correct, then there must be serious trauma in Lily's past.

The little girl's green eyes looked larger as they filled with tears. "I promise, Miss Grace. I didn't."

"I believe you." Believed she didn't know she had, anyway. Grace scooted back in her chair and opened her arms.

And then had another thought. If she really wanted to know the truth, maybe she could find it. She could discover everything she needed to know about Lily's past, and maybe the truth about the laptop, if she'd just allow herself to open her hand and press it palm-to-palm against Lily's.

But Lily crawled into her lap and held on. Now wasn't the time for delving into dark secrets. Right now, Grace just needed to be a steady, calming force in Lily's life, not a counselor digging into her past.

She told herself that was best. That it wasn't fear and self-protection that had her hesitating but care for the child.

She was lying to herself.

One more bit of evidence to add to the pile that proved she wasn't built for love.

She fixed breakfast and, once she'd settled Lily at the table to eat, said, "I need to pop over to Mr. Middleton's for a second. When you're finished, please get dressed."

"Yes, ma'am."

"Don't answer the door for anybody."

Lily rolled her eyes. "I won't."

Keys in hand, Grace made sure the door was locked behind her, then crossed the narrow lot to Andrew's door, thankful to see his BMW still parked in front of his condo. The air was crisp and cool, the faint scent of a wood fire floating on the breeze. At least the heavy winds had died down.

The other thing that'd kept her tossing and turning was the way she'd treated Andrew. Her shortcomings weren't his fault. She owed the man an apology.

She rang his bell, assuming he was already awake and getting ready for work. They often left about the same time. He could have been in the shower, though. Or maybe he was one of those guys who slept until five minutes before it was time to leave.

No, he always looked far too put-together for that.

She'd almost given up when the door opened. Andrew stood on the far side, wearing his suit pants, a pale blue button-down, and a tie hanging around the collar but unknotted. A smile spread across his features. "What a lovely way to start the day." He pushed open the storm door. "Come on in."

"I can't." She jutted her head toward her own door. "Lily. I probably shouldn't have left her alone, but—"

"Right. I'd come out but"—he looked at his bare feet—"it's a little chilly out there."

"I'm sorry. I wasn't myself last night. You were very sweet to bring dinner."

The smile stayed put, but his eyes squinted just a touch. "It was my pleasure."

"I think it was anything but a pleasure, but I appreciated you being there, even if I didn't show it."

He leaned against the jamb. "That's what we're doing, though, right? Having fun together is one thing, but if I really want to know you, then I need to be there even when it's not fun. It might not have been the lighthearted dinner I'd anticipated, but I'm glad I was there."

Her ears had snagged on his first sentence. "What *are* we doing?"

He stepped out of the house onto the cold concrete. When she started to back away, he lightly gripped her wrist. "I don't know what you're doing, Grace..." His words trailed, and his slight smile faltered. He swallowed and continued. "I'm falling hard."

Falling. Yes, that was an apt description. She needed to grab onto something before she crashed. "I just don't think now's the time..."

But he pulled her close and wrapped his arms around her. "Don't do that." The words were deep and low, and she felt his breath in her ear. He smelled of soap and shampoo and aftershave, masculine and sexy. "You don't have to do that."

Everything in her wanted to relax in Andrew's strong arms. But nothing had changed. She still needed to find Lily's family. She still wasn't good at this. Andrew still deserved more than she could ever offer.

"Whatever you're thinking right now," he said, "just...trust me. Trust that God did this for a reason."

God. God, Who'd been silent for so long.

She was formulating a response, something about taking it slow and focusing on Lily, when his lips trailed kisses from her ear to her mouth. She should not open up to him.

Her body wasn't obeying her mind, and she dove into his kiss.

All her arguments floated away.

He ended the kiss and leaned back, a grin teasing his lips. "I can think of no better way to start my day."

Right. It was morning. And cold. And...

She stepped back and looked at his bare feet on the cold stoop. "You must be freezing."

His eyebrows rose. "After that kiss? Are you kidding?"

"Go inside. You're going to catch pneumonia."

"Old wives' tale."

"I have to get back. Lily's by herself."

He leaned in and gave her a quick kiss on her cheek, then held her eye contact. "Go with me to the dinner Saturday night?"

He'd told her all about the events his company had planned for the following weekend. "Oh, I don't—"

"I found a babysitter. My friend Fitz's teenage sister is in town.

Fitz said we could take Lily to their house. Shelby will watch her, but Fitz and Tabby will be there too, so she'll be perfectly safe. She can even take Regis."

"I don't know those people, though."

"I know them. They go to our church."

Our church. As if she belonged there too.

"They're good people, Grace."

"But—"

"Do you trust me?"

She did, completely. She nodded.

"Then say you'll go."

"I guess—"

"Good. I'll call you later." Another quick kiss on her cheek, and he retreated inside, winking just as his door closed.

Brat.

~

GRACE'S HAND trembled as she tapped the button on her phone.

She'd left it on the kitchen table for thirty seconds to run to the bathroom, and that was when Ruby Lind had called. Thank heavens the older woman had left a message.

At the start of the third ring, Grace scolded herself for not keeping the phone with her at all times. She was usually so good to do that, but Lily was at school. If she'd missed her opportunity—

"Hello?"

"Hi. This is Grace Miller. Are you Mrs. Lind?"

"I am. A note was left for me to call you?"

"Yes, yes." Grace took a breath, trying to sound calm, not frantic. "I'm looking for an old neighbor of yours, Darla Springer. The lady who lives next door to you said you might have some idea where she or her family went."

"Did she now?" But the woman sounded more amused than annoyed. "Well, I do have a bit of a reputation for being a busybody." She laughed as she said the words. "Well deserved, I'm afraid."

"Nothing wrong with caring about your neighbors," Grace said.

"Exactly what I think. And anyway, Darla and I were more than neighbors. We were friends. Still are. Best friends since second grade."

Grace stifled the temptation to dive right into her questions, forcing herself to relax in her chair and close her eyes and listen, really listen. Because sometimes people needed to talk, and when you gave them the space to, they said more than they'd ever planned.

"I was Darla's maid of honor," Ruby said with a slow Texas drawl. "She was a matron by the time I walked down the aisle. Until a couple of years ago, we never lived more'n a mile from each other."

"So you know all her kids?"

"There was just the one, Annabeth. Prettiest girl in school, but so shy she hardly had any friends. According to Darla, the other girls didn't like her because she was gorgeous, and the boys were intimidated by her. I think they all mistook her shyness for snobbiness. Sometimes, beauty can be a curse."

Though Grace mostly wanted to know where Darla was now, maybe Ruby could tell her more about Annabeth's history. She was formulating a follow-up question, but Ruby kept talking.

"The girl was sure she'd found the love of her life in that football player she went to high school with." She tsked. "I could've told her from the start the boy was no good. Come from damaged stock, that one. His daddy's drinking practically kept the local bar afloat. That thing they say about the apple fallin' by the tree—that's the God's truth. I always said Annabeth was lucky that boy didn't claim her child as his own, and I wasn't wrong. He's got a houseful of 'em now, and he treats 'em all like dirt. His wife too. Least in that, Annabeth dodged a bullet."

Ruby must have been talking about Lily's birth father, not Myron. "What was the boy's name?"

A pause was followed by, "Listen to me, runnin' my mouth. Why do you want to know about Darla and Annabeth?"

"It's sort of a long story. I met a little girl I believe is Annabeth's daughter, and—"

"Lilianne? You know where she is?"

Ruby's reaction sent acid to Grace's insides. Maybe the police were looking for the child. Were they tracing this call? "I'm just trying to—"

"If you know where she is, you need to tell me right now. Darla's about gone out of her mind searching for those girls."

"Girls? There was more than—"

"Annabeth and Lilianne, of course. They been gone more'n six years now. Darla's heart about crumbled to pieces waiting for her babies to get home."

"Can you tell me what happened with Annabeth? Why she disappeared?"

"Well, it was that stranger who came to town, that man. Always a man. I mean, my Ron, he has a heart of gold, and Darla's husband was a good fellow. But so many of 'em anymore are slick as serpents. That man sure was."

"Do you remember his name?"

"Oh, let's see...Martin? Marvin?"

"Myron?"

"You do know them! Are they all right? Tell me they're all right."

"I don't know for sure that the little girl I know is Annabeth's daughter," Grace said carefully, though the evidence seemed to point that way. "But the man who claims to be her father is named Myron."

Ruby scoffed. "Father. Guy was a snake-in-the-grass photographer, promising Annabeth he could make her a big-time model, get her picture on the covers of magazines coast to coast. Darla did her best to talk the girl outta it, but she up and left with him, taking the child with her."

"Were Darla and Annabeth estranged at that point? Is that why Darla lost touch with her?"

"Nothin' like that. Darla didn't want her to go, but she loved her little girl. Hugged her neck when she left. Annabeth promised to come home for Christmas, to call and write, but she never did. She left with that photographer and fell off the face of the planet."

Grace rubbed her temples. "Okay, but…" Something didn't add up. "Darla knew the photographer's name. Could she not find him? He's still going by Myron Bowman, so—"

"Bowman? No, that wasn't his last name. It was…Williamson or Williams or something."

But he'd been Myron Bowman before Lily was born, a well-respected photographer. And he was Myron Bowman still.

Which meant that, when he'd met Annabeth, he'd been using a false name. Why?

"So you're saying Bowman's his real last name?" Ruby asked.

"If we're talking about the same person—"

"What makes you think the girl you know is related to Darla and Annabeth?"

"It's just a guess right now, Mrs. Lind. Can you tell me how to get in touch with Darla Springer?"

The woman paused a long moment. "Well, I ought to check with her before I give her information to a stranger on the phone."

Even the cautious answer had Grace's spirits lifting.

"How 'bout this?" Ruby said. "How 'bout I give her a ring and have her call you. I 'spect she'll do so in a jiffy."

"That'll work. Just please, tell her I don't know anything for sure. I don't want to get the woman's hopes up."

"Are you still in town?"

"I'm not. I'm from Washington State." Wasn't *in* Washington, but if this was all a ruse, if Ruby knew Lily had been kidnapped and was working with the authorities to find her…

Well, if that were the case, the FBI would have traced the call. They'd be barging through her door any second.

Too late to worry about that now.

"Alrighty, then," Ruby said. "I'm fixin' to call her, so hang tight."

Grace had stared at the phone off and on for an hour after she'd hung up with Ruby. When it finally dinged with a text, she snatched it up as if it held the meaning of life.

Well, she's not answering. I left her a message. I'll let you know when she calls. Sincerely, Ruby Lind.

Grace smiled at the salutation, not to mention the perfect punctuation. Apparently, Ruby wasn't much of a texter.

She tapped out a reply. *Thank you so much. I look forward to hearing from you.*

She spent the afternoon searching the internet for information on possible false names. Myron Williamson, Myron Williams, Myron Wilson.

She'd found a list of last names beginning with W and tried hundreds of them.

No luck.

Then she'd tried with different first names. Martin, Marvin, Mason.

For two hours, she typed random names into the internet search box, always with the addition of "photographer."

No hits.

Sure, she'd found plenty of photographers with similar names, but as far as she could tell, none of them led to the man Grace was looking for. The man who'd made sweet promises to Annabeth and led her away from home.

What happened after that? Had Annabeth become a model? Grace had searched for her name with no hits. She'd done an image search using the newspaper picture Andrew's friend had found. Again, no hits.

As far as Grace could tell, Annabeth had taken her daughter, left her mother, and then disappeared.

But Lily...Lilianne. She'd stayed with Myron.

A sick feeling filled Grace's stomach as she considered the implications. Maybe Annabeth hadn't left Myron at all. Maybe she hadn't left Lily in his care. And why would she? If she hadn't wanted to raise her child, she could have taken her home to her mother. But she hadn't.

Maybe something terrible had happened to Annabeth.

THAT EVENING, Grace leaned her elbows back on the picnic table behind her as she and Andrew watched Lily play on the playground. The sun was falling behind the trees, and though the temperature hovered in the upper fifties, the lack of wind kept it from being too chilly. As usual, the park buzzed with people. A group of what looked like middle-schoolers played basketball on the half court. One couple pushed a stroller, a golden retriever puppy straining at its leash. A group of older folks walked the perimeter. Though this condo complex was completely different from the neighborhood where Grace and her mother had lived before Mom's remarriage, it felt similar—a community of people who, though only connected by proximity, existed together in harmony.

When Mom remarried, Grace had lost her home. She'd lost that safe community. Barney's luxury house behind the big iron gates had never felt nearly as safe as that little three-bedroom surrounded by friendly faces.

To make up for her poor behavior the night before, Grace had invited Andrew over for tacos. She'd even fixed the meal herself. Well, with the help of Old El Paso, but it still felt like a win when both Lily and Andrew raved about the food.

Out for an evening stroll, Lily had met up with a few friends from school, and the girls were now crawling all over the playground while Regis kept vigil at the foot of the slide, never taking his eyes off Lily. The cast wasn't slowing her down at all.

"Ruby called me." Grace hadn't wanted to say anything where Lily might overhear, but the child was paying them no attention now.

Andrew shifted to face her. "What'd she say?"

"She knows where Darla is but won't tell me until she asks if it's okay. Apparently, Darla isn't answering her phone."

"That unusual?"

Grace shrugged. "I guess they've been friends since childhood." She caught Andrew up on everything Ruby had told her. When she was finished, Andrew stared past her, eyes narrowed.

"So you're saying Myron was using a fake name when he met Annabeth?"

"According to Ruby."

"But he was honest about his profession? That's odd. Why lie about one and not the other?"

"He was using his profession, though," Grace said. "He promised to make Annabeth a model."

"Right. But they didn't do their homework? Didn't look him up, check his credentials?"

Grace shrugged. "I'm sure Darla can give us more information when we talk to her."

Andrew turned his attention back to the children, but he seemed to be thinking pretty hard. Rather than interrupt, she followed his gaze, loving how easily Lily fit in. The child felt safe. Grace wished she hadn't taken Lily to Texas. Though she was glad that Lily had been there to confirm what they'd learned about her background, the trip had eroded her confidence. Which explained her poor behavior that week and the incident with the laptop. Speaking of...

"You might be right about Lily," Grace said.

"I told you he wasn't her father."

"That too."

"Have you called the social worker?"

"I will after I talk to Darla and confirm what Ruby said."

He studied her, squinting. "I don't understand the hesitation.

You should be calling the authorities to report him. You should be sounding the alarm."

"For all I know, he legally adopted her. I need to talk to Darla."

"He's a pornographer, so even if he did—"

"We haven't proved that yet."

Andrew blew out a heavy breath. "My friend's still looking for her picture. If it's anywhere on the deep web, he'll find it."

"It's amazing how long it takes."

He shrugged. "It's a big place. David tells me it's more than four hundred times larger than the internet. The difference is that it isn't searchable by your everyday search engines. It's not all bad stuff, I guess. The dark web is tucked in the deep web and hidden pretty well."

"Surely Myron's removed her image by now."

"If he sold pictures of her, then somebody has it. Probably many, many people."

Her dinner churned in her stomach at the thought.

Andrew nudged her shoulder. "You were saying I was right about something else?"

Thankful for the change in subject, she said, "It's possible Lily is having some kind of dissociative episodes."

He turned to face her. "I've heard that word. Isn't that…what do they call it? Multiple personality disorder?"

"The proper name is dissociative identity disorder, but that's the most extreme example. There's no evidence that Lily is suffering from that, but you could be right that she's moving my things and not aware she's doing it. I'll have to do more research to figure it out."

"Should she see a counselor? Would the state pay for that?"

"Oh, I don't know." She hated that she hadn't told him the truth about her relationship with Lily, but telling him she'd kidnapped the girl would only make him an accomplice.

"So you think she moved your laptop but doesn't know she did it?" Andrew clarified.

"She seemed genuinely perplexed this morning when I told her where I'd found it, almost afraid."

"Where'd you find it?"

"It was sitting on the kitchen counter."

The sun had set now, and it was hard to read his expression. In the gathering darkness, he said, "And there's no way somebody else came in and..." But his words trailed. "Obviously nobody broke into your house, borrowed your laptop, then broke in again to return it."

A shudder slid down Grace's spine. "Way to creep me out."

He chuckled and rubbed her upper back. "Sorry. You're safe here. Did you check the footage on your video doorbells?"

"I will now." She put amusement in her tone, but Andrew seemed serious. "You don't really think somebody broke in, do you?"

"No, of course not." He was quiet a moment, then added, "But it probably wouldn't hurt to have a look at those videos occasionally, just to be on the safe side."

She glanced at the videos every time her phone alerted her to someone's presence at her door. In the front, it was usually Andrew or somebody who crossed by her door a little too close. In the back, it was usually one of the cats that roamed the neighborhood, if not Oliver wanting in.

"Thanks again for installing those. They make me feel safer."

He slid his hand across her back and squeezed her shoulder. "Anything to keep you around a little longer."

She was in no hurry to leave Coventry. Eventually, she'd solve the mystery of Lily's past, find her grandmother, maybe even her mother. Eventually, she'd return the child to her family. And then, if she didn't end up in prison for kidnapping, maybe she and Andrew could have a future together.

She was afraid to hope, afraid to surrender to the feelings that were growing daily. But could she truly learn to love him?

She didn't know. She didn't know if she'd ever be whole enough to fully love anybody with the kind of love she'd heard about, the kind that changed lives. The kind that saved. She wanted to try, though. For Andrew, even for Lily...They were worth her effort.

"I've been meaning to ask you," she said. "Did you find what you were looking for in your father's company books?"

He groaned and dropped his head gently to where it rested against hers. "Unfortunately."

"What does that mean?"

He straightened but didn't back away. "Somebody's been embezzling."

"Oh, no. Your brother?"

His shoulders lifted and fell. "I don't have enough access to know the answer to that. Somebody will have to look at where the money went."

"How much?"

"If my math is correct"—she had no doubt it was—"then a little over eighty-five thousand."

She sat back. "Are you kidding me?"

"I wish I were."

"And you think Chet...?" Her words trailed as she remembered the half brother she'd met at the party, the impressions she'd gotten when she'd touched his palm. His dominant emotions had been loathing and fear.

Not greed, but had that lingered below the surface?

She hadn't hung onto his hand long enough to know. What she knew about Chet—both her impressions when they'd shaken hands and what she'd witnessed as he'd interacted with Andrew—didn't exactly inspire confidence. She wouldn't be surprised to find he'd been embezzling. She wished now she'd hung on longer. Maybe she could offer Andrew some insight.

Not that she should, but her loyalty definitely lay with Andrew.

He was watching her closely. Though his face was in shadow, hers was angled toward the lights surrounding the playground equipment, so he'd probably seen some of her thoughts in her expression.

"What do *you* think?" he asked. "Has Chet been stealing from our father?"

"I don't know, honestly."

"But it wouldn't surprise you."

"That doesn't mean anything. He's not your biggest fan."

"You don't have to have mind-reading superpowers to know that. But what else?"

"Nothing really. At their core, people are generally motivated by fear or love. Love in the general love-thy-neighbor sense, you know?"

He nodded.

"That's rare. Most people are more motivated by fear. In Chet, I definitely picked up fear. That doesn't mean he's stealing."

Andrew watched her another moment, then turned again to the playground. Grace should really get Lily inside and to bed, but she hated to end the evening—for Lily, whose giggles carried across the park—and for herself.

"It's very...ironic."

She turned to Andrew, trying to figure out what he was referring to. Had she missed something?

"I need to tell you something," he said. "You've been very honest with me about your past, and I need to do the same."

She hadn't been all that honest, not about the important things, but she settled for saying, "Okay."

"But first, I have another confession. I hope you're not angry with me for this. Or Cassidy."

Her friend's name twinged a nerve in her spine, and she sat up. "What about Cassidy?"

"After I left you last night, I went to see her." He ran a hand over his head. "Maybe I shouldn't have. I was concerned about our...interactions last night. I wondered if maybe she could shed some light on you, on why you might hesitate to get involved."

Grace was almost afraid to ask what he'd learned.

"She told me about Celia."

"Oh." She turned away, facing the playground but not really seeing it. The mention of the child's name still brought grief and shame, no matter how much time had passed.

Grace should have stayed after it happened. She should have faced it. She definitely should have talked through it with a counselor. Knowing what to do and doing it were two very different things.

"I'm sorry," he said. "I shouldn't have dug into your past. I was just feeling a little...desperate, honestly. Don't be angry with Cassidy. We both care about you. She was just—"

"I'm not angry. It's okay that you know."

"Do you want to talk about it?"

She shook her head. "Another time, maybe. It's just...it still feels so heavy."

"I'm sure it does." His words were slow and measured when he added, "You know it wasn't your fault."

"It was my job to bring her back from that dark place. I loved her the very best I could, and it wasn't enough."

"Sometimes, people are beyond rescuing. Sometimes, people are simply too broken."

"I wasn't."

He shifted to face her better, seemed to be waiting for her to continue.

So she did. "When my mother left me at the girls home, I was heartbroken. I felt like I would never recover. I felt unlovable. I mean, if my own mother didn't love me, why would anybody?"

Andrew he leaned closer and trailed his fingers down a lock of her hair, then down her arm until his hand settled on her elbow.

"But Mama Lucy loved me so well. Her love healed me. It saved me."

"She sounds amazing. I'm glad you had her."

"I wish Celia had had her. But Mama Lucy has health problems. She'd had to take a step back during that time for a surgery, then a long recovery. She left me in charge. I did my very best. I loved Celia—all the girls—the best I could. It just wasn't enough."

"You can't take that on yourself. You aren't the one who harmed that girl."

"You don't understand. I loved her, and I failed. Love is supposed to save, Andrew. My love was useless."

Andrew's head tilted to the side. "Your love—no one's love—will ever be that powerful, Grace. You can do your very best, love with all your heart, but people get to decide how to live, how to respond. Besides, your love doesn't save. God's love saves. We're made in His image, of course. But you don't have the power He has. You don't have the power to save."

"You don't understand."

That tender hand on her arm squeezed. "I think maybe *you* don't understand. You were never meant to save anybody. All you can do is walk with God and pray He does the work. If you think you're supposed to be that powerful, you're going to be disappointed. Every time."

Could that be true?

Was it possible that she wasn't supposed to be that powerful? She'd been given the gift—or curse—of being able to know more about people than most. But that wasn't a superpower. And even if it were, it didn't give her any power but understanding.

Maybe Mama Lucy's great power was her ability to love, but even she lost girls sometimes.

None to suicide, but plenty of girls left the home and returned to their lives on the street. More than one girl had thrown Mama Lucy's love in her face and stormed out the door.

Mama Lucy just kept loving.

Whereas, when Celia took her own life, Grace had run away.

"Here's another thing to think about," Andrew said. "God's love does save, and people reject it, and reject Him, every single day. Why would you expect different results?"

As the truth settled on her, the burden she'd carried for years dissolved and blew away on the cool autumn breeze.

When she focused on the man beside her, she saw his lips tip up in a smile and realized he was responding to hers. "You're beautiful when you're angry with me, but when you're happy"—he shook his head—"wow."

ONE OF LILY'S FRIENDS' moms approached the playground carrying a covered plate. Grace couldn't hear what she said, but Lily solved the mystery when she ran over. "Mrs. O'Donnell brought cookies. Can I have one? She says they're oatmeal raisin, so they're healthy."

"Just one," Grace said. "And you have ten more minutes."

Lily skipped back to the playground and accepted the treat. The girls settled on the merry-go-round to eat, and Mrs. O'Donnell wandered over to talk to the other parents at the playground.

Still feeling the glow after Andrew's compliment, and maybe after their conversation about Celia, Grace settled back against the picnic table.

"I was in prison for six months."

She snapped her attention back to him. If he'd told her he'd spent a semester on the moon, she wouldn't have been more surprised.

"Embezzlement." He let that hang in the air a moment. "I've been meaning to tell you, but it doesn't exactly come up in conversation.

"I didn't know what I was doing. My supervisor asked me for help with some accounting and offered to pay me overtime. More than overtime—way more than my per-hour wage, which he justified by saying I was doing more than I usually did in the job. Which was true.

"I was in financial trouble. Dad had cut me off, and I was struggling to put myself through school already. And then I started gambling. Sports betting. Football. I made a bunch of good bets, and then...That's how it happens. Beginner's luck turns south fast. I dug myself a hole, and the hole kept getting bigger. I was too embarrassed—prideful, I guess—to ask Dad for help. I told my boss, and he offered me the side gig, and I jumped at the chance to make the money I needed and help out my boss, maybe be considered for similar opportunities in the future. It was just a college job with an investment firm, but I was ambitious." His lips quirked. "I guess you knew that part already."

She stayed silent, unwilling to interrupt the flow of words.

"I had no idea that I was helping my supervisor cover for his stealing." Andrew took a breath while she processed what he'd said so far.

"The owner of the company figured it out." Andrew's voice took on a hard edge. "All the changes to the books had been made on my computer, with my login. I told the truth from the very start —that I'd done it at my boss's behest. He claimed I'd done it myself, and he'd figured it out after the fact. But he didn't turn me in, which made him an accessory at best. They checked both our accounts. I'd deposited the three grand. He'd deposited nothing in his checking account, but investigators found an offshore account.

"The DA didn't believe his story, but he didn't believe mine either. Both of us were convicted. And then, approximately five months and twenty-four days later, my sentence was overturned. My boss grew a conscience in prison, I guess. He admitted he'd lied to me. Which made me an idiot, but not a criminal."

In the darkness, she couldn't see his face and wanted to find some way to comfort him, to connect with him. But she stayed quiet to let him finish.

When he did, she heard a hint of amusement in his voice. "Not great for my pride, but by the time I stepped out of prison, my pride had been stomped pretty thoroughly." He turned to face her. "So, now you know."

"I cannot imagine how horrible that must have been. How long was your original sentence?"

"Three years. I might've gotten out early on good behavior.

Probably would have. But still, there's nothing like being trapped behind bars. It's...torture."

"I'm so sorry that happened to you."

He shrugged it off. "It's part of my story. My faith had been pretty paltry before prison. There's nothing like the cold, hard slam of steel doors to get the knees of the arrogant to hit the floor."

"You don't strike me as arrogant."

"If you knew me then..."

He let the words hang, still with that hint of amusement she appreciated, considering the gravity of the situation.

He turned back to the kids on the playground. She sensed he had more to say and waited. After a minute, he spoke. "I'd planned to be a physician, but I got kicked out of my premed program."

"You would have been so good at that. Why not transfer to a different school? There had to be a way."

"Believe it or not, that was one of the good things that came out of it. I realize now that I wouldn't have been happy as a physician. I love what I do, working with BNB, helping to bring innovation to the world of medicine. It's the perfect marriage of the things I love —biochemistry, technology, and business. So, even though prison was awful, I can't let myself regret it. The Lord used it."

"I love that attitude."

"Well, it's not like I'm ready to do it again or anything. In fact, I'd say my biggest fear is ending up behind bars."

She thought back to the times they'd been in the car together. The drive from Coventry to his father's house, the drive in Texas from the airport to Freedom Hill. Both times, cars had been whipping past, but he'd stubbornly kept to the speed limit. Now she understood. It wasn't just cautious driving. It was a desire not to get pulled over. Not to have a run-in with the police.

She wondered what Andrew had been like before the arrest. A risk-taker, if the gambling were any indication. He was still that, but she guessed that now his risks were more calculated, only taken after careful consideration. They weren't foolish or without purpose. And they were always legal.

"I'd only change one thing," he said. "My relationship with my father. He was so ashamed, so embarrassed by what happened. Our relationship had been rocky already, and my conviction only made it worse. Years later, and I'm still trying to heal it. And telling my dad that his favorite son is also guilty—"

"Ah. I see the problem."

"Not that it would be better to discover his son is incompetent."

"When are you going to tell him?"

"We're meeting in Concord for lunch tomorrow. The timing is terrible, but the prospective employees arrive Friday, so it's either tomorrow or next week."

"You can't carry that burden all weekend. You're wise to get it taken care of immediately." Grace's heart hurt for Andrew. All he wanted was to repair the rift with his father, and this was likely to make it worse.

Her hand itched to hold his, to feel what he was feeling. If she did, she would only be drawn closer to him, closer, when for days she'd been telling herself she should keep her distance. But she didn't want to do that. She didn't want to play it safe. She didn't want to run away from this relationship. Maybe he was right about love, that human love was imperfect. Maybe, despite her past and her mother's rejection and her stepfather's lust and Celia's suicide, maybe that part of her wasn't irreversibly broken.

Maybe she could learn to love like a normal person.

She slid her fingers over the back of his hand.

His gaze snapped to hers and held.

"Do you mind?" she asked.

He flipped his wrist, and she slid her palm against his.

Andrew was brave, braver than any man she'd ever known. He wasn't afraid of baring himself to her. He wasn't afraid of anything. She felt that fearlessness, despite what he'd told her. She felt the despair he remembered from prison. She felt the disappointment he'd picked up from his father time and again.

And then the feelings shifted. She felt his connection to her.

His desire. His love.

Reluctantly, she pulled her hand away from his, and his feelings receded. But they were replaced by hers, which were the same. Too much the same.

Andrew lifted that same hand and slid it against her neck, letting his fingers play in her hair. His voice was rough when he said, "Grace."

She leaned toward him, eager to feel his lips against hers again.

But the sounds of the laughter on the playground had her leaning away.

He groaned. She probably did too as he removed his hand from her skin and faced the children, then dropped his head back.

She bumped his shoulder with hers. "You okay?"

"You're killing me."

"Sorry. Unintentional. And reciprocal."

In the light from the lamp near the playground, she watched a smile spread across his face. "That does soften the blow."

They sat in silence for a few moments, but she couldn't put it off any longer. "I really need to get her home."

"I know. I've kept you out past curfew."

She started to stand, but he stopped her with a light grip to her forearm.

"Thank you. For listening to my story and not judging me too harshly."

"Nothing to judge."

He didn't loosen his hold. "And for trusting me enough to take my hand."

She did trust him. And the more she touched him, the more she trusted him. Her initial guess about Andrew was correct. He was a good and kind man.

"I think you had to trust me more," she said.

"I'm not afraid of you, Grace. I'm not afraid of you knowing... everything. I trust you with myself."

She wanted to be as trustworthy—as plain old *worthy*—as he seemed to think she was. She just didn't know if she had it in her.

CHAPTER TWENTY-FOUR

ANDREW PARKED at the far end of the restaurant's lot, in no rush to get inside. The low clouds overhead felt dark and foreboding, which he knew wasn't a harbinger of how his lunch with his father would go, even if it felt like it.

What emotions would Grace pick up if she were to take his hand now? Definitely not the hope and desire he'd felt the night before. But then, he wasn't about to enjoy lunch with the woman he was falling in love with.

Nope. He'd be sharing a table with Dad.

His phone had dinged with an incoming text during the drive, but Andrew hadn't dared to look. Texting and driving wasn't just dangerous, it was illegal. Now, he glanced at the screen.

Praying for you. Call me when you can.

That Grace, in the midst of all she was dealing with, had thought to text him—and pray for him—soothed his nerves. Whatever happened with Dad, he'd still have Grace when this lunch was over.

He grabbed his laptop case and made his way to the door.

It was a fancier restaurant than he would have chosen, but when he stepped inside, he understood why Dad had picked it. The tables were spread far enough apart that he and his father would have a modicum of privacy. The music being piped in over-head was barely audible. It was a white-tablecloth, crystal-glasses sort of place, a good place for a business lunch and a serious conversation. As much as Andrew might like to consider his relationship with his father otherwise, it was, at this point, mostly business.

Though Dad's kindness at the birthday party, the use of the jet...There was hope for more. Assuming Dad could forgive Andrew for the information he had to share.

Dad was seated on the far end of the large room beside a flickering fire in the hearth. He'd always seemed to take up more space than his five-nine, narrow-shouldered stature would suggest. But looking at him now, one would never guess he was a multimillionaire. One would never guess he ran a company that employed thousands. No, at that moment, Dad seemed like any other man. A father, a husband, a brother, a friend.

Truly, his money and success didn't make him better than others, even if people saw him that way.

Maybe Drew Middleton didn't deserve the pedestal people put him on because of his success, but he was Andrew's father. Much as he hated to admit it—probably wouldn't to another living soul—Andrew craved his admiration. He craved his affection.

As Andrew approached, Dad stood and held out his hand. "Son."

Andrew shook it, glancing at the half-full soda glass on the table. "I hope you haven't waited long."

"Traffic was light."

Andrew set his bag on the floor beside his chair. Dad was silent while Andrew studied the menu. When the server approached, he asked for iced tea. Before the woman left, Dad asked, "You ready to order?"

Apparently, they wouldn't be lingering. Andrew shouldn't have been surprised. "Prime rib and baked potato. Caesar to start."

Dad ordered the eight-ounce filet. After the woman walked away, he offered a wry smile. "Christine's got me on this diet.

Prime rib is not exactly a lean protein. I'd cheat, but she'll ask, and if I fudge, she'll figure me right out. I can't get away with anything with her."

Unfortunately, Andrew's mother hadn't been as good at discerning truth from lies. Andrew kept the thought to himself, rather ashamed he'd even had it. His parents had been divorced a long time. Mom had gotten over Dad's betrayal. Andrew needed to do the same.

But there was some primal protective instinct in a boy toward his mother, an instinct Andrew had never been able to squelch. Which accounted for at least a little of the animosity between himself and the man watching him from the far side of the table.

Watching him as if he'd guessed his thoughts.

Andrew returned to their thread of conversation. "Is there some health issue behind that diet?"

"Nothing to worry about."

That wasn't exactly an answer. He kept his gaze steady and waited for Dad to expound on that remark.

Dad sipped his soda and set it back down. "Blood pressure's a little higher than it should be. Cholesterol's above the normal range. They put me on blood pressure meds. They want to put me on a statin, but we decided"—by the way he emphasized the word *we,* Andrew figured Christine had made the decision for both of them—"that I should try to exercise and eat healthier and see if that brings the cholesterol down."

"You've been exercising?" Despite the workout equipment in their house, Andrew had never known his father to so much as walk around the block.

"I've been getting on that stupid elliptical thing. Feels so pointless, doing all that work and getting nowhere."

Andrew didn't bother to fight the smile. So like Dad to see it that way. "I'm glad you're following the doctor's orders."

"More like Christine's orders." He snatched a roll from the basket in the center of the table. He lifted it between them. "This'll be our little secret."

Andrew wasn't about to tattle to his stepmother about Dad's eating habits. He already had enough tattling to do that day.

Dad buttered the roll, took a bite, and set it on his bread plate. "I assume you have information for me."

Andrew took his time buttering his own roll, then taking a bite. He'd hoped they could at least enjoy part of their meal before getting to the reason for their meeting.

"Why did you ask me to look into this?"

His father sat back, eyes squinting. A long silence pressed between them before the server delivered Andrew's tea and set a fresh glass of cola on the table for Dad.

"Be right back with those salads," she said, turning away.

When she was out of earshot, Dad said, "What did you find out?"

Apparently, Andrew wasn't going to get an answer. Fine, then. He wasn't responsible for the results he'd found. He reached into his bag and pulled out the report he'd written up. Setting it on his lap, he met his father's eyes. "Somebody's been skimming off the top. Over the last eighteen months, he—or she—has taken a little over eighty-five thousand dollars."

Though Dad's expression barely shifted, Andrew didn't miss the tightening in the skin around his mouth, the slight widening of his eyes.

After a moment, Andrew continued. "It started small, a couple thousand here and there. But over time, the discrepancies grew. The biggest came in August of this year. Over the course of the month, just under seventeen thousand dollars were...redirected out of company accounts. Or...I'm making some logical jumps here. The money came in—the records show that. But when the totals were transferred to monthly books, they were smaller. Somewhere between the daily bookkeeping and the monthly records, money is being shifted." Which was just one of the many, many reasons companies used electronic software. And maybe the reason Chet hadn't converted his department to the software yet.

Andrew held the report across the table.

Dad stared at it as if it might sting to touch. But then, he snatched it and read.

Andrew sipped his tea, ate his bread, and tried to ignore the anxiety rising up his spine and tightening the muscles in his neck.

"Here you go." The server appeared carrying two salads. "Caesar"—she plopped one plate in front of Andrew—"and garden, Italian on the side."

Dad nodded to the empty place at the end of the table, and she set it there.

"Anything else?" she asked.

"No, thank you." Andrew added a smile, hoping his kindness made up for his father's brusque dismissal.

Dad had barely looked up from the report.

Andrew tossed his dressing with the salad, then forked and ate a bite.

It tasted fine, not that he could concentrate on the cool lettuce and salty dressing.

In his pocket, his phone vibrated, and he was happy for the distraction. He glanced at the screen and saw another text from Grace. *Still praying.*

She had perfect timing. He set the phone on the table. He'd prayed about this meeting for days. Whatever happened, he wouldn't be afraid. He had a Father who loved him no matter what, whether the man sitting across the table did or not.

Finally, Dad traded the report for the salad. "What's your best guess?"

"I don't have enough information to make an assumption." Andrew set his fork down and slid his hand around his cold glass. "All I have is what Chet gave me. I don't know where money was transferred to or even if it was. For all I know, that missing money is in a company account. For all I know, I uncovered bookkeeping errors."

"You don't believe that."

Andrew didn't flinch. "No. I don't."

"You think it's Chet."

Dad spoke the words as a statement.

Rather than respond, Andrew repeated his question from earlier. "Why would you ask me to look into this? You have an entire accounting department filled with very smart people, any one of whom could have found this information. Why not have one of them, or even Harrison, dig into the numbers? He's your CFO. Surely you can trust him."

Dad held his gaze over the table a moment, then looked at the flames in the fireplace beside them.

"Here's how I see it." Andrew leaned toward his dad. "Either Chet is guilty of embezzling company funds, or he's guilty of being monumentally stupid, allowing somebody else to do so. First or second, I don't know, but...Why me, Dad? We already have enough bad blood—"

"I knew I could trust you." Dad swallowed hard, his Adam's apple bobbing. "You and your brother have history, I know that. And I guessed you might find out something like this."

Andrew sat back, resisting the urge to cross his arms. Instead, he lifted his chin, preparing for whatever blow was about to come.

"Our relationship"—Dad motioned between them—"wasn't ever all that great, and it's only gotten worse."

Leave it to Dad to label it like he saw it.

"And you hate that," Dad continued.

Andrew felt more exposed under his father's knowing gaze than he had the night before when he'd held Grace's hand. Maybe because he trusted Grace wouldn't use her insights against him. He had no such confidence in his father.

Dad leaned forward, expression softening. "I hate it too, son. I hate it. I just don't know what to do about it."

"Maybe don't pit me against my brother. Don't throw us in a ring to watch us fight to the death."

Dad flinched as if he'd struck him. "Not what I was trying to do."

"Really?" He heard the skepticism in his tone and snapped his jaw shut.

Dad's voice was low when he spoke again. "Because you're trying to repair our relationship, I knew I could trust you. You have nothing to gain by making your brother look bad—or good, for that matter. Make him look bad, you risk damaging our already fragile relationship. Make him look good, you risk...well, making your enemy look good." The corners of Dad's lips tipped up, but the expression never quite turned into a smile. "You have no vested interest in the company except for what you'll eventually inherit. And you never seemed to care all that much about that."

Andrew cared, more than he'd ever admitted. Not because of the money but because it was his father's legacy. Back when Andrew had decided not to work for the family business, Dad had cut him off. At that point, Andrew had been convinced he'd inherit nothing. He'd been so furious, so desperate to prove to his father that he was worthy of him, that he'd caused himself all sorts of problems. Without his father's money, he'd had to figure out how to make his own way. He'd worked, he'd gambled, he'd gotten into ridiculous debt. He'd behaved like an idiot who didn't deserve his father's money.

Not that it was about *deserving*. Did a son really have to earn his father's love?

But he couldn't make his father love him. God help him, deep down, he'd always wanted that love, but he'd never been able to earn it.

Neither had Mom, no matter how hard she'd tried to keep the marriage together.

The thought of not inheriting any of the business, any of Dad's money...It had hurt him. In prison, he'd come to terms with it all. He'd learned to lean into his Heavenly Father's love.

But after Andrew's sentence had been overturned, his record expunged, Dad had relented on his vow to disinherit him just because Andrew refused to walk the path Dad had expected.

Andrew'd never counted on getting an equal share with his brother and sisters. And he didn't care. Or, at least, he tried not to. Chet, Angela, and Kate were the children of the favored wife.

They would inherit the bulk of Dad's estate, and that was fine with Andrew.

But Dad was right about one thing—Andrew cared very deeply about the distance that had grown between them. He wanted to repair it, not toss a grenade into the chasm and blow it to smithereens.

"You two still working on those salads?"

Dad hadn't touched his, but he pushed the plate away. After Andrew's quick, "we're finished," she lifted the plates off the table.

When she was gone, Dad settled his hands in his lap and leaned forward. "I didn't ask anybody else to look into MBC's numbers for obvious reasons. Chet's my son. He doesn't have the greatest reputation already, and I didn't want to put anybody in the position of having to tell me what they'd learned."

"Even Harrison?"

Dad's lips pursed. He shook his head but added no comment.

Was there some tension between Dad and his CFO? As long as Andrew could remember, they'd been the best of friends, sharing everything. Maybe that had changed.

"But you had no such qualms about putting *me* in that position."

"You don't want anything from me. Never have. You have no reason to lie to me." Dad's voice dropped an octave. "I trust you."

The truth of it settled deep. Andrew tried to be trustworthy, to live his life aboveboard. Since the false conviction, he'd done everything in his power to be a man of integrity.

And Dad had noticed. He tapped the report. "I trust your results."

"Now that you have them," Andrew asked, "what will you do?"

Dad leaned back and held his gaze a long moment. Then, he reached into his suit coat and pulled something out, which he held across the table. "I'm going to ask you for another favor."

Andrew groaned. "Please don't."

"Maybe it's Chet." Dad didn't break eye contact. "Maybe it's somebody else in his department. Maybe it's somebody else completely. If money's being transferred out, this should show where it's going."

Eyeing the flash drive, Andrew said, "You already knew what I was going to find."

"I guessed."

"You knew enough to bring that."

Dad didn't respond.

"What happens if I find out Chet's stealing from you."

"I'll fire him and send him on his way."

"No prison for the golden boy?"

Dad's hand dropped to the table. He looked wounded. "I would never send him to prison. And I'd have done anything in my power to protect you from that, whether you'd stolen from me or somebody else. I *did* do everything in my power. I just failed."

Dad had hired the best lawyers available. Unfortunately, the DA and the judge hadn't been convinced by Andrew's story. With his supervisor's lies and Andrew's fingerprints all over the records, the evidence had been overwhelming.

Dad's quiet, "At first," seemed to be an afterthought, spoken beneath his breath.

"At first?" Andrew asked. "What does that mean?"

Dad looked chagrined as he shrugged. "Nothing."

Andrew studied him, considered the words, realized what it meant. But it couldn't be true. Could it? He leaned forward. "Dad?"

He cleared his throat, straightened his fork and knife. "I might've had something to do with your boss changing his story."

"Telling the truth, you mean."

Dad's head bobbed, but he didn't seem fully convinced. Andrew would never know if Dad believed he'd been an unwitting pawn or an active participant in the embezzlement. He wished his father knew him well enough to know he'd never steal from anyone, but as Dad had said, they'd never been that close.

"I paid the guy a visit." His voice was rough and low.

"You didn't threaten him?" The thought of it had Andrew's

insides twisting. He had no affection for the man who'd tried to shift the blame to him, but he hated to think of his father sinking so low. And threatening somebody to get them to change a testimony —that couldn't be legal.

"Of course not. I just suggested that his kids might have a little more going for them if he did the right thing."

"You paid him off?"

"I offered him an incentive to change his tune."

When Andrew gave him a hard stare, Dad sighed and added, "I promised to pay off his house and start a college fund for his girls. He saw the benefit in coming clean."

Andrew was stunned. Dad held his eye contact across the table, unblinking. Too many emotions to name bounced in Andrew's brain. Shock, definitely. A hint of irritation that Dad had felt the need to step in and rescue him.

But Andrew had needed rescuing.

The irritation faded almost before he realized it was there.

"I don't understand," Andrew finally said. "Why didn't you say something? Why keep it a secret?"

Dad lifted one shoulder. "Truth is, I had people encouraging me not to do it. People who thought you'd gotten what you deserved."

"Christine, or—?"

"No, no. If it'd been up to her, she'd have had me make the offer before the conviction. I was so sure you'd be acquitted. I should have, though. I should've contacted your boss long before I did. As it was, it took months to get the sentence overturned. Thinking of you in that place…"

Andrew would have to process all his father was saying later. That his first emotion hadn't been shame or embarrassment. That he'd cared that much.

But right then, he wanted more details. "I know Chet didn't lose sleep over me being in jail."

"Not that I would have listened to his advice. And it doesn't matter now. I ignored everyone and did what I knew was right."

Everyone.

But the only person who held sway with Dad besides Christine was Harrison Ackerman. He must've been the one campaigning against Dad's getting involved.

Which meant, as kind as the man was, the person he'd called *Uncle Harrison* all his life must have thought Andrew was guilty as charged.

Andrew didn't even care, because Dad had gone against his oldest friend's advice and gotten Andrew's lying, conniving boss to change his story.

And probably then used his considerable influence to get the DA and the judge to agree to having the conviction overturned and Andrew's record expunged.

"Thank you." Andrew looked down to get his emotions under control. Swallowed and cleared his throat so they wouldn't fill his voice. When he looked up, he spoke again. "I had no idea, Dad. I thought his conscience just...I don't know how to...You saved my life."

The server with terrible timing returned and set their steaks on the table. "You two need anything else?"

Andrew couldn't force himself to speak.

Dad said, "Looks great. Thanks."

She faded away, and Dad set his hands on his lap and regarded Andrew across the table. "I did what any good father would do for a son he loves."

OF COURSE, Andrew had taken the flash drive and promised his father he'd try to figure out where the money had gone. How could he not, after what he'd learned?

He hadn't been overstating things when he'd thanked his father for saving his life.

Maybe Andrew's physical life hadn't been on the line, but in every other way, Dad had saved him. Why he'd kept that secret,

Andrew had no idea, but he was glad Dad had chosen to tell him the truth.

Unfortunately, as he'd explained to Dad after they'd finished their steaks, he wouldn't be able to look at the information on the flash drive until the following week. His life would be too busy between then and Sunday to do anything but hang on for the ride.

Once he settled in his car after lunch, he dialed Grace, but her voicemail picked up.

"It went really well," he said to the recording. "I can't wait to tell you about it. I'm headed to the office. Maybe I can stop by tonight?"

Despite the afternoon filled with last-minute issues and unexpected problems regarding the conference, Andrew's spirits stayed high. It was after six by the time he wrapped up for the day. Jacqui had left at five thirty. She made a concerted effort to be home for dinner with Reid and Ella every evening, no matter what was going on at the lab.

He admired how she always put her family first. Much as Dad loved Chet, Angela, and Kate, Andrew'd never seen that type of commitment toward them. When Andrew had been forced to spend time at his father's when he was a kid, Dad was rarely home for family dinner. Often, he wasn't home before Christine ushered them all to bed.

He thought of the family he'd like to have one day, the woman, maybe even the daughter. Maybe Lily's family wouldn't want her back. Maybe he and Grace could adopt her. And then add more to their brood, a child of their own.

He was getting ahead of himself. Way ahead.

But he'd make it happen. The more he thought on it, the more he was sure Grace was the woman he wanted. Forever. If Lily came with the package, even better.

Andrew shut down his computer, grabbed his laptop bag, and knocked on Braden's office door.

Braden waved him in, pulled his attention away from his laptop, and looked up. "Everything on track?"

"They start arriving tomorrow afternoon. Everyone should be there for the cocktail party. I'm looking forward to getting your feedback."

Braden tapped a stack of papers beside him. "Printed the résumés so we'll have them on hand. I'll be making notes. Hopefully, the people we like will be interested in moving to New Hampshire and are not just coming for the free vacation."

"We should know pretty quickly." That was the risk of the weekend, that they'd spend a lot of money to wine and dine people who had no desire to move to the mountains. But it was a risk worth taking. "Even if they only come for the weekend getaway, if we do this right, they'll at least consider what it would be like to live here."

"Agreed. You've done a great job putting it together. If they all don't want to pack their U-Hauls by Sunday, then it was never meant to be."

"Your idea," Andrew said.

Braden shrugged. "Which you brought to life way better than I ever would have." He shut down his computer and stood. "Leaving?"

They walked out together. They were halfway across the lot when Braden said, "You haven't said how it went with your father."

Andrew gave him an update, the joy of what he'd learned that day seeping into his voice.

Braden clapped him on the back. "He got you out of jail? That's something, man."

"I know." Andrew was still wrapping his head around it. "I'm not exactly looking forward to digging into the financials, but at least I don't have to worry about what I'm going to find."

"Maybe you'll be able to get Chet out of your dad's company permanently."

Andrew considered that, then shook his head. "Honestly, at this point, I hope he hasn't been stealing. For Dad's sake. I mean, even if he has, it's been going on right under his nose. That's an issue. But if I were Dad, I'd much rather find out my son's incompetent than learn he's a criminal."

"Either way, he's incompetent," Braden said. "I mean, if he's stealing, someone with half a brain would have been better about hiding it."

Andrew considered that, nodding. "The numbers will prove what they prove."

They reached Andrew's BMW first, and Braden leaned against the hood. "And Grace?" His eyebrows lifted, his amusement unmistakable.

"She's good. More than good." He didn't even bother to hide his smile.

"That's awesome. I can't wait to meet her."

"She'll be there Saturday night."

She was going to fit in perfectly. He had no doubt.

Back when Andrew'd been languishing in prison, he'd wondered if he'd ever get to live the life of his dreams. If he'd ever have a job he loved and friends he could confide in. He'd hardly had the courage to dream about a woman to share his home, his future, his bed.

God had been so good to him.

As he drove home, he felt lighter, freer than he had in years. Thanks to his conversation with his father, thanks to his friendship with Braden and the rest of the guys he'd met in Coventry, thanks to Grace, Andrew felt incredibly blessed and completely secure in a way he hadn't since he was a child.

Andrew and Grace had decided to meet at The Patriot for dinner. Shelby, Fitz's sister, planned to stop by to introduce herself so Grace would feel more comfortable leaving Lily with her.

He stepped into the restaurant to find Grace already there. He kissed her cheek before sliding into the booth across from her. A glass of iced tea waited for him.

She nodded toward it. "Hope that's okay."

"Perfect. Where's Lily?"

Grace tipped her chin toward the back of the restaurant. Reid and Jacqui sat across from each other in a booth. At a table a few feet away, Lily and Ella were bent over a screen, giggling.

"Soon as we walked in, Ella beelined over here. Reid and Jacqui don't seem to mind."

"I'm sure." In fact, they seemed to be enjoying having a minute to talk without Ella's constant chatter.

Grace returned her attention to him. "I'm glad it went well with your dad. Tell me what happened."

He filled her in on the meal he'd shared with his father and what he'd learned about his conviction being overturned.

"Your father did that? And never told you?"

"I know, it's strange that he kept it a secret from me."

"Wow, though. That's...wow. He must really care for you."

Andrew was beginning to believe that for the first time in a long time. "I think his friend—you met him. Harrison Ackerman?"

"I remember."

"I think he advised against helping me. Maybe Dad kept it quiet because he didn't want to have to defend his actions. I appreciate how Harrison is always thinking of Middleton Enterprises, and it's possible he thought my association with the company had already done enough damage."

The server came by and took their orders. He shouldn't be as hungry as he was after that huge lunch, but he'd picked up the scent of the fish and chips when he'd walked in the door. After Grace asked for a grilled chicken salad and homemade potato chips, plus a kid's macaroni and cheese for Lily, he ordered his meal.

Andrew pushed his unanswered questions to the back of his mind. He'd take them back out when he had time to examine them. "Dad kept it from me, and I'm guessing from Harrison and the management team. He didn't explicitly tell me to keep quiet about it, but I won't be making any public statements." Maybe he shouldn't have told Braden, but Braden wouldn't share the news.

"I won't tell anybody."

"You already know I trust you." He let that settle a beat, then said, "Any news from Ruby?"

She sighed. "She says Darla hasn't called her back yet, which is unusual. If she doesn't hear from her tomorrow, she'll call her brother. She did let where Ruby lives slip, mentioning how they always went to the Galleria when she visited. I looked it up. It's an oversize mall in Dallas. Of course, that's a huge metropolitan area, but at least it narrows it down."

"With that information, we should be able to track her down whether Ruby calls you back or not. I bet Dylan could..."

But Grace was shaking her head. "If we have to go that route, we can, but I'd rather wait for Ruby."

"Why?" It didn't make sense. They finally had a line on where Lily's grandmother was. Shouldn't Grace be eager to get in touch with her?

But he thought about what that would mean, and understanding dawned. He wrapped his palm around the back of her hand. "I know it'll be hard, but learning the truth, even if it means you have to give her up, won't it be a weight off your shoulders? And hers. I mean, you saw how heartbroken she was when she discovered nobody at that house."

Grace blinked a few times, then looked away. "Yeah. You're right."

"The longer you keep her, the harder it'll be to let her go." Even Andrew hated the idea of saying good-bye to Lily. He couldn't imagine how difficult it would be for Grace. "And maybe you'll find out Darla Springer doesn't want her. Maybe you could adopt her. Why don't you let me call Dylan right now? He helped Braden and Carly out last winter. I'm sure he won't mind helping with this. Finding lost people is his thing."

After a swallow, Grace shook her head. "I told Ruby I'd wait until she called me back. Maybe I'm just putting off the inevitable, but..." She shrugged. "I'm going to put it off one more day."

Andrew squelched his temptation to argue. What Grace had done by taking Lily in, and what she was still doing, trying to keep the child safe—who was he to tell her she was doing it wrong?

He let all his arguments die. "Just let me know."

Grace granted him one of those heart-stopping smiles. The woman didn't smile nearly enough. The more time he spent with her, the more he knew he wanted to keep making her smile as long as he lived.

Crazy to think such a thing about a woman he'd just met. But they'd known each other almost two months at this point. They'd spent a lot of time together. He couldn't imagine anything he could learn now that would change his mind about her.

She held his eye contact. They probably looked like lovesick teenagers to outsiders, but he didn't care.

He cleared his throat, figuring he knew the answer to his next question already. "I assume that means you haven't talked to her social worker yet."

Her eye contact slipped, and she looked up and away and kept her gaze trained on...nothing, as far as he could tell. "I'll do that after I talk to Darla. I just wish I could prove he's a pornographer." She met his eyes again. "No word from your friend?"

"I'll send a text right now." He pulled his phone from his pocket and texted David. No response, but David would get back to him as soon as he had something.

Much as he hated to think what finding images of Lily would mean regarding the sweet little girl, he hoped David would be able to prove Grace's suspicions. Then they could put away Myron for good.

After the server delivered their meals, Grace slid out of the booth and approached Lily's table, chatting first with the child, then with Jacqui and Reid. She returned, said, "She's going to eat with them," and took Lily's dinner and drink to the girls' table.

He was glad for the time alone with Grace, and not just

because, without Lily there, it felt like a real date. The last thing they needed was for Lily to overhear them talking about her so-called father.

Grace settled in and cut her salad into smaller pieces.

"Maybe Dylan could locate Annabeth," Andrew said. "I can see why you want to wait for Ruby to give you Darla's information, but surely they'd both be thrilled to figure out what happened to Lily's mother, regardless of how they came by the information."

Grace didn't look up to make eye contact, but he caught the slight tightening around her mouth.

A gnawing in his gut told him she wasn't saying something. Something he should investigate.

But this was Grace. She'd proved herself trustworthy over and over. And after all she'd done to protect Lily, even abandoning her home to do it, he refused to let suspicion get the better of him.

Before she could speak, he said, "It's okay. Once you hear from Darla, you can figure out what the woman's done to locate her daughter. Heck, maybe she's found her and Ruby doesn't know it."

Grace's smile held less wattage this time when she said, "Yeah, maybe."

"Tell me about where you used to live. I sort of figure it was down closer to Mass, considering you don't know this area very well."

"Oh. Um, yeah. Down by Manchester."

Her vague answer didn't do anything to assuage the suspicion growing in his middle.

When she added, "Goffstown," it didn't help. It sounded as if she'd only just remembered the name of the town where she'd supposedly lived.

What was up with her tonight?

And how did she end up in New Hampshire to begin with? If she'd come to be closer to Cassidy, then why not move immediately to Coventry?

He opened his mouth to ask, but she spoke first.

"Tell me the plan for tomorrow." Her voice was unnaturally perky. *Forced* perky.

Cut it out. What was wrong with him, suspecting her of something? He shook his head to rid it of the weird thoughts that were trying to ruin his night. And his relationship.

"You said something about a cocktail party?" she prompted.

"Yeah." He didn't want to talk about work, but she seemed eager to change the subject. "The hotel will serve drinks and heavy snacks—enough to replace a meal if the guests don't want to go out after. Jacqui's going to get us started, welcome everybody to the event and introduce Braden and myself, then point out the current employees, encouraging the guests to ask them questions. After that, we'll mingle, get to know each other."

"Are you spending the whole weekend there?"

"Unfortunately. It seemed like a good idea for all of us to stay at the hotel when I first proposed the idea. That way, we could be around to mingle with the guests at all hours. I'll hang around the hotel bar, chat up anybody who comes in."

"Have a few drinks?"

"I'm not much of a drinker."

"And Saturday?"

He explained the plans he and the event planner had put together, including a tour of the lab, a cruise on Lake Winnipesaukee, a cocktail party, and a fancy dinner.

"It sounds wonderful," Grace said. "I bet they'll be clamoring to work for BNB."

"That's the goal. That they'll want to work for us, and that they'll tell their friends. We hope to make the weekend an annual event, invite-only, so people consider it a privilege to be considered for employment in our lab."

"Color me impressed." Grace plopped her chin on her hand and gazed at him as if he were some kind of hero instead of the business manager of a small medical research firm.

Looking at the admiration in her eyes, his heart melted.

All his suspicions floated away.

CHAPTER TWENTY-FIVE

GRACE WAS TWENTY-SIX YEARS OLD, and she'd never been on a real date.

She'd been pursued by guys in high school, but she'd never found a single one attractive enough to spend an evening with. She'd had enough experience with boys and men—both personal and as a result of what she felt through other girls—to have little interest. In college, then working at the girls home, she brushed shoulders with men, but not one had ever convinced her to go out with him.

So maybe she didn't know what she was talking about, but this felt like a real date.

More than the birthday party had, perhaps because they'd been surrounded by people that day. And Lily had been with them.

And nothing about the trip to Texas had felt like a date, though romantic feelings had most definitely cropped up on that flight home.

But at that moment, sharing a meal with Andrew without Lily's near-constant presence, she thought perhaps she understood why her girlfriends had talked so much about this dating thing. This was nice.

Very nice.

Andrew took a bite of his fish, then sipped his iced tea and set it down. "Did you look at the video footage from the other night? Confirm nobody's been in your house?"

"Thanks for reminding me. I actually think I broke the back-door one."

His eyebrows lifted. "What happened?"

"The footage showed nothing, just black. I went to see if it was working, and there was a twig wedged in between the doorbell and the siding. A maple leaf was still stuck to the twig, blocking the camera."

Andrew's eyes narrowed. "That's bizarre. How in the world could that have happened?"

"You remember the wind that night. I'm guessing that's the culprit."

His lips pressed together. After a moment, he said, "A twig couldn't have broken the camera, though."

"I think I broke it when I yanked the twig out. The light wouldn't come on, and there's been no video since."

"And you didn't see anything on the recording?"

"Nope. It was dark, and then it was darker."

"Weird. I'll have a look when we get back."

"Thanks." She hated how the broken doorbell camera unnerved her.

"You seem troubled," Andrew said.

She shook her head quickly, laughing to cover her own foolish fear. "I'm fine. It was just a quirky accident with the doorbell. Nothing more."

He started to say something, but a young woman approached the table. She was pretty with a round face, long straight brown hair, and brown eyes. She looked perfectly at ease when she spoke to Andrew. "Mr. Middleton, right?"

He stood. "Hi, Shelby. Call me Andrew. Glad you were able to stop by."

Shelby turned to Grace and held her hand out.

Grace only hesitated a moment before taking it. If she was going to leave Lily with this girl, she needed to know her. When they shook hands, she got strange impressions. Shelby, trapped in a dark place, feeling terror. The image of an older, handsome man was accompanied by pure devotion and love. It was confusing because, though the dark place worried Grace, Shelby seemed open and kind, all her emotions bright and good.

Shelby'd lived through something horrible, but she'd come through it with her heart intact.

Grace could trust this girl.

"I'm Grace. Nice to meet you." She dropped Shelby's hand and scooted over. "Join us."

"Okay."

Shelby slid in beside Grace, who spoke to Andrew. "Go get Lily for us, would you?"

He did, and a moment later, they returned.

Grace and Lily got to know Shelby, who seemed genuinely interested in Lily's stories and answered all of Grace's questions. No red flags were raised.

After visiting for a few minutes, Grace stalled Lily's stream of conversation with a raised hand. "Why don't we let Shelby get on with her evening. You'll be able to talk to her Saturday night."

"Yay! We'll have so much fun!"

Shelby scooted out and stood beside the booth. After smiling at Lily, she turned to Grace. "I was supposed to assure you that Fitz and Tabby will be there all night, too, so there's no need to worry."

"Fitz is your brother, right?"

She nodded. "My parents died when I was a kid, so he's raised me since I was eight."

Ah. That was the man Grace had seen in the vision, the one who made her feel safe. "He must be a great guy," Grace said.

"The best. Super protective, and he takes that seriously. Always told me he became a cop mostly to give him an excuse to carry a sidearm so he could scare away the boys."

Laughing, she tapped her hip, and Grace forced herself to add her own chuckle, but there was nothing lighthearted in it.

Fitz was a cop.

He'd be there, with Lily, all night. What if he started asking questions? Cops knew the right questions to ask. What if he discovered her secret?

Seeing no way to gracefully back out at that moment, she said, "I guess we'll see you Saturday then."

Her gaze flicked to Andrew, and she caught him studying her through squinted eyes.

"Awesome." Shelby high-fived Lily, said good-bye, and walked back out the restaurant's door.

As they finished up their meals and Andrew paid the check, they agreed to meet back at Grace's house so he could look at the video doorbell.

Lily chattered all the way home, but Grace had trouble focusing.

Because Shelby's brother was a cop.

And Andrew had looked more than just curious at the restaurant. He'd looked suspicious.

IT WAS no easy feat settling Lily down after they returned from the restaurant. The child was in a good mood as she bathed and changed clothes, practically bouncing with joy after eating dinner with her "new best friend," Ella. She was even looking forward to going to Shelby's house Saturday night.

Grace hated knowing she was going to have to disappoint her, but there was no way she could leave Lily with Shelby and her cop-brother.

How had she gotten herself into this mess?

All she'd wanted was to keep Lily safe from Myron. She'd accepted that there would be consequences. She'd accepted that she might end up in prison. Her solitary, rather pathetic life hadn't seemed worth fighting for. To sacrifice it to save a little girl? She hadn't thought twice about her decision.

But now she had people she cared about, people who cared about her. People she'd been less than forthright with from the beginning.

She needed to call it what it was. She'd lied to them.

What would they think of her when they learned the truth?

Back in that little cabin, there'd been nobody whose opinion of her mattered. But everything had changed. She hated to consider what Cassidy and James would think about her if they learned she'd kidnapped Lily.

But Cassidy would understand. Cassidy would still love her.

It was Andrew whom Grace was afraid to lose.

How had she gone from living as a hermit to falling in love?

What was she going to do about it?

A little palm slid across her cheek. "Are you listening to the story?"

She smiled at Lily propped on the bed beside her. "Sorry. My mind drifted."

Lily tapped the page. "Sewer-ly? I don't know that word."

Grace read the word Lily pointed at. "Surely. As in *definitely*."

Lily studied the word and said, "Surely."

"Without the L-Y, it's just *sure*. Like, do you want to go to bed now? Sure!"

Lily shook her head. "I'm not done yet."

This was why she had Lily read aloud at bedtime. At any other time of the day, she'd hurry through the task, but when it was the only thing between her and lights-out, she took her sweet time.

Downstairs, the door opened and closed. Andrew called, "It's just me."

Regis hopped off the bed and ran to greet him.

Andrew had followed her home but then gone to his condo to change, promising to be back soon to look at the doorbell. She hadn't left the door unlocked but had told him to use his key.

Either he'd taken longer than she'd expected or he'd already been on her back porch to see what had happened.

Regis returned and curled up next to Lily. She continued reading, and Grace forced herself to pay attention until, finally, the book was finished. Lily said her prayers, and then Grace prayed over her as she did every night.

And, as she did every night, Lily said, "I love you."

Grace leaned over to kiss her cheek. She wanted to return the sentiment, but could she?

Was she capable of real love?

She was falling in love with Andrew—to the degree that she could love anybody. But was it real?

Maybe what Andrew had said was true. Maybe real love wasn't perfect. Maybe Grace could manage it.

Everything in her told her she loved this child, but could she trust her feelings? Other people's feelings seemed so easy to name and explain, but her own were jumbled and confusing.

The words *I love you too* were right there, on the tip of her tongue.

She couldn't make them come out. She leaned down and kissed Lily's forehead. "Sweet dreams, precious one."

Shutting off the light, Grace berated herself. Who couldn't tell a child she loved her? Her back against the hallway wall, she closed her eyes and spoke to the One who loved her completely. *Teach me how to love, Lord. Help me not only to say it but to do it, and do it well.*

God didn't answer, but she figured that prayer went right along with His will, and those were the kinds of prayers He delighted in answering. Feeling a little lighter, she walked down the stairs and peeked her head out the back door. "Making tea. You want some?"

"No."

The single-word answer was gruff, so unlike Andrew, who'd always been so kind. But he was working. Perhaps he was just focused on the doorbell.

In the kitchen, she started the water to boil and fixed two cups of chamomile anyway. Maybe he'd change his mind. When it was steeping on the counter, she stepped outside again and found Andrew kneeling in front of the spot where the video doorbell had been mounted, studying the wires with a flashlight.

"What's the verdict?"

When he didn't answer, rather than ask again, she changed the subject. Might as well get the hard conversation over with.

"I don't think I'm going to be able to go with you Saturday night."

His hands stilled, but otherwise, he didn't react. Didn't ask why. Didn't try to change her mind.

A sick feeling crawled up her throat.

"Shelby seems really nice, but I don't think it's wise to leave Lily at this point. If she is having dissociative episodes, I'm afraid being at a stranger's house will trigger them. We've finally gotten things back to normal this week."

Andrew used a tool that, she assumed, could tell him if the wires were getting power.

"I'm sorry to have to cancel on you." She waited a beat, two beats. Then added, "Maybe it's not too late to find another date."

"It's dead." He sounded off. Angry. Angrier than the situation warranted. Shoving the wires back into the hole, he said, "I thought maybe it was a connection, but I took it apart and re-installed it, and it still doesn't work. The wires are getting power." He stood abruptly, and she stepped back.

"I'm sorry."

"For what? What did you do?"

"What?" She was confused about the question. She might have thought he meant by backing out of their date, but the way he said the words—filled with accusation—told her they weren't talking about that anymore. Not that he'd been talking about it at all.

The night air was cold, and she hadn't grabbed a jacket. She crossed her arms. "I didn't mean to break it."

He studied her in the glow of the floodlight installed over her door.

She swallowed, unsure where his anger was coming from. Probably not the broken doorbell, but she said, "I'll buy another one. I can have it installed—"

"You think I care about the doorbell?"

"Why don't you tell me what you do care about, then?"

He rubbed his lips together. His Adam's apple bobbed. Then, he exhaled, the vapor hanging in the air between them before it dissipated. "Let's go inside before you freeze to death."

Though the air was frigid, the cold look in his eyes chilled her to the bones. She slid open the glass door and stepped in. She'd revel in the opportunity to spend more time with the man she'd eaten dinner with, but she wasn't looking forward to facing the one following her inside now.

He'd been suspicious at the restaurant, more than once. She'd seen that in his expression. One of the things she loved about Andrew was his openness. He didn't hide or pretend. She didn't have to touch his hand to know what he was feeling.

Now, standing beside her kitchen table, she saw fury.

"I'm not sure what I—"

"Was there something you didn't want me to see?"

"What? What are you—?"

"I don't have access to your doorbell's video footage. I installed them, but I wouldn't do that. I wouldn't spy on you."

"I know that. What are you talking about?"

"Unless it's not me you're worried about. Maybe you're worried about someone else getting access."

Though her hands were so cold she'd tucked them beneath her armpits to warm them, her face flushed with heat. She was afraid to say another word. Afraid of what he'd discovered.

He watched her with those squinted, suspicious eyes. "What are you hiding, Grace?"

"Nothing." But the word was breathy, filled with the fear she couldn't mask. She cleared her throat and went back to the source of this discussion. The doorbell. "I told you, there was a twig stuck in there. When I pulled it out—"

"How?"

"How...what?"

"How was it stuck in there?" He stepped out the back door, and cold air swirled around her feet as he bent down. When he stepped back inside, he laid the broken doorbell on the kitchen table. "Show me."

"I don't appreciate the third degree."

He pressed his lips closed.

She turned her attention to the doorbell and took a breath. She had no reason to fear. She hadn't lied. Not about that, anyway. She showed him the gap between the two pieces of the apparatus. "There was a twig stuck right here." She lifted it for him to see. A little of the twig's skin had scraped off on the spot, and she pointed it out. "I tried to separate these two pieces, but it requires a special screwdriver."

"Theoretically so people can't take the lid off, though you can buy the screwdriver online easily." Andrew's words came out monotone.

"I should have gotten the right screwdriver, but I figured, if the thing got stuck in there on its own, how far in could it have gone? Surely I could just pull it out. So I did. But it was stuck pretty good, and when—"

"Did you keep it?"

"Keep what?"

"The twig."

"Gee, Andrew, I didn't. I guess that would be destroying evidence, if you were a cop or something."

"If I were a cop, we wouldn't be...friends."

She noted the pause. Friends? Was that what they were? Ten minutes earlier, she'd have thought they were much more. Now she doubted they were even that.

But the other comment—about their not being friends if he were a cop. What did he mean by that?

He was still studying the broken doorbell as if it held the answers to all their questions.

"Like I said, I'll buy another one." Her words were coming out too fast. "I'm sure I can find somebody else to install it for me."

Very slowly, Andrew's gaze lifted to hers. He held her eye contact. She expected to see his care for her, his desire. But all she saw was anger.

"You've been lying to me all along."

"I didn't do anything to the doorbell."

"Not about the doorbell."

A bead of sweat trickled down her temple, but she dared not draw attention to it. She hadn't been honest, but she'd tried very hard not to lie. She didn't see any point in splitting those hairs.

She swiveled and stepped into her kitchen to put the counter between them, trying to buy some time to think, to figure out what he knew.

But he followed her, getting so close that she moved away, bumping into the sink.

"You need to back off."

He reeled as if she'd slapped him. He took a deliberate step away but kept himself between her and the opening to the breakfast room, crossing his arms. "Tell me the truth."

She didn't know what he knew. Didn't know where to start.

His gaze bored into hers, and she swallowed, knowing he was seeing too much but unable to hide from him.

"After the hospital, you told me you'd go back and pay the bill. Not give them your insurance information. Pay the bill."

"And I did. It's taken—"

"A foster child would have medical insurance."

She searched for an answer that would make sense. "I was trying to hide—"

"You wouldn't fly commercial."

"Myron could have—"

"Sure. Maybe he could have found your name among the millions of Americans who fly every day, but that's not why. You were afraid to use your real name. Ever since the day Lily broke her arm, I've known the name on the lease isn't your real last name.

Miller, is it? Nice and generic. I never asked because...because I thought I knew you."

For the first time, his hard expression faltered. She glimpsed something tender in his eyes, but it didn't hold.

"What's your real name?"

It was on the tip of her tongue. She wanted to tell him. She *wanted* him to know her, to fully know her.

But the hope that something real was developing between them felt as fleeting as the care she'd seen in his eyes. "You planning to Google me?"

"Yes, Grace—or Gloria, or Gina, or whatever the heck your name is."

"Grace. My name is—"

"You keep making excuses for why you haven't told the social worker what we've learned, but they're just that. Excuses. There is no social worker, is there?"

Grace scrambled but couldn't come up with a response that didn't reveal...everything.

"You don't want to get Dylan involved because he used to be a cop. You can't call the police and tell them what you believe about Myron."

"I did that. I called, but they didn't find—"

"You won't go with me Saturday night, and it has nothing to do with Lily's issues. You won't go because Fitz is a detective. You're afraid he's going to see right through you. Pathetic that it's taken me this long to figure out the truth, but then, Fitz is happily married to a kind, *honest* woman. He won't be blinded by attraction."

Andrew gave her one long, appraising look, and then stepped back, dropping his arms. "Tell me the truth."

She didn't know what to say. She prayed for wisdom, for guidance, but the Lord gave no answer. Had He abandoned her too?

"You can tell me the truth," he said, "or I can call the police right now."

She squared her shoulders and pulled in a deep breath. When

she blew it out, she released all of her hopes for a home in Coventry, for a normal life, for a relationship with Andrew. This had never been about her.

It had always been about protecting Lily.

"I let you believe I had *legal* custody of Lily. I don't. Lily and I became friends, and one day she took my hand."

Andrew's eyes narrowed. He understood what she was saying, but his hard stare didn't soften at all.

"I called the police." Her voice wobbled with emotion she couldn't contain. "They searched his house and questioned Lily, but she didn't tell the truth. The police found nothing. I'm sure they would have continued their investigation, but that night, Lily came to my house after dark. She told me her father was packing up, that they were leaving. She begged me to hide her. If he'd left with her, he'd have disappeared. He'd have set up in a new town and continued to exploit her and who knows how many other children. I couldn't let that happen."

Andrew swallowed hard, blinking a few times. At least he still felt affection for Lily. At least that was something.

"So I took her. I just...I took her. By the time we loaded the car, he was there. He had a shotgun. I think it was a shotgun. Or a rifle. I don't know. I aimed my truck straight for him. His shot went wild because he had to dive out of the way. He'd have killed me, but we got away."

Some of the color drained from Andrew's face.

"I called the police. They said he'd taken off but assured me they were still looking for evidence. They didn't seem to realize that I'd taken Lily. I didn't tell them. I couldn't because...Because they'd have taken her back, given her to Myron or stuck her in foster care. Maybe thrown me in prison. She was safe with me. I knew that. All this time, I've only been trying to protect her."

"You kidnapped her."

"I had no choice. Don't you see? If I hadn't—"

"It's a felony, Grace." He faltered at the name.

"My name is Grace. Grace Leann Mullen. Leann was my

paternal grandmother's name. Mullen is my father's name. You can Google me if you want. I do so daily. As far as I can tell, nobody is looking for me. Or Lily."

"You can't know that. And even if they're not, what do you plan to do? Just...just dump her on her grandmother's doorstep and then come back here and resume..." His voice trailed. "No, you wouldn't come back here. You'd just disappear again."

"That wasn't my plan."

His eyes rounded. "Your plan! What plan? You obviously—"

"Keep your voice down. Lily is sleeping."

Please, God, let her be sleeping. Let her not be hearing this.

His shoulders hunched, and his hands curled into fists. A moment passed before he relaxed and blew out a breath. "You have no idea what you're facing."

"I'm trying to save a child's life. Her life is worth that."

"There has to be a better way."

"If there is, I don't see it. And it's too late. We're here now."

"Last night, you and I sat right down there"—he pointed in the direction of the playground—"and I told you my biggest fear."

She whispered the word into the space between them. "Prison."

"Do you understand what you've done?" He ran a hand over his mouth and down his stubbly chin. "You've made me an accomplice."

"You didn't know. They wouldn't—"

"You think that matters?" Again, his volume rose. He lowered his voice and added in a whisper-shout, "You think they'll care that I didn't know? That they'll even listen?" He muttered a curse word under his breath. "I put you on a private jet. I flew you across state lines."

"You didn't—"

"I didn't know the last time, either, and I was convicted and sentenced to prison. If not for my father..."

Another curse word. He ran his hands over his head, mussing his neat hair. "My father. We're finally starting to repair our relationship. He's not convinced I didn't embezzle money, but he's forgiven me. This will...this will destroy it. Forever. I'll never win his respect after this."

"Andrew, I never meant—"

"You meant to lie to me. Over and over and over, you absolutely meant to lie to me."

"I was trying to protect—"

"I get it. Okay? I get it. But I won't do it. I love Lily, I do, and I cared for you, but I won't be involved in this."

Her heart hooked on one word. *Cared.*

Past tense.

Very carefully chosen past tense.

It was all she needed to hear. It was over between them.

This little fantasy in Coventry.

This idea that she might have found a forever home.

It was all over.

"Let me by." Her words came out calm but confident.

Andrew shifted out of the way, and Grace stalked past him and through her living room, where she yanked open her front door. "It's time for you to go."

He brushed by her but turned on the stoop to face her. He kept his voice low. "For her sake." He paused, blowing out a breath. "For both of your sakes...I'm leaving in the morning. I won't be back until Sunday afternoon. Be gone by then, or I'll have no choice but to call the police."

CHAPTER TWENTY-SIX

ANDREW HAD A TERRIBLE NIGHT.

It was already shaping up to be a worse day, and it was barely seven-fifteen in the morning.

Hot rage crawled up his back and settled at the base of his skull. He rubbed his neck and told himself to cool off. Never mind that the temperature hovered in the twenties. Never mind that it was actually supposed to snow.

Step one in attracting new employees to New Hampshire... Don't let them experience snow in *October*.

He cursed the weather. Took a deep breath. Lifted a prayer. And then pushed the button to start his BMW. Again.

Nothing. Again.

His check-engine light had come on the previous evening, but he'd ignored it. He'd once driven a car with the check-engine light on for an entire year. He'd figured he could make it through one weekend.

He slammed his palm against the steering wheel, ignored the pain that seared his hand, and let out a string of curses the likes of which he hadn't heard since prison.

Sorry. A pathetic prayer. Nevertheless, he added, *But come on! Seriously?*

He had no idea what was wrong. Sure, he could install a doorbell—

Don't think about that. Don't think about her.

But he knew next to nothing about cars.

He popped the hood, climbed out, and stared at the engine.

It was all chrome and black. There was no neon sign indicating the problem.

He pressed his lips together to keep from saying aloud the ugly words bouncing off the walls of his brain.

"Hey!"

He spun as Garrett approached.

His friend froze and lifted both hands. "Just coming to see if you need help."

He hated to consider the look Garrett had seen on his face. "Sorry. Stupid car won't start."

Wearing sweatpants and a T-shirt and somehow not shivering in the cold air, Garrett approached and stood beside him, focusing on the BMW's innards. "What happened?"

"Pushed the button. Didn't start."

"Did you try unplugging it and plugging it back in?"

Andrew heard the amusement in Garrett's voice but couldn't find any humor.

Garrett added, "Works with my laptop. Sometimes." After a moment, he asked, "What's the proper amount of time for us to stand here pretending like we know what we're looking for?"

Andrew slammed the hood closed. "I gotta call Braden, see if he'll give me a ride."

"I can take you."

Even though Garrett lived just a few doors down from him, and even though they went to the same church and hung out with the same group of guys every Monday night, Andrew didn't know him very well. He knew Garrett worked with his hands—plumber, electrician, HVAC repairman? Andrew couldn't remember. He had no idea how Garrett spent his days.

"You have nothing better to do?"

"Better than helping out a friend?" He shook his head. "Come on."

While Andrew retrieved his laptop bag and waited at Garrett's passenger door, Garrett grabbed his wallet, a bottle of water, and a sweatshirt from inside the house. He tossed the sweatshirt in the tiny half-backseat behind the cab, settled the water bottle in the cup holder, and started the pickup, an older model Toyota Tundra that looked well cared for and held a faint scent of sawdust. Two minutes later, they were on the highway headed toward Plymouth.

"Hope I don't smell," Garrett said. "Just finished my jog."

"That explains the stench."

When Garrett glared, Andrew chuckled. Garrett's blond hair was messy, but in that artful way that made guys look like they didn't care about their appearances. His UNH T-shirt looked well-worn, his gray sweatpants not designed for fashion but function. Women probably thought he was good looking. He was probably the kind of guy who had women falling all over themselves. Not that Andrew cared. He only wanted one woman.

Had wanted.

"So," Garrett said, "you wanna tell me what the problem is?"

"Uh, my car wouldn't start?"

Garrett glanced his way, one eyebrow lifted.

Andrew offered no other explanation for his bad mood.

They drove a mile or so, slowed by the traffic. The truck had finally heated up enough to blow warm air, and Andrew was beginning to thaw.

"How's it going with Grace?"

The rage he'd been fighting since the night before heated him all over again. "It's not."

Another glance from the driver.

"You should keep your eyes on the road."

"I can walk and chew gum at the same time. What happened?"

"Nothing *happened*. It's just not going to work."

"Ah. She dumped you."

"She didn't dump me. It wasn't like that."

"What was it like?"

"It was like, none of your business."

Unfazed, Garrett simply said, "Okay."

Andrew dropped his head against the headrest and closed his eyes. "Sorry. It's just...She lied to me."

"About?"

"It's a long story."

"Is it the lie that makes you mad, or the story behind the lie?"

An insightful question he didn't choose to answer.

"Do you understand why she lied? Does it make sense to you that she chose to lie, even if you wish she hadn't?"

Again, Andrew chose not to answer.

"Braden had something like that happen with Carly. She lied to him—or, I guess, just kept something from him. Something important. I don't know if you know the story. But, in time, he understood why she hadn't been forthright from the beginning. I think that made it easier for him to forgive her."

Braden had told Andrew enough of his history with Carly for him to piece together parts of it. Considering Desi was born just a few months after their wedding, and considering Braden hadn't seen Carly for years before that, it wasn't that complicated to figure out at least some of what she'd kept from him.

"Of course," Garrett said, "in that case, the issue was the lie, not the story. Now, if it's the story—"

"You're not gonna let this go, are you?" Andrew opened his eyes and faced his friend.

"What else do we have to talk about?" Garrett nodded toward the long line of traffic slowing them down.

If Andrew had left on time, he'd have missed this congestion. The few minutes he'd lost would end up costing a lot more. "Tell me about your job. What do you do for work?"

Garrett chuckled. "Nah. That's boring. Do you understand why she lied?"

"If she hadn't, we would never have gotten past introductions,"

Andrew said. "So it's the lie, but it's also the story. And the reason for the story. It's all of it. Okay?"

Garrett's perpetually amused expression dimmed. "I see."

Andrew sat back and closed his eyes again, praying for…He didn't even know what. He needed God to sustain him like he hadn't needed in a long time. Since prison. Because he was exhausted, and upset, and angry, and he had an important weekend ahead of him, but all he could think about was Grace.

Grace and Lily, and the fact that they'd be gone by the time he returned to his condo.

He'd never see them again.

Which was for the best. He was taking a risk by giving them two days to disappear. If law enforcement found out he hadn't called them immediately, Andrew could be tried as an accomplice. But he had to give her a head start.

The thought of Lily being returned to the man who'd exploited her made him sick to his stomach.

The thought of Grace in prison…

"You okay?"

He opened his eyes again. "I'm fine."

"You groaned, man. I know I don't drive a Beemer, but I'd still rather you not hurl in my truck."

"I'm not sick."

"Heartsick, I think."

"What is this, the Hallmark Channel? Should we stop to have a heart-to-heart over a cup of Earl Grey and a scone?"

"I would but"—Garrett lifted his water and took a swig—"gotta rehydrate."

An Uber driver wouldn't have so many questions.

"So, it's unforgivable?" Garrett asked. "What she did?"

"Seriously?"

"I'm just saying—"

"It's not *unforgivable*. It's just…hard to explain."

Garrett tapped the *UNH* emblazoned across his chest. "I know it's not Ivy League, but I think I can keep up."

"Let me rephrase. I'm not going to explain it. It's her story, not mine." And the last thing Garrett needed was to become an accomplice in Grace's crime. Andrew couldn't even hint at what he knew. Because Garrett knew the same people Andrew knew.

Dylan was a former cop.

Fitz was a current detective.

"But if you can forgive—"

"I can forgive," Andrew snapped. He could. He would, eventually. "Doesn't change anything. It's not going to work with Grace. It's not like I bought a ring or anything." Not that he hadn't been considering the proper amount of time he'd have to wait before he could propose. Not that he hadn't been thinking about forever.

He'd imagined a wedding, his mother, Christine, and his father, all watching him proudly.

His father...

He hated to consider how Dad would react if he found out about Grace's past.

What it would do to Middleton Enterprises if Andrew got arrested again.

As much as he understood why Grace had done what she'd done, as much as he admired her for her sacrifice, even loved her for it, he couldn't risk going to prison again. He didn't think he'd survive a second stint behind bars. Didn't know if he'd want to.

"Can we please talk about something else?"

Garrett paused a long moment before he asked, "You got your big thing this weekend, right?"

"Don't want to talk about that, either." He'd thought of little else for weeks. All the plans were made. It would work out the way it worked out. There was nothing new to discuss. "What about your work. Didn't you tell us once you're trying to start a general contracting business?"

"That was the goal."

"Was? Why the past tense?"

Garrett's lips flattened into a line. He flipped on his turn signal. "This way, right?"

"Yeah. I'll guide you."

But they still had a good ten minutes before they'd reach the lab.

When Garrett said no more, Andrew said, "What? You grill me about a girl but won't talk about your job?"

"It's been frustrating. Supplies are limited. Workers are hard to come by. And now we're going into winter, so there'll be few jobs until spring, if then. I'm running out of capital. Honestly, I have no idea what I'm doing. I've been framing since I was in high school. My uncle taught me carpentry, and I'm good at it. He's the one who paid for me to go to college. If I hadn't, I wouldn't even consider becoming a contractor. My dad thinks I'm just trying to prove the education wasn't a total waste of money. Dad never thought I should go. Didn't think I'd cut it."

Huh. Andrew had thought *his* father was unsupportive, but at least he'd never made Andrew feel less than. Sounded like Garrett's dad could learn something from Drew Middleton.

Garrett continued. "Maybe I should just focus on the framing and forget the rest."

"Is your dad right? Do you want to be a contractor, or are you doing it to make your uncle happy?"

"Yeah, I want it. But—"

"You're gonna give up, just because it's hard?"

"Hard doesn't cover it. I don't have any experience. Without contacts and references...I'm getting up there in age."

"What are you, twenty-seven, twenty-eight?"

"Thirty-five."

"No kidding?"

"I know I don't look it. But yeah, if I start now, by the time I make it a success, I'll be forty."

"You're going to be forty either way. Wouldn't you rather be there doing what you want?"

His friend shrugged, adding nothing.

"You should give up then," Andrew said.

Garrett's lips stretched in a smirk.

"If you're willing to quit so easily, then you're not cut out for it. You know how to always reach your goals with no risk of failure? Set your sights really low. Never dream. Never try. As soon as it gets hard, pretend you didn't care and change directions."

"Thank you, Zig Ziglar."

"The man's a genius."

That earned a snort.

"Another option," Andrew said. "You could ask for help. Do you know *how* to be a general contractor?"

"Sure. I've worked with enough of them, been watching what they do. There are some pretty bad ones out there. To tell you the truth, I think I'd be good at it."

"So you've got the knowledge, you just need to get started. Tell me about your business plan."

Garrett glanced his way, looking chagrined. "You know, get jobs, do them well."

"You don't have a business plan," he clarified.

Garrett just shrugged.

"After this weekend, I'll have lots of time on my hands." And lonely evenings loomed on the horizon. "Let's say we get together and come up with a plan and figure out how to get from here to there."

"I mean, yeah. That'd be great. If you got nothing better to do."

"Better than helping a friend?" He tossed Garrett's words back at him. "As long as we skip the tea and scones, I'm in." Not that Garrett would be any replacement for Grace, but at least he'd be company. At least one evening wouldn't be spent staring out the window at the empty condo across the lot, wishing things could have been different.

CHAPTER TWENTY-SEVEN

GRACE MANAGED to keep herself together long enough to get Lily to school the next morning.

Much as she'd tried to stir up some anger toward Andrew, she couldn't. He was right. She'd put him in a terrible position. She should be grateful he hadn't called the authorities right away. Would he, after she left? Or would he let her go, pretend he never knew anything. Pretend he was as surprised as anyone else to discover Grace and Lily gone.

She hoped the latter. She hoped she wouldn't have law enforcement always just a hair's breadth away.

But she didn't know for sure. So, though she wanted to put it off as long as possible, she and Lily would be leaving Coventry the following day. Grace just needed enough time to make a plan. She wasn't willing to spend another six months moving from hotel to hotel, constantly looking behind, constantly sure the police or Myron were right on her heels.

She still liked the idea of France. There was something refreshing about the idea of starting over in a foreign country. If they headed to Canada, flew to England, and then bought a car and drove across the Channel...It could work.

They could disappear.

She wasn't as enamored with the idea as she'd been a few weeks before, back when Andrew was nothing more than an attraction.

Before she'd fallen in love.

Love. That was what it was. Much as she'd feared naming it, she knew now exactly what she felt. What else besides love would hurt so much? What else besides love would feel like her heart had been shattered into tiny, unrecognizable pieces?

She'd asked God to show her what love was, and He'd answered in a big way.

In the future, she'd need to be more specific in her prayers. This was not how she'd wanted to learn the lesson.

Besides, if she had the good and real kind of love, she wouldn't have opened up just enough to get Andrew to care for her, but not enough to tell him the truth about what she'd done. Maybe she *felt* love, but in the action-verb sense of the word, she was pretty lousy at it.

It didn't matter. What mattered was Lily and keeping her safe.

When she got home from dropping Lily at school, telling herself to pay no attention to the BMW still parked in front of Andrew's condo, she turned up the heat. It was freezing outside, and the chill was seeping through the walls.

This was the coldest it'd been since she'd come to New Hampshire. There was even snow in the forecast.

Lily would love that.

Maybe watching the snowflakes fall would lighten her mood as they drove away from Coventry for the last time.

Blinking back tears, Grace sat at the kitchen table with her laptop and started looking into what it would take to get them to France. They could test their passports at the US-Canada border. If they worked there, then she'd be less concerned about trying them on a flight. Or maybe she'd get Canadian passports. It'd taken months for her to figure out how to get good papers in the US. Could she do it faster in Quebec?

In any event, they'd have to find a way to get to France.

There were plenty of places available in the French country-side, but she wasn't going to rent one yet. No, the less of a trail she left, the better. They'd find a hotel in London and go from there.

It was a plan. A partial plan, but the details would fill in as they went.

She wanted to do the right thing by Lily. That was all she'd ever wanted.

The thought had her deflating.

What was the best thing for Lily? To grow up in France with a woman who didn't know how to love? To leave everything she'd ever known, including her native language?

To never reconnect with the family that, according to Ruby, desperately sought her return?

Ruby seemed to know her friend. There was a reason Darla hadn't returned her call, but it wasn't because she didn't care.

Lily would be better off with her grandmother than she'd ever be with Grace.

As hard as Grace would try to love her, she'd fail. She'd fail over and over, just like she'd failed with Andrew. And Celia. And her mother.

Grace's love had never been good enough.

Gently, she closed the laptop on the idea of France.

On the dream of keeping Lily forever.

She couldn't be Lily's.

She'd never be Andrew's.

She might have left that secluded cabin in the woods, but soon enough, she'd be more alone than ever.

What did people mean by the term *a good cry*?

Once her tears were spent, all Grace wanted to do was curl up in bed and sleep for the rest of the day. Because she knew what she had to do, and stealing Lily and moving to France wasn't it.

They were going to Texas. If she had to knock on every door in the state, she was going to find Lily's grandmother. If the woman wanted Lily, then Grace would leave the child with her.

After that...

It didn't matter. All that mattered was getting Lily back to her family.

She forced herself to sit up, to stretch, and to climb out of bed. Regis, who'd cuddled up beside her, woke and followed her, sitting dutifully outside the bathroom while she threw some cold water on her face.

She was going to miss Regis. Grace had wanted a dog when she was a child, but her mother'd never given in to her begging. Barney probably would have gotten her a dog, but she'd never been dumb enough to ask him for anything.

Once she became an adult, she'd lost the desire for a dog, but this little spaniel had wormed his way into her heart.

Just one more thing she'd have to learn to live without.

In her bedroom, Oliver looked up from his spot at the end of the bed, blinking at her.

"When we find Lily's grandmother, it'll just be you and me again. I bet you'll like that."

But Oliver and Regis had become friends. And the cat loved Lily.

Even the cat would be sad when this was all over.

Grace packed her clothes in the large suitcase. Most of Lily's would fit in the smaller one that had come with the set. She couldn't pack any drawers that Lily might open and discover empty. But Lily wouldn't open any of them if Grace left her pajamas on the bed for her.

She tossed them there, then set aside a warm outfit for Lily to wear the following day.

When she'd done as much as she could without cluing Lily in to her plan, Grace went downstairs to consider what she wanted to keep from the kitchen. No sense replacing the more expensive items—the toaster oven and cookware she'd purchased.

She flipped on the TV, something for her to focus on besides the heartbreak that was tearing her to pieces. She didn't know what she was going to do next. She didn't know where she'd go, only that she'd start heading toward Texas and pray Andrew wouldn't tell the police about Darla Springer until Grace could locate the woman and deliver Lily to her.

After that, assuming Grace didn't end up in jail, she had no idea what she'd do. She'd considered returning to her cabin in the woods, but would Myron look for her there?

She didn't want to face the man, not ever again.

And though she loved Mama Lucy, she wasn't going back to the girls home.

Mom had moved to California after Barney's death, not that Grace wanted to be near her mother. She'd forgiven her, but that didn't mean she trusted her or wanted her in her life.

No, there was nothing drawing Grace back to the West Coast. She'd end up somewhere, and it wouldn't matter where, because nobody would miss her or long for her. She could fall off the face of the planet, and nobody would notice.

Trying to shake off her little pity party for one, she stepped outside, shivering in the bitter wind, and froze on the front stoop.

Andrew's BMW was still parked in front of his condo.

This was his big weekend. What was he doing home? Was he sick? Hurt? Maybe she should check on him.

She took a few steps toward his place, then stopped.

He was a grown man. He had friends and family and coworkers and a church. He didn't need her.

Forcing her gaze away, she trudged to the back of her SUV and lifted the hatch to retrieve the boxes she'd picked up at the U-Haul store after dropping Lily off at school. She slammed the cargo door and hurried back inside.

She spent the day packing and planning. She and Lily would see a movie after school, then eat out. Grace's goal was to bring Lily home late and get her in bed right away so she wouldn't realize the cabinets were all empty. And most of the drawers. And the closets except for the boxes Grace would stack in them. She'd go to sleep early, too, so she'd be well rested for the drive.

It was a plan. Maybe not a good plan, but it was what it was. If Lily discovered they were leaving, then Grace would deal with the fallout, though it would be much easier to put the child in the car when she was half-asleep so that, by the time she awoke and threw the coming fit—and who could blame her, being forced, again, to leave a place she loved?—they'd be miles away from Coventry.

There'd be no going back. There'd be no room for second-guessing.

Grace finished and was hiding the last of the boxes in the front closet when her phone rang. She slammed the closet door and hurried to the table where she'd left it. She snatched it and answered without looking at the caller ID.

Deep down, hoping it was Andrew. Hoping he'd called to take back everything he'd said the night before.

"Is this Grace Miller?"

Not Andrew's voice. She pulled the phone away from her ear to check the number. A 972-area code.

Phone pressed against her ear again, Grace said, "This is she."

"My name is Rex Thompson." He had a deep voice that made her think he was an older man. He spoke with a Southern accent. "I'm Darla Springer's brother. I got a call from a former neighbor of ours from Freedom Hill, Ruby Lind. She said you might have information on Darla's granddaughter, Lilianne?"

Grace pressed her hand to her chest as if the action might protect her heart from the coming blow. She squeezed her eyes closed but worked to keep her voice even. "It's possible," she said. "I need to speak with Mrs. Springer. Is she available?"

"I'm afraid she can't talk." The man's voice grew lower, gravelly. He cleared his throat, but emotion remained when he said, "She was mugged the other day. Some punk stabbed her and stole her purse. We're just lucky somebody found her as fast as they did or she'd have bled out in the parking lot."

"Is she going to be all right?"

"They say so, yeah. She just lost a lot of blood and hit her head when she fell. She's been in and out of consciousness for a couple days, but the doctors think she's gonna recover."

"Did they catch him?"

"Not yet, but we're praying."

"I'll add my prayers as well," Grace said, meaning it. Poor Lily had already lost so much.

"What can you tell me about Lilianne?" Rex asked.

"Look, I don't know you. I don't know Mrs. Springer, either, but...I'm sorry. I really need to speak to her before I give you any information."

The man was quiet a long moment. Then, he must've covered the mouthpiece on his phone, because his voice was muffled, spoken to someone else. She heard him say something, then a woman responded, but Grace couldn't make out the words.

The conversation lasted a minute or two. When Rex spoke again to Grace, he said, "Here's the deal. I'm gonna have my daughter take some pictures and text them to you, pictures and whatever else I can think of to prove to you that we are who we say we are. I think telling Darla that we found her granddaughter will go a long way to helping her recover. She's been looking for her girls for years. She's never given up on finding them. Even when the rest of us..." The words trailed, and a deep breath was followed by, "And I'm sure as shooting not gonna"—his voice cracked—"not gonna let this chance of bringing Lilianne home to her family get away. Okay?"

Grace was willing to keep an open mind. "All right. I'll call you back after I have a look."

She ended the call and sat heavily in the chair.

This was good news.

This was great news for Lily.

Even if it tore Grace's heart to shreds, she wouldn't regret it.

Her phone dinged, dinged again. Dinged multiple times.

She studied the first image that came in. A woman lying in a hospital bed, ashen skin, a bandage wrapped around her head. She looked old, but on further inspection, she wasn't really—maybe in her fifties. All this time, Grace had been picturing a grandmotherly type—stooped and gray-haired—but of course Darla wouldn't be that old. After all, Annabeth must be around twenty-six. If Darla'd been twenty-five when she was born, that would only make her fifty-one.

Darla's eyes were closed and ringed with bruises.

The next photo was of a man crouched beside the woman, looking at the camera. No smile. The text that followed it read, "Rex and Darla."

Next, a link to a newspaper article. *Woman Attacked, Left for Dead in Grocery Store Parking Lot.* She skimmed the details, which tracked with what Rex had told her. The accident had happened on Wednesday, two days prior.

The next image was of a Texas driver's license belonging to Reginald Theodore Thompson. No wonder he went by Rex. The address was in Flower Mound, Texas.

She looked it up and found it was a suburb about halfway between Dallas and Fort Worth.

Next, Darla Springer's driver's license, which listed an address not far from her brother's.

Then, a screenshot taken from a cell phone showed missed calls from Ruby Lind, the caption reading, *Darla's phone. Ruby called me this morning when Darla never called her back.*

Rex and his daughter had left no doubt in Grace's mind that Rex Thompson was exactly who he said he was.

One more image came. The caption read, *Darla's home screen image.*

Grace studied the faces in the snapshot. The woman was Annabeth, blue eyes and beautiful smile. On her hip, a toddler girl with the biggest, prettiest green eyes Grace had ever seen.

The newspaper photograph had been grainy. Grace had thought the child looked like Lily, but she'd never been fully convinced.

But this...She ran her fingers over the familiar face, but the image blurred with her tears.

This was Lily's family. These were Lily's people.

All this time, Grace had wanted to find them, and now she had. Why did she feel so sad?

She pulled her emotions under control and dialed.

Rex answered on the first ring. "Well?"

She bit her lower lip to keep it from trembling and wrapped her free hand around her stomach to hold herself together, hoping her emotion wouldn't carry in her words and knowing it was too much to ask.

No matter how little Grace asked for, it was always too much.

"I believe you are who you say. And the photograph...it's Lily." Her voice cracked, and she exhaled and pulled in another breath, needing to be rational a few more minutes. "It's definitely Lily. We can be there in a couple of days. We'll just—"

"Days? No, no. You need to get on a plane right away. Marcy, can we send this lady cash or get her a ticket or something." His voice brimmed with emotion. "You hear that, Darla? We found her. We found your baby granddaughter. She's..." His voice sobered. "She's okay, right? Lilianne? She's okay?

"She is. She's beautiful and smart and..." Tears streamed down Grace's cheeks, and she wiped them on her sleeve. "She's perfect. She's had a rough time. I'll tell you everything I know when we get there. But we won't be flying. I'll start driving tonight. It'll take us a few days."

"No. We'll meet you. Just tell us where. My daughter's sitting right here. She says she'll fly to where you are. We need to get our Lilianne back immediately. Today, if possible."

Grace squeezed her eyes shut. Praying, crying, wishing... wishing everything could be different. She swallowed her emotion. "We're pretty far from the airport." It was true, wasn't it?

Manchester was over an hour away. It was too late to get on a flight for Texas.

All excuses, but she grasped them like a float in the ocean.

"Tomorrow," she said. "It'll have to be tomorrow. I'll bring her to you."

Would Lily be safe if she was returned to Texas? Grace would have to tell Rex and the family everything she knew and trust that they could protect Lily.

Once Lily was settled, Grace could leave her with them.

Rex's pause on the other end of the phone was overly long. "Look, if it's money, we don't have a lot, but we'll give you—"

"I have all the money I need, Mr. Thompson. It's that I'm on the East Coast, and I'm a ways from the closest airport, and it's not exactly a hub."

"Where are you, exactly?" he asked, voice filled with suspicion.

She could see no reason to lie but wasn't ready to get too detailed. "New Hampshire. I promise, I'm not going to keep you from Lily. I tracked you down, remember?"

"That doesn't mean anything. If we're about to get a ransom note, I'll call the FBI so fast your head'll spin."

She checked her watch and then slipped on her jacket and headed for the door. She needed to calm him down, but she couldn't be late to pick up Lily. "Sir, it's an hour later here. If we headed to the airport immediately, we wouldn't get there until six thirty at best, and that's if there's no traffic. Assuming there's a flight to Dallas tonight—which I highly doubt—we wouldn't get there until very late. Lily's just a child. She needs to understand what we're doing. She needs time to process it. She's been through a lot. The last thing she needs is another trauma. I promise you, I'm not going to ask you for money or anything else. I'll pay for the flights to get us there. I'll send you the flight information as soon as I have it. I can rent a car and bring her to you, or you can meet me at the airport. I won't be leaving her right away. We need to talk, and I need to be sure she's all right." She waited, but he said nothing. She settled in her SUV and waited for the call to switch to Bluetooth. "I've risked everything to keep her safe. You're going to have to trust me to do so for one more day. Okay?"

"Yeah, okay. Would you mind sending me a picture of your driver's license?"

"I will. I'm leaving now to get her from school, but I'll do it from the pickup line."

Finally, the man seemed convinced that Grace wasn't about to steal his grand-niece. She ended the call and backed out of her space, once again wondering about Andrew's car, which still hadn't moved.

He must be sick. Very sick, if it meant missing the weekend he'd spent months planning.

She forced her gaze forward. Forward and away from this condo, the community she'd found, and the man who'd come to mean so much. He'd made it clear how he felt about her now. No matter what happened with Lily, once tomorrow came, she'd be gone, and she wouldn't be coming back.

GRACE WAS LATER than normal when she reached the school and got into the pickup line. Once she parked, she pulled her driver's license from her wallet, snapped a photo, and texted it to Rex Thompson.

Her phone lit up with a response almost immediately with another photograph, this one taken at Christmastime, evidenced by the decorated tree in the corner of the living room. It was a big family picture. She enlarged it to study the faces, picking out Darla and Rex. There were others who looked to be about the same age as them or older. Rex had his arm around a woman, his wife, she assumed. There was another older couple tucked among adults who were younger by a generation. Some in their thirties, she guessed, others in their twenties. There were a couple of teenagers, and in the front of the group stood a little boy and two girls around Lily's age. Studying all the faces, Grace picked up the resemblance to Lily in the shape of the eyes, the cheeks, the mouths. Two of those pictured even had green eyes.

This was Lily's family. Her real family.

Another text came in, and she stared at Andrew's name, a spark of hope warming her insides.

But the text only read, *From David. You were right. You need to report it ASAP or I will. Contact David directly and let me know the plan. David's right—Lily's safety trumps everything.*

Was this evidence of what she'd known about Myron all along? Based on Andrew's remarks, it must be. If so...did he really think she wouldn't report what she learned? This was exactly what she'd been searching for all along. But Andrew no longer trusted her. Perhaps she shouldn't blame him, but irritation flared, and with it, the desire to defend herself.

She shook it off and responded. *Darla called. Taking Lily to Texas tomorrow. After Lily is safely with her family, I'll contact the police and tell them everything.*

He responded with a thumbs-up.

Nothing else. No kind words, no regret at how things had ended, no request for Grace to let him know how it worked out.

Apparently, the thumbs-up said it all.

She clicked the link he'd forwarded.

At the top of the PDF document was a note.

What follows are the images I found that match the one you sent me. These were taken off a server deep in the dark web, all offered for sale. I don't believe the seller is the same person who took the photos. I believe he bought the images and is reselling them—which isn't legal, but who's going to turn him in? I can explain to the police how I concluded that.

Since I have an inkling where this child is, I will be reporting what I've found to law enforcement by the end of the day unless you are planning to do the same. Happy to work together, but not willing to wait. This child's safety trumps our friendship. Please advise.

Following that was David's full name and phone number.

The images that filled her screen had been cropped to hide Lily's body. She thanked God that David had done that. Even still, she saw Lily's face and far too much skin, even after the images had been edited.

She scrolled through the pictures quickly. At the bottom of the page were multiple web addresses, all hyperlinked. Above them, the words, *Sources. Enter at your own risk.*

The line of cars moved forward toward the kids standing just inside the school's front door, and she inched ahead. She'd be at the front of the line soon, and then with Lily all afternoon. She clicked the phone number.

He answered on the first ring. "This is David."

"My name is Grace Mill—" She tripped, considered the implications, and then restarted. "Grace Mullen. I'm Andrew's friend." *Was* Andrew's friend. "I don't know how much he told you about what we're—"

"Not a lot, he just asked me to see if I could find the girl, and I did." The man sounded almost angry. "I wasn't sure what I was gonna find, but seeing what's been done to that girl...I don't know if you clicked any of the source links, but—"

"I know what you found. I've located Lily's real family today. The man who had her—his name is Myron Bowman. He's been passing himself off as her father, but the photograph you sent of Lily with her mother led Andrew and me to the place where she was born. According to a friend of the family, Lily was born before her mother met Myron. We've been working to locate her real family, and they contacted me. They live in Texas, and they've been searching for Lily and her mother for years. I'm taking Lily to them tomorrow, and when I do, I'll turn over all this information and tell the police everything I know."

"Why not call the police now?"

It was a fair question, and she considered the option, but it wasn't the best way to go. "I need to get Lily to people who have a legal right to fight for her. If I contact the police now, there's a chance they'll put her in a foster home here in New Hampshire. I don't know the procedure. If she's with her family, then I can't see anybody trying to take her away from them. But if she's with me... It's just complicated."

"Don't you have an obligation to tell the authorities what you've learned? I thought you were her foster mother."

Right. Of course he thought that. It was what she'd led Andrew to believe. She skirted the question. "I'm going to tell the police everything. But I have no reason to believe that Myron Bowman is in New Hampshire. So telling the police here or telling the police in Texas...It's not going to matter one way or the other."

More than a few beats of Grace's racing heart passed before David said, "Tomorrow, then. I expect I'll hear from someone in law enforcement by the end of the day tomorrow."

"Tomorrow's Saturday, so—"

"Look, Ms. Mullen." She wondered if he'd used her name as a warning, reminding her he knew who she was. "The cops don't take weekends off. I'll hear from someone by the end of the day tomorrow, or I'm calling the police myself. Fair?"

"Very fair, David." Grace pulled forward in the line, and Lily stepped out from the crowd of kids. She said good-bye to a friend and hurried to the SUV. Grace was quick to say, "Thank you for all you've done. I can't tell you what it means to me, and to Lily."

She ended the call just as the back door opened. "Guess what! Gabby brought her new puppy to school for show-and-tell. He was so cute! A little golden retriever with the floppiest ears you've ever seen. And I got to hold him!"

Grace smiled at the precious child in the rearview mirror, recalling the reserved girl who'd sat on her porch, silently coloring, back in Washington. She'd hardly spoken. She'd hardly made eye contact.

Now, Lily was smiling, feeling at home in the world. She was excited about life. She felt safe.

Leaving Coventry would be hard, but finding her real family, people who loved her and had been searching for her for years? Things were only looking up for Lily.

No matter what happened, Grace wouldn't regret anything.

She'd protected Lily from Myron Bowman, and she was about to return her to her family, where Lily would be able to grow and flourish surrounded by people who loved her.

Whatever happened to Grace at that point, it would be worth it.

CHAPTER TWENTY-EIGHT

WAKING FROM A SOUND SLEEP, Grace fought to open her eyes. Her lids felt like sandpaper.

She couldn't have asked for a better last day with Lily. After school, they'd gone to Meredith and seen the only kids movie showing at the three-screen cinema. After the movie, Lily had picked out a restaurant where they'd eaten pizza—half pepperoni, half pineapple. And then they'd found a giant arcade, where they'd played mini-golf, competed at bowling, driven race cars, and enjoyed every age-appropriate game imaginable.

And though she'd tried to get herself to do it all day, she'd never quite gotten around to telling Lily about Darla and the family in Texas, who were waiting eagerly for her return.

She'd tell her the next day, on their way to Manchester. It wouldn't be a lot of time for Lily to get used to the idea, but at least she'd sleep that night.

Grace had figured she'd toss and turn, but by the time she'd gotten Lily to bed and finished her nightly cup of chamomile, she'd dragged herself to her mattress. Which didn't make much sense, considering she was about to lose the only person in the entire world who loved her back.

What had woken her?

She glanced at her phone. Eleven o'clock, meaning she'd fallen asleep less than an hour before. Why in the world—?

Oliver meowed loudly from the floor beside her bed. Sometimes, Grace could swear the cat was talking. At that moment, it sounded like he was saying, "Now." As if he ran the household. Which, she had to admit, when he wanted something, he did.

Because there was nothing as irritating as the sound he made when he wasn't happy.

"What do you want?"

He responded with another meow.

"Fine." She flipped on the bedside light, swung her legs over the side of the bed, and stood, feeling off-center and unbalanced. What was wrong with her? Was she sick?

She couldn't be sick. On Sunday, after she delivered Lily to her family, then she could collapse and sleep for days. But not until then.

After shoving her feet into slippers, she followed the cat down the hall, turning on the overhead light as she passed. Downstairs, she went through the living room and into the kitchen.

The cat's water bowl was full.

He'd finished his food and had never wanted more than the dishful she gave him every morning and evening.

Again, Oliver issued a moan he probably believed sounded like a roar.

"I'm not afraid of you."

He turned, flipping his tail her way, and approached the back door.

"You don't want to go out there, buddy. It's freezing."

But Oliver slid behind the curtain, meowing again.

"Fine. See for yourself."

Reaching past the curtain, she unlocked the door and opened it, and the cat dashed outside while bitter air swirled within.

She slammed it quickly and locked it. She'd give him five minutes.

After turning on even more lights, she started pulling boxes out of the front closet so they'd be easier to load into the SUV come morning. Lily hadn't noticed anything amiss. Maybe it had been cruel for Grace not to warn her, but no matter when she told Lily they were leaving Coventry, it would be hard. Why make the child dread it? Grace was doing that for both of them.

Their flight left at seven forty-five. They'd need to leave the condo by five in order to get to the airport on time. Grace planned to have everything she wanted to keep loaded in the SUV so she wouldn't have to return to Coventry. She'd fly back to Manchester to get her SUV after she left Lily with her family. Where would she go from there?

She'd figure that out when the time came.

Boxes stacked by the door, she stepped into the half-bath beneath the stairs. After finishing up and washing her hands, she returned to the back door and peeked outside.

No Oliver.

She slid the curtain back and flipped on the light, expecting to see the cat running to the door to get back in. What halfway intelligent animal would choose to be outside on a bitter night like this? Snowflakes drifted through the illumination cast by the floodlight and fell to the small back yard. The snow must have just started because there was no accumulation, yet it was starting to stick. The weathermen had predicted it wouldn't begin until morning. Maybe they'd changed the forecast. Grace checked the weather and, sure enough, it was predicted to snow all night.

Great. They'd need to leave even earlier so they could take their time on the roadways. New Hampshire crews were good at keeping the roads passable, but there was no sense cutting it close.

Where was that cat?

She opened the door and whisper-shouted, "Oliver."

But the cat didn't come running.

She had half a mind to leave him outside. Would he be all right? He'd stayed out all night plenty of times before, but not in a snowstorm.

What if he didn't come home by the time they left for

Manchester? She'd paid to take both animals on the flight to Texas. Regis would sit with Grace, but Oliver would ride in the cargo area. He'd hate it, but what choice did Grace have? She didn't want to return to Coventry, and she hadn't told anybody of her plans. She'd call Cassidy after everything was taken care of, but not before.

Emitting another loud yawn, Grace gave up waiting. If Oliver didn't return by morning, then she'd have to ask Cassidy to look after him until Grace returned.

She wasn't about to abandon one of the few living beings who cared if she lived or died.

She blamed her melodrama on her fatigue as she issued another yawn.

She closed and locked the door, then turned toward the staircase and took two steps.

And froze.

Oliver.

He was in the living room, licking his paws and looking at her as if she were insane.

Maybe she was. Because she hadn't let him in.

Acid filled her stomach.

Her hands shook while her mind raced to process it.

It made no sense. How could Oliver...?

Was Grace sleeping? Was this a dream? A nightmare?

Had she let him in already and forgotten? She was sleepy, but...No, no, she'd remember that.

Maybe Lily...Of course. Lily must've come downstairs while Grace was in the bathroom and let the cat in.

Which meant she'd seen the boxes.

Oh no.

Grace dashed up the stairs and down the hall, stopping in Lily's bedroom doorway. She stared at the empty bed.

"Lily?"

The bathroom door was wide open, the light off.

Grace's room was empty.

"Lily! Answer me."

But the child didn't answer.

"Regis," she called. The dog was too obedient not to come or, if he couldn't, bark or start scratching or...something.

But Regis wasn't there either.

Surely, surely Lily wouldn't run away.

The boxes might have frightened her, but how could she have seen them, decided to run, gotten out of the house, all in the seconds Grace was in the bathroom?

Somehow, she had. It was the only thing that made sense.

Grace dashed back down the stairs and out the front door. Her phone jingled, the notification that she was on the stoop. A notification she hadn't gotten moments before. Lily hadn't gone out the front. She must've slipped out the back, letting Oliver in on her way.

She rushed to the back door, where the video doorbell was gone.

Oh God, oh God. Lead me. Where is she?

Stepping out the back door, she called for Lily, for the dog. No response. In her slippers, Grace dashed through the tiny yard, opened the gate, and peered past the grassy area at the playground at the far end of the row of condos. No footprints in the thin layer of snow.

No sign of Lily and Regis.

No sign of movement whatsoever.

She focused on the trees, trying to see past the edge into the dark forest. No child, no dog.

She dialed 911. "The child in my care," she said when the dispatcher answered, "I think she's run away." Standing in the middle of the grassy area, she turned in a slow circle, seeing but not believing.

Would Lily run away?

Back in Seattle, she'd run from Myron when she'd seen him packing the moving trailer.

She'd had a plan. She'd run to Grace.

Maybe...Maybe she'd run to Andrew's house.

The woman on the phone promised to send someone and asked her to stay on the line.

Grace trudged back toward the house, registering the cold seeping through her thin pajamas and slippers but barely noticing it. "I can't. I've gotta make some calls."

She hung up and, with trembling fingers, dialed Andrew. If Lily wasn't there, she'd try her friends. She had all their mother's phone numbers.

His phone rang and rang before, finally, voice mail picked up. Her heart sank. "I saw your car. I don't know if you're home, but Lily's run off." She stepped inside the house and closed the door. "I need your—"

A hand clamped over her lips.

An arm wrapped around her waist.

It was a nightmare, the worst kind of nightmare. The kind that was true.

She fought and managed to free her mouth and screamed.

She was yanked back against a broad chest, his hand over her mouth.

He held her head tight with one hand and wrestled the phone from her hand with the other.

"You can either stop fighting and see Lily again"—he dropped her phone on the hardwood floor and wrapped his arm around her middle—"or you can keep it up and die right here, right now."

Her blood froze at the voice.

Myron Bowman had found them.

Grace's reality shifted.

She'd been wrong. About everything.

No, not everything. She'd been exactly right about Myron Bowman. If anything, she'd underestimated his capacity for evil.

"Do you want to change into something warmer?" he asked,

still holding her against him. "If you do, you'll stop fighting me. I don't want to kill you. And I'd prefer not to have to carry your unconscious body."

She forced herself not to move, though the instinct to fight was not easy to quell.

"We're going to go upstairs," he said, "and I'm going to give you two minutes to put on something weather-appropriate. We'll be outside for some time. Understand?"

She nodded, unable to speak with his hand still over her mouth. He was wearing leather gloves, and the scent of them filled her nostrils.

"I'm going to move my hand," he said. "You're not going to scream. For everything you do that goes against my wishes, I'll punish Lily. Tell me you understand?"

Again, she moved her head up and down.

He lifted his palm from her face and gripped her cold arm. "Upstairs."

She turned to face him. When she'd first met him back in Seattle, she'd thought him rather attractive with his blond hair and blue eyes. He was fit and trim, older but without a lot of wrinkles. He'd smiled that day, looking for all the world like a normal human being.

Now, she saw past the facade to the depraved monster beneath.

He never loosened his hold as they walked up the stairs together.

"Is Lily okay?" she asked.

"She's cold, so the faster we get this done, the better."

Grace stepped into her bedroom and saw a step stool in the center.

"You made things complicated by waking up. I thought you'd sleep more soundly after your tea."

What was he talking about?

"I should have slipped in a bigger dose."

She turned to face him. "Dose? Of—"

"Just a sleeping pill. A pretty strong sleeping pill, which I'm sure would have worked if not for that stupid cat. Assuming you drank all your tea. Did you?"

Her tea? He'd slipped something into her tea?

"I put it in your cup," he said. "A crushed up white pill in the bottom of your favorite white mug. There was a risk you'd see the powder, but it was a slight risk at best. I did it before you got home last night." He gestured to the clothes folded neatly on her bureau. "Get moving."

"You have Lily. I'm not going to run or fight. Can you step out while I change?" The thought of changing in front of him sent a wave of nausea to her middle. But that wasn't what prompted the question. Her handgun was in her purse. And her purse was in her nightstand.

A wicked grin spread across his mouth. "Why bother?" He reached her in two steps, spun her around, and pulled her back against his chest. "It's nothing I haven't seen before."

Myron lifted his phone so Grace could see the screen. On it, she saw the top of their heads.

His hand on her chin, he lifted her face to the light fixture, and the image on the phone showed her looking up.

Myron grinned like a madman.

"I wondered if you'd bring your boyfriend up here, give me some footage I could sell. But you're too chaste for that, aren't you?" His voice lowered, rumbling in her ear. "Have you ever been with a man, Grace? I'm hoping my guess about you is right. I'm hoping I'll be your first."

She squeezed her eyes closed against the image on the screen, but the one he'd put in her mind remained. *Please, Lord. Save us.*

"And if you're thinking of getting to your gun, don't. I took it out of your purse when you were sleeping." Myron let her go. "Change your clothes." He leaned against the doorway and crossed his arms, watching.

Praying frantically, she turned her back on him and slipped into her jeans, the short-sleeved top—chosen because of the weather in Dallas—and the cardigan as quickly as she could. She'd planned to wear a cute pair of flats but instead grabbed the fuzzy boots she'd worn that day. She sat on her bed to pull them on.

Behind her, she'd heard the squeak of the stool. He was retrieving the camera. Were there others in the house? Had he already gotten those? While she'd been outside looking for Lily? While she'd been downstairs moving boxes?

Or while she'd been in a drug-induced sleep?

He'd come into her house, he'd taken Lily and the dog, and somehow, she'd slept through all of that. Who knew what else he'd done?

She turned to find him at the door, the stool leaning against the wall nearby. She was dressed, but she needed to stall a few more minutes. The police were on their way. They could get him to tell where he'd left Lily. They'd mount a search. They'd find her.

Lord, bring the police fast. Please.

She asked, "How did you find us?"

That sinister smile returned. "Find you? I never lost you." He gestured her toward the hallway. "Let's go."

The thought of walking out with this man, of not fighting for her life, kept her feet rooted to the floor. "How did you know where we were?"

"The dog's collar. It's embedded with a GPS chip. Lily doesn't go anywhere without her dog. When you two got on that plane the other morning, I would have been worried, except you'd left the dog here. I knew you'd be back."

He'd seen that. He'd seen everything.

"Get a move on. We don't want sweet Lily to freeze to death, do we?" He made a show of looking at his watch. "It's been fifteen minutes. It's awfully chilly out there." Again, he gestured with his fingers for her to come.

The thought of Lily got her feet moving. She stepped past him into the hall and down the stairs.

"Put your coat on, and gloves," he said.

Her jacket was draped over the couch in the living room. She slipped it on.

While she was still pulling on her gloves, he grabbed her upper arm and turned her toward the back. "This way, where there's no camera."

"It was you, wasn't it? With the doorbell camera?"

"Of course. The trick was getting to it without being seen. I had to do it late at night when nobody would be looking, approach from the side. I disabled the camera with an icepick, then shoved the twig in there to make you think it was an accident."

"Smart."

"I am that." At the back door, she reached for the handle, but he tightened his grip on her arm. "We're going to walk silently across the complex. On the off chance anybody sees us, they'll think we're out for a late-night stroll." He took her hand in his, and she thanked God for the gloves. "If something happens, if we don't make it to where we're going, Lily will freeze to death before anybody finds her. So, paste a smile on your face. Got it?"

She dipped her head and opened the door.

They stepped past the gate and onto the grassy area that separated her condo from the row behind. He angled her not in the direction of any parking lot but toward the park and playground and, beyond that, the thick forest.

She had no idea where they were going, but one thing was certain. Myron had a plan, and he was way ahead of her.

CHAPTER TWENTY-NINE

ANDREW HADN'T CONSIDERED how much Jacqui, Braden, and he would learn this weekend about the students they were thinking of hiring. Andrew had gotten to talk to every student for at least a few minutes. He'd been impressed by their intelligence and ingenuity. When the cocktail party had broken up, rather than end the evening, the group had moved into the hotel lounge to continue their conversations.

But once the band played and the alcohol flowed, the students started showing their true colors.

Which, for most of them, wasn't bad at all. From his perch at the end of the bar, he scanned the room. A few of the women and two of the men had been dancing most of the evening, sober and looking like they were having a great time.

The guy Andrew had pegged as the most serious was in a deep conversation with two other students, one male and one female. There were lots of hand gestures and nodding heads. Whatever they were talking about, they seemed to be enjoying the discussion.

One student, whose résumé had really impressed him, had ordered a round of shots for their table and, when her roommate for the weekend refused hers, drank them both, back-to-back, slamming the second down and then belching.

At the moment, she was slumped over a table in the corner. Andrew prayed someone would get her out of there before she lost the liquor and the rest of the contents of her stomach all over the floor. Considering the way she'd been hanging off every man who'd paid her the slightest bit of attention, he wasn't going to be the one to help her back to her room.

A guy who'd come off as a schmoozer was currently sweet-talking a local girl just a few barstools down. If he started leading her to the elevators, Andrew was going to intervene and send the girl on her way. BNB definitely wasn't footing the bill for that kind of behavior.

Maybe that was overstepping, but seriously. This was a business event. The students needed to learn what was appropriate and what was—most definitely—not.

Someone bumped his shoulder, and he turned to find Braden at his side. "Drinking alone?"

"Me and my water"—he shook the glass—"ice, I should say. I've asked the bartender three times for a refill."

Braden turned to face the crowd. "What's going on with you today?"

"Nothing."

His friend just lifted his eyebrows.

"Nothing I want to talk about tonight. I just want to get through this weekend. Speaking of, the party planner canceled the boat trip and scheduled us at the ski area. They're gonna hook us up with sleds on the bunny slope for anybody who wants to do it. She's trying to get them to operate the lift so we don't have to climb."

"Sounds like fun."

Andrew shrugged. He'd try his best to enjoy it, and when that failed, he'd fake it, like he'd done all day.

"Come back to the table," Braden said. "We're gonna head up in a minute, and Jacqui'll want to hear about the plans."

"You can tell her."

"*You* can tell her," Braden said. "She'll have questions, and I'm not your go-between."

Braden wasn't fooling Andrew. Jacqui wouldn't have a single question about the plans for the following day. Her job this weekend—which she'd outlined quite clearly—was to go where they said and be available for conversation. Braden was just trying to get Andrew to rejoin the fun.

Not that any of this had been even the slightest bit fun.

He was ready for bed, but he wouldn't go to his room upstairs until Jacqui and Braden excused themselves. Without Grace, all Andrew had was his job. He'd better not screw it up. "I'll come back when I get my water."

Braden studied him a long moment before returning to their table, where Carly waited for him next to Reid and Jacqui. All coupled-up. Third wheel, fifth wheel—either way, Andrew was the odd man out. Story of his life.

He got the bartender's attention and lifted his empty glass.

The woman nodded. "Sorry. Just a sec."

He'd heard that one before.

Bored and exhausted, he pulled his phone from his pocket and saw he had a voicemail. Grace?

Why would she be calling—and at eleven thirty at night?

Something must be wrong.

He lifted the phone to his ear, but the music was too loud. He heard something about Lily. Running off? Was that what Grace had said? He paused the message, left his glass on the bar, and hurried to the hotel lobby, a small area with a seating area and a coffee bar.

He restarted the message.

Lily had run off. In the middle of the night? Grace said, "I need your..." And then silence.

And then, Grace screamed.

Acid filled his stomach, raced through his veins.

Phone pressed to his ear, he heard a scuffle, a grunt.

The message ended.

"You all right?"

Andrew swiveled.

"Whoa." Reid lifted his hands and backed up. "What's wrong?"

"Something's happened to Grace. And Lily."

Reid's eyes narrowed. "Tell me what—"

"Here." Andrew couldn't explain. He needed to think. He hit the play button and shoved the phone into Reid's hand. Leaving him in the lobby, he ran back into the lounge and got Braden's attention, waving him over.

When Braden stood, Andrew rushed back to Reid, who held out Andrew's phone with one hand, his own phone pressed to his ear with the other. "Maybe an abduction," he said. "I'm not sure exactly." He met Andrew's eyes. "Got 911. What's the address?"

Andrew told him, and Reid repeated it to the operator.

Braden reached them. "What is it?"

While Andrew caught him up, Carly and Jacqui joined them in the lobby.

"I'm going to find them." Andrew clenched his fists to still the trembling, turning toward the front doors.

A hand clamped down on his shoulder. "I'll drive you," Braden said.

"I can—"

"You don't have your car."

Right. Right. His car was at home, which was why Grace had called him. She'd thought he was there. If only he had been.

Braden kissed Carly's cheek. "I'll be back. Stay here where it's safe." They'd brought one of Carly's sisters for the weekend, who was upstairs with the baby.

Reid gave Jacqui a quick hug. "Sit tight and do what you need to do here."

"Be safe and keep us informed." Jacqui reached for Andrew's hand. "We'll be praying."

He couldn't force words past the gratitude and fear clogging his throat. He nodded and ran out the front door, his friends on his heels.

By the time they reached Braden's truck, Andrew'd dialed Garrett.

He answered as they climbed in. "Dude, do you know what time—?"

"Something happened. Grace called. I think she was...I don't know. Attacked or something. At her condo. I'm on my way, but can you—?"

"On it. I'll call you back."

Andrew ended the call, dialed Thomas. Told him the same thing. Thomas lived in the same complex, just a few buildings away. He promised to head to Grace's place.

Who else? Who else could he—?

"Fitz." Braden said.

From the backseat, Reid said, "Calling now."

"I'll try Dylan." Andrew dialed, and Chelsea answered, her voice sleepy.

"It's Andrew. I need Dylan's help." He couldn't be bothered to be kind or polite. He just needed...

He needed Grace. He needed Lily. He needed them to be safe and healthy and well.

"One moment," Chelsea said. Seconds later, a deep voice rumbled on the line. "What is it?"

Andrew told him about Grace's message.

"Any idea who'd do this?" Dylan asked.

Andrew barely hesitated before spewing the whole story. About Myron Bowman and the proof they'd found that the guy was a pornographer. About Lily's family in Texas, the family who'd been searching for Lily for years. About how Grace had come to get custody of Lily. "She just took her. She didn't know what else to do. And when I found out..." He squeezed his eyes closed and rocked forward, resting his head against the dashboard. "I should have been there. I should have told her..."

"There's no time for that now." Dylan spoke in what Andrew

had no doubt was his soothing, we've-got-this-under-control cop voice. He hadn't been on a force in years, but apparently the habits weren't forgotten. "When we find her, you can tell her anything you want. Have you called the police?"

"Reid called 911."

Behind Andrew, Reid said, "Grace did too. They're already there."

Andrew swiveled to face him. He put his phone on speaker so Dylan could hear.

"When I called," Reid explained, "they said they'd already gotten a call from that address and had sent officers. And when you didn't answer, Garrett called me. Said the cops are already in her condo."

Dylan must've heard because he said, "Good, good. Maybe they've already got it managed. When will you be there?"

Andrew looked around at where they were. Despite the snow, Braden was keeping their speed well above the legal limit. "Ten minutes, tops."

"Meet you there."

CHAPTER THIRTY

DESPITE THE FACT that they were holding hands, supposed to be looking like they were out for a stroll, they'd hurried across the open area to the woods. They probably hadn't been visible for a full minute. What were the chances anybody had seen them?

Slim. Very slim.

You're the God of miracles, though. Save us.

They'd stepped into the thick forest and walked a few hundred yards along a trail. They were moving fast enough to stay warm. The snow fell steadily, silently, all around. In the places where it didn't get caught on branches and needles overhead, it was already starting to accumulate.

Myron's flashlight beam bounced ahead on the trail. Aside from that, the forest was dark and deep. After about ten minutes, Grace spotted the outline of some sort of all-terrain vehicle. It had a high top and a plastic windshield. The doors had been removed, or maybe it'd never had doors to begin with. As they approached, Myron aimed his flashlight at the flat cargo area behind the two front seats, where a pile of blankets had been dumped.

No, not a pile. Just one blanket, and it shifted as they approached.

A bark cut through the silent night, and Regis poked his head out.

Myron said, "Regis, quiet."

The dog silenced immediately. She shouldn't have been surprised at that. Myron had been the one to train the dog so well. Regis was much more Myron's dog than Grace's.

She hurried forward to pull the blanket away. Lily lay beneath, hands and feet bound, a gag in her mouth.

Turning a glare on Myron, she snapped, "You're a monster."

"Leave her be. We'll be where we're going in a few minutes."

"She's freezing."

"It's a subzero blanket. She'll be fine."

Lily's eyes were wide and terrified, blinking their fear.

"At least let me take off the gag."

He seemed to consider that, then nodded. "I can be reasonable."

Grace didn't bother to argue as she removed the too-tight cloth from Lily's face. "Are you all right, sweetheart?"

Even with the gag removed, Lily only nodded, gaze flicking from Myron to Grace and back.

Grace leaned close and whispered so quietly she wasn't even sure Lily would hear. "I called the police. They'll be—"

"Enough of that." Myron yanked Grace back with a hand on her shoulder. "Get in."

Settled in the passenger seat, Grace turned and patted Lily's hip through the blanket. "It's going to be okay, sweetheart. Just sit tight."

Beside her, Myron gave Grace a pleased look, almost smug. "This is going to be better than okay."

He cranked the engine, and it rumbled to life louder than a lawnmower. Didn't he worry about the sound carrying?

But the snow muffled everything. And they were pretty far from the condos now. What else was out there? She tried to remember the area around the community she'd called home. There was a neighborhood not too far away, but it was in the opposite direction. As Myron drove forward, if her internal compass was correct, they headed not parallel to the main road but deeper into the woods, farther from any structures she'd seen in Coventry. Farther from the lake. Farther from town. The trail angled up, and they climbed an incline that had to be the back side of Mt. Coventry, the side not facing the lake and the town. The road became steep, the engine roaring to keep up the pace.

Except where the headlights cut through the darkness, the night was black. Snow flitted in the bright beams and flew over the vehicle. Cold wind and icy flakes blew through the open sides.

Grace turned to the back and saw that Regis had crawled from beneath the blankets and had his paws propped on the edge of the cargo area, looking out at the dark woods as if checking for predators.

Lily remained huddled beneath the blanket. Grace patted her hip, and the child pulled the blanket down and peered up at her.

The fear had drained from her eyes, replaced by the numb expression she'd worn when Grace had first met her.

How quickly, how thoroughly, Lily had been pulled right back into the role Myron had for her, not of treasured daughter but of valuable commodity.

Despite everything Grace had done to try to protect her, she'd failed. She'd utterly, miserably failed.

Because, as much as she'd tried to encourage Lily before, she had little hope that the police were going to find them. Myron had planned every step of this. Even on the off chance that somebody had glimpsed them walking into the forest, these woods went on for miles and miles in every direction. They were crisscrossed by logging trails and narrow roads. Grace guessed Myron had a car up ahead. They'd be loaded in and driven away, and nobody would ever know where they'd gone.

Lily would once again be used as Myron's meal ticket.

Grace...Who knew what would become of her, but based on the threats he'd made and the look in his eyes, Myron had plans for Grace as well.

Still, she smiled at Lily, tried to fill her expression with a confidence she didn't feel. She'd been uttering prayers since the first moment she'd realized Lily was gone, a constant stream of *please God*, and *help us*.

Now, she gripped Lily's hip through the blanket and closed her eyes. *Lord, You know everything. You are our strong tower, our very present help in times of trouble. We are in deep trouble now. Please, be our help. You are the Rescuer. Rescue us. Without You, we are lost.*

Help me to be what Lily needs right now. Whatever happens, help me shield her. Protect her.

Help me love her well.

If only Andrew had answered the phone. If only she'd had the opportunity to hear his voice one more time.

The vehicle hit a bump, and Grace gripped the side to hold steady, not letting go of Lily.

Regis bounced and flew off the back.

Lily screamed.

Grace yelled to be heard over the engine. "Regis fell. We have to stop."

But Myron only glanced at her, a strange look in his eyes.

"You have to stop. Lily needs him."

Without taking his eyes off the road, Myron smiled. "She has you now. She doesn't need the mutt anymore."

"But he'll freeze to death."

Myron only shrugged, never even slowing.

Lily's scream died, but she propped herself up to see.

Regis ran behind them on the trail. Though Grace couldn't hear him barking, she imagined the sounds in her ears.

Protect Regis, Lord. He's been such a good friend to her.

They rounded a corner, and Regis disappeared from sight.

For the first time since she'd discovered Lily missing, tears filled Grace's eyes. Regis was gone, and Grace feared the dog would be just one of many tragic losses before this was all over.

Assuming it ever was over.

CHAPTER THIRTY-ONE

GRACE DIDN'T KNOW EXACTLY what she'd expected.

A car. A long drive. She'd had vague thoughts about being shoved in a trunk. She didn't have irrational fears of small places, but she still didn't relish the idea.

She definitely hadn't expected this.

Myron had driven them through the thick woods along a trail that twisted switchback-style up the mountain. At the top, they'd exited the worn track to a path that seemed barely wide enough for the all-terrain vehicle.

That was where she dropped the glove.

She'd been thinking about it for miles. Thinking that, as long as they stayed on the wide trails, there was a chance they'd be found. But when they left it, that was when things would get dicey.

Her hands had been shoved in her jacket pocket, but she managed to get her right glove off. She'd held onto it for what felt like miles and miles and miles.

And then, Myron slowed considerably and made a turn, gaze fixed ahead.

She'd flicked the glove over the side of the ATV.

She didn't dare look to see where it'd fallen, praying it had landed in the middle of the path. Praying the wind wouldn't blow it away.

Not that anybody would think to check the woods behind the condo. Surely the police would start looking on the roadways and highways, not on the four-wheeler paths used for recreation.

The path opened to a lonely structure in the middle of nowhere. They approached from the back, where Myron pulled the ATV straight into what looked like a newly constructed shed, likely built for exactly that purpose.

Rather than untie Lily, he simply hoisted her into his arms as if she weighed no more than a sack of groceries and nodded to the back door. He shone his flashlight that direction, and she saw it was a house.

"Ladies first."

What choice did she have? She started across the snowy yard toward the back door.

He tromped behind her. When she reached the door, he said, "Go on in. It's unlocked. Switch is on the left."

She stepped into an empty room, flipped on the light, and crossed to the far side near the window, putting distance between herself and Myron. The house was warm, the sound of the furnace humming in the quiet.

He angled to get himself and Lily into the house and closed the door with his foot. Holding Lily in one arm, he turned the key already in the keyhole, pulled it out, and pocketed it.

The acid in her stomach rumbled in fear.

Lily's eyes were open, but Grace saw nothing there. No fight. No light. Lily had resigned herself to this fate.

Grace looked around the dilapidated space. Dull and cracked linoleum was coming up from the subfloor at one corner. Based on the tacky, tarnished brass light fixture hanging from the stained ceiling in the center of the room, this was an eating area. It held the scents of mold and dust and something long dead.

She peered through an opening on the far side of the room and saw countertops and a stainless refrigerator that looked new.

"You like the place?" Myron asked. "It still needs a lot of work. I've focused my efforts elsewhere." He crossed through the dining area and into a hallway, where he pulled open a doorway and yanked a string. A bulb hanging from the ceiling lit up.

He turned back to Grace. "I know what you're thinking."

She wished she were less predictable in that moment, but she was sure he did.

Run.

And at the same time...

Lily.

"Even if you tried it," Myron said, "you'd fail. I haven't done much cosmetic work, but all the windows have been nailed shut. With time and the right tools, maybe you could manage to get one open, but it wouldn't be easy. Sure, you could crack the glass, but you see how it is, all those little panes? These are old windows, and those panes are real. So for instance, those"—he gestured to the windows in the small room where they'd just stood—"are actually nine panes of glass in a wood frame. You'd have to break all nine panes and then remove the wood in order to get out. Could you do that before I caught you?" He shrugged. "I wouldn't try. Even on the off chance that you got away and didn't freeze to death trying to find help, Lily and I would be long gone by the time anybody got here. And I'd have to punish our sweet Lily for your choices."

Still in his arms, Lily didn't react to the words.

He lifted her and kissed her forehead, leaving his lips against the child's skin for far too long, never taking his eyes off Grace.

"Come on now." His voice was low, almost seductive. "We both know what you're going to do. A woman who blows up her entire life for the sake of a girl she barely knows is not about to give up on her now."

Grace stared at the doorway and the void beyond. She could make out the tall walls on either side. It was a staircase to the basement.

Something told her that if she went into that basement she'd never come back out. That the sunshine she'd felt on her face that afternoon had been the last sunshine she'd ever feel.

But this was what she'd signed up for. She'd told Andrew she'd give her life to protect Lily. In a million years, she'd never imagined that this was how it would end. Seclusion, probably. Prison, possibly.

But being imprisoned by this man?

It had never crossed her mind.

If it had, back when she'd lived in her cabin in Washington, if she'd known this was the endgame, would she still have snatched Lily and run?

She hoped so. She hoped she was that kind of person.

Lily was barely responding now. She'd shrunk so deep into herself that Grace hardly recognized her. But the real Lily, *her* Lily, was still in there. She was still worth fighting for.

Grace turned and glanced at the dark windows, wishing she could see the snow falling lightly on the other side. But that didn't matter. All that mattered was staying with Lily. Protecting her as best she could.

She stalked past Myron and down the steps.

Myron clomped behind her, then stepped past her through the dank room. Concrete all around, metal poles reaching from the floor to the beams, supporting the structure. A few wide, squat windows at the top of the walls showed the black night. A brand-new washer and dryer sat below one of them.

Metal shelving units lined the long back wall, filled with tools and paint cans and cleaning supplies.

Still holding Lily, Myron approached the shelving unit, reached through to the back of one of the supports, and lifted a lever.

Then, he swung the whole thing into the room.

It was a door. A door nobody would ever find.

He held it open for her. "Welcome home."

With lead in her feet, she stepped through. Myron came in behind her and pulled the door closed.

The room was completely dark.

In the silence, Lily screamed, a heart-wrenching sound that nearly weakened Grace's knees.

"Quiet, now." Myron's words, uttered gently, had the desired effect. Lily had learned to obey him immediately.

Overhead fluorescents flickered to life.

Unlike the unfinished basement area they'd just left, this space looked shiny and new. White walls, a queen-sized bed, camera equipment all around. Screens for backdrops. Props. Giant lamps and reflectors. A computer with an oversize screen. Cameras mounted on two tripods.

The studio.

Myron opened yet another door, this one metal and equipped with locks. "You two'll be in here. It's not the nicest accommodations, but it'll work."

She stepped inside and stopped in the middle of the room. Two twin beds, a nightstand between them, a bureau, and a normal interior door. She peeked through it.

A full bathroom. Everything looked new, from the chrome fixtures in the shower to what she guessed were peel-and-stick tiles on the floor. Not fancy but clean.

A linen closet was stocked with towels, soap, shampoo. Even feminine hygiene products.

He'd thought of everything.

"Come on in and sit down," Myron said.

Grace stepped from the bathroom to find Lily on one of the beds. Myron was cutting the duct tape off her hands and feet. "There, sweetheart. That must feel better."

Lily stretched her hands and twisted her feet around.

Myron lifted her left arm and surveyed the cast. "We're going to have to figure out how to get this off."

"The doctor said her arm would be good as new in another week or two," Grace said.

Myron stood, the movement so sudden that she took a step

back. He crossed the room, not stopping until he was inches from her. "How could you let that happen?"

Seriously? The man who'd just tied Lily up and left her to freeze was angry about a broken arm?

"It was an accident."

"Do you have any idea what she's worth? If I find a single mark on her—"

"Do you?" Grace should probably shut up, but anger stirred in her chest like a kettle of water coming to a boil. "She's worth far more than you'll ever understand. She's infinitely valuable."

"You think I don't know that?" The wild look in Myron's eyes had Grace swallowing. "She's my inspiration. My muse. Do you have any idea what I've sacrificed for her?"

"Not *for her*," Grace said. "For you. For your pocketbook."

The anger in his features relaxed, and the expression that replaced it was almost scarier than the rage. "Not for money. It's about so much more than that. You have no idea of my talent. My genius. Someday, Lily's pictures will grace the walls of museums. Someday, they'll see the beauty. The world, with all its puritanical ideals, isn't ready yet, but someday, adults and children alike will gaze at what I've created. She'll be immortalized, as famous as Mona Lisa and far, far more beautiful."

"You're insane."

He just shook his head. "You're just like the rest of them. You don't understand." He gripped her arm and manhandled her to the bed, where he pushed her to a sitting position. "It doesn't matter if you understand or not. You'll take care of her. You'll make sure no harm comes to her. You'll make her happy." He licked his lips. "I think you'll make us both happy."

As cold fear dripped down her back, Grace could think of nothing to say.

But Myron turned in a circle, then gave her an expectant look. "Impressive, right?"

His moods shifted faster than winds in a storm.

"How did you do it so fast?" she asked because, why not? Why not make conversation? Why not pretend to care? Maybe she could gain his trust. Maybe…

She had no idea what to do. What he expected of her, or if she'd be able to provide it.

She only knew she was at his mercy.

"You were in that condo," he said. "If you'd moved into another hotel, I would have watched and waited, but you seemed pretty settled here from the start. Lily was going to school, so I figured you wouldn't be leaving anytime soon. I could take my time. I bought this place and started preparing it for you."

He sat beside Lily and pulled her into his lap.

She went willingly, not fighting him, and popped her thumb into her mouth.

He settled in to talk. "I made myself a fixture in town. The new guy who'd just moved here from Windham, working on my vacation home, hoping to get it ready for spring. Chatted up the locals. I fit right in. Had a contractor out to give me an estimate on the kitchen. He already updated my bathroom." He looked around the space, pride puffing his chest. "Did this myself, of course. Couldn't have anybody figuring out my secret." He knocked on the wall behind him. "Completely soundproof. I could have the whole Coventry PD on the other side of this wall, and you could scream your head off, and they'd never hear you." He turned back to her with a proud smile. "Even went to The Patriot for lunch today. I had a nice chat with James. You know James, right? Married to Cassidy? She's the reason you're here. I needed to know if you'd told them about me, but James was oblivious. Andrew probably knows about me, but it doesn't matter.

"I've been trying to figure you out all along. Ever since the first time I followed Lily to your house, I've been trying to get to know you, to find out what kind of person you are. Going through your things, *moving* your things. It was all just a ruse to see how you'd react. Watching people, filming people…It's what I do."

What was he saying? He was the one who'd been messing with

her things? That day he'd shown up at her place to get Lily, claiming Lily hadn't told him where she'd gone...

Lily *hadn't* told him. But he'd known. "So you're saying..." She tried to reconcile his words with what she knew. "When my hairbrush went missing in Denver..."

"That was me, of course. Every place you've been, I've been. The cameras you saw today? I had 'em at your cabin in Washington. At that extended-stay hotel in Kansas City. Except places you only stayed a night or two, I installed cameras."

She closed her eyes, accepting the horror of it. How many times had she accused Lily? Had Lily known? Maybe not for sure, but perhaps she'd guessed. When the laptop went missing and then showed up, Lily had seemed afraid.

Grace glanced at the girl, who hadn't reacted to anything Myron said. She'd checked out. Maybe it was better that way. Grace wished she were as oblivious.

"You took the laptop," she said.

"After your little jaunt to Texas, I needed to know what you'd learned. It definitely stepped up my timetable. I still didn't plan to make a move for a couple of weeks. I figured with Darla dead—"

"She's not dead." Maybe Grace shouldn't have said it, but the man was so smug, so sure of himself.

He waved off her words with a flick of his wrist. "Of course she is."

"She's in the hospital, but she's gonna make it. And she knows I have Lily. She and her family aren't going to stop until they find her."

Myron took that information in with narrowed, assessing eyes. After a moment, he shook it off. "Doesn't matter. They'll never find you. See, the key is to always do the unexpected. For instance, I know you called your boyfriend earlier. But despite the car in the parking lot, he wasn't home. He was in Plymouth, just like he said he'd be. No idea why his car was there, but I've been watching the camera in his place all day. No movement. So I wasn't worried when you called him. He's probably at your place now. It's gotta be crawling with cops. They'll start canvassing the neighbors. Know what they'll find out?"

Though she'd figured the question was rhetorical, he seemed to be waiting for an answer. "What?"

"There's been a 'suspicious van'"—he made air quotes with his fingers—"in the area. Missouri plates. I bought it back when you were in Kansas City. Drove it up here. But when I've been going back and forth to town, I've been driving my boring black Honda Accord with the New Hampshire plates. I'm guessing the police have put out a BOLO on the van. They'll find it parked in a lot in Manchester. That's where they'll hit a dead end.

"Best part of my plan? We stay right here. They'll be chasing their tails all over the state, and we'll be right here, just a few miles away, and nobody'll ever know."

Again, he paused to give her a moment to react. He'd obviously been dying to tell somebody how clever he was.

Did he really expect her to praise his ingenuity?

"If there's nothing else," she said, "Lily needs her rest."

He glared through narrowed eyes.

She should play along. If she wasn't rescued soon, she'd have to learn to. But she didn't have it in her tonight. Because he was right. Nobody would find them. If she couldn't figure a way out of the windowless room, that basement with the metal doors and the heavy deadbolts, she and Lily would be at this man's mercy forever.

CHAPTER THIRTY-TWO

ANDREW STOOD in the parking lot between his and Grace's condos and watched the activity. Cops had swarmed in, some in uniform, others in plain clothes. Some of the uniformed ones were knocking on doors, others going in and out of Grace's place, seemingly doing nothing.

Not nothing. Surely.

An older, overweight man who'd introduced himself as chief or sheriff or something was snapping orders and making calls.

Fitz and Dylan had introduced themselves and offered their aid. Dylan had jogged away to help with the canvassing.

Fitz had gone inside.

The rest of Andrew's friends—Braden, Reid, Garrett, Thomas, and James—were there, primed to jump in.

But there was nothing to do.

Grace and Lily were gone.

The first cops had entered through the unlocked back door—where the video doorbell had been broken. He'd told one of the cops about that, and the guy'd given him a knowing look, a look that said, *if only you'd replaced it immediately.*

Nobody needed to say the words. Andrew'd failed them. He knew that.

He knew.

Braden's hand gripped his shoulder, but Andrew stepped away. "Don't. I can't..."

"I understand."

Maybe he did. He'd faced something with Carly. Andrew'd never gotten the details, but Carly had been taken, and Braden had feared he'd never see her again.

But pain wasn't like spare parts. Pain wasn't interchangeable. Pain was uniquely designed for the person who experienced it.

So no, Braden didn't understand how he felt.

He didn't understand the regret settling in Andrew's being like tar, so sticky and heavy it would never be scraped away.

Dylan jogged down the sidewalk and approached the one in charge as if he had information.

Andrew moved that direction, desperate for news.

"...a navy-blue van. Missouri plates." Dylan rattled off the plate number, and the chief/sheriff guy repeated the information into a phone.

When Dylan turned to Andrew, he had a look on his face that made Andrew's heart pound. Hope. The man had hope.

Andrew needed it, desperately.

"Lady on the next block said she's seen a van around. A few others mentioned it as well. Nobody ever saw anybody get in or out. It was picked up on her security camera, so we were able to pull a plate number."

"Great."

"It's a good lead," Dylan said. "Chief Cote's already put out a BOLO—a be-on-the-lookout. Someone'll see it."

Chief Cote. He was the guy in charge. "She saw the van tonight?" Andrew asked.

Dylan shook his head. "But that doesn't mean anything. He probably just parked somewhere else tonight, maybe somewhere closer. I figure they went out the back door, crossed the little yard, and went around to the front of one of the condos on the other side of the development. We're knocking on doors, seeing if anybody saw anything. We'll find them."

Andrew wanted to feel the hope that Dylan obviously felt. He tried to conjure it, but the truth was too strong. "This guy...He won't be that easy to find."

Dylan's eyes narrowed. "Why do you say that?"

"Let's say you're right, that the van belonged to Myron Bowman. That means he's been here for days. Why wait until tonight? And why be so obvious? I mean, could he drive a *more* suspicious vehicle than a dark van with out-of-state plates?" Andrew shook his head. "No. No, if it was him, then it was a ruse."

"Not all criminals are masterminds," Dylan said. "Most aren't all that smart at all."

But Bowman had managed to pass Lily off as his daughter for years, and nobody had known. He'd managed to find Grace and Lily despite all of Grace's precautions. "This guy is, though. He's smart."

"But he was rushed," Dylan said. "The boxes. You saw the boxes, right?"

Andrew didn't want to think about those boxes, all stacked neatly by the front door.

"He must've known she was packing," Dylan said. "He didn't want to lose her again."

Nobody had asked Andrew about that. Though all his friends had to have been wondering, not one had brought up the obvious fact that Grace had been about to move away for good.

"Do you think she saw him?" Dylan asked. "Was that why she was leaving?"

"Grace found Lily's grandmother. She was taking her there."

"It's one thing to take a trip to Texas," Dylan said. "It's another thing to relocate permanently. Unless she wanted to stay near her. Or was she going to fight for custody or something?"

None of what had transpired between himself and Grace would make any difference in finding her. He didn't say anything

Chief Cote called, "O'Donnell!"

Dylan turned back to the chief, and they moved away from Andrew.

He should stay close, listen to what they were saying. But for what purpose? They knew what they were doing. At this point, Andrew could offer nothing of value.

His other friends surrounded him again.

He needed air. He needed to think and pray and...and be alone.

He brushed past the guys and marched to the end of the row of condos. Turned toward the back and walked around to her door.

It was quieter back there. Though lights were on in condos all around—the police hadn't worried about waking the neighbors—he didn't see a soul.

He stared at Grace's tiny yard, his breath fogging in the frigid air. If there'd been footprints, they were gone now, all covered by a growing layer of snow.

He spun slowly. A car could have been parked in any of the lots, or down by the playground. Not a suspicious van but something nobody would look twice at.

A distant noise had him turning toward the woods. There was nothing back there. Nothing for miles and miles and miles. Yet...

Was that a dog barking?

He tried to make out shapes, seeing trees and more trees, wondering if he'd lost his mind. Maybe he had.

His dress shoes were not designed to traverse snow-covered fields, but he ignored the cold seeping through the Italian leather and started toward the sound.

The ambient light from the condo complex reflected off the fresh snow. He was still a good fifty yards away when he saw the outline of a small dog.

He jogged toward it.

The dog didn't run his direction, though, just stayed where it was, barking all the more. Was there something there?

A body?

Andrew's stomach twisted. Bowman was only after Lily. Grace was disposable. And she'd caused him worlds of trouble.

Please, God. Don't let her be dead.

But what would keep the dog out there, on this frigid night, except one of the people it loved?

Andrew slowed as he approached, afraid the little spaniel would bolt. Was it...? He inched closer and realized it was definitely Lily's dog. He called, "Regis, come."

The animal didn't move closer, and its barks only became more furious.

Andrew approached, but when he got within a few feet, Regis dashed into the woods.

Andrew followed, looking around but seeing nothing unusual. He pulled in a breath and blew it out with a prayer of gratitude. Not a body. Not yet, anyway.

Garrett's voice came from behind him. "That the girl's dog?"

He turned to see that Garrett and Thomas had been following at a distance.

"I have no idea where it's going."

He stepped into the woods. Behind him, Thomas made a call, telling somebody what they were doing.

"It's probably nothing," Andrew said to Garrett. But hope pounded a drum in his chest. Why would the dog be in the woods? He was a good dog, a smart dog.

Okay, he wasn't Lassie. They weren't about to find Timmy at the bottom of a well.

But Regis was loyal. He loved his girls. If Lily and Grace had gone this way, maybe Regis could lead Andrew to them.

Anyway, he had to do something.

He started down the path, but Garrett's grip on his arm stopped him. "Let's run back and get the four-wheelers from the shed." Garrett did enough work for the development that they'd given him keys.

"We're not going to be able to go faster than the dog," Andrew said. "What difference will it make?"

"You never know what we're going to find. Better to have them and not need them than—"

"Need 'em and not have 'em." Andrew scooped the dog up and followed Garrett and Thomas to the shed.

Seven minutes later, Andrew set the dog—who'd been practically snarling at him the entire trip to get the machines—back down on the path.

Regis bolted into the woods.

Andrew took the lead in his ATV, and Garrett and Thomas followed.

They were both dressed for the occasion, wearing jeans and a winter coat and boots. When Andrew had first arrived home, someone had gone into his place and found his wool overcoat, so at least he had that. No hat and gloves, though, and his thin suit pants weren't exactly weather-appropriate. His fingers were so cold, they felt like they were going to freeze and fall right off his body.

They rode slowly, barely faster than if they were walking, following the dog. Ten minutes passed, twenty.

And then, Regis stopped in the middle of a clearing.

He turned in a circle, sat on his haunches, and whined.

Andrew braked, peering into the darkness. There was nothing there. Nothing but trees, trees, and more trees.

He approached the dog and looked down at it. "Where are they?"

Somehow, Lassie would have found a way to answer.

While Garrett and Thomas climbed off their four-wheeler, Andrew walked around the edge of the clearing. He turned to Garrett, who was standing in the middle of the space, but his friend only shrugged.

Andrew glared at the dog again. "What is this supposed to be, some kind of clue?" Fury rose, heating him far more than the coat did.

Garrett and Thomas watched, saying nothing.

"Sorry I dragged you guys..."

But he caught sight of something. Maybe it was the angle. Maybe the different perspective.

He stalked across the clearing and peered down at the mostly snow-covered ground.

But it wasn't all covered yet. A lot of the snow had settled on branches and needles overhead.

He pulled out his phone and aimed its flashlight, bending to see better.

It was a muddy spot at the edge of the path. And there was the distinct impression of a tire.

Thomas crouched beside him. "Four-wheeler?"

Shrugging, Andrew stood and looked for more tracks. The path itself was covered with snow, but here on the edge...

He saw another impression in the leafy bracken. "I think he turned around here."

"If it was him," Garrett said. "People use these trails all the time."

"I know."

Thomas said, "But the dog led us here. There must be a reason. It can't be a coincidence."

It could be, though. *God, now'd be a great time for You to light a path or speak through the dog. Would that be so hard? You made a donkey talk.*

God was silent, and Regis only panted after the long run, but Garrett was nodding. "So the guy parked here, got the girls, and walked them back through the woods to this spot. Got on a vehicle and drove...where?" He looked around, but there was nothing in any direction.

Thomas was staring at the trail that continued up the back side of the mountain. "Further," he said.

Garrett yanked his phone from his pocket. Swore. "No service."

Andrew checked too and got the same result.

Thomas said, "Nothing."

Andrew walked a few feet farther on the path, the dog at his

ROBIN PATCHEN

side. Regis was letting him lead now, as if he knew where he was going. He'd probably only get them lost.

The thought had him yanking his phone from his pocket again. He might not have phone service, but the GPS should work. He had an app that tracked his jogs. He turned it on so he'd have an idea of where he'd already looked. He studied the map to get a sense of where he was.

No landmarks, no roads, no nothing for miles and miles.

But there had to be something. There had to be.

"We should go back until we get service," Thomas said. "Call and let the police know what we found."

"I'm not going back." Andrew settled Regis on the ATV's seat and climbed on next to him. The dog was no tracker, but maybe he could be of help. "You two let them know what I'm doing."

"What are you planning?" Thomas asked.

"This has to lead somewhere."

Thomas and Garrett shared a look. Thomas said, "These trails go all over the mountain. We're going to need help."

"Fine. Go get help. I'll be out here until I find them."

Thomas whipped his gloves off his hands and held them out. "I'll have someone bring me a pair."

Andrew took them and yanked them on. "Thanks."

Thomas pulled something else from one of his parka's pockets. He extended it to Andrew.

A handgun.

"You know how to use that?"

Andrew took the weapon. He didn't know enough about guns to know the caliber or make or anything like that, but he knew how to check the safety and the magazine. It was fully loaded.

"One in the chamber," Thomas said. "Don't use it unless you have no choice. I'll be back with help. If you find them, sit tight and wait. Let the police handle it."

Good advice, but it came from a guy who'd given him a gun. Mixed messages at best.

Andrew shoved the gun in his pocket. He was about to get

moving when Garrett lifted the dog and sat in his seat, settling Regis on his lap.

"Let's go."

Andrew wasn't sorry for the company.

Thomas lifted a hand, and Andrew gunned the engine.

He had no idea what he was driving them into, but he couldn't worry about Garrett or himself at this point. If Grace and Lily were at the end of this trail, Andrew would find them or die trying.

CHAPTER THIRTY-THREE

GRACE GOT Lily to brush her teeth and change into pajamas Myron had left in the bureau, along with neatly folded jeans and sweaters. He'd bought clothes for Grace as well, but she wasn't about to put them on. She tucked Lily into one of the twin beds and read to her from a book he'd left in a nightstand drawer.

The nighttime routine felt surreal, and as little as Grace wanted to get comfortable, to play into Myron's bizarre plan, Lily needed normalcy. She needed to feel comfortable and safe, even if she wasn't.

Grace didn't know what else to do.

When the book was finished, Lily said her prayers, asking God to bless each of her friends, her teacher, Grace, and Andrew. When she prayed He'd protect Regis, her monotone voice cracked.

Grace laid beside her, wrapped her arms around her, and sang a lullaby.

Long after Lily's breathing evened out, Grace stayed, needing the child's presence probably as much as Lily needed hers. When she was sure Lily was in a deep sleep, she prowled the room, opening every drawer, checking every cabinet. She needed a weapon. Something heavy or something sharp. Anything she could use to take Myron out.

If he were wounded badly enough, she could search his pockets, get the keys, and get them out of there.

She could see no other way of escape.

She was sitting on the bathroom floor looking through the first-aid kit she'd found in the cabinet beneath the sink, hoping for a pair of scissors to cut gauze or medical tape, when the door creaked. Expecting Lily, she pasted on a smile and looked up.

Myron was leaning against the jamb. "It came with scissors. I took 'em out. It was a conundrum I had to solve. If one of you gets hurt and I'm not down here, how can you let me know? I didn't want to risk an intercom. What if you used it when somebody was here?" His smile was relaxed and confident. "The first-aid kit should work until I check on you."

She shoved it back in the cabinet and closed the cabinet door softly. "You should keep your voice down so you don't wake her."

"She's a heavy sleeper," Myron said. "You must have learned that by now."

"Still..." Her voice trailed as Myron stepped closer to her and held out his hand.

"Come on." He wiggled his fingers. "I don't bite."

She pushed off the floor and stood without taking his hand.

"You're a stubborn one, aren't you?"

The bathroom was already small, but with him in there, the walls inched inward. She moved back but bumped into the edge of the tub.

He moved closer. "That's okay." His voice was low, seductive. "Lily was stubborn once too. She learned. You'll learn." He took Grace's hand.

And she saw again all the images she'd seen in the spring. Lily in pose after pose after pose. There were other children as well, but the bulk of the images were Lily.

She felt Myron's triumph, his pride, his arrogance. His sheer and shocking narcissism.

The man truly believed he was unique, special, set apart from the rest of humanity—and he was, but it was his depravity that set him apart. To Myron, his photographs of children were art, a *gift* to the world.

She yanked her hand away and sucked in a deep breath. She needed space, but he was right there. Watching her through narrowed eyes.

"What was that about?"

"I don't like to hold hands," she said. "It makes me feel weird."

Lily's words.

"Why?"

"It goes back to my childhood," she said. "Everything will be better if you don't hold my hand. Okay?"

Still, the eyes were narrowed. "You'd think, with your psychology background, you'd have gotten over that. But you never earned more than a bachelor's, right?"

He backed up, and she pulled in a deep breath as if she'd been deprived of oxygen.

"Me, I never needed college. They didn't have anything to teach me of import. I was always better than my teachers at the only thing that mattered, capturing beauty through photography." He backed to the bathroom door. "Come on."

"Where are we going?"

He offered no explanation, just waited for her to comply with his commands.

She stepped past him into the small bedroom, where Lily was sound asleep.

But Myron didn't stop there. He pulled open the metal door—it didn't seem to be locked—and led the way into the studio.

She froze at the entrance. "What do you want?"

"Pull that door closed," he said. "She's a sound sleeper, but we don't want to take any chances."

Grace did as Myron asked. Anything to protect Lily. The door closed with a click. She pushed, and it opened again.

"We won't keep it locked when we're out here. We need access to her, and she to us. She is just a child, after all." A smile spread across his face. "You're fortunate, Grace Mullen. If you were ugly or fat or old, if you didn't have so much going for you, I'd have killed you in the woods and left your body for the birds. But you're attractive. You're not like Lily, of course. You're not perfect. And you're not like me, obviously."

Like him in what respect? Insane? Egomaniacal?

"But you've been a good mother to Lily," he said. "I'm going to let you continue in that role. We're going to be a family, the three of us. And we're going to be happy." He clicked on a lamp aimed at the bed, which shone in the glare. He looked through the lens of a camera on a tripod, adjusting a few settings. He didn't look at her when he said, "Don't worry. I just want to get a sense of the potential. I'm not sure yet how I'll use you." When he glanced her way, a gleam lit his eyes. "I mean, I have *some* idea, but I'm talking about merchandise." He added a wink as if it might put her at ease.

Every nerve in her body trembled.

She would scream if she could get the sound to carry up her throat. A pathetic squeak issued from her mouth.

She backed up a step, then another.

Looked around for something, anything to use as a weapon. She reached for a black pole leaning against the wall. It was a couple of inches in diameter, probably a part to one of his many stage lights or easels. She lifted it.

But he was there, his hands wrapping around her from behind. "I'll need to be more careful about what I leave lying around." He removed the pole from her hands and let it fall to the concrete floor, where it clanked as it bounced.

"Good thing we closed that door." Myron's breath was hot against her ear. "Now would be a very inopportune time for Lily to wake up." He gripped Grace's arm. "Come on. Onto the bed for me."

She stopped at the edge, her body refusing her brain's commands.

"It would be better for you"—Myron leaned close—"if you'd do what I say. And better for Lily."

Lily.

This was all about Lily.

She sat on the mattress.

Mercifully, Myron returned to the camera. "Beautiful," he said. "You look so..." He snapped a few photos, then leaned out and leered at her. "You know what I'm going to do to you, don't you?"

Cold fear had her crossing her arms.

"I love that," he said, snapping more pictures. "The fear is palpable."

He kept talking, telling her the things he planned for her, for them. The more he talked, the more excited he became, the more photos he snapped.

She kept sitting there, apparently looking exactly as he wanted her to look. She had no idea what he was seeing through that camera lens, but she assumed the vision he had barely resembled the truth. There was no beauty in this moment. Only fear and horror on her part. Ego and lust on his.

But she'd play along. The longer he spent on the far side of the camera, the better.

CHAPTER THIRTY-FOUR

Andrew almost missed it.

At first, he'd thought it was a leaf, but as he'd approached, as the headlights on the four-wheeler had illuminated it better, he'd realized what it was.

He parked and swept the item off the ground.

"What is it?" Garrett asked.

He held the thin leather glove up for his friend to see. "It's hers."

"You're sure?"

Grace had worn these gloves at Dad's birthday party. Thank God, *thank God* it hadn't been covered in snow.

He lifted it to his face and breathed in the scent. It didn't smell like Grace. This wasn't the movies or some romance flick. It wasn't even warm. But knowing she'd been there, right there...

Where was she now?

He gazed at the thick woods all around. The path continued further up the mountain, but if Myron had taken her that way, then why drop the glove here? Why not a mile back or a mile forward?

There was a reason.

Regis hopped from the four-wheeler and ran up and down the trail, pausing often to sniff, acting as frantic as Andrew felt.

Garrett, on the other hand, was gazing deep into the woods. "That way"—he pointed to the right—"leads to more trails." He turned to face the woods to the left. "I have no idea what's in that direction."

While he spoke, Regis ran into the woods not far from where Garrett had just indicated. Andrew followed, pushing a low-hanging branch out of the way. "There's a path here." He crouched down, studying the ground. Maybe tracks.

Maybe wishful thinking.

Still, this had to be the way. He yanked out his phone to call the police. Still no service.

He approached the four-wheeler. "Come on."

"Hold up," Garrett said. "If Thomas gets the cops to follow us, we need to show what direction we've gone." They found some fallen branches in the woods and dragged them back to the trail. Together, they arranged the branches in a very crude arrow pointing to the path.

Garrett stepped back. "No way they'll miss that."

Andrew peered into the darkness ahead. How far would they have to go from there? If they took the ATV, would Myron hear them coming?

But it could be miles further.

What to do?

Before he voiced the question, Garrett said, "I think speed trumps stealth." He didn't say what Andrew was thinking, that Bowman had a good lead. That most likely all they'd find was an empty road. Most likely, they were already too late.

Lead us, Father. Take us to them.

Twenty minutes later, the ATV bounced in a hole in the middle of the woods and stopped.

Andrew cut the engine.

Garrett jumped off to survey the damage. "I think we're stuck."

"There's that higher education at work." Andrew climbed off the machine to confirm what he already knew.

Up ahead, the trees were too close together to maneuver the ATV through anyway, the ground too covered in brush.

Somewhere, he'd lost the trail. Had it been seconds before, or minutes? He'd been certain he was going the right way, and then worried. And now...

He muttered a curse word under his breath, feeling the need to be quiet despite the fact that the over-loud ATV would have announced their presence for miles.

"It can't be too far behind us," Garrett said. "We could push the thing out and backtrack."

The area was too narrow to turn the vehicle around, assuming they could get it out of the hole.

The dog scampered beside him.

"Which way, Regis?"

But the dog just whined.

"Lassie, you are not." Andrew lifted his phone, praying he'd have service.

No deal.

He lit the flashlight and aimed ahead. Maybe the path had veered one direction or another, but they weren't far from it. Best case scenario, just go forward. If Myron had brought them up here, surely there was a road somewhere.

Idiot. Shaking his head, he navigated to the app he'd opened earlier, which marked the route he'd taken. According to it, he'd gone more than five miles.

But to where?

He expanded the map to get a wider view and found a road. It wasn't named, but he saw a winding absence of trees that indicated something. He held the screen out for Garrett. "About a half mile ahead."

Garrett took the phone from his hand, then looked around as if there might be a road sign somewhere. "I think I just figured out where we are."

"Yeah?" He looked at the screen to see what his friend was seeing, but nothing had changed.

"There's a house up here. Dilapidated and in desperate need of work, but it's got great bones. I tried to buy it to fix up and sell. The owner lives in Hawaii, so I figured he'd be eager to get it off his hands. I reached out to him, but he wasn't willing to let it go. Must have history with the place or something."

"When was this?"

"Six weeks ago, maybe two months."

He doubted Garrett knew the renter's name but asked anyway.

Garrett shrugged. "No clue. Sorry."

Probably didn't matter. Myron was likely not using his real name. Andrew tapped the screen. "Where is it?"

Garrett shifted the map this way and that, then held it out to him and pointed to a spot on the screen. "It's hard to see, but I think that's it."

Less than half a mile away.

"Let's go."

They'd been walking for what felt like an hour when his flashlight beam bounced off something metal.

It was a detached garage with a side door. Quietly, he opened that door and saw a Polaris inside, one of those fancy off-the-road vehicles.

His heart pounded a steady stream of hope.

He turned to see Garrett at the edge of the structure, facing away. He joined him.

A house. A house in the middle of nowhere.

"This is it," Garrett said.

Light shone through a downstairs window. More light seemed to come out of the ground.

The basement. The lights were on in the basement.

The rest of the house was dark.

"They're here," he said.

Garrett nodded but said, "Maybe."

Andrew checked his phone. Still no service.

Well, he wasn't about to sit there and wait for help to arrive. If Grace was there, he was going to find her.

He pulled the handgun from his pocket and slid the safety off.

Garrett gripped his arm. "What are you doing?"

"I'm getting inside that house. What do you think?"

"You can't just break in, man. We don't know for sure that—"

"There's an ATV in there. If they're not here now, they were at some point."

"Maybe. But what if you're wrong?"

If he was wrong...

Then it would be breaking-and-entering.

"I'll apologize and explain and hope they go easy on me."

"Dude, you're gonna land yourself behind bars."

Andrew winced at the thought. He'd told Grace his biggest fear was going back to prison. Turned out, he'd been wrong about that.

He was living his biggest fear. If they didn't find Grace and Lily, he'd never get over it.

He studied the house. Breaking down a door would be loud, and who knew what Bowman would do if he heard the noise?

They needed a distraction.

CHAPTER THIRTY-FIVE

GRACE KNEW Myron wouldn't be content with taking photographs for long. She should have tried harder, posed for the camera. When he'd started to manipulate her this way and that, she should have played it up. Maybe, if he'd gotten lost in his *art*, he'd have forgotten the rest.

But even though he'd been clear about his plans, she hadn't had the stomach to pretend.

When he stepped from behind the camera, his dark figure almost hidden on the far side of the bright lights, she'd known what was coming.

He moved to a different camera, looked through the lens, and then stepped away.

He would be filming this.

Better me than Lily. The thought brought a modicum of comfort.

He approached the bed, anticipation in his features.

She scooted away until she reached the corner, pulling her knees to her chest.

He crawled onto the bed and yanked her feet out from under her.

She'd known he was strong, much stronger than she was, but the strength in that one move sent panic to her throat.

He hovered over her, whispering, "Feel free to fight. It'll make a great show."

And then, he lowered himself to kiss her.

She told herself to remain still as a stone, to not react. But her instincts kicked in. She knew the camera was picking it all up. Knew he'd probably enjoy watching a replay later.

Intellectually, she knew, but she fought him anyway.

He seemed to love it. Though he could have easily overpowered her, he allowed himself to be pushed away. It went on for hours and hours, or so it felt, him trying to take her clothes off, her fighting to keep them on. Him trying to kiss her, her turning her head. Him trying to touch her, her squirming away.

She had no hope. She knew that. She knew he'd eventually tire of the game. When he did, she wouldn't have a chance of escape. He was bigger and stronger. She could feel his caged strength when he gripped her wrists. Whenever she got them loose, she knew it wasn't by her own power but by his mercy.

No, not mercy.

Showmanship. That was all, nothing more.

Even knowing all that, she fought him. And when she peeked —she mostly kept her eyes closed, and not just because of the bright lights overhead—and got a glimpse of him, she knew he was enjoying every second of it.

But then something shifted. She felt a change and opened her eyes. The amusement was gone from his face, replaced by dark lust.

He yanked her hands over her head and pressed his palm to hers, pinning her in place.

She felt what he felt.

Lust and possession and power.

Terror filled her heart and ripped a scream from her mouth.

He laughed, the sound low and vibrating in her ear. "That's

good. Don't worry about waking Lily. This room is soundproof too."

He loved it. She could feel how much he loved her terror. She tried to hide it but couldn't.

He slipped his hands off hers, and the darkness lifted from her mind, but not her body.

His fingers moved over her middle, reached the button on her jeans.

She tried to squirm away, but he wasn't playing anymore. He pinned her to the mattress, and she was powerless to stop him.

A bell rang.

Loud and shocking.

Myron stopped, propped himself up on his arms.

She tried to wiggle out from beneath him, but he slid his hand over her neck and squeezed. "Be still." She obeyed, and he let up the pressure the tiniest bit.

The bell rang again and again.

A doorbell. It had to be, though it was magnified as though through a speaker.

Maybe it was. This room was soundproof, so he'd need a way to know if somebody was at the door.

But it was the middle of the night.

Myron let out a stream of curses and climbed off her. He straightened his clothes and patted down his hair.

The bell kept ringing.

He walked to the doorway. It had a combination lock, and he punched the buttons. She couldn't see what numbers he hit from where she was lying.

The door clicked, and he pushed through it.

She bolted off the bed and shoved her foot in the doorway.

The bell was still ringing incessantly, which had to explain why he hadn't noticed the door didn't close behind him.

Whoever was out there was determined.

Maybe it was the police?

She heard him pound up the stairs and across the floor over her head.

Heart racing, she reached for one of the pillows on the bed, but her arms weren't long enough to reach. There was nothing else.

She slipped off her boot and shoved it in the doorway, then grabbed a pillow to put in that space to keep the door open.

She pushed through to the basement. The door upstairs would be locked. She'd heard it slam.

The window, though.

She grabbed a stool from Myron's studio, shoved it beneath the window, and climbed up.

The doorbell stopped ringing. Voices filtered in.

Was the rest of the basement soundproof? She considered screaming, but would that bring help, or just bring Myron back?

The window wouldn't open.

But, unlike the ones upstairs, this only had the one pane. It was tiny, and she wasn't sure she'd fit, but Lily could.

She ran through the studio and into the bedroom, where Lily lay sound asleep.

"Wake up, sweetheart."

She grabbed the child's clothes and started shoving her feet into her sneakers.

Lily was half awake.

"You have to wake up. There's somebody here. I'm going to lift you out the window, and you're going to run to the front of the house and scream. Tell the man you need help, that you've been kidnapped."

Lily shook her head. She looked terrified.

"You have to, honey. It's the only way."

As soon as the glass broke, Myron would come running. Lily would have to get out fast.

Grace found a sweater and shoved it around Lily's shoulders, then lifted her and carried her through the studio, setting her down a good distance from the window. "I'm gonna break it and then lift you out, okay? You'll run that way"—she pointed to the right—"to the front of the house. Hear the voices? I think it's the police."

She had no idea if it was the police. She hoped so. She hoped it was somebody looking for them.

Sending Lily out to who-knew-what? It was dangerous.

But nothing was as dangerous as staying in that basement.

Lily shook her head hard. "I can't leave. He'll be mad."

Grace crouched down to Lily's level. "You have to get out of here."

Her little head shook.

"Don't you trust me?"

But Lily's eyes only widened further. And who could blame her? Grace hadn't protected her. She'd promised, and she'd failed.

Grace needed to know how to convince Lily to go. She needed to see into her heart. She swallowed her fear, took a deep breath, and gripped Lily's hands.

All the ugly things came—the pictures Myron had taken of her, the way he'd manipulated her, treated her like a possession. She felt fear and shame. But behind all that came bright and beautiful emotions. Love and tenderness and kindness. She saw herself in Lily's eyes, a protector. She felt Lily's love for her.

And her uncertainty. If Grace didn't love her, could she be trusted?

She let the child's hands go and slid her palms over Lily's little cheeks. "I love you, sweet girl. I love you with all my heart." They might have been the truest words Grace had ever spoken. "I need you to be safe. You are priceless and worth protecting. Please, please trust me. Please go out that window."

Eyes still round as marbles, Lily said, "What about you?"

She didn't know if she'd fit and didn't think she'd be able to hoist herself up. "Tell them I'm here. They'll rescue me. You can do it, darling girl. You can do it. Okay?"

But the voices had faded. Footsteps pounded on the floor overhead.

The door at the top of the stairs opened.

Grace grabbed Lily's hand and, snatching the pillow from the floor, let the door to their prison shut. She pulled her through the studio and into the bedroom. "Wait here." After propping the bedroom door against the pillow, she grabbed the metal pole from the floor where Myron had dropped it. Positioning herself beside the entrance, she lifted it.

Because of the bright lights still aimed at the bed behind her, she was in shadows and prayed it would be enough cover.

Myron reached the bottom of the steps and uttered a curse word, pounding across the space. He pushed through the thick metal door and paused to let his eyes adjust to the light.

She swung the metal pole like a baseball bat.

It connected with his head, and he went down.

She stood over him and hit him again, a scream crawling up her throat. It escaped as the rod connected with his skull a second time.

He didn't move.

She stepped back, hands trembling.

She'd done it.

But he moaned and rolled to his side. She didn't have long.

"Lily!"

The child stepped out of the bedroom.

"Come on. Let's go." She lifted Lily and stepped over Myron into the basement, expecting him to grab her foot or do something to take her down.

He didn't. Thank God.

She wanted to pull the hidden door closed to lock Myron in, but his body had fallen half in the doorway, and she didn't dare move it.

She dashed up the stairs, but the door was locked. She banged on it, screaming.

But nobody was up there. Whoever'd been there was gone.

She had to get Lily out.

She hopped over Myron again. This time, he grabbed ahold of her jeans and yanked.

She shook him off and somehow kept her balance as she

hopped away. She grabbed the pipe, swung it at his head again, and rushed past him to the window. With rage and fear still coursing, she smashed the end into the glass.

It crashed loudly, pieces raining on her.

She used the pole to clear the edges, then turned to Lily, who was cowering against the far wall, thumb in her mouth. "Come on, sweetheart. Let's get you out of here." After that, she'd get the keys out of Myron's pocket. But not until Lily was safe.

And if somehow, Myron stopped her from escaping? She wouldn't think about the miles and miles of forest out there. Somebody'd been at the door. Somebody would find her.

Please, God. Please.

She hoisted the child in her arms. Lily didn't protest, but it was harder than Grace had thought it would be to lift her high enough. She didn't want to stand on the stool, afraid they'd both fall.

"You can do it, sweetie. Just pull yourself up."

"I'm scared," Lily said. "It's so dark."

A gloved hand came through from the other side. "I got you."

Andrew?

It couldn't be.

He said, "Take my hand, sweetie." And then, "You okay, Grace?"

A million questions filled her mind. Her heart seemed to swell to twice its normal size.

Before she could respond, Lily was pulled from her arms.

Grace peered up at the open window, and Andrew's face filled it. "We're trying to get inside. If you want to sit tight—"

"No." She turned toward where she'd left Myron. He was lying still. Had she knocked him out? Maybe. "I need to get out now, before he wakes up."

She moved the step stool into place and climbed on top, but looking at the small window, she said, "I don't think I'll fit."

"There's plenty of room," Andrew said. "Give me your hands."

He held his through the window. He'd taken off his glove, probably to get a better grip on her. She'd feel everything he was feeling.

She didn't even hesitate before she slid her palms against his. While he pulled her through the window, the bottom scraping against her middle, she reveled in the feelings filling her heart.

Relief, gratitude. And love.

CHAPTER THIRTY-SIX

THE SECOND GRACE cleared the window, Andrew swept her into his arms and held her tight. She held him back, and he wondered if they'd ever be able to let go.

Lily hovered beside him, holding Regis in her arms, kissing him and cooing. The dog was going crazy licking her face and wriggling to get away like Tigger on steroids.

Lily was safe. Grace was safe.

Andrew couldn't push words past the emotion in his throat.

He backed away, but Grace didn't release her grip.

"Sweetheart, where is Bowman?"

"I hit him, hard. In the head. A couple of times."

"Where? Is he alive?"

She glanced behind her at the basement window. "He was when we left him."

Her voice cracked, and he could feel her sobs. "It's okay. You're okay."

Garrett approached. "No keys in the Polaris. They must be in the house."

"We'll have to break the door down." Andrew gripped Grace's upper arms and pushed her back so he could look at her. "Are you all right?"

She nodded, took a deep breath, and then scooped Lily up, dog and all.

Thirty seconds of weakness, and she was strong again.

Wow, he loved this woman.

"Grace," Garrett said. "Did you see keys? Or maybe a cell phone?"

She shook her head. "The keys to the thing we drove here in, they're in his pocket. Can't we just take your car? How did you get here?"

"Same way you did," Andrew said.

Garrett looked back at the house. "So we break it down. Door or window? Or we could go through the basement."

"The door to the upstairs is locked," Grace said. "You won't be able to get into the house that way."

Andrew started toward the back, pulling out the handgun. "You suppose I could shoot the lock off, or does that just work in movies?"

Garrett chuckled. "Let's not try it."

"The windows are nailed shut," Grace said.

"Maybe we can break the door down, or—"

"No need." Garrett ran toward the street, calling over his shoulder, "I think the cavalry's here."

Andrew had never been happier to see the glow of red and blue lights. Sure enough, the police had arrived.

A *click* drew his attention to the house.

The back door was pushing open.

Grace had her back to it, facing him, Lily in her arms.

Neither of them saw what he did.

Bowman stepped onto the back stoop, the barrel of a long black gun raised.

"No!"

Andrew tackled Grace, pulling all of them down.

The blast of the shotgun exploded in his ears.

Somebody screamed.

Andrew rolled off Grace, made it to his knees.

The pistol was in his hand before he'd registered his need for it. He aimed.

Bowman charged, screaming obscenities, the long barrel of his gun swinging their way.

Andrew fired.

The man took another step forward, two.

Andrew fired again.

The gun was aimed at Andrew's chest.

He braced for the impact.

Squeezed the trigger once more.

But the shot went over Bowman's head as the madman stumbled, fell face-first into the snow.

Someone was still screaming. Screaming.

There were shouts in the air.

"Drop it! Drop it now!"

A police officer rounded the house, gun aimed not at Bowman but at him.

"Drop it." Another man came around the house. His voice was low and calm. "You got him, son," Chief Cote said. "They're safe. Drop your weapon."

Andrew let the gun fall at his knees. He lifted his hands.

But before the police reached him, Grace threw her arms around him and held him tight.

Was she okay? He couldn't make his voice work to ask the question.

Lily gripped him from behind, her tiny head pressed against his shoulder. She was saying something, but he couldn't process the child's words.

It was okay. They were okay.

He shifted to pull Lily into an embrace, slid his other arm around Grace, and buried his head in her hair. Maybe that would hide the tears.

~

"JUST STANDING out there in the open like that?" Fitz shook his head. "Stupid rookie mistake."

Andrew lay on a gurney in the back of an ambulance. He was fine, despite the cuts the paramedic kept calling gunshot wounds.

He'd been shot. Shot.

He hadn't even felt it.

Even as he'd held Grace and Lily, he hadn't felt pain.

No wounds on either of them, thank God. None that he could see anyway. Though the look in Grace's eyes had him wondering what she'd gone through. He didn't want to think about what Bowman had done to her.

She was in the back of another ambulance, telling some stranger what had happened.

She would tell Andrew everything eventually. Now that Bowman was gone, there was no need for secrets.

"You gotta take cover." Fitz was standing at the back of the ambulance, oblivious to the snow in his hair or Andrew's wandering thoughts. "Unless you've checked to make sure the perp doesn't have a pulse, you gotta assume he's still a threat."

"Why don't you write all your tips down for next time?" Andrew suggested. "I'll study them. You can give me a quiz, make sure I've got it."

Fitz just smiled that irritating Hollywood-leading-man smile. "Let's hope there's not a next time."

Amen to that. Beyond Fitz, a car door slammed, and Andrew sat up to try to catch a glimpse of Grace.

The paramedic pushed him back down. The action had his shoulder throbbing, thanks to the gunshot wound.

Wounds. Plural. Which explained why he couldn't move his left arm.

Andrew did his best not to flinch but knew he'd failed when Fitz chuckled. "Sure, take on a madman, no problem. But a little pressure on your boo-boo—"

"Don't you have anything else you could be doing?"

"Sadly, no. Local cops are handling it. They let me come along as a courtesy."

"Not feeling like a courtesy to me," Andrew grumbled. "How'd you guys figure out where we were, anyway?"

"Thomas came back and told Cote about the dog and the trail. He and two of the cops rode up the path and found the marker showing which way you'd gone. Cops radioed it in. Not a whole lot of structures up here, so we headed this way. But you guys couldn't wait."

"Wasn't like we knew you were coming," Andrew said.

"How'd you get Grace and Lily out?"

"Garrett went to the front and rang the bell and banged on the door, hoping to distract Bowman while I got inside. But the door and windows were sealed tight. I could hear Garrett and Bowman talking around front while I looked for another way in. There was a light on in the basement, so I went that direction. I was almost there when I heard the front door slam.

"I ran to the front and saw Garrett standing on the stoop. He said the guy told him to get off his property or he'd call the police. Garrett didn't want to give away that he knew who he was, so he apologized for bothering him."

"What was his excuse for knocking on his door in the middle of the night?"

"Said he was looking for a lost dog and saw the light on."

Fitz glanced at the house. "It was dark when we drove up, just that dim basement light."

"Yeah. Garrett and I were trying to decide what to do next when I heard a crash. Grace had broken the basement window. She was trying to lift Lily out." Andrew remembered seeing Lily's little hand. Seeing Grace. Getting them both to safety. His heart raced as if he were in that moment again.

"I pulled them out," Andrew finally said.

"And then stayed out in the open. Sitting ducks."

Andrew glared at him. "Are you trying to help?"

Fitz chuckled. "Just saying, I'm glad you're alive. I think God must've been watching out for you. What's that saying about how He takes care of babies and fools?"

"Feel free to run along."

Fitz wandered away, chuckling, and Andrew shifted his attention to the paramedic. "Are we done here?"

"Try to relax," he said. "It'll take an hour to get to Plymouth."

"I don't need a hospital," he said.

"Gunshot wounds get infected. It'd be really dumb to die of sepsis because you don't feel like taking a trip to the ER."

Sepsis? He'd heard of that. So fine, he'd go to the hospital. "Can I just go check on—?"

"I'll get her for you. The lady, right? The blonde?"

The paramedic called to someone. A few seconds later, Grace climbed into the back of the ambulance, concern marring her beautiful features. "They say you're going to the hospital."

"Stitches and antibiotics. That's all I need. Is Lily all right?"

Nodding, Grace kneeled beside him and rested her head against his chest. "Thank you. Thank you for coming. Thank you for—"

"Don't thank me."

She lifted her head to look at him.

"I'm so sorry about everything I said. I was an idiot. I should have supported you."

"I shouldn't have lied to you. I put you in a terrible position."

"For good reason."

She slid her finger on the back of his hand, looking at him for permission. He slid his palm over hers.

Closing her eyes, she laid her head on his chest again. He wasn't afraid for her to know how he felt. Gone was his anger toward her. Gone was his fear of prison. Gone was all of it.

He felt overpowering gratitude that she was alive. And more. So much more.

She leaned back and kissed his cheek. "Me too. All of it." She took a deep breath, smiled, and said, "I love you too."

CHAPTER THIRTY-SEVEN

ANDREW WAS BORED, though considering all he'd gone through in the previous couple of days, bored wasn't all bad.

Grace and Lily had been to the hospital to visit him earlier that day and the day before, but they hadn't stayed long. Not that Grace hadn't wanted to, but she'd been focused on Lily and her emotional health. Which was right and made sense. Didn't make him long for her any less, though.

He was still in the hospital because the doctors were paranoid. They'd told him the wounds in his shoulder and upper arm would all fully heal, and he'd recover. Bowman had shot him with a shotgun, which explained how one squeeze of the trigger had left so many holes, all of which could get infected.

He felt fine. He told that to every nurse who came in, and they all smiled and patted him on his good shoulder and pretended he wasn't demanding to leave.

Which he wasn't, not really. He had way too much to live for to die now.

Fitz pushed through the wide door. "Knock knock."

Dylan came in behind him.

Cop and former cop—they both had that same back-straight, eagle-eyed look about them.

"So, you knew she kidnapped the girl," Dylan said, getting right to the point.

Fitz shot a look at the other man. "I thought you agreed to let me handle this."

Dylan shrugged, never taking his eyes off Andrew.

Andrew laid his head back and closed his eyes. "I'm feeling a little lightheaded."

"Sure you are," Fitz said.

Andrew opened his eyes to the sound of a chair scraping. Dylan sat, and Fitz stood at the end of the bed.

He'd confessed everything to Dylan in his frantic phone call Friday night. He'd been surprised the cops hadn't come by the day before and had half-hoped Dylan was going to let it go.

Nope. They'd decided to wait until Sunday. It was fine. Whatever happened now, Andrew would handle it. If he faced criminal charges, so be it.

He prayed Grace wouldn't. She'd already given so much for Lily. Would she have to give her freedom as well?

"I found out Thursday night," Andrew said.

"And told her to run." Dylan stretched out his long legs in the chair. "I'm just spitballing here. You didn't want to turn her in, but you also didn't want to be a party to kidnapping. That's why her boxes were packed, right? It took me a little while to put it all together."

"Is she going to be charged with anything?"

Fitz fielded that. "The child was never reported missing. Not by the mother or grandmother or Bowman. The county in Washington where they lived isn't going to be interested in pursuing charges, not after how they botched the search."

That got Andrew's attention. "What do you mean?"

"Once Cote saw the basement where they were held," Fitz said, "he put in a call to the detective in the little town in Washington where she used to live. He told her what happened and asked how thoroughly they'd searched the basement in the house there and described Myron's modifications. The detective there issued another search warrant and found a hidden room. It was empty, of course. But that must be where he hid the evidence when the cops searched after Grace reported what she'd learned."

"Grace saved Lily," Dylan said. "Nobody disputes that. And she's been working hard to find the girl's family. They're itching to get her back, but Grace refused to leave until she knew you were all right, and she also refused to turn Lily over here. She insisted she needs to accompany her to Texas and see her settled."

Andrew'd known that part already. He planned to go with them and had already asked Jacqui for the time off.

He'd missed the conference he'd worked so hard to put together, but Jacqui and Braden and the other BNB employees had handled it. Apparently, it'd gone well and many of the prospective employees expressed an interest in moving to Plymouth.

With the weekend behind them, Andrew could afford to take a few more days off. They were hoping to leave for Texas on Wednesday.

Darla Springer had waited years for Lily's return. She could wait a few more days. She'd be stronger, too, more recovered from the knife wound that'd almost killed her.

"All that to say..." Fitz paused, probably for dramatic effect.

"Just spit it out."

The detective smiled. "Obviously, she's a hero, and I guess in some sort of weird way, you are too. You saved their lives, Grace saved Lily's. Nobody's going to charge either of you with anything."

The words lifted a weight off his chest.

Dylan set Andrew's laptop bag on the adjustable tray. "Your computer, as requested."

"Thanks for grabbing that for me."

"No problem. You need anything else?"

He had his laptop, which would give him access to all the records Dad wanted him to look into. Since he had nothing but time, he might as well solve that mystery.

"One more thing." Fitz's fingers curled over the plastic rail at the end of Andrew's bed. "The cops have been going through Bowman's images."

Andrew's disgust must've shown on his face because Fitz added, "Yeah. I'm glad that's not my job. But they found something that, uh…" He shook his head. "The mom. Annabeth Springer? We think he murdered her. He took photos of a body. They're matching the images with those they have of Springer before she left with Bowman. Police are trying to figure out where they were taken so they can find her."

Dylan said, "At least now the family will know."

"What a monster," Andrew said. "The guy convinces Annabeth to leave her mother, then, when she's cut off all contact with everybody she's ever known, murders her. There's nobody to report her missing and no way to trace her, even if the parents want to. Then he's got the kid, free and clear."

"Sick," Dylan said.

"Nobody'll grieve Myron Bowman." Fitz shook Andrew's hand. "Well done."

Dylan squeezed his good shoulder, and the two men walked out, leaving Andrew to consider all he'd learned.

And to dig into his father's business finances.

CHAPTER THIRTY-EIGHT

GRACE HELD one of Lily's hands. Andrew held the other. Together, they walked up the walkway to the little house in Flower Mound, Texas, Regis on their heels.

The door opened, and Darla Springer filled the opening. Grace had expected her to look grayer, sicker, but her skin was pink and healthy just a week after Myron stabbed her. Somehow, though his intent had been to kill, the knife hadn't hit any vital organs. She might've bled to death if someone hadn't found her quickly. Only God could have orchestrated those things. Grace could almost imagine His hands stopping the blade from penetrating too far, then turning a woman's head to notice Darla on the pavement.

Lily froze at the sight of her grandmother. Even though Grace had told her where they were going and who they were going to see, Lily still seemed stunned.

She pulled away from Grace and Andrew and stepped forward.

Before Grace could feel the loss, Andrew's arm slipped around her waist.

Together, they watched Lily approach Darla. She stopped a few feet away. "Nana?"

Darla crouched down and held her arms open. Tears streamed down her cheeks. "Darling Lilianne. I've missed you so much."

Lily's cast had been removed the day before, and her arm was as good as new. She ran to close the distance and fell against her grandmother's chest, wrapping her little arms around the woman's neck.

Beside Grace, Andrew tightened his hold and kissed her head. There was nothing to say.

The child she loved with all her heart didn't belong to her. Never had.

She'd loved and lost enough in her life. Her mother. Though the woman was still alive, Grace had lost her love a long time before. Her father. Celia. Now Lily.

At one point, she'd thought she'd never be able to love again. She'd believed her love inadequate, faulty. She'd believed herself flawed because her love had never been enough.

But she'd been wrong.

Her love would never be the kind of love that saved. But it was good and worth sharing.

Even when it hurt.

This hurt. Wow, did this hurt.

With Lily's hand in hers, Darla stood. "Come on in, beautiful girl. Meet the family." When Lily stepped inside, Darla faced Grace and held open her arms.

Grace stepped into them, accepting the hug, feeling Darla's sobs against her shoulder. "Thank you."

Words clogged in her throat. All Grace could do was nod.

They went inside to find that the family was all there.

Grace and Andrew were introduced to Lily's great-uncle and cousins of every age and size.

Except for the children, who seemed more stunned than anything, every member of Lily's family cried.

After some awkward questions and conversation, Lily found a girl about her age—her cousin Brittney—and disappeared with her and the young boys down the hall. Regis padded behind them, delighting the children.

They all seemed perfectly at ease.

A few more pieces of Grace's heart seemed to crumble and fall away.

The teenagers slumped down on sofas to look at their phones.

And the adults went into the kitchen, where they focused on Grace and Andrew as if the two knew the secrets of the universe.

Which they didn't, but they knew enough.

It was Rex, Darla's brother, who started. "Tell us about this place he took you and Lillianne."

Grace's gaze flicked to Andrew, who scooted a little closer to her. He must've seen the emotion in her expression because he described the place and how they'd found it as Lily's family leaned in with rapt attention. "He'd built a false wall in the basement. Behind it was his studio and a little bedroom for Lily and Grace."

Darla's face paled while Rex's turned bright red. "What kind of man shoves a kid into a windowless room like that?" he demanded.

Grace swallowed hard. "One who only thinks about himself and his needs. A narcissistic psychopath."

"What'd they find there?" Rex asked.

"Boxes and boxes of photographs. Printed photographs, old-school style. And all the evidence of his..." Andrew's voice trailed.

But Darla and Rex and the rest of the family knew what Lily had been forced to do.

"The good news is," Andrew said, "there's zero evidence that Lily's been assaulted."

"There's that." Rex laid his hand on his sister's shoulder. "It could be worse."

Darla's head bobbed, tears dribbling down her cheeks. She didn't say much. She had to feel conflicted. Thrilled to have her granddaughter home while grieving the daughter who'd never walk through the door.

Once they told the family all they knew, Grace hugged Lily good-bye and promised to see her the next day.

She planned to hang around for a few days until Lily got settled. And then she'd return to New Hampshire with Andrew and try to figure out how to go on with a gaping hole in her heart.

CHAPTER THIRTY-NINE

ANDREW STEPPED onto the private jet where his father, Chet, and Harrison Ackerman waited. He greeted all three with handshakes. He'd have hugged his dad if his shoulder and arm didn't still hurt so badly.

"Let's sit," Dad said.

They did so at the table where Andrew, Lily, and Grace had been less than two weeks before. Felt like months, but a lot had happened since then.

"I assume you have an answer for me." Beside him, Dad's gaze flicked to Chet and Harrison on the other side of the table. "And I assume we all needed to be here to hear it."

Andrew set his bag on the table and pulled out the report he'd drawn up.

Chet's eyes were narrowed as if he were annoyed, but the way his lips were pressed together, tight at the corners, gave away that he was nervous.

Harrison, on the other hand, looked comfortable. Cooly confident. "Why'd we have to fly all the way to Texas for this?"

"Dad wanted the information ASAP," Andrew said. "Grace needs to hang around here another couple of days until Lily feels comfortable, and I'm not leaving her alone."

Andrew'd woken up Saturday morning to find his dad at his hospital bedside. Grace had called and filled him in. It wasn't as if they'd had some deep man-to-man heart-to-heart. They hadn't needed to.

Dad's thoughts had been so clear that they might as well have been printed in a cartoon bubble over his head. Andrew'd gripped his hand, and Dad had squeezed, and it was enough.

Now, Dad looked at him with an expression that could only be described as pride.

And Andrew's heart swelled just a little. It wasn't perfect, their relationship. But then, what relationships were? It was better, and it'd keep getting better. Despite what Andrew needed to tell him.

He set his hand on the paperwork and addressed his brother. "Bookkeeping isn't your strong suit."

Chet glowered at him. "I don't know what you think you found, but—"

"I've been doing some digging, even made a few calls. You're actually pretty good at some aspects of running a business. You've expanded into new markets, signed new clients."

Chet leaned back against his chair. Apparently stunned that Andrew had said something complimentary, he seemed to be waiting for the punch line.

There wasn't one, though. Chet wasn't a complete incompetent.

"But admit it. You're not so great at the books."

Chet didn't argue. His shrug was all the agreement Andrew was going to get.

Andrew turned his attention to Harrison. "You didn't want Dad to get me out of prison."

Harrison's lips stretched into a smile. "I thought you were guilty. To be honest, son, I still do. The last thing we needed was a criminal working for us. And I knew your father'd give you a chance."

"That might be true," Andrew said. "But I think it's also true that you like your position at the company. You have a lot of power."

Harrison seemed unfazed. "I don't know where you think you're going with this."

Andrew turned to Dad. "You wanted me to take over. When I bowed out, you wanted Chet to take over. But what happens if Chet can't because he's in prison for embezzling?"

Dad turned to Harrison and held there. He didn't say anything.

Andrew slid the report to his father, who skimmed it.

Then Dad's gaze went back to Harrison, his eyes filled with confusion.

And hurt.

Andrew focused on Chet, the only one at the table who didn't know what was going on. "Harrison was supposed to be teaching you how to keep the books."

Chet's shoulders dropped. He looked at their dad, then back at Andrew. "He was trying. I wanted Dad to think I'd gotten over...I have this thing, dyscalculia. It's like dyslexia, only with numbers. No matter how hard I try, I just can't seem to make them work."

"I knew about that," Dad said. "It's why I asked Harrison to help you. I didn't realize..."

Harrison was seated between Chet and the window, and though he made no move, Andrew could feel the man's desire to escape.

He was glad Chet either didn't feel it or didn't care.

Andrew got to the point. "Harrison's skimmed just under a hundred grand since Chet took over. He did his very best to make it look like Chet was the guilty party, but I followed the trail." He leveled his gaze at the man he used to call *uncle*. "You're good. I'm better."

Harrison held Andrew's gaze, then turned to Dad. "Obviously, they're in on it together."

The accusation wasn't worth responding to.

Andrew stood and looked down at the three men. Chet seemed

relieved, a little embarrassed. Harrison was pulling himself together, about to come up with some long story about how Andrew and Chet were trying to swindle their father.

It'd probably be amusing to watch, considering that the brothers had never even been able to shovel a driveway without arguing.

But Dad seemed heartbroken. He loved his sons. But he loved his oldest friend too.

"All the evidence has been forwarded to your assistant," Andrew said to his dad. "I considered sending it straight to the authorities, but that's up to you."

Dad stood and wrapped Andrew in a hug, which Andrew returned with one arm. The other ached where Dad had squeezed, but he wouldn't have missed that hug for the world.

"I love you, son."

Andrew stepped back. "I love you, Dad." He gripped Chet's shoulder. "Let's try a little harder, okay?"

Chet shrugged. "Whatever." But his lips twitched like he might smile. "Thanks for not, you know…"

"Pinning the whole thing on you out of sheer pettiness? Don't think I didn't consider it." But he kept amusement in his tone. "At the end of the day, you're the only brother I have."

He didn't bother to speak to Harrison. There was nothing to say.

He left the three men to sort out their issues on the long flight back to New Hampshire. Maybe it wasn't the kindest way to handle this, having them come to Texas, but Dad had insisted. Now, he'd have to deal with the fallout.

Maybe, someday, Andrew would accept his dad's offer to take over at Middleton. Maybe he and Chet could even learn to work together.

For now, Andrew was happy at BNB. He was happy in Coventry. And he was happy with Grace, who planned to stay right in the condo across the lot.

It was enough. For now.

CHAPTER FORTY

GRACE DUMPED the contents of her new favorite mug into the kitchen sink. This one had been imprinted with a photo of herself and Lily, a gift from Andrew a few weeks earlier, just because.

When she left Lily with her grandmother, she'd felt a hole rip open in her heart, a hole she'd been sure would never be filled. But, somehow, the hole didn't make her weaker.

There was an old saying that a bone would grow back stronger after it had been been broken. She didn't know if that was true, but she was starting to realize that, when a broken *heart* was treated properly, it did grow back stronger.

Hers was, anyway. Because rather than running away and cutting herself off from society after losing Lily, she'd run home to Coventry and allowed herself to be surrounded by friends, some of whom she'd not even met before.

Somehow, she had a community here. People she was just starting to get to know but already cared about. Not just Cassidy and James, though they were a part of it. But friends of Andrew's from work, from church, and from the condo development. They'd gathered around Andrew when she and Lily had been taken.

And gathered around Grace when she'd come home from Texas without the child she'd fallen in love with.

So, yes, there was a hole in her heart. But it was shrinking. Or maybe her heart was just expanding into it, thanks to all the wonderful people who'd become her community.

Thanks to Andrew, who'd offered a shoulder to cry on more than once. Who'd distracted her. Who'd encouraged her to work at the youth center.

She'd agreed to help out while Cassidy was on maternity leave. Cassidy hadn't had the baby yet, but in the course of training and preparing, Grace remembered how much she loved working with young people. It was hard and messy and sometimes heartbreaking, but it was rewarding.

But the hole was filling, mostly thanks to God, Who'd held her close and whispered truth into her ears—truth about who she was and Whose she was. About her gift, her value, and how He loved her.

Her bell rang, and she opened the door.

Andrew stood on the other side. Before she could say a word, he pulled her into an embrace and kissed her senseless.

When he backed away, he looked down at her with that smoldering expression that'd only grown warmer in the month since they'd returned from Texas. It took her more than a moment to get her bearings.

"I missed you," he said.

She giggled like a girl. "I saw you yesterday."

"An eternity."

"Goofball."

He helped her into her wool coat. She slipped on her gloves, not because she feared holding his hand—she loved holding his hand, though it could be distracting—but because it was downright frigid outside. "Why are we doing this again?"

"It's tradition."

After she locked up, they walked hand-in-hand toward the park. Others who lived in the development were making their way to the common area, where a giant Christmas tree had been erected. Grace had helped decorate it the day before, not even minding when the pushy Mrs. O'Malley came along behind her and "fixed" what she'd done.

Barely batting an eye when the nosey Mrs. Peterson fished for details about her relationship with Andrew.

They were a part of her circle now. Moms and dads and kids and single people and retirees, all doing life together in this weird little community.

She loved it. Loved everything about it.

How had she ever thought she was meant to live separated from the world?

The lies she'd told herself, the lies that'd been whispered into her ear by a very busy and very cruel enemy, were just that. Lies. Slowly and carefully, Grace was learning to replace those lies with truth.

She was valuable.

She was lovable.

She was fully capable of love.

Andrew squeezed her hand. "I wish I could read your mind the way you read my emotions." He gave her an expectant look.

That was the deal they'd made. He shared everything with her. The least she could do was open herself up to him.

"I was thinking how much I love this. How I was barely living before I met Lily." She bumped his shoulder with her own. "And you."

"Did you talk to her this morning?"

"Yeah. She's so happy." Grace's voice cracked on that last word, not with sadness but with joy. It had cost her to give her heart to Lily, and then to give Lily back to her grandmother. But what she'd gained, what Lily had gained, had been worth every tear.

"I bet theirs was a joyous Thanksgiving."

Indeed, it had been. Grace had heard the tears in Darla's voice when she'd told her about the day with all the family.

"Ours was too," Grace said. "I wouldn't change a thing." They'd gone to Andrew's dad's for the holiday. Apparently, Andrew had spent every Thanksgiving and Christmas with his mom since he'd been old enough to make the choice. But this year his mom told him to make other arrangements and booked herself on a cruise.

Grace loved her, that older version of Andrew. Full of life and joy. She seemed genuinely thrilled that Andrew was repairing his relationship with his dad. And she'd welcomed Grace like a long-lost daughter.

Andrew's family were good, kind, and generous people. Knowing the man, she wasn't at all surprised.

The tree-lighting ceremony was typical. Short and sweet with the president of the condo association thanking those who'd done the work. Moments after the sun went down, the tree lit up.

It wasn't Rockefeller Center, but it was pretty.

And then the group huddled closer and sang "Silent Night."

Listening to all those voices raised in honor of Jesus...She couldn't help the tears that streamed down her face.

Life was so good.

When the song was over, she turned to Andrew to thank him for insisting they go, but the place where he'd stood was empty.

He was kneeling. Looking up at her with sparkles in his eyes. The reflection from the tree, yes.

And love. Pure love.

Slowly, he tugged off her gloves, then took her hands so she could feel what he was feeling. "I was happy before I met you," he said. "I had everything I needed. But then you came into my life and showed me this whole new part of myself. You taught me fear-lessness and sacrificial love. I'm not perfect. Neither are you. But I see glimpses of the perfect creature God created in you. I want to be a part of that. I want to walk alongside you and watch you grow into the woman He made you to be. I want you alongside me as I try to grow into the man He made me to be. Our love will never be perfect. But it can be good. I think we can be good...together. Will you marry me?"

She couldn't force words past the emotions clogging her throat. She managed a nod.

"Yes?" he clarified.

She swallowed. "Yes. Yes."

He slipped a diamond ring off the end of his pinky and slid it onto her finger. It was beautiful, but it was nothing compared to the man who'd given it to her.

He stood and wrapped her in his arms. After a kiss that didn't last nearly long enough, he backed away, turned to the crowd, and shouted, "She said yes!"

And then, somehow, they were surrounded by friends. Jacqui and Reid and Ella, Braden and Carly and their beautiful infant girl. James and Cassidy, whose coat would no longer close over her baby bump. Tabby and Fitz, along with Fitz's sister, Shelby. Even Chelsea and Dylan had made it, the gorgeous heiress and her redheaded husband.

Garrett, Thomas, and other neighbors watched.

Andrew's father slapped Andrew on his back. "Well done, son."

Christine pulled Grace into a hug.

Even Chet was there, standing near his sisters and their families. He looked a little happy for his big brother, maybe a little jealous. But he was trying.

That was all anybody could do.

"I hope you don't mind a crowd," Andrew said. "But this is your family now." He didn't just mean the Middletons. He meant all of them. The friends. The neighbors.

Family. She hadn't realized how badly she'd longed for a family...how badly she'd needed one...until she came to Coventry.

She'd given up Lily, but look at all she'd gained.

"I couldn't be happier, Andrew Middleton."

He wrapped her in his arms again and gave her the first kiss of the rest of their lives.

THE END

⁓

I HOPE you enjoyed this story about Grace, Andrew, and Lily—not to mention Regis and Oliver. If you did, then you won't want to miss getting to know Aspen and Garrett. Join them and the rest of the Coventry crew in *Inheritance of Secrets*. Turn the page for more information.

Inheritance of Secrets

"I didn't do right by your mother. Find her and do what I never had the courage to do."

Her father's deathbed confession changed everything for Aspen Kincaid. The mystery of her mother's disappearance was unsolvable, or so she'd believed.

It seemed her dad had lied to her all her life.

After inheriting a house in New Hampshire—a house Aspen hadn't known her father owned—she travels thousands of miles, desperate to fulfill his dying wish. But some residents of Coventry don't want Jane Kincaid's daughter digging into things they think should remain buried forever.

Renovating the secluded old house on the mountain should be the next step in Garrett McCarthy's contracting career, but Aspen's arrival in town stirs up old animosities in Coventry that he'd known nothing about. All he wants is to complete the job, hoping it'll open doors to new opportunities. But when he's asked to keep an eye on Aspen's activities, he feels he can't refuse. How can he honor his beautiful, vulnerable client and remain loyal to the people who need his help?

Join Aspen and Garrett as they attempt to solve a thirty-year-old mystery—without becoming its latest victims.

ALSO BY ROBIN PATCHEN

The Coventry Saga

Glimmer in the Darkness

Tides of Duplicity

Betrayal of Genius

Traces of Virtue

Touch of Innocence

Inheritance of Secrets

The Nutfield Saga

Convenient Lies

Twisted Lies

Generous Lies

Innocent Lies

Beauty in Flight

Beauty in Hiding

Beauty in Battle

Legacy Rejected

Legacy Restored

Legacy Reclaimed

Legacy Redeemed

ABOUT THE AUTHOR

Robin Patchen is a *USA Today* bestselling and award-winning author of Christian romantic suspense. She grew up in a small town in New Hampshire, the setting of her Nutfield Saga books, and then headed to Boston to earn a journalism degree. After college, working in marketing and public relations, she discovered how much she loathed the nine-to-five ball and chain. After relocating to the Southwest, she started writing her first novel while she homeschooled her three children. The novel was dreadful, but her passion for storytelling didn't wane. Thankfully, as her children grew, so did her writing ability. Now that her kids are adults, she has more time to play with the lives of fictional heroes and heroines, wreaking havoc and working magic to give her characters happy endings. When she's not writing, she's editing or reading, proving that most of her life revolves around the twenty-six letters of the alphabet. Visit robinpatchen.com/subscribe to receive a free book and stay informed about Robin's latest projects.